Weirdbook

VOL. 2, NO. 10 ISSUE 40

Features

From the Editor's Tower, by Doug Draa. 2

Stories

Iconoclasm, by Adrian Cole 3
Have a Crappy Halloween, by Franklyn Searight 17
Early Snow, by Samson Stormcrow Hayes 37
The Dollhouse, by Glynn Owen Barrass 39
Elle a Vu un Loup, by Loren Rhoads 49
Bringing the Bodies Home, by Christian Riley 62
Restored, by Marlane Quade Cook 67
Nameless and Named, by David M. Hoenig. 70
Playing A Starring Role, by Paul Lubaczewski 81
And the Living is Easy, by Mike Chinn 86
The Prague Relic, by Paul StJohn Mackintosh 92
The Circle, by Matt Sullivan. 113
Sanctuary, by John Linwood Grant 121
The Giving of Gifts, by Matt Neil Hill 134
The Santa Anna, by Jack Lothian 146
The Dread Fishermen, by Kevin Henry 154
Blind Vision, by Andrew Darlington 165
The Thirteenth Step, by William Tea 177
This Godless Apprenticeship, by Clint Smith 184
Waiting, by John W. Dennehy 195
Pouring Whiskey In My Soul, by Paul R. McNamee 203
True Blue, by Darrell Schweitzer 213
The Treadmill, by Rohit Sawant 222
The Veiled Isle, by W. D. Clifton 232

Poetry

Gila King, by Jessica Amanda Salmonson 249
Necro-Meretrix, by Frederick J. Mayer 250
Grinning Moon, by Frederick J. Mayer 252
The Burning Man, by Russ Parkhurst 253
Silent Hours, by Russ Parkhurst 254
The Old White Crone, by Maxwell I. Gold 255

Artwork

J. Florêncio. . . . . Front Cover
Allen Koszowski. . . . . Illustrations

Weirdbook #40 is copyright © 2018 by Wildside Press LLC. All rights reserved. Published by Wildside Press LLC, 7945 MacArthur Blvd, Suite 215, Cabin John MD 20818 USA. Visit us online at wildsidepress.com.

From the Editor's Tower

This is it! Our tenth regular issue! That's 10 issues plus a themed Annual in just a little less than three years. I honestly thought that when I started the re-launch that we'd be lucky to do two issues a year. I never imagined that we'd take off as quickly as we have. I think that this is due solely to *Weirdbook's* fantastic contributors and the marvelous stories that they produce. It also doesn't hurt that no other magazine of Weird Fiction publishes so much pleasing entertaining material as we do.

I think that all of you will enjoy our selection of stories and poetry this time around. you see many familiar names and just as many new one. All of them together covering the entire gamut of Weird fiction!

I'd like to point out that *Weirdbook* is a truly international magazine. Even though we are an English language magazine, our contributors are not confined to the Anglo-sphere. In the past three years we've published stories from the US, Canada, the UK, Australia, Germany, Italy, Spain, Israel, and India! We've truly gone global is a very short time.

And as always, I hope that you enjoy reading this issue as much as I enjoyed editing it.

Take care and God bless!

—Doug Draa

Staff

PUBLISHER & EXECUTIVE EDITOR

John Gregory Betancourt

EDITOR

Doug Draa

CONSULTING EDITOR

W. Paul Ganley

WILDSIDE PRESS SUBSCRIPTION SERVICES

Carla Coupe

PRODUCTION TEAM

Steve Coupe
Sam Cooper
Shawn Garrett
Helen McGee
Karl Würf

ICONOCLASM
By Adrian Cole

They told me the next morning the church had burned to the ground. As though the fires of Hell itself had dragged it stone from stone and baked it to ashes.

I was propped among fat pillows in the hospital bed and I'd stopped coughing my lungs up. I was lucky to have survived the smoke—when the Police had found me, sprawled unconscious on the car park in front of the inferno, I was barely conscious.

A nurse gave me some porridge and a cup of tea, and I could talk again. I told her I felt fine. Which was true, although my head throbbed when I got up to go to the toilet.

"The policeman gave me this, Father," said the nurse, handing me a notepad and pen. "He said if you felt up to it, could you make a few notes about what happened. He'll be back this afternoon."

I got back into bed and nodded. They would need an explanation. Whether they accepted it or not was up to them. I thought about last night and started writing.

* * * *

Another Sunday evening service was over and I sat in silence among the pews. The congregation had left, the last echoing step replaced by the sly creeping of night. Already the temperature had dropped; the sky outside the stained glass was a deepening hue of winter grey. A draught eddied among the seats, like the first small wavelet of an incoming tide. It sapped the last of my energy.

Somehow I felt as if I'd been in a physical conflict and lost. My bones ached. I got up slowly, pulling my cassock tighter around me.

The people who had come tonight—the usual, diffuse crowd—had been uncomfortable. Probably with me. I'd never thought of myself as an inspiration to my flock, but lately my disaffection must have communicated itself.

I often thought of them as the epitome of despair. Mavis and Ben Rand, a prematurely aged couple whose teenage son had got in with a bad crowd—drug users—and died from using a dirty needle; Lorraine Stead, whose husband had often beaten her and finally run off with another woman; Dixie Pike, a gaunt youth beaten up by drunken homophobes; the Johnsons, a West Indian family, scarred by racial abuse; Tracey and Lisa, two local prostitutes. And all the others, all with their private pain, or broken dreams, looking for something to ease the passage of their days.

I told them that God cared about them and if they believed, he'd prepare a place for them when all this was over. I doubt if I sounded convincing any more. Maybe once I had. Not now.

I walked slowly down the nave towards the doors, preparing to lock up for the night. I should have been alone in the sepulchral gloom but a shadow between two pillars moved. I hadn't realised there was a figure there.

"Evening, Father," said the man, his voice carrying in the still air. He was dressed in dark, sombre clothes, a jacket that was marginally too tight for his broad chest, and he wore a loosened tie. He looked dishevelled. I guessed him to be about forty. I'd not seen him before. The eyes were sharp, the expression more alive than those on the dull faces gathered here earlier.

"I was about to lock up," I said. It was uncharitable of me, symptomatic of my general *malaise*, I suppose.

"Can we talk?" said the man, unperturbed. He spoke as though he didn't expect to be put off. I wondered if he were a policeman. He had that manner. "Though by all means lock up," he added, indicating the tall doors.

I saw no point in argument and performed my task slowly, relieved to shut out the growing darkness and whatever curdled within it. The midday weather forecast had said there was a possibility of snow, cold winds from the east.

"How can I help you?" I said to the waiting man, though he must have sensed my lack of enthusiasm.

He shook his head, an odd smile crossing his face. "I've come to help you, Father."

"I don't understand."

The man studied his surroundings, like an estate agent weighing up the pros and cons of a building he was about to put on the market. He could see the long scabs of flaking paint on the walls, the lengthening stains of water penetration up among the beams. Like many of its kind, the church cried out for money to restore its failing health. If it had been human, it would have needed hospitalization.

"Your faith isn't helping you, is it, Father?"

The man knew how to poke a nerve. I'm sixty, though my body feels older, protesting at the slightest cold. Every day it gets harder.

"You want to talk to me about it, Father?" The man smiled apologetically. "Now—there's a thing. Me asking you for a confession."

Strange choice of words, I thought. And yet I did want to share my thoughts. I studied the man. In spite of his slightly untidy appearance, he had a certain vitality, a confidence born out of his relaxed manner. The hushed, sepulchral aura of the church had no visible impact on him: he might have been in a supermarket after hours. There was an odd smell to him, earthy but not unpleasant and I could see now he was unshaven, weather-beaten in the way that farmers are, incongruous in this area.

"It's difficult to explain," I said.

"I'm sure it is, but nothing you tell me will surprise me." He waved me to a pew, sitting down himself, an arm resting along the back of the wooden seats. He was oddly relaxed. His clothes were musty, as if he had been rolled in grass or caught in a deluge and not dried off fully. His shoes were scuffed, a little muddy. I had the ridiculous idea that he would have made a good scarecrow.

I sat, looking at the altar beyond us and the tall, wooden statue of the Saviour behind it, sagging on its cross. Its blind-eyed face was haggard, drawn in pain. Its acute misery seemed even more wretched than usual, its despair, like that of the congregation, hopeless.

"The city is changing," I said. "It's fallen into its own kind of darkness. I can't combat it. It's like an illness, a pestilence. As a priest, I suppose I'm expected to say it's the work of Satan. If I'm honest, I don't really believe that."

He let me talk. I needed to.

"If I were dealing with divine and satanic forces, my faith, my psychology would be my strength. Against what's out in the city today, they're ineffective. At first I thought it was a kind of possession. I've seen such things and the Catholic faith has a long experience of them, well documented. "

"Yet you don't think this is the work of a demon or some other related satanic force." His face remained impassive.

"No," I said. "It's people. It comes from within them. Satan would be a poor excuse for it." My grip on God's hand had been loosened. If I let go altogether, what would it mean? There was only darkness outside what I had once believed in.

"It's about power, Father. An expression of energy, if you like. Vast and timeless, well outside the confines of humanity. Humanity is just one expression of power. The thing is, humanity has grown arrogant, like the Lucifer of your legends, rebelling against its Creator. Man has created gods and devils all down through the centuries. They come and go. Your God and Satan aren't any more than a part of this procession. They're being superseded, like all those before them. Same with all the other religions of the world.

"The energy I'm talking about endures. It's not shaped by goodness or evil, or by the will of man. It's not a pestilence, it simply *exists*. In purely local terms, it's an integral part of the landscape. It was here before the first men set foot on the hills and in the valleys. It's not confined by time, which is, after all, a human concept, a human conceit."

"Some might call it God," I said.

"Be careful, then. You have a preconception of God, dressed in rules and paraphernalia gleaned from a score of hybrid religions. Your God is a conglomerate and, in the end, moulded to suit you. You think he'll reward you if you obey his rules—rules, ironically that man has devised, though he'd claim otherwise. I'm speaking of something outside of all that.

"The earth stores energy that exudes power and feeds on it. Over the years, man has rooted himself here, ultimately building this city. It's risen up from the earth, using its stone, its minerals, its riches. And, unwittingly, its power. The city blankets the earth, smothers it. But the primal energy survives all this, dormant but alive. The city has drawn power up into itself, initially unconsciously. But the city is organic."

I found the concept disturbing. "You're saying—it's alive?"

"Absolutely. It provides a body for the old power, the energy. Just as it houses electricity, so it pulses with life from the deep earth. And power is never dormant for long. It's restless, vividly alive, burgeoning like a forest. Feed it nutrients and it will evolve. That's its sole purpose."

I weighed the words slowly. It would have been easy enough to dismiss them as the outpourings of a crank, but I felt myself seduced by them. "How does this affect the people of my parish?"

"They come to the house of your God and find it empty. They're losing what they believed in. It's redundant. They're confused and apprehensive. There's a problem. Heresy, blasphemy, whatever you want to call it. The truth is uncomfortable."

The man got up slowly and brushed down his jacket, straightening its creases. "I didn't come here to take anything from you, Father." He walked casually towards the locked doors. "Perhaps it's time for you to cast off the chains that bind you."

Put my life's commitment aside? I thought. Quit my safe harbour and sail out into—what?

I walked the man to the doors, conscious that his shoes were leaving smears of mud on the carpet, that rich, loamy smell still pungent. I unlocked and unbolted one of the doors and followed the man outside. The church was built on a hillcrest and from here we looked out over a view of the cityscape.

It wore its night glow; a garish mantle fuelled by a million lights, and from below came a constant throb of sound, fused from every vehicle and engine within the sprawl of buildings and streets. The man had said the city was organic, alive. Studying it now, it was easy to believe it. That unbroken buzz of noise was like the sound of a beehive, an uninterrupted dynamo.

"You need to make a choice," said the man. "Your god is said to have performed miracles through his son. Perhaps that's what you need. Something to help you make that choice."

There was a challenge in his expression, but then he walked away quickly, before I could respond, across the gravel of the small car park to where a solitary vehicle had been parked. It was an old van, its white paint chipped, its fenders dented. The man slid back the door to the driver's seat and got in, closing the door behind him. In a moment the engine grumbled a few times before it came reluctantly to life.

I watched the van drive away to the gates and beyond, its diminishing sound absorbed into the city's night hum.

A choice. A new, darker god, is that what he meant?

After I'd secured the church for the night, I left and made my way through the streets. The night air was cold but invigorating; it was thick. I could taste it, metallic, slightly acrid. Shadows eddied around me as though my movements had disturbed them. Isolated sounds superimposed themselves over the general throb—the thump of a door closing, an individual car or bus, a brief chorus of voices.

Alive, the man had said. My senses were more finely tuned than they had been for a long time. The buildings no longer seemed dead brick and stone. It was suddenly easy to imagine them as the bones of something living, a superstructure that was every bit as alert and functional as a human body, a vast organism, its blood the life of its inhabitants, the machines that they activated and the power they generated through it, electricity, gas, water. I could feel my own body echoing the vibrations of this macrocosm.

I walked more slowly, more cautiously, increasingly wanting to savour the experience, to be filled with it. *A new baptism.* Power. The old power that had been here, in the land, since the beginning. It was down there, in the bones of the earth, in the rocks and soil, the bedrock; the immense pumping organ, the heart of a world. I listened to it, fascinated, my own heart echoing the rhythm. I wanted to laugh, to shout, sing, express my oddly exultant state.

I entered the cramped general store where I picked up a few days' supplies of foodstuffs and a Sunday newspaper. The headlines were depressing. Ironically they snarled their outrage at the acts of a certain Bishop—I knew the man, a hateful, hypocritical monster—and his involvement with several young boys. A paedophile, a stain on the Church he served, another transgression, all blows to my already failing allegiance.

Inevitably, I added a bottle of whisky to my shopping. It had become a habit. I'd been telling myself for too long I didn't need it, but the truth was, I did.

As I paid for the goods, I looked up at the television mounted behind and above the counter. The local news was being broadcast, though no one in the store paid much attention. Something on the screen caught my attention.

A battered white van. Battered for a reason. It had been in a crash. I listened to the voice over the pictures.

"...*just after midday. Police are not sure how the van came to leave the road, although the recent flooding and subsequent residue of mud are thought to be responsible. No one else was hurt in the accident, although if the van had not collided with a street light it may well have driven into at least one of the terraced houses. The driver of the van has not yet been identified. Police are calling for any witnesses to come forward...*"

I gaped at the van—the same van that had been parked outside my church less than half an hour ago. It wasn't possible. The van on the TV was a write-off. The one I'd seen must have been an identical one.

I left the shop, bemused. The feeling of elation I'd experienced earlier had been replaced with one of deep unease. Around me the city seemed very quiet, as if it were listening to my thoughts, trying to pry into my mind. I was no longer in accord with it. Embraced by the darkness of an alleyway, I took a long swig of whisky and felt the brief solace of its fire. I was tempted to drink more, but it wouldn't be sensible, given my resolve to understand the mystery of the crashed van.

I went to the nearby police station. Inside the air was stuffy, over-heated. A few staff moved around, immersed in the tedium of their work. At the reception counter, a lone sergeant pored over notepads and documents.

"Hello, Father. What can we do for you?"

"I saw something on the television news. About a van crashing. At midday? A man was hurt."

The sergeant nodded slowly. He knew about the incident. "Yeah, sorry to say, it was fatal, Father. What do you know about it?"

"Where is the van?"

The sergeant studied me. I could see my agitation puzzled him. "Out in the yard, Father. Now, what's this all about?"

"I'm not sure. I saw the van earlier—and the driver." I decided against saying when it had been. "It came as a bit of a shock to see it on TV."

"Who was the driver? Can you identify him? He's at Whitelands Hospital. Mortuary."

"I don't have a name. I'll go there. Can I see the van first?"

"Sure." The sergeant called one of the passing constables. "Derek. Show the Father that van. The white Bedford that got smashed up earlier."

The constable took me out through some doors to a yard at the side of the station. There were several vehicles parked, but no van. The constable walked to the far end of the yard. Something had thrown him.

"They must have towed it away, Father. That was quick work. I didn't know the forensic guys had been here. I'll find out where they took it. Could have been one of a number of places. It was a complete write-off so it'll get scrapped eventually, but not until the case is investigated. If you don't mind waiting."

"I think I need to get to the hospital. I might be able to identify the victim."

I gave the police a statement, left the station and went home, getting my car out of the garage, my thoughts still locked on the accident. It must be a different van. They were common enough.

My car, an old Fiesta, spluttered as if reluctant to perform, but I coaxed it out through the streets. I felt strangely isolated, almost suffocating in the car. I was cold and uncomfortable throughout the five mile journey to the hospital. It was a relief to enter the deliberately baked atmosphere of the building. Light glared, the reception area wide and impersonal. There were people seated around. Some looked up at me. Most of them were immersed in their own private dramas.

"There was an accident," I told the receptionist. "One of my parishioners. He was driving a white Bedford van. He crashed and I understand from the police that he died."

"Oh, yes. I'm glad that you've come, Father. I don't think they've been able to identify him." The woman shuffled documents and tapped at a computer keyboard as if the machine would divulge the information if only she could hit the right keys. "Did you know him?"

"I'll know if I see him."

The woman nodded, as though she understood the situation perfectly, lifting a telephone receiver and dialling. She exchanged brief, quiet words with someone and then put the phone down.

"Mr Morgensen will be down in a moment. He's the surgeon dealing with the case." She smiled neutrally, disinclined to make small talk. It suited me and I waited quietly, looking out through the glass front of the hospital to where the night pressed in. Somehow, in the brightly lit interior, I felt vulnerable to that darkness.

The surgeon appeared, a tall, saturnine man, who seemed unmoved by the grim events. "I gather you knew the deceased, Father?"

"I'm not sure. I saw a man earlier today who might be the victim of the crash. I don't have a name, but if I can help in any way—"

"Of course," said the surgeon, nodding patiently. "No one has come forward and we're at a bit of a loss, to tell the truth. There was nothing in the man's pockets to identify him. I'll take you through." He led the way along numerous corridors and passages until we reached a door marked MORTUARY. ADMITTANCE TO STAFF ONLY.

"Father, I should warn you, the accident inflicted some very bad injuries on the man. He is recognisable, but you may find this a little disturbing."

"I'd know him by his clothes."

The surgeon nodded uneasily. "Ah. Good. Very well." He opened the door and led me through to an annex of the mortuary where a number of steel beds were arranged in rows, each of them covered in a white sheet. Some of the sheets had been draped over bodies, vague but recognisable human shapes. At the end of one row, the surgeon stood beside a bed. There were traces of blood on the white sheet that covered it.

A mortician materialised, his face masked, his eyes studying me.

"The van crash," said the surgeon, as though speaking in code. "Is this him?"

The mortician shook his head. He motioned us to follow him. We were at the end of the room, where there seemed to be empty beds only. The mortician looked around him as though he had lost his bearings.

"Something the matter?" said the surgeon.

The mortician studied the beds and stepped back a few paces, reading the label on one bed, but shaking his head. He tried a few others.

The surgeon looked at me. I could see something was clearly amiss. I said nothing, waiting. Moments later the mortician took the surgeon to one side and held a nervous but muted conversation with him.

I knew intuitively what was wrong. The man was not here. Just as the wrecked van had not been in the police yard. Disappeared. Taken back by the city. I frowned at the thought. Maybe there had been a mistake.

"I'm sorry about this," said the surgeon, as the mortician disappeared.

"Perhaps the man was not as badly hurt as people thought," I said. *The man I saw*, I thought, *was fine—scruffy and a bit worse for wear, but no more than that.*

The surgeon was evidently torn between his professional commitments and the need to prevent anything embarrassing from leaking out. He looked baffled, but spoke calmly. "Well, there's certainly been a mix up, Father. If you'd like to wait in the foyer, we'll sort this out."

I allowed myself to be led back to the reception area and sat at a table. Someone brought me a cup of coffee. I would have preferred a mouthful of whisky. My mind was on the man who had visited the church. A police detective, I'd thought. Reconsidering our meeting, it seemed odd that a detective would be driving such a battered old van. And of course, the police would have known if one of their own was missing.

It was half an hour before the surgeon returned. He was no longer the calm, detached person he had been earlier. His face was drawn, tired. He eased me to a quiet corner of the foyer and spoke in hushed tones. "This is rather difficult, Father. There've been some complications. It looks as if the victim of the crash has been transferred. It isn't supposed to have happened, but occasionally these things do occur. I think the best thing you can do is go home and we'll contact you as soon as we have any more information." His expression suggested he didn't want any further discussion.

I merely nodded. I just wanted to get away.

Outside, the air had turned bitterly cold, a stark contrast to the baking heat in the hospital. I hurried, shivering, across the car park to my vehicle. It took several attempts to start it, but I got it moving and away. My thoughts were as numbed as my body. There had been a crash—the police and the hospital staff had all confirmed it. So I hadn't imagined it. But how could it possibly have been the same man who had come to the church? It couldn't have. Of course it couldn't.

Unless he'd survived the crash. But no, even if he had, the van had been a complete write-off. The man couldn't have subsequently driven it to the church. When I'd met him, he showed no signs of having been involved in an accident.

The streets closed in as I drove homeward, black arteries of the city, blocked with cars parked up for the night. The city was in a different mood now, as if its corporate breath were drawn, anticipating something. I wanted to lock myself away until morning.

I pulled up at traffic lights, the only vehicle around, isolated in the red glow of the stop light. It seemed to be locked, an unblinking eye. I looked at my wing mirror and saw movement in its glass. Another vehicle coming up behind me.

White.

A cold hand seemed to touch my neck and I felt a churning in my gut. I needed that drink.

White.

I tried to turn in my seat, restricted by the seat belt, unable to see clearly. The red light changed to orange and quickly to green. The vehicle behind pulled out and around before I could respond as it overtook me.

White.

I ground the gears as the van—the white van—turned left at the crossroad and out of view. My car juddered forward and without thinking I swung it around to the left, in pursuit of the van. It was already fifty yards or more ahead of me, gathering speed. Smoke swirled out of its exhaust, cloudy in the cold air. It was an old van, its paint chipped, its rear fender dented.

It's the same van, I knew. This is deliberate. The man is trying to make a complete fool of me. Why? What does he have to gain by this?

What had he said as he left me? Something about—a miracle. To help me make my choice.

I tried to accelerate enough to catch up, but always the van kept its distance, swerving recklessly around corners, bumping over the pavement edges, narrowly missing parked cars. If this was how its driver flogged its engine, it was no wonder that it had crashed. No, that wasn't right. This van hadn't crashed. Not the way the van on TV had done.

It was only after we'd raced through the streets for some distance I realised where we were. The church was not far up ahead. If the van drove up to the church, its driver wouldn't be able to avoid me. It must be what he wanted.

I slowed the Fiesta, taking the final bend carefully. I felt anger welling in me, infuriation at being toyed with. The gates to the church car park were open and the white van hadn't slowed. I could see it by the church, as though it had been eager to race up there, a dog let loose from its lead. I followed cautiously, eventually pulling up yards from the van. Now there was no doubt in my mind that it was the same vehicle that my visitor of earlier had driven.

I got out of the car and walked towards the van's driver's door. It was open, but exasperatingly there was no one inside. I looked around me. There was no movement and a deep silence had settled over everything. Above me the church loomed in the night, lightless and sombre. Below the hill the city throbbed gently, a breathing giant. Its mood had changed. Like the air, it was gathering itself.

"Hello!" I called. I walked up and down outside the front of the church, feet crunching the gravel, but there was no reply. I went to the church doors and realised that one of them had been opened. Unlocked, not forced, though that was impossible—I knew I'd locked it. I scowled at it. It seemed to be a night of impossibilities. Only the caretaker and I had keys. Jeffers must have come back for some reason.

Gently I eased the door open, calling his name. There were no lights on inside. In the gloom I could make out the pews, the pillars, but not much else in the way of details. No one was here, that was obvious. But if Jeffers had been here, surely he wouldn't have been that careless that he'd have left without re-locking the door. He was a meticulous man, almost irritatingly so.

I flicked a light switch. At once the church was bathed in a brilliant glow. There was no one visible. I walked down the aisle, calling out once more, but there was no response. I could see, though, that someone had been here—the carpet was muddied in places. Far more than it had been, as if several people had been here.

I reached the altar. Some of the candle-holders, large brass objects, had been moved, one of them actually over on its side, its thick wax candle lying on the floor, snapped in half. It was only then, looking up, that I realised what the intruder had come here for. Amazingly, the wooden statue of Christ on the cross was missing. Yet its *weight*—

I looked around in horror, realising there were other signs of disturbance and damage. Whoever had moved the tall wooden icon had struggled with it and carelessly knocked into not only the altar but other furnishings. A curtain had been torn down from its runners. Carpets were rucked up. Surely it would have been beyond one man to move it? For all my recent doubts and uncertainties I could only feel outraged at the theft.

After a brief search of the main body of the church—there definitely was no one here—I went back outside and stood on the steps, baffled. Beyond the car park, below the hill, it was as if countless invisible eyes were watching me, eager to see how I was going to react to this crisis. I could hear something nearer at hand, over to my right where there was an overgrown area, perhaps half an acre, beyond the graves and headstones. A light glowed there, flickering. The sound came again—kids! Messing about. Not for the first time they'd lit a fire. Could they be responsible for the damage in the church?

Angered, I went through the headstones and down the roughly beaten path to the overgrown area. Brambles threaded through banks of grass and low shrubs. The kids had heard me coming and after a moment they scattered like rats from a bin. It was a frequent game they played to relieve their boredom. I heard them laughing as they fled into the labyrinth of weeds and tall grasses. I knew from experience it would be pointless trying to pursue them. Their taunts and laughter grew fainter as they ran off back down the hill towards the streets and buildings.

I reached the fire. The kids had made it from a few gathered bits of dead branch and rotted planks, heaped neatly—safely as it happened—into a low cone, the grass around it flattened so that the fire was contained. At least they'd had the sense not to risk it spreading and causing real havoc. There were buckets of sand in the church: I'd put the fire out easily enough. I stared at the flames for a while, as if their dancing colours would impart something to me.

The missing statue! Were they burning it?

I got closer to the fire and peered more closely through the stinging clouds of smoke. The statue was as tall as a man and equally as wide. Thankfully there was no sign of it on the heaped wood and it would have taken a significant time to burn down to ash, so it couldn't be here. If the kids had brought it out here, it must by lying around somewhere in the long grass. I had to find it.

As I walked around the rim of the fire, my foot caught on something—a three foot length of metal. It was a spar of some kind, dragged from a nearby derelict factory. The kids must have been using it as an impromptu poker. I picked it up and started using it as a beater to work my way through the high grass and tangled brambles. They almost snared me with thorns like teeth. I worked methodically around the fire, going slowly outwards.

I'd been bent over, immersed in the task, for long, fruitless minutes, when I realised I was no longer alone. Someone was studying me from the other side of the fire.

Smoke billowed, thickened by the breeze, obscuring my view. I assumed it was the van driver.

Still clutching the length of metal, I circled the roaring fire. The man was very still, thickly wrapped in shadows. Flames licked around and over him. I moved closer, wary of the intense heat, my face dripping with perspiration.

"Do you mind telling me what on earth is going on?" I said, unable to keep the rising anger from my voice.

The man remained motionless.

I closed with him, between him and the fire. "Look, I don't understand—your van was on the TV, in a bad crash. You must have—" My words choked off as I realised what it was I was looking at. *The statue*. Christ on the cross. Except that there was no cross. And the arms were not raised up, nailed to the crosspiece: they were hanging down at the statue's side. Not cut off, but in a different position. I gaped, coughing in the smoke. It must be a different statue. That, or-

It moved. I couldn't see the face or the eyes, the head still bowed in wooden agony. It stepped forward, its arms lifting slowly with a sound like the movement of branches in the wind. Wooden fingers opened, reaching out slowly, as if experimentally.

I couldn't stagger back without blundering into the fire. Panic raced up inside me like rising bile. At last the statue's face was revealed, those blind, wooden eyes, holding the torment of centuries, locked in that carved visage. Step by step the thing came to me, imbued with impossible life, impossible *energy*.

Galvanised by sudden, sheer terror, I lifted the metal bar and struck out wildly, fuelled with excessive strength, wild energy. The metal smashed into the looming shape, connecting with one of the statue's shoulders so fiercely that the wood split. Again I struck and again the wood split under the force of my blows. The arms swung at me, fingers almost finding my shoulders; I swerved aside, almost losing my balance, conscious of the flames behind me. I struck out at the legs of the statue, hitting the polished wood with renewed ferocity. All the frustration and tension of the day—no, the years, a lifetime!—drove me on so that a kind of hysterical joy took a hold of me. With each blow I shed a memory of pain, the beatings of my childhood, dressed as religious punishment, the mental torment of sexual guilt, the misery of failure to meet the dictates of my demanding god. All the disappointments of my flock, the desperate lives, the unrewarded search for peace of mind—I shaped my fury from it.

It made no difference. The statue's sudden life force was undimmed by my attack. Though it cracked and split in a dozen places, wounds that did not bleed, it was an automaton, one hand finally gripping my shoulder, squeezing as if it would snap the bone, its own power desperate, as if it knew it would lose me—my soul—if it failed here.

I dropped the metal bar, staggering back to the very edge of the fire. Instinctively I pulled a spar of wood free and used it as a weapon. Embers flurried from its burning end as it smacked into the face of the statue. In that hot glow, the blind eyes swivelled, fixed in an expression of deep sorrow, regret at the act of assault. *Pity me*, they said.

I drove the burning point of the weapon into that face over and over again until the statue's wooden skin caught alight. The face contorted even more, as if it felt the pain of the fire. Its mouth hung open, smoke belching from it. I was able to scramble to one side, staring in horror at the statue as it stood before the fire, hands closed over its face in an attempt to beat out the flames licking up from it.

Snatching up the fallen metal spar, I swung it with every last vestige of anger at the neck of the statue. I struck at its legs and drove the point of the spar into its spine. The statue blundered forward, its movements almost human, its disorientation complete. It stumbled and fell, face first, into the flames. At once there was a conflagration, as though the wood of the statue had been soaked in oil. I drew back from the intensity of the blaze, realising I was shouting at the top of my voice. Around me the night echoed that sound, gleeful and exultant.

I lurched away from the inferno, watching the writhing shape within it, boiling with white hot fire. There were no screams, no sounds but the crackling wood and the hungry roar of the flames. An arm rose pathetically, a silent, impotent gesture.

Eventually there was another sound, more distant. The van! I was certain it was its engine coughing to life. I blundered through the grass, realising as I staggered back up to the church how exhausted I was, my clothes glued to me as if they would drag me to my knees. The van was shuddering to life, black smoke pouring from its exhaust. It seemed to be crouching, about to spring away like some predatory creature of the night.

I reached the gravel, shouting at the invisible driver. Behind me I could hear movement in the grass and I turned to see the bent shape of something stumbling towards me, an arm outstretched, an arm that glowed with fire, shedding streamers of white smoke.

The statue! It had risen from the flames, driven on by God alone knew by what fanatical power, still reaching for me. I could hardly lift my legs, my own energy drained. Somehow I got to the church doors and went into the inner darkness. Somewhere among the pews, I slumped down, coughing, my eyes streaming. Light flared behind me as that horrific, still blazing shape groped its way into the church.

As it came forward, the fire from its torso licked out and began to feed on the woodwork. In no time the first pews caught alight. I sagged down, unable to find the strength to get up. This was going to end in an inferno, and it would be my pyre. I must have blacked out at that point.

I came to, I don't know how much later, and found myself being dragged across the gravel of the car park. I saw only the legs of the man who had rescued me from the church—the church that was now ablaze, its flames reaching dozens of feet up into the night sky. Nothing would quell that blaze. The church would be gutted.

It was the van driver who'd pulled me out. He let me fall prone and I caught again that pungent smell of earth, the soiled clothes. I was stretched out on the ground, my face in the gravel.

I saw the man's feet move away towards the parked van, its engine still throbbing. He got into it and shut the door. Moments later the vehicle pulled away and I watched it slowly disappear down the slope towards the city and as it left, it seemed as though it was gradually sinking into the earth.

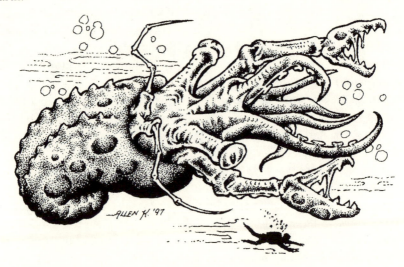

Have a Crappy Halloween
by Franklyn Searight

Robbie, kneeling on the carpet, thumbed his shooter, sending it into the circle of string, unerringly striking the gaudiest marble. It was done with the skilled precision of a ten year old boy who had devoted much of his life to developing his skills.

The lad was good—-very good, as his chums, who had lost their stash to his seemingly magic thumb, would grudgingly attest.

"If you paid as much attention to your school work as you do to your pastimes, you'd have a much better chance of making something of yourself in life," his mother had told him a week earlier, fed up with the manner in which he wasted his leisure time.

"Awe, Maw," he retorted, "I have my entire life to learn stuff. There's only so much time during the day I can spend at aggies."

"Too much time, if you ask me," responded Gertrude Epstein. "Balancing your time is important, but put the most essential priorities first."

"I do, Maw, and marbles is the most important activity on my list."

"I know, and schooling seems to take up less and less of your time. You want to be a lawyer someday, don't you, or maybe a doctor?"

"I'll do better, Maw. I'll get all "A's" on my next report card."

Mrs. Epstein smiled and left to pour him some Kool-Aid and arrange a platter of Oreo cookies to nibble on. "I'll be happy," she said, under her breath, "if you bring home a report card with C's and B's on it."

Robbie shoved the pile of marbles he was using back into the circle and started all over again, using his shooter to knock them out. This would be his last practice session until after dinner. He had been engaged with the glass spheroids for a while, anyway, and was looking forward to taking a stroll down the block. Maybe, if he was lucky, Becky Wilkins would be outside, riding her bicycle, and she might even talk with him for a few minutes. He finished the game he was playing, winning again, as he always did and put the sack of aggies away for a while.

Tonight was the night, his favorite evening of the year, the night for which he had waited an entire three-hundred sixty-four days, each one passing so very, very slowly. Tonight, the bats and goblins would fly and the black cats and haunts would walk the streets as though they owned them.

Tonight was Halloween.

Robbie was not just enamored with Halloween; Christmas was also a favored time of the year and came in as a close second, in his estimation. He always looked forward to the festive season with enthusiastic anticipation, enjoying the bright colors better than the drab darker ones of All Saint's Day. And the presents he would receive, well, what more can one say? Even the foods were in a close race for first place: The hallowed sweets were closely tied with the yummy pastries of Christmas, topped with sticky delicacies and interiors filled with gooey, finger-slurping goodness. Considering everything, though, the night of spooky haunts would always be best, in his estimation.

If Robbie was to have his own way, it would be Halloween for two thirds of the year and Christmas for the remainder. Further, when his education was finished, he would like to have a job in a marble factory, perhaps filling bags of glass globes for Santa's elves, rather than work at a law office. His second choice would be a professional who participated in marble tournaments, to earn a living.

He slipped into his lightweight jacket, just heavy enough to break the wind, and walked outside. He stood on the porch for a minute, looking around to see if some of his chums were outside, playing. None of them was to be seen and nether was Becky, who was the cutest and sweetest girl in the world—- compared, at least, with any other adolescent in the fifth grade class they shared at school. He would never admit it, of course, even if flaming sticks had been driven into his fingernails. In years to come he intended to ask Rebecca to be his girlfriend and she would accept. He felt himself blushing at the thought.

It had been only two months ago when both, invited to the same birthday party, found themselves opposite each other in a circle where spin-the-bottle was being played. Robbie had been ecstatic when the bottom of the bottle pointed to the girl and the top to him, but tried not to show it as he went over and kissed her on the cheek. Rebecca, in turn, had wiped her face with the back of her hand as though she had been licked by a lizard. The lad would always remember the episode in his young life and the surreptitious admiration he had felt toward her he believed would never diminish.

He sat on the porch swing for a couple of minutes, deciding what he would like to be doing. He still had a good three hours before 'The Night' would begin and so far the neighborhood was relatively quiet. Still, he could sense an unseen and unfelt tension building in the air he was certain would grow stronger and stronger until it exploded. Or was it just his imagination?

Maybe Becky was on the next block riding her bike.

He meandered down to the sidewalk, enjoying the crispness of the cool air and did not stop until he had gone past a dozen houses, almost to the end of the block. On one side of his pathway, running between the sidewalk and the street, was a shallow ditch. The water, when it was present, during and after a heavy storm, flowed along in the ditch and under each driveway on its way to the end of the street and the catch basin. Where the water moved under the driveways, it went through cement conduits.

All in all, Robbie believed, the open trench was not a very attractive sight, although when he was a little boy he enjoyed wading in it until his parents yelled at him to stop. There were a few houses on his block where the owners had installed, at their own expense, a conduit from their driveway to the next driveway, through which the water would flow. The area between the driveways filled with dirt and grass grown over all. Robbie thought this setup made the landscaping much more attractive. He believed the entire drainage ditch, going down the entire block, should be covered-in and when he mentioned this to his father, he had been told someday the city would take on the project when it had the money to spend.

Robbie was so used to the partially uncovered ditch in front of his house he never gave it a second thought and today was no different than any of the others—-at least not at the beginning and not until he had passed the first two houses to his right and saw the same man again, the one he had noticed hanging around the neighborhood for the last month or so. His chums had also seen him and had made of him an entertaining topic of neighborhood conversation.

He was an old guy, a seedy looking character who wore tattered, unkempt clothing so shabby it might well have been hand-me-downs passing through a succession of owners. On top of his head rested a wide-brimmed, disheveled slouch hat looking as though it had been worn repeatedly for many years. Out from under it peeked stringy, uncut hair snowy white in some place and a dirty gray in others. The community youngsters suspected he was a homeless gent, as no one had any idea where he resided, or even if he had a home in which to live.

As Robbie was returning home, he saw the peculiar man sitting on his neighbor's driveway, near the street, his legs dangling downward inches above the ditch, his head cocked to one side as though he were listening to something. Perhaps someone under the driveway was talking to him, Robbie thought and was tempted to giggle at the amusing notion.

The stranger paid no attention to the young boy as he walked by without slowing his steps, pretending not to notice him, as though he was not even there. At the last second, however, the lad looked down at him and was surprised to see the man looking up at him with eyes seeming to be empty, with nothing substantial behind them. It was too late to avert his own eyes and he realized he should not have looked at him at all.

The boy shrugged his shoulders and continued down the street, going past his own house toward the end of the block, not wanting the weird dude to know where he lived, glancing over his shoulder a couple of times to see the man was still there and still looking down into the trench.

He stopped suddenly, before reaching the corner, struck by a weird thought: Was it possible the man lived down there, somewhere under the driveway where he had taken up residence? It was a silly notion, but if the guy did not live in the conduit, where did he live?

Naw, he thought, it was an absurd idea, but a funny one to consider. Who would want to live in a place like that? He turned the idea over in his mind a few times, liking the taste of it, like some dessert his mother made for him he did not feel was quite right until he chewed on it a few times. He had looked into the conduit under his driveway by his own house on differet occasions in the past, climbing down into the ditch and peering into the concrete channel. There had been nothing of interest for a young boy to see, nothing to entice him to crawl inside and explore around. Sunlight penetrated into the opening a couple of feet, where a few pebbles and leaves could be seen which had not been washed away, before the interior had dwindled away in to darkness. Someday, he thought, when the man was not around and it was clean and dry down there beneath the driveway, he would take his flashlight, drop into the ditch, crawl in for a foot or two or three and shine the light around. What might he find?

Robbie looked around one more time as he reached the corner, wondering if the man had dropped down into the trench and crawled into the conduct under the driveway, but he was still there. He concluded the outsider had no more interest in exploring it than he did.

He turned at the corner and walked along the side street a few steps and then came back and concealed himself behind a huge elm tree. There he decided to stay for a while, himself unseen, watching the man and wondering if he was going to sit there for the rest of the day or do something else. If he left, maybe he would be able to follow behind him for a distance.

Robbie stayed there for a spell as the sun slowly made its way to the western horizon. He was still thinking of the weirdo stranger, his rich imagination running wild, still wondering what he was doing there. He was still intrigued and amused by the notion he had fabricated of the man dropping down into the ditch and crawling under the driveway, unknown to the residents of the block. The young man was actually disappointed when the man did no such thing. There was still a trickle of stagnant water in the passageway, remnants of yesterday's rain; not enough to drown anyone, but enough to make it uncomfortable if one attempted to crawl into it.

He turned momentarily to watch a dog running down the street carrying a stick and when he looked back again he saw the man was no longer there.

Had he really been sitting there, or was his presence nothing more than a curious illusion?

Of course not; others, besides himself, had seen the creepy guy.

But which way had he gone? It was a question Robbie could not answer. If he had come his way, the boy would have seen him. If he had gone in the other direction, he would still have seen him and Robbie would be able to follow him to find out where he lived. What most likely happened, the lad decided, was the man entered one of the nearby houses, but he could not be certain of it, either.

Drat! He knew he should have been more alert, watching more closely and not allowing his attention to be diverted elsewhere at the wrong moment.

And then, suddenly, he noticed the man on the other side of the street slowly waddling away in the opposite direction. For a few seconds, the lad considered following him, to see where he went, but decided a more prudent course was to stay away from evil. It was a chunk of advice in which he strictly believed, something he learned from one of his parents, he could not remember which one. It was something just coming to mind at the moment because, unquestionably, the stranger was one of the most incarnate characters of evil he had ever seen.

Still, in some secret part of his mentality, in the wild flights of his imagination, he daydreamed of discovering the man had set up housekeeping under one of the driveways. There might be a bed and a couch in there, maybe a make-shift stove upon which the man could fry hamburgers when it was time for dinner. Yeah, it was probably what he would like to eat— just like Robbie did.

The boy was in no hurry to return home, not yet. He was a youth who enjoyed listening to his own thoughts and partaking of the fanciful flights they took where most adults would not want to go.

His reflections now returned to the coming of Halloween night. It was a special time of the year during which he was able to watch the varied leaves turning into their finest garments of red and yellow and orange before giving up their grip on the branches and settling softly to the ground. He found no enjoyment in raking them, of course, but when the last leaf was finally gathered, he participated in another joy: leaping into the mound and scattering the fallen ghosts of autumn around again, making it necessary for him to clean them up once more. He loved the entire scenario repeating itself year every year.

Robbie also loved the smell of rich earth turned over and exposed; of small fires in the streets chewing the roughage fed into them; the smell of smoke with a special tang to it; and the cries of childish joy as the younger ones stood about chatting with their playmates, anxiously waiting for darkness to fall and for trick-or-treating to begin.

The sight of goblins and ghouls, of vampires and werewolves and witches, stirred Robbie's blood, as he approached the steps of his porch, whipping his senses into a frenzy. He also enjoyed the more humorous costumes like princesses and queens and, now and then, someone like Rebecca Wilkins who once dressed as an old grandmother, wearing the remains of a white mop on her head.

He loved the special scenic effects used to decorate the neighborhood: the hollowed-out pumpkins seen aglow on gloomy porches, along with black cats and gravestones erected on the lawns, and even the more elaborate homes made up to resemble haunted houses.

At Robbie's urging dinner was early that evening so he could get an early jump on the other beggars patrolling the streets. Every moment would be precious to him as it meant one more piece of candy for his sack. He rushed through his meal with greater speed than usual, ingesting a hotdog with frantic haste, his mind focused almost exclusively on the coming hours.

The youth donned his cowboy outfit, which seemed to fit a bit more snugly than he remembered it and he wondered if his mother had shrunk it in the wash or if he was outgrowing it. He placed his ten gallon hat atop his head, which was more like a five, leaned it at an awkward angle and strapped the holsters holding his six-shooters around his waist. He completed his ensemble by pinning a deputy's star to his chest.

Twilight was well advanced, the shadows clustering ever thicker, when he grabbed his flashlight and the pillow slip he intended to stuff with tasty treats and started out. It was six o'clock, the agreed upon time throughout the neighborhood for trick-or-treating to begin. Only a few lights were aglow and then, almost simultaneously, welcoming porch lights were switched on, turning the area into a magical wonderland. The residents were ready for the tidal wave of costumed children advancing upon them.

His first stop was the house next door where Timmy Thomas lived, his seven year old playmate who would be joining him for the night's scavenging, the arrangement made earlier in the day by their mothers. Timmy was a good scout, a little naive, Robbie thought, but a fun loving chap with a good heart who looked up to him as though he were an older brother. If they came upon the usual school crowd the older boy hung out with and frequently walked with on Halloween, the little tyke would fit in with the group just fine.

He cut across the lawn to the youngster's porch, noting the bright orange pumpkin, large as a beach ball, illuminated by a lit candle inside and carved to resemble a gargoyle, or something. Jack-o'-lanterns were a favorite with Robbie, who was fascinated by the intricate sculptures the makers crafted.

He waited beneath the porch light as Mrs. Thomas slipped a popcorn ball wrapped in cellophane into his bag and his younger partner, already dressed up as a pirate, took his flashlight and slung an empty, floppy sack over his shoulder and came outside.

"Thank you, Mrs. Thomas," he said politely, acknowledging the treat. He usually tossed away foods wrapped in cellophane, or otherwise unprotected, not willing to take a chance it had not been tampered with by someome. His mother warned him of such delights being doctored with noxious solutions, or even with razor blades embedded in them, something he wanted to avoid. He cringed at the thought of biting into an apple and feeling the cold steel of a blade slicing through his mouth and tongue. Everything he bit into would have to be in the wrapper in which it came from the store. Mrs. Thomas, of course, would not give him such a treat, so he felt safe in enjoying it at a later time.

"C'mon, Timmy," he said. "Time's a wasting!"

"Have a good time!" called Timmy's mother, as the boys left the porch. At the same time as they descended, three other fellows were climbing up the steps to take their place, crying: "Help the poor", their sacks opened wide. One was a taller teenage boy, nearly as large as Robbie's dad, costumed to look like a tramp, his face darkened with ashes or soot, or maybe even shoe polish. The other two were smaller, one dressed as an Indian Chief, a rubber tomahawk slipped into his belt and the other wore a white sheet draped over his head, with large eye holes cut into the fabric through which he could see. Robbie did not think he knew either of them and suspected they might be children driven into the area from a less prosperous neighborhood.

On to the next house they went, where Mrs. Costello slipped Mound Bars into their sacks, and then on to the next and the next and so on until they were at the end of the block. They followed much the same routine: climbing porch steps, yelling "trick-or-treat" or "help the poor", whatever they were inclined to say at the moment, pounding doors or ringing doorbells if the occupants did not come to the door quickly enough.

Their bags grew heavier and heavier as more houses were visited and more delights were handed out to them. Many of the dwellings had a jack-o-lantern sitting on the porch or gaping at them through a window, each one with a light inside and each one showing the individual creativity of the carver. Ghoulish faces, funny or happy expressions, tormented features, faces with bulging eyes, absurd noses and other assorted features.

Robbie was amazed at the wide variety of pumpkin teeth on display:

small choppers, large and wide grinders, some squared off at the bottom, others sharply spiked as though they had been in the maw of a shark and some specimens with serrated teeth like the blade of a buzz saw. Many of the teeth they saw looked ferocious, ready to administer an awful bite to any of the beggars who dared to get too close. The hungry, creepy, sharpened teeth represented this special day in the very best of ways, the two boys believed.

On one occasion the home owner had a pail of water on her porch, filled with apples for which the children were invited to bob. Robbie excused himself, explaining he had a cold, which he really did not have, but Timmy was eager to dive in to claim his prize and emerged from the dunking with an apple in his mouth and his hair dripping and plastered down.

Some of the lawns they passed were drearily decorated with tombstones, wooden caskets, flying bats hanging on strings and a wide assortment of other ghoulish gadgets designed to strike horror into the hearts of the younger folk. A few of the adults answered the doors dressed in costumes of their own making, werewolves and vampires predominating and others in costume guiding their little tykes around the block. Robbie believed many of the older people enjoyed the evening just as much as the children did and, in some cases, perhaps even more, remembering their early years when they strolled the streets themselves on All Hallows' Eve.

Orange, yellow and black seemed to be the predominant colors of the Special Night and seemed to be everywhere. Even earlier in school the children in Robbie's fifth grade class were assigned the task of drawing and coloring a Halloween picture and Robbie made full use of the traditional hues of the festive holiday, splashing them all over his creation.

"Too much orange," his teacher had said, passing his desk. "You're wearing out the crayons!"

"Awe, Mrs. Nowak! It's Halloween!" he asserted. "I'm only using three colors for my scary picture!"

His teacher smiled. "You're right, Robbie. Forget what I said. These are the best colors for the season, so use all of them you want to."

One of his classmates had invited him over to his house for a party after school to celebrate the big day, urging him to wear a because their garage would be decorated to resemble a haunted house, advising him they would tell scary stories and watch . Afterwards, they would go outside and sit around a bonfire, thinking up funny to play on their neighbors. It sounded like loads of fun to Robbie, but he passed on the invitation, explaining he probably would not have the time, but he would be there if he did.

Forty minutes later the two boys were back on their own block, this time on the other side of the street and slowed down when they spied a man coming toward them. Robbie recognized him right away, even in the darkness—-the homeless man that had been spied lurking around the area. He was dressed in costume as a hobo, still wearing the same splotched, slouch hat, limping as though he had sprained an ankle.

"Hey, boy!" said the man, his voice harsh and grinding. He stopped before them and took off the knapsack he had slung around his head. "Got a special treat for you here, kid.

"Wanna make a trade?"

Robbie was in a state of consternation! Never talk to strangers was a warning he had been taught throughout his young life, an admonition he had promised to never forget. But now his mind was confused, suddenly befuddled and he was unable to think coherently. He had taken one step toward the stranger when the caution lights went on like a sparkler on the Fourth of July.

Robbie tried to avert his eyes from the man's own and found he was unable to do so. They had a penetrating quality about them the lad was unable to ignore, drawing the boy into them with a hypnotic quality.

"A trade?" he finally asked, his voice not much louder than a whisper. "What kind of a trade?"

The man opened up his sack and held up a hefty cotton pouch, tied at the top with a draw string bulging as though it had been filled with small rocks. The word 'marbles' was emblazoned on the outside.

"Your bag of candy for this sack of marbles!"

"It's a great deal," thought Robbie, sorely tempted to make the exchange. "There must be hundreds of them in there, enough marbles to last me for years."

"Boulders, puries, steelies, cherry blossoms, commies, shooters, cats eyes and aggies—-plenty of each," said the eccentric man, rattling off the different names as though he were a waitress reciting a menu's selections. "Can't go wrong with these, boy."

Robbie was sorely tempted. He could always get more candy but, then again, he really had all the marbles he needed.

"I…I…I…think I'll keep my candy" decided Robbie after careful reflection. "Plenty of marbles at home."

"Suit yourself, boy. Some other lad will enjoy having these."

The man shoved the bag back into his knapsack. He turned and strolled away saying, "Have a creepy, crappy Halloween!"

"Did he say what I thought he said?" Robbie asked Timmy as they walked away and up to the next house.

"I think he wished you a Happy Halloween," was his partner's answer.

I must have misunderstood him, Robbie decided.

"Still, I'm sure it wasn't what I heard," reflected Robbie, but he made no issue about it with Timmy. "The gent had not been all that clear, not with his gritty, sandpaper-like voice," he concludeed.

Robbie had a further thought after thinking the situation over. "Maybe I should have made the trade after all." He was tempted to call after the man and tell him he changed his mind, but when he looked again, the stranger had already disappeared down the street.

"Oh, well, it's too late now," Robbie thought. "The bag was probably filled with stones anyway."

The hobo was soon forgotten as they continued their progress down the street passing an assortment of witches, goblins, cats of assorted sizes, ghosts, space aliens and numerous haunts, too many to count on both hands. They had pillaged nearly to the end of the block when they saw a group of giggling girls leaving a porch and coming toward them. Robbie's heart began to flutter a little faster at the sight of a pretty princess wearing a tiara and attired in a flowing gown of blue. He recognized her at once as Rebecca Wilkins, the cute girl in his class he had been watching for all evening.

"Hi, Becky," he called out to her. "Your sack filled yet?"

"It's getting there," she answered.

"You know the cowboy, Beck?" asked one of her friends, a skinny girl dressed up as Raggedy Ann.

"Sure. He sits behind me in math class. I don't know his name."

"Hurry up," said Cat Woman, another of her companions.

"'Bye," called Rebecca, as the trio continued on their way.

Robbie wondered how it was possible she had not known his name. They had been in classes together for the last few years and the teacher had used his name nearly every time she had called on him.

This was a stupefying problem, he reflected, until the thought came to him she might have been just teasing him, or she was pretending she did not know him lest her friends think she had an interest in him. Robbie was learning an important lesson at his early age in his understanding of the opposite gender. He, himself, would never indicate a fondness for any girl; it simply was not done. His chums would tease him unmercifully, even though they also might secretly have such feelings. Could it be Rebecca was like other girls her age, furtively having feelings for certain boys they would give anything not to reveal? It could be so, Robbie decided and gave the incident no further thought.

An assortment of other youngsters passed them as they trod along, their legs growing more tired, porch steps becoming higher and their goody sacks heavier and heavier. Robbie was continuously amazed by the variety of costumes he saw. The fellows, some he knew, some he thought he knew but was unable able to penetrate their disguises, and others who were total strangers, were seen as Frankenstein, Spider-Man, Ninja Warrior, Captain

America, Superman and so on. The girls, in turn, had their own favorites, being partial to witches, Bat Girl, princesses, Cleopatra, gypsies and so forth. He even spotted one dressed as Velma from Scooby Doo, which made him chuckle.

"It's been a grand evening," Robbie declared to his little friend at the end of the block, crossing the street and making their way back to Timmy's house.

"Is it always like this?" asked the smaller lad.

"It always has been," the older boy declared.

They parted company when Mrs. Thomas opened the door and Timmy slipped inside, beginning to lower his heavy pillow even before he was through the door. He thanked Robbie for taking him around and his older friend retraced his steps back to the sidewalk and over to his own house. He could hardly wait to tip the contents of his sack onto the living room floor, emptying it and seeing what treasures he had garnered throughout the evening.

Robbie was quite happy when he went to bed, expecting to dream about Mound Bars and Clark Bars, Hershey Bars, Tootsie Rolls and Chuckles, along with a large assortment of other scrumptious delicacies. But sweet dreams somehow eluded him and were replaced by visions of the peculiar vagrant in the slouch hat who worked his way into different scenes as the principle dream character on center stage, or lurking around in the shadows, but making clear his presence. They were horrid dreams waking him repeatedly throughout the night.

Still, Halloween had been a blast and he went to school the next day with his usual enthusiasm, although somewhat weary from his near-sleepless night. He arrived a little earlier than usual and stood outside the wide school door with his classmates, waiting for the bell to ring and school to begin. Most had something to say about the goodies they had gathered the evening before; tales of playful pranks were shared and nifty costumes described they had worn or seen others wearing. Spooky stories were exchanged and jokes told before the students filed into the institute.

Two pieces of candy had been slipped into Robbie's lunchbox by his mother, reminders of the fun he had enjoyed. School was humdrum, as usual and the boy had trouble keeping his eyes open during the last class of the day. He was not the only one; many of the others had stayed up later than usual, wanting to savor every ounce of magic they had experienced the night before. Becky was absent in the morning, disappointing Robbie who had the notion of offering her some of the candy he had brought to school——a Hershey bar, with nuts, he knew was one of her favorites.

She was also absent from the afternoon session.

The neighborhood was quiet at the hour of his return home from school, everything as normal as Jell-O, and it was not until he noticed the slightly perceptible odor drifting from beneath the driveway two doors away from his home, he suspected something might be amiss. The ditch in front of the particular home had been fitted with a cement culvert and covered with dirt and grass. A smattering of leaves now covered the area, but Robbie knew the passageway was still there, unseen. The smell was not terribly obnoxious, but something dimly reminded him of ripening fruit. The nearer he came to the driveway and the waterway beneath it, the more noticeable it was. When he went out to play later on, it was even more pronounced and a bit more pungent.

The following day the aroma was worse and Robbie began to suspect a dog had been hit out in the street and had somehow limped or crawled into the tunnel for safety, or perhaps to die. Could be a cat, too, he considered. The scent was more noxious and nascent and he hoped the wind would soon dispel it. He had heard it might rain during the night and he thought maybe the stream of water flowing through the ditch would wash away whatever was in it.

It did rain in the evening, a downpour lasting for nearly half an hour, but when Robbie passed by the ditch the next morning there was still the same odor, lingering languidly about. The rain had dispersed much of it and he believed it would soon disappear altogether.

Rebecca Wilkins was absent from school again during day, which was surprising to everyone because up until this time she had enjoyed a record of perfect attendance. Robbie noticed some of the teachers getting together from time to time and whispering among themselves and a couple of unknown men, dressed in suitcoats and ties came inside the school to talk with the teachers and some of the children.

Returning home after school, Robbie passed the hidden culvert and stopped to cover his nose. The smell was worse than ever. Maybe a horse had crawled into the tunnel. He was certain there was something in there, something dead and rotting away.

It did not occur to him later, not until after he had gone into his house and sat down for a snack of milk and cookies, that it might be Becky, missing from school for the last two days. Was she under the driveway?

He soon learned a search for her had been underway ever since she had not returned home on Halloween night. Not only was a hunt being conducted, but also an investigation was being made. Had the preteen girl run away? Had she been abducted? Was she staying at a friend's house, neglecting to tell her mom? Up until nightfall, the quest throughout the neighborhood by frantic parents, concerned neighbors and the police, was conducted but none of the searchers had been able to locate her.

The following day, Edgemont Park, a few blocks away, was carefully scrutinized for any clue leading to the missing girl. Residents were interrogated and children asked if they knew of her whereabouts. The inquiry branched out, spreading into other neighborhoods further away and into other community parks. It was there the searchers were hopeful they might find some hint of her whereabouts and it was there they concentrated much of their manpower, looking under logs, scattered mounds of leaves, heaps of vegetation, digging and moving the earth where it seemed to have been disturbed.

Nothing was found.

"She's probably ten thousand miles away by now," one of Robbie's older friends theorized. "Maybe twenty thousand."

"Maybe a space craft landed and she was forced to go on board," suggested another of his chums. "Might be galaxies away, by now."

Later on, while going from the kitchen to his bedroom upstairs, he overhead his father speculate with, "…probably abducted and in another state by now."

Were they talking about Becky? Robbie wondered, continuing up the steps.

During the evening, around the dining room table, Robbie mentioned the culvert and the offensive odor to his parents. They set down their forks, stopped eating and turned to look at each other questioningly.

"Come to think of it," said Dad, "I did notice something peculiar after parking the car and walking to the front door. That what you're talking about, son?"

"Probably," said the boy, agreeably. "What do you think it might be, Dad?"

"No clue. Maybe a dead dog or cat. Maybe a squirrel. Whatever it is, it's not likely to still be alive."

"What can we do about it, Dad? Should we go under the driveway and pull it out? Drag it to the dump?"

Mr. Epstein laughed shortly. "No, nothing we can do, son. They have city workers who attend to such things."

"Like cleaning up after road kill," his mother contributed.

"Yeah, like that," agreed Dad. "I'll call in the morning."

* * * *

It was midafternoon of the next day before the city workers, a crew of two, arrived at the Costello's house to investigate the complaint. They arrived in a city truck, identified by signs on the side-door panels as the Jefferson Water and Sewage Department and left the vehicle. They took a few steps toward the house, stopped, crinkled their noses and then continued to the door where they informed the home owner of what brought them there.

They failed to see Robbie sitting on the porch, eating an apple, watching every movement they made.

"Wow!" said one of the men, waving his hand around his head to clear away the surrounding air carrying the offensive reek. "Smells like a dead cow around here, Manny."

"More like an elephant," offered the other, an older man with an insignia on his shirt the boy was unable to read from the porch.

"Whatever it is, it's probably been around here for a long time."

"I don't see nothing in the ditch; it's probably coming from under the driveway."

"This would have been a good day to call in sick and take the day off," said the first.

"We might have to call in sick anyway," said the second man, walking along the ditch and looking carefully for whatever was giving off the odor. "I'm already beginning to feel nauseous."

"Me, too. Probably not a good day to call in, though. They'd probably send us out again tomorrow and the stink would be even worse."

"It's a nasty job all right," said Manny. "Awful job——one of the worse I've had to deal with."

"It is for me, too."

Manny removed the cap he was wearing and wiped his hairless pate with a handkerchief. He stopped at the driveway and held his nose. "Yeah, it's coming from down in there, all right, or further along; sooner we get started, the sooner we'll be finished. Get a couple of flashlights and some tools, Chewy."

The young man, apparently the second in seniority, did as he was instructed, going back to the truck for the equipment they would need. Meanwhile, Manny dropped down into the ditch to look as far as he could into the conduit tunneling beneath the driveway. Visibility was limited and he told Chewy, who handed the rake down to him.

Neither of them had noticed Robbie, sitting on the porch, chewing the last bite of his apple, taking it all in.

Chewy handed one of the flashlights to his partner and jumped into the ditch to join him, bringing the shovel and rake he had brought along with him, while Manny directed his light into the opening of the conduit.

"See anything, Manny?" the young assistant asked.

"Nothing. Don't see a damned thing. Whatever it is, it must be further in than the light reaches. Gimme the rake."

With the instrument in hand, Manny reached in, extending it as far as it would go, then pulled it back towards himself. A few dead, moldy leaves adhered to the tines. Two more attempts produced about the same results.

"Damn! It means you'll have to crawl in there, Chewy."

"Me? Why me? You're slimmer than I am. Won't be as hard for you."

"I'm thinner, yeah, but I got the rheumatism and you don't. 'Sides, you're a young man and I'm pushing sixty. 'Sides...'" he paused for long moments, hesitant to continue.

But Chewy knew what he would say if it was necessary: Manny had more tenure than he did and, on this job, he was the boss. He told his partner in charge.

"Well, I didn't want to put it that way. I think of us as co-equals. But it's true: I been on the job longer'n you have and I've had plenty of jobs as bad as or worse than this one."

"S'pose you're right, but you'll owe me a coffee later on."

"Just a coffee? Hell, I'll buy you a beer. Now get in there—and take the rake with you."

Robbie continued to sit there on the porch, barely moving, deeply engrossed in what was going on and now chewing vigorously on a stick of gum with some of its flavor left. He wanted to question the men but held off, reluctant to interfere with their work. What would they find? Anything? The dead animal he first imagined? A herd of rotting skunks?

Becky?

He stopped guessing, aghast at the thought. God, it could not be Becky in there! Could it?

Chewy slipped on a pair of rubber gloves and began to crawl and wriggle into the opening under the driveway, shining the light ahead of him and dragging the rake behind him.

"Yuck," he exclaimed. "Even with the flashlight, it's dark in here. And soggy—-the ground is wet, mushy and slimy, like an enormous snake was crawling in there."

"Snakes ain't slimy, Chewy. Rotten vegetation, probably; but if you do spot a snake, get the hell out of their...and quick...unless you know it's harmless."

"Don't worry about it, Manny. I won't stop to chat with it."

"It's about twelve feet from one side of the driveway to the other, Chewy. You shouldn't have to go in any deeper."

"I'm not so sure. The ditch on the other side, the one for the house next door, has been covered in. Whatever is smelling so bad might be in there, much farther than I can crawl."

Chewy was making progress. Eventually, he was all the way in, up to his ankles and then even they disappeared from sight.

"This's about as far as I can go, Manny," he yelled back after a minute, "and I haven't seen a damn thing yet. It's narrowing down and I've reached the end."

"Well, the drain must continue on beyond, doesn't it? We can't see it 'cause it's covered with dirt."

"Yeah, it does, but I'm not going any further—-might get wedged in there and can't get out. Whatever is making the awful smell must be in the next trench, all covered with dirt and grass."

"Smells worse, does it?"

"Worse than before. Indescribably noxious! I'm not coming in here again without a mask to wear, for sure."

"It would help, I guess, but it doesn't matter anymore. The lawn beyond the driveway will have to be torn up and shoveled out in order to reach whatever's causing the stink and it's not our job. I'll put in a requisition to have the work scheduled when we're back at home base. Just to be sure, though, stick the rake in front of you one more time and see what you can drag out."

A couple of minutes passed, during which time Chewy could be heard grunting and uttering nonsense talk as he poked and prodded.

"What cha see now?" Manny asked impatiently.

"Nothing yet. I'm all the way in now," Chewy called back. "The rake reaches another five, six feet or so beyond the end of the driveway and into the area covered over with dirt.

"Still can't feel anything, though. Maybe another push…

"Oh, oh, there's something there. Something bulky, bigger than a dog though. Can't drag it out, not without a lot of leverage I can't get in this position. Probably just a huge boulder."

A minute later he continued with: "I can feel it ahead of me with the rake, but I still can't get to it, or drag it out."

"What'cha see, Chewy?"

"Can't see anything and the light's starting to dim."

"Old batteries."

"Ya know what? This might be a body of some kind. It feels resilient when I poke at it—-not at all like a big rock. Too bulky to be a dog, though."

"Can you hook it and drag it out?"

"Naw, too heavy. This isn't a fresh kill, though—-sort of squishy. Still, it might be a person here—-a small one."

Robbie had left the porch and walked closer to the workers, quietly so as not to draw attention to himself. He had been holding his breath and with the words made by Chewy, he let it all out in a whoosh.

"Oh, God" he thought. "It's her! They've been searching all over and she's been here all this time!"

"Use the rake to grab it by the clothes and yank it out!"

"Nothing doing. Don't feel any clothing, either. Besides, this might be a crime scene. I don't want the coppers after me for destroying evidence."

"Then you get yourself out of there, Chewy. I don't mind telling you: this is a nervous business and I'm very uneasy. We'll go back and file a report. Probably have to dig out a lot of lawn beyond the driveway to see what's under there, but we'll let the big guys take care of it. It's out of our pay scale."

"Now it's 'we' and 'our' is it?"

"Course, it's we! Nothing to do but call it in, report it to the authorities and let them take over. Probably have to break up the concrete conduit to get what's in there, outta there, and then conduct their investigation."

Chewy wiggled backwards until he was out of the water way, shaking his head and pulling the rake along with him.

"Something's there all right," he said, climbing out of the trench. "A bit too far away for me to see anything, but by the feel of it by the rake, it's fairly large. You can just see a tiny shred of dark brown clothing clinging to the tines. Makes me awfully suspicious. It's a body of some kind, all right and more than likely, a person…a small person."

Shred of brown clothing! The news caught Robbie by complete surprise and he did not know what to think. Becky had been wearing a bright blue gown!

"Nice to have a partner like you, Chewy. You talk common sense—got a head on those narrow shoulders."

"Maybe I do. This is a job now for others—-not for us."

"Good job, Chewy," said Manny approvingly. "C'mon. We have a phone call to make and a report to fill out."

* * * *

It took little time for the word to spread among the authorities, the searchers and, eventually, the entire neighborhood and municipality. Within half an hour, city crews were out again, parking up and down the street and meeting with the police who had quickly assembled. Soon, workers began to uncover the Costello's storm drain. Others arrived to break up the cement conduit when it was reached and then smash through it with heavy mallets to reveal what was inside.

Soon, yellow tape, labeled 'Crime Scene' every few feet, had been strung all the way around the area and the gathering multitude was ordered to stay away. Pedestrians had to walk in the street, around the sectioned-off area to get where they were going and when Robbie's father drove up, returning from his work during the day, he found it necessary to park his car further down the street as many people milling about did not want to move out of his way. An assortment of men and women, boys and girls, had gathered more quickly than buzzards to a fresh kill.

Robbie had wiggled through the crowd, inching his way forward until he was in the front. The first thing he saw were pieces of ragged brown clothing, now in shreds and placed nearby was a brown, slouch hat he recognized at once.

Inside the yellow-taped area, a few men were probing and prodding the earth, examining everything uncovered with careful detail and carefully examining every inch of the grass removed. When the top of the cement encasement had been destroyed and the debris moved some distance away, a body had been revealed. It was not, however, what they expected to find. What they discovered were the remnants of a desiccated skeleton, enclosed in brown pants and shirt so badly frayed and tattered little remained, as though they had been in the conduit for many years.

The bones were removed, one by one and assembled on a white sheet, placed in the position they would have been attached to in life. There they could be seen by the people nearby, properly arranged, each bone separated from the other. The fragmented revulsion was in, what the newspaper reported the next morning, a deplorable condition, lacking any flesh or skin or ligaments to bind them together.

The coroner had been called in and arrived in time to stop one of the men, attempting to get some idea of the size, from piecing the bony remains closer together and made him leave the discovery alone. The skull, however, had already been moved closer to the spine. A large selection of pictures were taken from various angles and the gruesome remains loaded into a basket, moved to a city vehicle and transferred to the morgue where forensic testing would begin.

"There's something else in there," one of the detectives whispered to his superior officer. "They're removing it now."

One of the workers laid the additional form found in the culvert off to the side. It was completely covered, but Robbie judged the form to be about the same size as Rebecca Winston and swallowed hard. His heart began to rise in his gorge and choke him, although there was no certainty it was her. It still might be a large dog or animal under the covering that had lived and died in the area, but Robbie was now certain it was his classmate. No one but Rebecca had been reported missing,

During a pause in the proceedings, Robbie overheard the coroner, one of the workers and an inspector talking together and listened carefully so as not to miss a word.

"Any signs of sexual molestation?" asked the officer.

The coroner shook his head. "Naw. No preliminary signs, at least. No marks on her, no bruising and her clothes intact. I'd be surprised if we find anything."

The boy had only a nebulous idea of what they were talking about and decided he would ask his father what they meant when he returned home.

When the three men saw him loitering about nearby, they stopped talking and told him to scram.

Robbie heard later on, before the fall of darkness, the search party had been called off and told to go home, with no further word.

"What do you think, Mom? Is it…could it…?"

Mom had no answer, no opinion and neither did Dad, but their faces were glum and worried looking and they picked at their food as though they had consumed a ten course meal twenty minutes earlier.

* * * *

It was Rebecca Wilkins who had been found. School was cancelled early the next day when the identification was confirmed and the news revealed to the public. It was the body of a child, gender easily determined, identified by her parents and by the blue clothing she had worn Halloween night. Grief counselors spent hours at the school the next day, talking with those in need of their services: adults, including teachers, but mostly children, especially the victim's friends. They remained there for the rest of the week.

What had happened Halloween evening? The police were determined to find out, to locate the perpetrator and see to it justice was done. So far they had no suspects, but believed they soon would. They were adamant in their assurance. The mother of the little girl had been prostrated soon after her disappearance and the latest revelation sent her into a near coma. Her father had little to say, but anyone could tell by his features he was a stricken man, morose and vacant eyed.

Robbie hoped they would soon determine who was responsible for the calamity and shove him off the Empire State Building. Teams of policemen walked the neighborhood, knocking on doors, asking the homeowners if they knew of anything strange occurring in the neighborhood for the last few weeks and about any strangers they might have seen loitering about. Robbie was eager to tell what he knew of the homeless man who had offered to exchange with him a bag of marbles for his candy, but a couple of days passed before they got around to him.

The authorities were completely befuddled about the skeleton found, determined to be of a male. Who was it? Where had he come from? Where had he lived? They had no idea. By its position in the tunnel, the young lady must have crawled around it in order to get further in, or she had been shoved all the way into it, and the skeleton crawled in behind her.

The goodies she had gathered were not there and the authorities wondered what could have happened to them. In their place was discovered, next to the body, a pair of pink ballerina slippers, finely crafted. It was a pair Rebecca had not owned, according to her parents, although she did have an intense interest in taking dancing lessons and specialized in the ballet.

Robbie wondered, too. He had seen her outside trick-or-treating during the night, and exchanged a few words with her when her bag was nearly filled. What had happened to it? The boy thought of the vagrant who had offered him marbles for his candy, which he had declined. Had the man come upon Becky and offered her the pretty slippers for her candy? If he did, had she accepted? What would have happened to him, he continued to wonder, if he had accepted the man's trade? Would the homeless creep have kept the candy and not given him the marbles, then slaughtered him before shoving him into the culvert? If he had taken Robbie as his prey, would he then have left Becky alone to continue her happy Halloweening? Or would he have throttled both of them? Robbie did not know and could only conjecture.

"How could the brute know Becky liked the ballet?" he murmured aloud.

"The same way he knew I like marbles," he answered himself.

Robbie thought back to the brief glimpse he had of the skeleton before it had been covered up and imagined its bony fingers clutching a bag of marbles.

The community's fears, anxieties, astonishments and unanswered questions died down as the days and then the weeks passed, but Robbie continued to wonder about the strange man who had never been seen again around the area.

The 'Special Day', for Robbie, would never be quite the same. For him, it would always be the crappiest Halloween of all.

Early Snow
by Samson Stormcrow Hayes

I listened as the newscast made the startling announcement: Halloween was cancelled. I looked out my window in disbelief as all of my hard work disappeared beneath the heavy snowfall. Because my home was set so far from the main road, I liked to reward the brave souls who ventured down my long drive with a yard full of spooky skeletons and monsters. It helped that I also handed out full sized candy bars, but apparently not this year.

The next morning, there were hardly any traces of my decorations beneath the blanket of snow other than a few lumps that were pumpkins and gravestones.

I felt bad for the kids, especially my next door neighbors who lived a hundred yards up the road. Megan and Graham loved Halloween as much as I did and I know they were looking forward to showing off their costumes for me.

By dusk, the snow had stopped, but the temperatures continued dropping until they were well below zero. I turned up the thermostat and returned to my horror-thon of films. I was just finishing the *The Omen* when a knock on the door surprised me. I peered through the window. It was Megan and Graham dressed as a fairy princess and a knight.

"Trick or treat," they chanted.

"You shouldn't be out in this weather. Where are your parents?"

"They said we could come over," said Megan.

They held up their homemade bags waiting for candy. I tossed them each a few chocolate bars and invited them inside.

"You're not even wearing your winter coats," I said.

"We wanted you to see our costumes," said Graham, waving his plastic sword.

"They're very cute, but come in before you catch your death of cold."

Just then my phone rang. It was their mother, Sarah.

"Are they there?" she asked.

"Yes, they just got here."

"Oh, thank goodness. They snuck out after dinner and I just hoped and prayed they were going there. We'll be right over with the car."

"Take your time, I'll make them some hot cocoa until you arrive." I hung up the phone, but when I turned around they were gone. I quickly hit redial.

"They must be on their way back," I told Sarah. "I'll go look for them and meet you outside."

I grabbed my coat and flashlight, but as soon as I left the house, the cold gnawed at my exposed flesh like a hungry animal. How could those kids stand it, I wondered. Maybe that's why they ran home.

I shined the flashlight through the trees, but there was only the swaying of dead branches. Looking down to find their tracks, I made a chilling discovery. There were no footprints other than my own. The surrounding snow remained undisturbed.

I ran through the trees toward their house, the thick snow pulling at my feet, slowing me down. It was only when I reached their back door that I discovered tracks leading at first toward my house and then slowly drifting deeper into the woods. I followed the trail while I heard Sarah and Ryan running behind me, their voices desperately calling out their children's names.

"This way. They're over here," I called.

The tracks led further into the woods and then toward a ravine. It was at the ravine's edge that they ended. Looking down, I could see their tiny bodies lying still in the snow. By the time the police dragged us all inside I had frostbite on my nose and fingers. When I told the authorities that I had seen the kids, they were skeptical since the tracks never made it my house. There was just one thing they couldn't explain. If they never made it to my house, how did my candy bars end up in their frozen hands?

The Dollhouse
by Glynn Owen Barrass

Since her escape from the compound, Concubine had wandered many miles, first through the fog-shrouded, rubble-strewn cities the humans once called home, then the wilderness beyond, a poisonous wasteland filled with the skeletal remains of forests and abandoned, rusted cars.

The compound: far behind her, always close to her thoughts. A gargantuan underground labyrinth of torture and slavery, her sole purpose for being had been for the fulfilment of Matriarch's entertainment and lust. "Slave no more," Concubine had repeated many times since her escape. It was her mantra, her anthem of freedom.

When she had stumbled across the strange new community, she was cautious at first, then happy, and now…Concubine was caught between remaining in ennui or continuing her journey across the wasteland.

The day she arrived, Concubine had been wandering the old subways, the poisonous fog on the surface having driven her underground. After a few dozen miles of waterlogged tunnels, she ventured to the surface and found a town populated exclusively by synthetic humans.

'Welcome to Synth-Town!" the ripped, faded banner above the rusted iron gates had proclaimed. Within, Concubine discovered a town fallen to ruin, and some distant ancestors.

Built in the shape of an octagon, the town was split into two halves. The outer half, surrounded by a sagging iron fence, consisted of houses flanked by white picket fences. All stood in various states of disrepair. Roofs crumbling, their walls collapsed and the windows broken, the lawns between the rotting fences had long ago degraded to bare earth that bore the leafless remnants of trees and bushes. The inner half hadn't fared much better. Consisting of damaged public buildings and shops, it was centred by a small octagonal park of wasteground and dead trees.

Despite the decrepitude, the town still had functioning electricity. At night, every building stood illuminated, the streetlights, where not broken, lining the roads in bright fluorescent lines.

Night had fallen, and the town's lights were just flicking on. Seated at a circular aluminium table outside one of the cafés surrounding the park, Concubine sat with one of her ancestors.

The model was female, her white ceramic shell moulded with fake breasts. The majority of her clothes were long gone, rotted off by the elements, but a ring of tattered pink material hung around her neck, a cracked red leather high-heeled shoe remaining on one dainty right foot. Her head was bald, white as a skullcap where not spattered with muck. Some of the synthetics wore wigs, mainly the ones stuck indoors away from the elements. This one's was long gone. Her eternally smiling, mask-like face stared at Concubine with well-detailed, faux human eyes quite unlike her own opaque blue orbs.

Like her companion, Concubine sat naked, her production line number, '96,' tattooed in black above her left breast. Although deathly pale, Concubine's artificial skin appeared more human than her companion's, except where the damage from her travels had scarred and pitted the flesh to reveal the endoskeleton beneath.

Concubine had named this one: 'Angie,' and written it in black marker above her left breast. The other, two hundred odd machines around town were marked in similar fashions.

Angie raised a white teacup filled with dirty water to unmoving lips, pantomimed drinking, then placed the cup back in its saucer.

"Have you seen those horribly garish pink Flamingos on Miss Willoughby's lawn?" the synthetic said in a crackly voice.

Concubine scowled. Angie had a dozen pre-programmed conversations in her repertoire, but the 'Flamingo Gossip,' kept reappearing at regular intervals.

"No tell me," she replied in a bored tone.

"Well…" Angie looked around for eavesdroppers before leaning forward, "when my—ktzzzz-tzzzz-eighteen-corlyktzzzz." As the garbled mixture of buzzing and words continued, Concubine shook her head. Being outside had severely damaged many of the synthetics voice boxes, Angie not the worst of them.

"Tell me later," Concubine said and stood from the table, leaving Angie to crackle and gossip as she stepped towards the park.

Other synthetics crossed her path as she walked across the asphalt road surrounding the park: a male model wearing a ragged blue suit tipped its non existent hat to her, while three females, dressed in the tatters of jeans and jumpers, walked by with linked arms, giggling and chatting in broken voices.

The wrought iron fences surrounding the park were thick with rust, the gate creaking loudly as she opened it to step upon the gravel path. A pavilion stood a hundred feet away at the path's termination, its octagonal, brown-trussed roof held up by sagging wooden beams. The whole structure was rotted, and probably only a few months away from complete collapse.

The park stood as populated as the rest of town. As she crossed the path she saw five pretend dog walkers wandering its environs: three brandished empty leads while two dragged the skeletal remains of dogs behind them. Concubine shook her head at the sight of those small, bony relics. When she reached the pavilion, she scooted over the gate and stepped upon the sand-covered floor within. Directly at its centre was a steel manhole cover leading to the bowels of the town. A place of computer terminals and generators, this was Concubine's fourth visit since its discovery a few days earlier. Following her previous footsteps through the sand, she paused before the lid to scan the surrounding area. Not that she needed to be cautious, the town's inhabitants didn't seem to care what she did. So far none had interrupted her or tried to halt her ingress.

Concubine knelt, and with her knees pressed into the sand for leverage, she took hold of the handles welded into the cover, and pulled. She grunted, for it was heavy, but nothing her enhanced strength couldn't deal with. Placing the cover onto the sand, she next gripped the edges of the hole and lifting herself, found the ladder rungs below with her feet. She turned, lowered herself further inside, and finding the top of the rungs with one hand, then the other, climbed down into the darkness.

It took ten feet of climbing to leave the darkness behind, ten more through the basement's antechamber before Concubine reached bottom. Here wall mounted, lozenge shaped lamps illuminated the room in a stark white light. Concrete walled and empty, the antechamber stood bisected by a pair of arched doorways. The one to her right led to the generator rooms—a gently throb and hum of machinery issued from that direction. She turned and headed towards the other doorway, her footsteps slapping lightly, invoking tiny echoes as she entered the tunnel. The dark tunnel, twenty feet long, led to a brightly lit room. After a few seconds of walking, Concubine paused at the doorway.

The room was square, its concrete walls lined with lamps except for the one facing her, which stood fronted by a large, yellow plastic console. The recessed sides of the console held floor to ceiling, flickering arrays filled with red lights. Between these, at eye level, stood a flat-screened monitor embedded in ribbed yellow plastic. As she crossed the dusty floor the screen activated, illuminating blue. Concubine paused before the console, raised her right hand, and quested with her fingers across the warm surface. Finding a recessed hole, she pressed her forefinger inside. The hole held a needle, and pushing her finger towards it she experienced momentary pain as it pierced her flesh.

The room disappeared, replaced with an endless violet void filled with descending, multicoloured streams of data. When she first found the mainframe console, Concubine had used the touchscreen interface for entry, then, in her browsing, she had discovered the wetware inlet.

As she hovered in the mainframe's inner data, she considered the town's purpose. Some data packets had hinted at it being a 'showcase,' a place for humans to visit and examine the synths before purchasing. *Purchased for what? Servants? Or like her, a slave for sex?* The beings above were just so basic, and yet the mainframe had been built with access for more advanced models, like her. Concubine sighed, and a virtual representation of the sound filled the void. Human history was mostly unknown to her, although she had pieced some of it together *back the compound*. The most she knew was that when Matriarch and her ilk arrived on Earth, war and devastation had followed, the human race being decimated as a result. At some point Matriarch had found an undamaged synthetic factory, and co-opting it for her needs, had her human followers restart the production lines to create hardy soldiers and toys for her entertainment.

Concubine moved forward between the streams. Her virtual left shoulder brushed one and the data for subroutines, the synths finger movements, momentarily filled her mind. These were of no interest to her. Neither were the subroutines for mannerisms and the other basic programming streams she passed. Since finding the mainframe, Concubine had formulated a plan to upgrade the synths, give them some semblance of free will, and life. If she succeeded, she would remain in the town, teach them, help them. She turned left between more streams until she reached the one dealing with fine motor skills. Weeks earlier, while secretly exploring the mainframe back at the compound, Concubine had learned to add fighting arts and covert skills to her programming, just like the Hunter and Assassin models possessed. Today she wanted to test these skills on the synths above ground, for she believed their bodies were capable of better, quicker movements. After that she would attempt something more difficult, more ambitious, and tackle the streams containing personality to see if they could be given free will.

Touching the stream, Concubine searched until she reached the point she had stopped at yesterday. *Here we go*, she thought, and accessing and scanning her own subroutines, chose to add Brazilian Jiu-Jitsu to the synths programming.

As she was copying and pasting code, she experienced an odd sensation, almost as if she were being watched. Concubine paused what she was doing, said, "Hello?" and glanced around the stream. It was odd, and not the first time this had happened. *There couldn't be another AI here, could there?* Whatever it was, it was gone now, and she returned to her programming.

* * * *

The cafe surrounding her was a wreck of broken tables and smashed glass. The last synth standing, a red wigged, grey suited man she had christened 'Harold,' took up an orthodox boxing stance.

"You wanna play? I'll play," Concubine said, and matched his move. She licked her split lower lip, tasting faux blood on her tongue. She threw a flurry of left and right handed jabs that the synth dodged, followed by a right cross that he didn't. Off balance for a moment, Harold shook his head and danced back between the bar's upturned tables. His following heel kick would have been devastating, if Concubine hadn't seen it coming. With two hands she caught his raised left leg an inch from her jaw, gripped his ankle and twisted. He toppled sideways, hitting the floor loudly. He was stunned, out.

Surreptitious footsteps sounding behind her, Concubine reacted by stepping forward and turning to face the new threat.

Blonde haired 'Joe,' dressed in a blue mechanics coverall, waved a broken bottle menacingly.

"Really?" Concubine grinned and performed an inside crescent kick, impacting the left side of his head. Joe went down, hard, stunned on the floor.

"Phew, haha! It worked," Concubine said and examined her fallen foes.

Including Harold and Joe, who were patrons, the café held two worker synths.

The waitress, Doris, was down behind the counter; Geoff the cook beneath a table to her right.

She kicked a piece of broken chair at her feet and thought, *But the mess, damn, I should have made them fight outside*. "You four," she said, "when you come to, cease combat functions and return to you usual programming." Harold shuddered where he lay, the faux unconsciousness she had programmed to make the fight safer on the synths having run its course.

He rose, glanced around the room, then returned to the remnants of the table near the door. Concubine followed his progress, watching him pause before the broken table then stand there motionless. *At least he didn't try to sit down on nothing.* She giggled at the thought. *Would the staff synths clean up the place, repair it even? Probably not without new programming.* Doris was limited to wiping down tables and tending to orders. Geoff the chef: he played wash up and put plastic foodstuffs on plates.

Despite the mess, she was pleased at how the encounter had gone. The synths could be programmed, and with fairly complex routines at that. From behind the counter, she heard Doris shuffling about, and at this, decided to leave the four to their regular routines. She stepped towards the glass exit door, and as she passed, Harold went to tip the missing hat she had knocked off during in the fight. "Good morning, Miss," he said.

"Harold it's been a pleasure," Concubine replied and left the café. The success invigorated her, so much so she felt it time to take things up a notch and reprogram the synths en-masse. It would take some time, she reflected as she strode across the street towards the park, but wasn't time the thing she had most on her side?

* * * *

It's been a long night, Concubine thought as she climbed the final rungs of the ladder and stepped into the pavilion. Still, she had achieved so much in the twenty-two hours down below. A large percentage of the synths were now reprogrammed with new skills. A few, using her own code as a basis, now had vastly improved cognitive architecture. It would take an examination of the reprogrammed synths to see how that had worked.

The sky beyond the pavilion was black with clouds, making the park a shadowy, gloomy place. She stepped over the fence and walked quickly through the trees, her anticipation growing at every step. *It is so dark though,* she thought, and looked past the trees to the clouds, clouds that actually appeared a little too uniform for her liking.

"Oh no," Concubine said, and froze. Around her, massive beams of light flooded the park, the white spotlights issuing not from clouds, but from Matriarch's wide transport ships.

"Oh, hell no."

The spotlights not only illuminated the park, but the army of synths between the trees. Concubine saw Hunter models armed with machine guns, Assassins bearing swords and knives, and most dangerous of all, Matriarch's elite bodyguards. The one at the forefront stood naked but for a long, tattered crimson cape and a brown leather belt bristling with weapons. His flesh painted dark brown, his head resembled a charred skull. Concubine had seen him before: Ténèbres, the Matriarch's champion.

She bit her lower lip, scanned the faces staring back at her. *We have the toy soldiers,* she thought, *so where is the general?*

One of the spotlights flickered, and a dark shape began descending through the light.

Matriarch!

All of Concubine's courage, all her bravado left her at the sight of the huge, oval-shaped, alien horror. Her front a mass of silvery tentacles, Matriarch's unseen rear held a dark brown carapace, the bat-like wings folded and tucked within the shell. Her head, a large brown globe topping the oval, held an array of glowing green eyes that found Concubine as she descended.

Concubine could run from the army, but Matriarch's eyes, embodying her judgement, her ownership, there was no escaping them.

The world around Concubine seemed to freeze as Matriarch descended to the street. When she reached the asphalt, the army of synths went to their knees as one.

Concubine's legs wobbled, her knees turning weak in the presence of her creator, her god.

The eyes continued to scrutinize her. Concubine stared back transfixed, until movements near the base of Matriarch's torso caught her attention. The shivering tentacles parted, sliding away to reveal a naked, teenaged girl. She had short, raven black hair, the black number 'zero' tattooed above her left breast. Beneath a slanted fringe, her eyes were opaque green orbs.

This was Matriarch's avatar, 'Zero,' her interface with a bipedal world. Concubine had spent much of her life sating the needs of that faux human form.

Zero stepped forward with slow languid movements. Although unseen, a long fleshy tube connected the synthetic being to the alien, sharing every lust, every sensation, an umbilical cord linking machine to flesh. She breached the gap between them and paused a few feet away. She wiped a stray hair from her cheek, and smiled.

"The computers below connect right to mine," she said in a melodious voice, "I found you through the network." She held her slender arms out to Concubine. "You know, things haven't been the same without you." She tilted her head, her face expressing a child-like image of innocence.

Despite her reservations, her fear and hatred of Matriarch, Concubine felt an overwhelming urge to step forward, to accept that embrace. It was so strong she had to physically stop herself from moving.

No, she thought. *Slave no more.*

Zero lowered her arms, rested them against her hips and sighed. Her lips twisted, transforming her friendly smile to a sadistic one.

"There is no way out of here," she said.

A figure appeared to Zero's right, the tall, looming form of Ténèbres. He stopped, lowered his head and glared at Concubine.

"You can come in one piece or many," he said, and his hoarse voice reminded her he wasn't a synth like the others, but rather an enhanced human.

A swift gauge of her options, and Concubine saw only one. She ducked right and ran.

Zero laughed, followed by Ténèbres booming the words, "Seize her!"

She shivered as she passed Matriarch's hulking form, long tentacles whipping towards her that she dodged to escape through the park. As she ran, footsteps, issuing from her left and right, closed in quickly.

Ahead Concubine saw a dog walking synth.

Damn. She hated doing this, after all the work she had put in.

"Davy, attack/defend," she said, and the synth dropped his lead to charge towards her pursuers.

As she reached the park gates, Concubine shouted, "Everyone, attack/defend," and every synth within earshot stopped what they were doing and rushed to protect her. She leapt over the fence and saw the three girls, Angie, and half a dozen other synths home in towards the park.

She flinched as gunfire issued behind her—Matriarch's soldiers would make short work of the synths, Concubine had no illusions there.

"Everyone, attack/defend," she repeated as she reached the alley between Café M and The Pepper Mill Bistro, and heard doors slam open as more synths answered her call. She increased her speed through the narrow alley, her bare feet stamping across the floor as she weighed up her chances of escape.

Not very likely, she thought as she left the alley to enter a residential street lined with houses. Now they had her scent, there were only two choices she could see: surrender or die.

In a flash of speed, something dropped from the sky above her, making her freeze to the spot. The object hit the street and made a crater in the asphalt, the impact shaking the ground and almost making her fall.

Ténèbres, she realized in fear.

Engulfed in his cape, his head lowered, the champion gripped his sword two handed. He looked up and stared at her with eyes like glowing coals.

Her feet shuffled, she wanted to run but in which direction? He had her and they both knew it.

Noting her indecision, Ténèbres rose to his feet, his full height looming over Concubine's smaller form. He reached into his cloak and removed a brown handled wakizashi with a rusted blade. Tossing it forward, balancing the end in his hand, he said, "Take it. If you defeat me, you will be free."

She reached for the sword then stopped. "I can't win against you. You know that."

Ténèbres grimaced, nodded, and replaced the sword on his belt.

"We subdued your automatons," he said, "they're coming back to the compound, with you."

Concubine waved her arms in horror. *No.* "No! Leave them! They're of no use to you."

"Matriarch wants what Matriarch gets," he said, and there was no gloating in his voice, just a kind of sad resignation. "What do you care? You already proved they're disposable to you."

Yes but that place, she thought, *destruction would still be better than that*. Now Concubine found another option, and it pained her to the core to make it.

"Take me then. I'll go willingly and promise to serve, if Matriarch leaves the synthetics here, unmolested and free."

Ténèbres nodded. "An admirable choice," he said, then raising his hand to his ear, said, "She'll surrender if we leave the old machines alone." He tilted his head, listened for a few seconds, then lowered his hand.

"Approved," he said, "Matriarch will honour that." He sheathed his sword, said, "Follow me," and strode past her towards the park.

Overwrought yet resigned, Concubine followed him towards the alleyway. She stepped quickly, her mind filled with trepidation as she tried to reconcile herself with her fate.

"You have to allow me to reset the synths," she asked, "and I'd like help repairing any damages."

"Okay," he agreed without turning. Ténèbres left the alley with Concubine close on his heels. Beyond it she saw Hunters and Assassins, their weapons trained on disabled synths. Some synths had bullet holes, a few were missing limbs. The sight filled Concubine with regret that she hadn't just surrendered, instead of panicking and getting them crippled or destroyed.

She saw Angie on the ground and paused. A red headed female champion, naked but for a pair of frayed tan stockings, stood over her, a katana aimed at her face. As Concubine changed direction and turned left, Ténèbres halted and said, "What are you—"

"A minute," Concubine replied. The female champion turned at her approach, revealing a scarlet domino mask upon her expressionless white face.

"I'm sorry Angie," Concubine said, kneeling to take the synth's limp hand. The damage didn't appear too severe—just three shallow, horizontal gashes across her face.

She gripped the hand tighter and said, "Angie, cease combat functions and return to you usual programming."

The synth twitched where she lay and raised her head. She said, "Have you seen those horribly garish pink Flamingos on Miss Willoughby's lawn?"

Despite everything, Concubine grinned.

* * * *

The floor vibrated, tingling against her feet as Matriarch's ship rose from the town. Concubine approached the cell's circular window and watched as the park and buildings shrank rapidly below her. When the town was nothing but a blot on the landscape, she turned away to face her small, metal-walled cell. The sight of her imprisonment didn't upset her. In fact, she hadn't given in to despair, and wouldn't any time soon. Concubine had a plan. If the compound's mainframe was linked to the one beneath the park, then with a little luck, she could continue her work on the synths.

Slave turned liberator. It was a good plan. Good enough.

Elle a Vu un Loup
by Loren Rhoads

Alondra DeCourval set her carpetbag on the dock. The July day was clear and cloudless. Bright golden sunlight sequined Lake Huron, almost too sharp for her eyes.

A man in a red windbreaker hurried over. "Are you going to the island?"

"Yes." She offered him her ferry ticket.

"Just a day trip?"

Alondra smiled. "No. I'm staying the weekend."

He didn't take the ticket from her hand. "Do you have reservations?"

"One of the bed and breakfast owners is a friend of my family's." That wasn't exactly true. The owner had known her guardian, had in fact written to Alondra about the problem on the island. But Thomas Lenaghan planned to leave the island for the night, like all the others. Supposedly he had reserved her a room.

"Ah," the ferryman said, "you have family on the island." He took her ticket, tore it partially, handed it back. "You'll be the only one going over. Sit anywhere you like."

She climbed the gangway. The two-story ferryboat could have accommodated a hundred passengers on its hard wooden benches. Alondra was grateful that it would make the trip solely for her. The stairs throbbed beneath her feet as she climbed to the upper level and chose a seat by the railing.

She'd hardly settled before the ship pulled away from the dock. Alondra stared out at the delicate suspension bridge spanning the Straits of Mackinaw. It made her think of an aeolian harp, each cable ready to sing when plucked by the wind. The bridge stretched from Michigan's lower peninsula to the less populous upper one, joining the state's two halves and bypassing the island entirely. Until the lake froze over for the winter, the only way to reach the island was by boat. This weekend, the ticket clerk had warned, there would be no ferries running after sunset. Alondra would be stranded on the island until morning.

Lulled by the sparkle on the water and the thrum of the engine, Alondra closed her eyes to enjoy the sun on her face. She'd need her strength to face whatever perils lurked in the night.

* * * *

The landing dock was thronged with people waiting for ferries off Mackinac Island. Mothers clutched their children near; kids hovered over cats in carriers or tugged on dogs' leashes. With the sun still high above the horizon, the queue was orderly, but Alondra wondered how the mood would change when shadows crept in.

An unfamiliar voice called her. She searched out the man. His hunched posture and protuberant Adam's apple made her think of a turtle, but his brown eyes were kind.

As she neared, the stranger said, "I was sorry to hear about your uncle's passing."

Victor hadn't been her uncle, but if the family connection gave Lenaghan more confidence in her, so much the better.

"It was a terrible loss," he continued. Alondra sensed that he meant to the world. She didn't disagree. She just hoped that someday she could bear someone's condolences without feeling pain twist in her heart.

"Here are my keys." Lenaghan put a ring into her hand. "The address is on the tag. Make yourself at home. If you take one of the rooms toward the front of the inn, you'll have a view of the water."

The people around him turned to stare at Alondra, taking in her black jeans and black leather jacket, the cascade of jewelry at her ears and throat, and her red, red hair. Someone muttered, "Here's a pretty morsel," to mean-spirited laughter.

Alondra pretended to ignore them. "Thank you, Mr. Lenaghan. When do you return?"

"Three days. Monday. Same as these other brave souls."

Alondra smiled gently. "I understand there aren't any cars on the island?"

"That's right." Lenaghan suddenly moved away as the line advanced toward the ferry.

When she caught up to him, Alondra asked, "Can I rent a horse or have the stables closed?"

"Brighton won't leave the island. He's the one who owned the horses savaged two months ago. He might not rent to you, but I'm sure he can use money, if you know what I mean. Just know that he'll sleep in the barn with a shotgun. You don't want to startle him after dark."

"Where is he located?"

Lenaghan lurched after the line again before he could respond. Alondra found herself nearly back to the ferry. Then Lenaghan pointed up a side street, past the village's tourist shops. "He's on Cherry Street. Do me a favor, though. Don't mention my name." Lenaghan grimaced. "Gossip is the best entertainment we've got. He'll find out soon enough, but knowing that I recommended him because of his money troubles won't help you."

Alondra thanked the guesthouse owner and turned back toward the island. An undercurrent of anger trailed her as she walked past the line of islanders abandoning their homes and jobs at the height of tourist season. Better to leave than to face whatever had been stalking the island for the last six months, expanding in appetite from pets to horses to a seven-year-old boy.

Better to leave, Alondra understood, than to reveal—or be thought to be the one to reveal—to the outside world what was destroying their livelihoods and peace of mind. She understood the mentality of closed societies too well.

The island rose before her in a series of tiers. Nearest the water lay the strip of Victorian-styled fudge and T-shirt shops. Behind that stood a ring of guesthouses. Halfway up the hill sprawled the whitewashed ramparts of the historic fort, decommissioned after the Civil War, now a state park. Atop the hill glittered mansions of the wealthy: hoteliers and auto barons who summered on the island before the current troubles began. Alondra wondered how many of the mansions sported For Sale signs now.

A pair of chestnut horses stopped in front of her. Shielding her eyes against the island's flawless sky, Alondra looked up to see the wagon driver in white shirtsleeves and old-fashioned black garters with a top hat on the bench beside his thigh. His hair was sunny blond above sky-blue eyes. "Taxi, miss?"

"I'd appreciate it."

He hopped down and steadied her arm unnecessarily as she climbed up into the wagon. "Where to?"

"Do you know the Tides Inn Bed and Breakfast?"

"Sure, but Lenaghan's left the island."

Alondra raised the key ring. "I have a reservation."

Some strange shadow crossed his face, but the driver nodded. He climbed back up and clucked to the horses, which ambled forward.

Alondra leaned forward to ask, "You're not evacuating, then?"

"Those fools got nothing to be afraid of." In another era, he might have cursed or spat, but now he only jiggled the reins, urging a faster mosey from the chestnut pair.

* * * *

The Tides Inn was grander than Alondra expected. The Victorian-era inn stretched along the street, decorated with turrets, a veranda, and a widow's walk. An enormous lilac shaded the front like a lady's fan, its deep green leaves glossy. The B&B exuded a sense of being completely vacant. In fact, the whole street was deserted, except for the seagulls spinning lazily overhead.

Alondra took the taxi driver's extended hand as she stepped down from the wagon. She thought he might let her go without a word beyond naming his fare, so she asked, "I've got nothing to be afraid of?"

His gaze met hers, before dropping to the money in her hand. "Don't go wandering at night," he advised.

"What about that boy?"

"Probably a custody thing, like the papers say. Mainlanders come up here to escape their troubles, but most bring their problems right along with them." He offered the flicker of a smile. "You've got little to fear, down here in the village."

"Thank you." Alondra walked carefully around the front of the horses, smiling up into their blinkered eyes as she passed. Then she mounted the wooden steps and let herself in to the bed and breakfast.

* * * *

The inn was over-decorated in a historically accurate Victorian way. Framed antique photos of the island crowded the entryway, followed by a sitting room jammed with chintz-covered armchairs. The variety of floral patterns in the room hurt Alondra's eyes.

She didn't bother to choose a bedroom, since she didn't expect to spend much time in it. The sitting room sofa looked comfortable enough. She sat on it to sort through her carpetbag, tucking certain items into the pockets of her leather jacket.

* * * *

The stable, scented with hay and saddle soap, brought back memories. Alondra paused in the doorway, letting her eyes adjust to the mote-filled light filtering through the barn's high windows. It had been a long time since she'd been around horses. She hadn't realized how much she'd missed them.

"Help you, Miss?" a man asked sharply.

"How much to rent a riding horse for the afternoon?"

"They're not for rent today."

Alondra turned until she found the figure leaning against a stall's doorway. The horse inside the stall pressed its head against the man's shoulder. He reached up to scratch the horse's jaw.

The image helped Alondra grasp that Brighton's hostility rose out of affection for his animals. She moved to stand where a dusty sunbeam could strike the diamond pendant she wore in the hollow of her throat. "That's a shame. I came all the way up here to discover the whole island is practically abandoned. Isn't there anything to do here this weekend?"

"Lady, don't you read the news?"

"It's been full of stories promising that there's nothing wrong here, just a series of sad coincidences."

As the word left her lips, her gaze found the new stall door across the way. Its paint didn't match the surfaces around it. On the wall at the back of the stall—up over Alondra's head—was a long gouge, where a hoof struck it. What would panic a horse enough to kick that high?

Across the barn's central aisle, a gray horse with liquid black eyes batted extravagant lashes at her. Alondra scratched under his forelock. "Hello, handsome," she purred. "Your name must be Moonshadow."

"Moon Calf is more like it. He's too dreamy to be much of a saddle horse." The stable master drew nearer, watching Alondra charm the horse. "You ridden much?"

"I grew up on horseback. My mother bred Arabians in Upstate New York."

He stood close enough that she could see the gold hoop in his right ear, the curls of black fur at the unbuttoned collar of his plaid shirt. He looked more Eastern European than the British name labeling his stable.

"I worked on an Arabian farm on my way through school," he said. "What was your mother's name?"

Alondra hated to resort to name-dropping, but she needed to borrow his horse. "Cassandra DeCourval. If you met her, you'd probably remember."

"I do."

Alondra was used to the admiration in men's voices when they recalled her mother.

"You can have him for a couple hours, but you'd better be back here no later than four. Sunset comes before nine thirty and we're under curfew… more like martial law. Anyway, you don't want to run into any trouble with the local yahoos." He pronounced the word "yay-who." He named his price. Alondra fished her wallet out of her leather coat.

He saddled the horse for her. Rather than beginning with the bridle, he let the gelding take the bit last, before leading him out of the stall. Alondra stroked the horse's nose again, gazing into his black eyes. Then she stepped up onto the block, hooked her foot into the stirrup and swung her leg over. It had been much too long since she'd ridden, but it all came flooding back.

Brighton handed her the reins. "Normally, they want horses kept off the Lake Shore Road, so you're not competing with the bicycles, but they won't get in your way today. You'll have enough time to take the circle road around the whole thing. That's six miles. It's real pretty on the other side of the island, peaceful, not built up like over here. But be back by four."

Alondra checked her watch and nodded. "Thank you, sir."

She nudged the horse forward to ride out. The protection glyph painted above the doorway didn't escape her notice.

* * * *

Alondra stopped for lunch in a shady place overlooking the lake. It was nearly two o'clock. She hadn't seen another soul on the state-numbered "highway" that ringed the island. The silence was almost unnerving.

She looped the gray gelding's reins around an aspen tree and left him to graze while she sat in the tall weeds at the edge of the road. Black-eyed Susans and purple coneflowers nodded in the faintest breath of breeze. A bumblebee hummed to himself.

Across the empty blacktop, waves the color of beach glass lapped gently. Across the water, Alondra saw Michigan's upper peninsula. Once it had been mined for copper and steel, but now it was mostly wild land. She'd heard it was beautiful there.

She hadn't been mentally prepared for the distances between one mass of land and the next up here. Which was foolish: she remembered that the Great Lakes were visible from space. Knowing that and experiencing it were two different things.

She opened the sack lunch she'd packed in the supermarket on the mainland. She cut the under-ripe D'Anjou pear into spears and dipped them into the peanut butter.

Alondra scanned the waves, half expecting to see a seal. The water was as vacant as the island trail had been. She hadn't anticipated how lonely she'd feel surrounded by water.

The gelding nudged with his nose. Alondra offered him a carrot stick, but he was more interested in the jar of peanut butter.

* * * *

As they turned off the paved road onto the flat dirt track, Moonshadow tossed his head, glad to be out of the sun under the shadow of the oaks. He picked up the pace now that they'd turned back toward home.

A tingle at the back of Alondra's neck alerted her that they skirted the old battlefield. During the War of 1812, the British had captured the fort on the mainland side of the island. Fighting to recapture it had been fierce. Alondra shivered, despite the day's warmth. She usually avoided battlefields. The blood-soaked soil forever changed the vibrations of the land. Too often, ghosts lingered over their forgotten remains. One could spend an entire lifetime repatriating dead soldiers. In fact, one of Victor's friends—bereft after World War II—had done so. Alondra preferred to help the living.

The horse stumbled. Alondra thought they were going over. She yanked her feet out of the stirrups, preparing to jump. Moonshadow caught himself awkwardly, whickering in pain. He couldn't put weight on his right front leg.

Alondra patted his neck. "Let me get down."

He stood as straight as he could, flesh shivering beneath her hands. Alondra swung her leg over and stretched her toes to the ground. The long drop would have been an even longer fall.

She walked in front of him, stroking his muzzle, and stopped with her shoulder against his. Then she placed both hands around his foreleg and pulled his hoof upward, resting it against her knees so she could look at it.

The horseshoe still seemed firmly attached. She pulled a ballpoint out of her pocket and cleaned some dirt away.

An old iron nail barely protruded from Moonshadow's foot. She couldn't tell how long the nail was or how deeply it pierced. If she pulled it, she'd have to find something to clean the wound and a way to bandage his foot until they could get back to the stable. The pain from the nail wouldn't kill the horse, but blood poisoning might.

Damn. She wished she'd kept to the Lake Shore Road now. Odds were better that someone would come across them there, if anyone else was out roaming the island. Unfortunately, they'd come far enough it was too far to double back. She'd just head south as best she could. Eventually they would reach water.

Alondra checked her watch: almost three. Maybe, when she didn't make her four o'clock deadline, Brighton would come after her. After his horse, at least.

She had a long sip from her water bottle, then poured some into her cupped hand. The horse lipped it up gently. Alondra patted his cheek. "I'm sorry this happened. We'll take it easy, but we can't stay out here and wait to be rescued. Let's get you home."

Holding the reins, Alondra started up the path at an easy stride. Moonshadow limped after her.

* * * *

Alondra noted the lengthening shadows, but didn't remark on it to the horse. All the island's animals had undoubtedly scented the fear throughout the day, as the human evacuation took place around them. Even if they didn't respond to cycles of the moon, they had to recognize this wasn't an ordinary day.

She hadn't intended to be caught out like this. It was one thing to walk into danger alone, but the large, wounded herbivore was another matter.

She hadn't brought weapons, for pity's sake, only charms and some knowledge of what she was facing.

The island was a maze of riding trails and nominal roads, none of which ran directly south over the rocky ground. Climbing was hard on the horse, but climbing down—when more of his weight rested on his injured foot—was going to be brutal.

* * * *

Finally they reached an overlook. Between the oak boughs, she saw the village spread below, still a good distance away. The sun sank into the arms of the suspension bridge. Crimson painted the sky, reflecting in the lake.

A gutteral engine revved as the last ferry chugged out of the harbor. Alondra wondered how many islanders remained behind, whether they were armed like Brighton. Were the stalwarts sleeping on their boats, secure that the beast wouldn't cross running water?

Old-fashioned streetlights twinkled on in the empty streets. Somewhere, a dog barked. The lack of automobiles made a kind of quiet that Alondra hadn't heard in a long time.

A breeze raised goosebumps over her humid skin. A spot on the horizon burned magnesium white, heralding moonrise to come.

Time to climb down *now*.

* * * *

Returning to the village proved difficult. Somewhere they turned left when they should have gone right. Alondra found the bluff's edge, but the way down was a steep multi-story wooden staircase. In peak condition, the horse could not have faced it.

They'd reached the mansions overlooking town. Perhaps the wisest thing would be to hide, but Alondra didn't like the idea of leading the horse onto someone's hardwood floor and trying to barricade the picture windows. The mansions didn't look defensible.

She couldn't afford much time to look for a hiding place, especially if the odds weren't good she'd find one. Then her eyes caught the signpost pointing off into the trees: Garrison Road. That must lead to the old fort. If Alondra could get them past its gate, the fort had to be impregnable. It probably had working stables and hay that she could offer long-suffering Moonshadow, who needed water, a blanket, and to get off his swollen foreleg.

"Let's hope this works." Jiggling the reins, Alondra started down Garrison Road.

The road soon dwindled to what seemed like a path between the trees.

It looked very lonely. The clear island air was silent except for the syncopated clip-clop of Moonshadow's shoes. Alondra's nerves twanged when she realized the rising moon cast black leaf-shadows at her feet. A sign pointed to the cemeteries, half a mile away.

It wouldn't hurt to pray, she decided, even if she didn't have much to offer as a sacrifice. "Well protected may I be as I roam, beautiful Diana, for I walk with your blessing. May you quench the lust for blood and transform it into love of thee."

When Alondra reached the whitewashed rampart around the fort, she found her courage again.

A mournful howl ripped through the still evening. Moonshadow huddled beside Alondra. She patted him as calmly as she could. If she'd been alone, she would have made her stand here, with the wall at her back.

Before long, she and the horse reached Saint Ann's Cemetery. Its stone gates opened to the left of Garrison Road. The graveyard shimmered with tiny blue and amber lights. Fewer ghosts than she expected sat on their tombstones. The horse whickered softly, tugging the reins as he tossed his head.

"If you'd had an opinion about the path, you should have voiced it half a mile back," Alondra scolded gently. "You know this island better than me." Then she promised, "They won't hurt us. Come on. Maybe they'll help."

"What'd you do to that horse, Missy?" an invisible man asked from a tablet tombstone beneath a holly bush.

"He stepped on a nail as we crossed the old battleground."

"That'll be the death of him," the ghost predicted. "The wolf will smell the blood as well as we can. Easy pickings."

Alondra refused to let him frighten her. "We need to get into the fort. Give me directions to the nearest gate."

"No time," the man argued. "That wolf is smart. He knows there's no hunting down in the village, where people wait with traps and guns. He'll prowl the highlands, looking for fools caught out in the dark. If you're not a fool, stake the horse out and run."

Running was the last thing on Alondra's mind. Despite the sweat beading on her forehead in the humid evening, she slipped her leather jacket on and patted through its pockets, reassuring herself where everything was stashed.

"What do you know about wolves?" she taunted him.

"Used to hunt them, when the British still owned this land. My family moved my grave twice until I landed here."

He moved out of the shadows. The moonlight showed black blood smearing his buckskin jacket. A darker shadow hid where his throat had been.

"Is this wolf your kin?" Alondra asked. "Is that why you're delaying me here?"

The trapper laughed. "I been dead a long time. Watching you run screaming through the dark woods while your lame mule gets eaten will entertain me for a while to come."

Alondra led Moonshadow deeper into the graveyard, where a big old oak spread its branches. As luck would have it, she stumbled over a fallen limb sturdy enough to serve as a club. She lashed Moonshadow's reins loosely to a branch overhead, so he could free himself once she had the wolf engaged. Then she gathered kindling.

After the first warning howl, the woods remained eerily quiet. The wolf was already hunting them. He knew better than to panic his prey.

Alondra built a small fire with her club extended into its heart. She kept close, so she could grab it out.

Once small flames licked through the twigs, she looked around at her surroundings. An antique rosebush, loaded with fragrant pink blossoms, decorated the grave of Melody Carver, who died at sixteen years, four months, and 22 days.

Taking a candle stub from her coat, Alondra lit its wick with a twig from the fire. She dripped wax atop the headstone, then set the candle upright. "This light I offer to the memory of Melody Carver, plucked from the joys of life too soon." Alondra drew her silvered knife and cut several blooms from the rosebush, stripped them of thorns and tucked them into her braid.

"*Elle a vu un loup*," a voice whispered nearby, its French old-fashioned. Still, Alondra took its meaning: Melody had lost her virginity before she died. Alondra shrugged. Graveyards were more gossipy than small towns.

The horse whimpered and danced, scenting the predator outside the firelight. Alondra pulled her club from the flames and held it aloft, watching for the glow of the wolf's eyes. In the old days, that reflected light had been considered a mirror of the flames of hell.

The animal stood not far away, black lips pulled back. A white mask stretched around its burning eyes. It was smaller than she'd expected, maybe three-quarters grown.

It launched itself at her.

Alondra swung the club up to protect her throat. The wolf crashed into her, knocking her dangerously close to the campfire. Alondra rolled, pinning the wolf between her body and the flames.

Its jaws snapped shut close enough to her that hot spittle splashed her face.

With her left hand, Alondra drove the hypodermic needle down like a knife.

The surprised wolf yelped. He kicked at her with his hind legs, desperate to escape. Thank goodness she wasn't fighting a cat with sharpened hind claws. Instead, her coat took the worst of the damage from his dull canine toenails.

Wrenching the needle out before it snapped, Alondra flung herself clear. She prayed the one syringe would do the job. She wasn't sure if the wolf would let her close enough for a second shot.

It scrabbled in the dirt, trying to get its suddenly nerveless legs beneath it. It nipped at its forelegs, trying to bite some sensation back in. Throwing its head back for a wail as frightened as any human child's, the wolf turned icy blue eyes on Alondra. Its gaze had lost focus.

Alondra was barely aware that Moonshadow had broken his lead and vanished into the shadows. She was glad he wouldn't see what she planned to do next.

She retrieved the coil of rope from the tree crotch. Tying a hangman's knot, she looped the rope over the wolf's back feet and cinched it tight. It took her several tries—she was shaking from her near escape—to fling the free end of the rope up over a branch high enough for the work to be done. Then she hoisted the paralyzed wolf out of the dirt and lashed the rope to a branch.

The wolf panted, its tongue lolling between slack jaws. Its saliva traced an arcane pattern in the dirt.

She brushed sweat from her forehead with the back of her hand. Adrenaline left her jittery. She had an hour for the work, if the drug and the firelight held out. She wanted to be finished before the wolf woke up.

Alondra turned the hanging wolf so his belly faced the firelight. She grabbed a thick handful of fur in her left hand, twisting to draw it taut, and made a shallow cut with her silvered knife.

The fur grew wet and warm in the darkness. Alondra's mouth watered at the smell of blood. She swallowed hard and kept cutting.

* * * *

Men shouted through the darkness. Alondra saw flashlight beams bouncing toward her as they ran toward her campfire. She wiped sweat from her eyes with a bloody hand and kept cutting. *Almost there.*

"Sweet Mother of God," a man groaned.

A shotgun bolt was drawn back. "Step away," another man ordered, "or by God, I'll kill you where you stand."

As long as she stood beside the wolf, Alondra knew she was safe. "At this point, he's just tranquilized. If my knife slips, he'll be dead. Please don't shoot us yet."

"What in God's name are you doing?"

The silvered knife had lost most of its edge. Alondra tore the wolf skin the last couple of inches. A belt of bloody hide, six inches wide and as long as the wolf's belly was around, hung over her shoulder, congealing in the darkness.

She lifted her hands in mock surrender, unable to see if the shadowy posse relaxed. Her thumb brushed one of Melody's pink roses, hanging askew in her braid. Alondra plucked the rose and forced it into the wolf's mouth.

The change washed over its face first. The boy was maybe sixteen, hair bleached blond by the summer sun. His nose was a little too long and straight to be truly handsome. She couldn't see the color of his closed eyes, but she bet they were blue. Muscled by hard work, his bare arms hung down to in the cemetery dirt.

The men rushed toward her now, untying the boy, easing him down to the hallowed ground. Completely drained, Alondra sat down with her back to someone's headstone. She couldn't count the men, but her initial suspicion was probably correct: seventh son of a seventh son. Scion of the kind of good Catholic family that one rarely encountered any more.

A water bottle nudged her shoulder. Alondra took it, grateful it was already opened, and splashed the emerald ring on her left hand. The emeralds burned their true deep green. The water wasn't poisoned. She tipped back her head and drank deep, letting the water wash blood from her face.

Brighton said, "We found Moon Calf limping down Hoban Road as we came up from the village."

"There's a nail in his foot. I was afraid to take it out."

"That was wise. Did he throw you when he stepped on it?"

"No. He was a complete gentleman."

A bespectacled man stopped in front of her, silhouetted against the fire. Alondra could tell he wasn't related to the others, many of whom shared the boy's blond hair and long nose.

"What did you give him?" the man demanded.

"Ketamine." Alondra rubbed her tired eyes. "It was easiest to get and probably easiest for you to counteract."

"There doesn't seem to be any bleeding where you cut that…pelt off of him."

"I only cut the wolf's skin. The boy was still the boy beneath it."

The first voice she'd heard, moaning a prayer when he thought his son was being butchered, asked, "Does that mean he won't turn into a wolf any more?"

"Never again," Alondra promised.

The men startled her by dropping to their knees. "Praise God," they breathed as one.

Typical, Alondra thought.

Bringing the Bodies Home
by Christian Riley

The plane has crashed, the copilot is clearly dead, all radios are down, and Otis is stuck in the cockpit. He tries to disengage the forward hatch, but the metal hinges must be bent—nothing gives. The windows? Impervious up to a 30mm round, and his sidearm is only a Browning 9. Gone are the days of having a cabin door, at least on cargo planes of this line. But there's a reason for that detail—the solid wall of titanium behind him—a damn good reason.

If there's a bright side to this morning, it's that Otis is still alive, and the plane's homing beacon has turned on. Luck of a million quasars if the rescue team arrives in time. And the view? At least it's interesting. A hundred or so yards away lay the Sea of Silence, an expansive black drum forming the horizon. Otis thinks it looks as quiet and still as every author has penned it to be. They've been writing about that wave-less ocean since Sentinel Command first found this planet, some three decades ago.

Three decades—that's a long time to be fighting a war. Turns out the Secretians were tougher, and smarter, than Sencom had first suggested. Victory seemed promising in the beginning, the first few years, at least. They hit those buggers hard, hit 'em damn hard. Seemed as if they had the war bagged. Then, out came the secret weapon. It was everyone's opinion that the Secretians had gotten desperate.

For Otis, it seems ironic. As a kid, playing at war, he and his brothers each had a "secret weapon," something they saved for special occasions, down to the last man sort of thing. Otis' favorite, Jimmy had made up. He called it the "Turn-cloak," and when activated, the nearest enemy went on his side, started fighting previous teammates.

A taste of irony, but still, not the same. Not even close. They don't have a side, other than their own. Sencom, the Secretians—fair game the lot of them.

Otis unbuckles and checks himself for damage, unintentionally gazes at the copilot's broken form, his body tin-canned by a malfunctioning ejection seat. Old Eddie…

Otis never liked him. He was the worst copilot, boring as shit, had the personality of a box of rocks. *Is that what they call a mixed metaphor?* Otis wonders—then, doesn't care, as it beats anything Eddie ever came up with. Their first day out, Otis told his funniest joke, and Eddie, he just gave back a blank stare. Been rocky ever since. And there is nothing remotely decent about that, considering the nature of their job: hauling bodies home from the war. A guy could stand a bit of fun, surrounded by all that grief, and danger. But now? Well, Otis suspects he'll be getting a new copilot, assuming he survives this ordeal. Cheers to the bright side!

Speaking of bodies: if memory serves Otis correctly, the Sea of Silence has swallowed quite a few over the last thirty years. Ships, and planes, interstellar modules—they've all been shot down over that watery graveyard. The last one, not even two weeks ago, in fact. It was a Frigate Carrier, Tsudo Class...the *SCS Miyaki*, Otis remembers. Had over five thousand personnel onboard when it went down—took them all to the bottom of that ghostly sea. *What a way to go.* Then, with a sidelong glance, Otis looks over at Eddie—bloody sack of pulp that he now is—and after, the titanium wall behind him. There are, of course, worse ways to meet one's end. Much worse.

Looking away, Otis studies his control panel, makes a few inquiries: cabin pressure good, CO_2 scrubber functioning, redundant life support systems sound, on hiatus. Not bad, considering the crash landing. Then he checks his Cryo-containment settings, in the unlikely scenario that he may need to go into a state of hibernation, assuming...well...assuming the worst.

There's a depressing thought. Going into Cryo-state comes with a mandatory of ten, uninterrupted years, allowing for a proper deep freeze, and safe incubation period—not to mention a painless defrost. Otis thinks about his wife, his two sons, even his dog, Harry. Ten years is a long, long time.

His last memory with his family, he was sitting—

Thump!

Otis leans forward, double-time. That sound, it came from the back, behind him—behind the titanium wall. It's not much of a surprise, now that he coldly wraps his mind around the noise. Although, he does check his wristwatch. Seems to him that, despite the engine failure, and the crash landing, he should still be in the green zone. As far as Otis knows, complete transmutation never occurs in less than thirty-six hours, and the loadmaster had been quite clear about where these bodies had come from. And, more importantly, when they were pulled out from the Gray Wastes—the Secretian's *secret weapon.*

Clang!

Well, so much for certainty. Instinctively, Otis recoils back into his seat, attempts to make himself smaller. In his mind, he does some rough calculations, trying to figure out when the rescue party should arrive. Enemy lines are six thousand kilometers to the east. Forward base, where he departed from, that's a good three thousand, give or take. No major conflicts or operations within this sector. All in all, they should be here soon. Somebody should.

Ca-chunk—shkreeuh!

That last sound—the sound of tearing metal. In his mind's eye, Otis pictures scabrous hands ripping through the plane's fuselage. It won't be long now, this he knows. If only he could conceal himself in some way. If only there was a place to hide. He glances again at Eddie: the luxury of a quick, painless death, no doubt.

If they see Otis, and observe him for what he is—a living morsel—the bodies will stop at nothing to get at him. Some of them, Otis may recognize. May even know. As a general rule, he never looks at the complete cargo manifest. What's the point? The job is depressing enough on its own. Why add company to the misery?

Seconds later and silence prevails, but there is nothing comforting about it. The proverbial calm before the storm, as Otis waits, motionless, like the blank sea before him. Will they buy it?—him playing 'possum, playing dead. He thinks again about his family, then sees a shadow cross the ground on his left. They're coming.

He watches through slitted eyes, sees the mangled forms stagger forward, past his periphery. Six, seven, then the last one—eight creatures now, wandering in the forefront of the plane. Otis' heart rattles in his chest, an engine in overdrive. These are vile specters, abominations of humanity created through their own deaths, from a gray sludge of God-knows-what. And, they're beyond dangerous. Beyond deadly, even—if ever there was such a thing. Just one of these guys, Otis recalls, tore to shreds an entire A-Team of Brunt Force operatives.

Collectively, the bodies turn and stare at the cockpit, as if one of them had given a command. Otis swallows hard, feels the sudden urge to piss. He tries to remain calm, comatose, his eyes a hair's width apart. They might be able to get at him—collectively—rip the glass away from the cockpit, pull him out and onto the ground, pick him clean straight down to the bone, crunch on that, suck the marrow dry. Otis has no doubt that they would certainly try, if they had the faintest inkling he was alive.

He holds his breath. He holds his breath, and waits. He knows that Cryo-state would do an even better job at disguising his "liveliness." He thinks about his wife and kids, his dog, tries not to think about the worse, when suddenly, the bodies turn their backs on the plane and shamble off—toward the Sea of Silence.

What is this? Otis thinks, opening his eyes. He watches as the bodies shrink into the distance. They reach the flat water, plunge into obscurity, are gone—nothing but faint ripples now.

Otis exhales, relaxes. He leans forward, peers outside, double checks the manifest, finds the number "8" on the cargo line, relaxes some more. "What a fucking miracle," he says.

Now, it's all about the wait. And, Otis waits. He waits for hours. He falls asleep, which eats up a few more hours, wakes up, checks the time, falls asleep again. When he wakes the second time, he realizes he's been grounded for over twelve hours, which takes him well past the green zone, and into the red. Any rescue team now would have to know this. They'll be coming in fully armed, a squadron or two, prepared to deal with eight ravenous carcasses. *What little they know*, Otis thinks.

His stomach churns with hunger, (speaking of ravenous). Otis reaches behind his seat and pulls out a small gear bag, dumps its contents onto his lap. He finds three protein bars, a carb-shake, and a canister of fat tablets. Halfway through his second protein bar, he hears a distinct sound in the distance, pauses chewing. He cranes his ear toward the sky, then smiles. It's the sound of a Nakajimi 2160, coolant-pressed, twin-drive engine: standard fitting for the *Horsefly* troop carrier. Not one, but two, which means that Otis was correct with his assumptions: the cavalry would be coming.

He watches as the turbo-copters pass overhead, circle the scene, then land roughly two-hundred yards down the beach, to his left. He sees the soldiers storm out, form a defensive perimeter, guns up and ready—easily a hundred men. One of them raises an arm, then they all move forward, toward the crash site.

Otis yawns, stretches. He looks around for any personal effects he'll want to take with him, grabs the photo of his wife taped near the control panel, shoves it in his front pocket. He glances over at Eddie…*grim*. Otis feels a little bit sorry for the guy, just a little, then looks away, notices something in the distance, on the horizon.

It's the Sea of Silence.

It seems to be…*boiling?*

What the fuck?

And then: the breaking of the surface, the rise of hundreds—no—thousands of grotesque black heads, flailing pale arms, ragged torsos and warped legs, a massive wall of rot scrabbling out of the surf. Otis blinks, doesn't believe his eyes.

The surge of bodies erupts onto the beach and lurches forward, the soldiers now noticing, now panicking, upon being waylaid, their path back to the transports no longer unrestricted. Discipline breaks as a firestorm of bullets scream into the army of death, fooling Otis not in the slightest. The worst…the worst has now arrived, and Otis has no other options but to…

A lot happens in the short seconds it takes him to dial in the Cryo controls. The cost of ten years echoes inside his head, bangs out a migraine an inch behind his eyes. A gruesome, howling massacre unfolds on the sandy beach a hundred yards away. And the suspicion that this plan, this last ditch effort—to capsulate and freeze his body—will most likely prolong his death by mere minutes, if even that, crosses Otis' mind.

He activates the Cryo sequence anyways, feels an immediate blast of cold wind dash across his face. He squeezes his hands into white fists, as the translucent casing slowly slides down and seals him in. As his body goes heavy, and his mind and vision begin to fog, suddenly, Otis thinks he sees movement at his right. He swears it's Eddie's legs, shifting and twisting, but he can't move his head to be sure; and that can't make sense, because Eddie popped on the way down. And then, just before Otis' eyes clamp shut, and his conscience drifts away, does he really hear a whisper in his ear? Someone saying, "I never liked you, either." Otis swears it's Eddie's voice, but he can't open his eyes to be sure, and that too makes no sense, as Eddie never got hit by the gray sludge, and…

Restored
by Marlane Quade Cook

Scarlet velvet showed dusky in the dim corner where it hung. A lazy drapery ran nearly six feet high and drooped in crimson folds on the cold floor. A man's pale hand drew the drapes, and from behind gazed a pair of brooding eyes, dark and very well captured. The canvas was more than five feet high, and he gazed at the subject as if she were standing behind a window. A murky window, though. The painting was dark and grimy with age, except for the face and those cold, lovely eyes. He stepped back, scrutinizing the artwork with the aid of the room's dim light. He was still considering having it restored, and yet…was worried it would change the painting too much. He had grown attached to the murky quality of the canvas. He gazed back into the eyes. They met his, so intensely he almost shuddered. He shifted his gaze to the dark Grecian hair, unbound, and statuesque form clad in diaphanous black. The image was so lifelike it seemed to breathe. And move. And then with a shiver of realizing the impossible, it struck him: she did. Her movements were sinuous, but almost ghostly as she drifted from the heavy frame. She stepped lightly to the floor as if she'd just entered through a door, rather than from the painting's frame. She was close to him once more, so close, and real. Her intense eyes burned into his, the dark hair flowed over her shoulders, there was the sense of another person close by, the displacement of air and sound caused by a physical body, the glimpse of the woman's form he could see but was still hidden in its flowing garment. Her dark lips did not smile, yet curled, beckoning. Her hand did not seek his, but yet he felt himself holding hers, drawing her closer, feeling her warmth, her seduction…and then he found himself standing in front of the painting once more, staring at the dim figure of a woman swathed in black. He thought there was something triumphant in her expression, but he merely shuddered at his vivid imaginings, for such they must be. He shook his head and drew the velvet curtain, still unsure what to do with this strange object.

A few days passed, and once more he felt drawn, as if by an unheard call. He mocked himself inwardly for returning to the painting once more, but found himself standing in front of it again. He vaguely wondered if the throat and arms seemed clearer, shining more lifelike from the murk of time. The colors in the iridescent sky were more vivid. The Hellenic landscape with olive trees—all the details and forms were clearer. It was as if an invisible restorer had been hard at work, saving the painting from the ravages of time. But his thoughts ended as she stepped forward once more, and this time, her lips did part, just slightly, as she leaned toward him. A gleam of ivory teeth beckoned him forward as the dark eyes pleaded and demanded at once.

"What do you want?" He asked in a hoarse whisper

"To be free," answered a breath so soft it echoed through the cold air indistinctly. It could have been nothing more than the wind.

"How?"

Another fleeting flash of teeth, but then she was back in the painting once more.

He was not sleeping well, and had begun to notice strange aches and pains that had never bothered him before. He suspected the beginning of an illness. He resolved to end this foolish preoccupation with the painting and have done with it. He would take it to an art broker and have it valued…. soon.

A few days later, he felt it drawing him back to the remote room once more, and he was like an addict returning to the source of his turmoil. Now she stood clear against the background, regal and seductive, eyes beckoning but haughty.

"Come," she seemed to whisper, "come and set me free," and this time when she stood before him she drew closer and closer, and he felt he should move away but was powerless to move. The dark eyes burned hungrily as she softened against him, sliding her hands up his chest. She leaned forward, dark hair brushing his face. The dark lips, so deeply red, parted in a sigh as they grazed his skin.

* * * *

In a cold remote room of an old house hung a set of red velvet drapes. It seemed to be a showcase or hiding place for a prized painting. But upon closer investigation, the taste of the painting was morbidly grotesque, and baffled the heirs of the house as to why it was kept. For although large and ornately framed, clearly quite old and badly in need of cleaning, if not restoration, the painting featured the distorted form of a man who seemed to be in the grip of agony or death throes. This odd, tormented figure, so poorly arranged as to be off-center, one onlooker remarked, was but dimly visible in the grime of the painting. The age-stained background was a neoclassical landscape, iridescent skies and faraway Hellenic temples on a windswept hillside dotted with olive trees. On this incongruous background writhed the figure of a man captured in a state of agony, mouth shrieking silently, hands clawed and back arched as if trying to escape his fate. Onlookers shook their heads in bemusement. He stood out so oddly in his contemporary clothes. They shuddered at the morbid posture and silent cry. Why, they wondered, would anyone paint such a thing?

Nameless and Named
by David M. Hoenig

The evening air was warm and sultry as Abdul Amjad the spice merchant moved through the Damascus bazaar. The pouch at his belt was overfull and heavy from the sales of the day—as was usual, for such a successful businessman—and the substantial profit brought a pleased curve to his lips as he moved through the dwindling marketplace crowd.

"Peace be unto you, Abdul," said a heavyset man sitting under a colorful canopy which proclaimed his own wealth to all of the bazaar.

The sudden sight of his friend caused the small smile on his face to blossom like a flower to the sun. "And unto you, Mahmoud! How fare you this evening?"

"I am…uncertain, my friend."

Abdul stopped, surprised at the unexpected, weighty response. "Whatever is wrong? Was the perfume business today unsatisfactory?"

Mahmoud smiled. "No, Abdul. On the contrary, it was wonderfully rewarding. But what has happened since has made me pensive about my current state. Come, sit. Take some tea with me?" He produced another cup from below the low table at which he sat, then gestured to the saffron and indigo pillows on the ground beside him.

"I would be honored to share your tea, as well as any burden which troubles an old friend." The spice merchant sat across from his friend and watched Mahmoud as he poured the fragrant brew.

"Then I would ask you to hear my story and judge as to whether I have been wise or a fool."

Abdul took a sip. "Excellent, as usual, but I have never known you to be a fool, Mahmoud. Indeed, you are one of the shrewdest colleagues I have. *Yallah*, tell me what has happened."

The perfume merchant shifted his considerable bulk to a more comfortable position, though his expression remained anything but. "I sought out a Dervish who came to the bazaar this day, to ask if he would be willing to offer a prayer on my wife's behalf."

"But no! Not you?" Abdul let out a delighted laugh. "My old friend Mahmoud did this? The man known widely as the 'Puff Adder', so deadly shrewd in your bargaining, sought out such a fable?"

The perfume merchant looked nettled and drank another cup of tea with irritation. "I know how it seems, but the situation is desperate."

Abdul drained his own cup, then extended it to the other man for a refill. "I am sorry, my friend. What happened then?"

His friend poured. "I told him that I was desirous of God's help in the matter of my wife's health. The Dervish agreed, and danced a frenzy. Let me tell you, I have seen such before, my friend, but this one was special." The troubled look settled on Mahmoud's face again. "When he finished and came to me, he said: 'You must donate a day's earnings to someone desperately unfortunate, and the sooner the better for your wife's health. Believe me when I tell you that even the matter of a single day may be of great importance.'"

"Your wife has been ill a long time, Mahmoud..."

"She's been worse, much worse recently, my friend. There is pallor to her face now, and a bluish tinge to her lips, and the physicians have no remedy left that they have not tried. If nothing is done, she will go with God soon, great be His name."

"No! Please tell me you didn't..."

Mahmoud looked up. "I did. I took the healthy profits of the day and gave them to the beggars by the docks without a single qualm at the time."

Abdul broke out into delighted laughter, but sobered immediately at his friend's scowl. "Please forgive me for my reaction at this distressing time for you and your family. Is your wife any better since you have given so charitably?"

"No; and that is why I am so troubled."

"Then I fear you have been a fool, dear Mahmoud."

"I, too—apparently hope breeds it. *Insh'Allah*, I suppose."

"Truly, it will be as God wills it." Abdul stood. "Peace be unto you."

"And also unto you." Mahmoud stood as well, and the two embraced.

The spice merchant left the canopy of his friend's shop for the walk home, but before Abdul had gotten halfway, he felt a sudden tug at his money pouch. He grabbed for the sack even as he whipped his head around to look at the thief. He did not see the face, but instead only a fist moving rapidly which struck him full on the jaw.

The sudden shock and pain left him reeling backwards even as he felt something at his waist give, and then he was falling, dazed. Abdul tried to scream, but all that emerged from his mashed lips was a wheezy, indistinct burble. He half-lay in the dust of the street, his vision blurred by tears of pain and frustration. As blood dripped from his injured mouth to stain his robes, he struggled to sit up.

Then there was a helping hand upon his shoulder, and he began to shake off the dizzy feeling.

"Are you badly injured?"

Abdul looked up into the face of…"A Dervish? But, how…?"

The ascetic face was furrowed with concern as he examined the spice merchant's injuries. "I was passing this place to find a meal when I witnessed the very end of the attack. Are you alright?"

"Yes, yes, I am simply…" Abdul paused, memory returning abruptly. He dropped his hand to his waist only to find his bulging purse missing. "No! By the Prophet, but I've been robbed!"

The Dervish helped him to stand. "Would you like me to help you find the Sultan's guards that you may seek justice?"

The merchant, eyes casting every which way for the thief, locked eyes on the holy man hungrily. "Would you offer a prayer to God on my behalf?"

"I could do that for you, my friend. For what would you beseech Him?"

"I want the one who stole from me to be punished for his evil! He should die in agony for what he's done to me."

The Dervish's eyes grew distant, and he stepped back. "No, this I will not do."

"But you must!" Abdul wiped blood from his lips and showed it to the holy man. "You have prayed for my friend Mahmoud, and for others I have no doubt. This thief has hurt me and taken all my wealth, and he must be punished. It is only fair, I say!"

"This is not justice, it is only rage."

"I've lost everything! And I beg you to pray for me and…"

The Dervish interrupted him with a single raised finger. "I will pray on your behalf, but not for the vengeance for which you hunger. You are too quick and vehement in your anger, and selfish, that you would see worse than justice done. Instead I will pray for guidance for you." He stepped back and began his dance.

Abdul watched irritably. "'Guidance'?" His mouth throbbed and his thoughts were on the loss of his fortune, not the prayer. He would have to start over again, take out loans…and in the course of his distraction paid little attention to the astounding efforts of the holy dancer, or to the pure, unfettered joy of his prayer. He barely realized when the Dervish had finished, holding one final pose on the ball of his right foot while he held his left above his head with both hands for an impossible amount of time.

Impatient, Abdul scowled. "Well? What message does God send me?"

The Dervish made no immediate response. With slow grace, he returned to the ground, as though a magnificent bird after flight, and his distant gaze focused once again on the bloodied merchant before him. After a moment of scrutiny, he sighed. "If you wish to regain the riches of your life, you must journey south from the city, into the desert. At midnight, you will find a dune and must lie down upon it; then you shall contemplate the naked heavens which lie above all our earthly desires. There you will wait for the gifts which shall surely shower down upon you, and thus provide the means to recover far more than you have lost." He turned in a swirl of robes and was off at a pace swift as the wind.

The merchant was startled by the sudden movement and called after him, but the holy man moved so quickly and without a backward glance that he was gone before Abdul could begin to follow him. His irritation only grew. "Preposterous!"

He looked around, only to see no one but himself in the darkened street. Full night had fallen, and he was absent of a single coin. He felt his injured mouth again, and venomously cursed the thief who had robbed him as he considered what to do.

To go home would be devastating, Abdul realized, for he would have to tell his wife about his misfortune. The great and proud merchant embarrassed, laid low by a common criminal: his neighbors would hear of it and see him with his injuries, and the stories would spread like fire. He would be the laughingstock of the quarter, perhaps even the entire city. No, he could not go home.

But neither could he find a rooming house—not without coin. "Better I should die," he grumbled. It would save him the shame of his predicament, and others would not laugh at that degree of misfortune.

Or you could follow the Dervish's instructions, came the sudden unbidden thought. Abdul tried to dismiss it, but next to dying or returning home to embarrassment, he could not deny that it looked to be a fine option. The more he struggled with his dilemma, the more he wanted to believe that the Dervish's advice might, somehow, offer redemption. And so he began walking.

Soon he had left the city behind, and was out in the dry scrubland of the desert, and still he walked. He kept an eye on the sky as he trudged along, and while the desert cooled quickly, his efforts kept him warm enough. He continued south, and at midnight did, indeed, come to a dune.

He lay down upon it and opened his eyes. The stars were like jewels in the blackness, bright and hard and clear. The dark sky stretched from horizon to horizon, as though he were under a great dome of the heavens.

And then he felt the sharp sting in his right thigh.

He sat up with a cry, and saw a huge, fat-tailed scorpion by his side, one far larger than he had ever heard story of in fact or legend. "No!" he whispered in horror, but he already felt the fire in his leg which was said to herald certain death.

"Oh, but yes," whispered the scorpion.

"What?" Abdul tried to look that way but a sudden convulsion thrust him flat onto his back upon the dune. He tried to speak again, but could only exhale weakly as his muscles began to seize and lock.

The huge insect moved along his side, up to where his head lay, and he heard the clicking of its legs as it came. "This seems a surprise to you?" it asked.

"Buh, buh, buh, Der, Der, sai, sai…"

"Yes, but the Dervish said what? Something to do with a message from God, perhaps? Or maybe it was about regaining wealth?"

"Gi, gi, gi, gi…"

"Ah, yes, that was it! Gifts to be showered upon you as you lay under the naked stars! Well, friend Abdul, how do you like them? What? Nothing to say? Well then, allow me to tell you a story as you laze there…

"At the time of creation, God said to each creature: 'You will be according to your nature, and the purpose of your nature will be to educate man'. And I asked: 'But Lord God who is good, why should you fill me with venom and death?' And God replied: "You will be according to your nature, and your purpose shall be to educate man.' And for many ages of the Earth I have wondered on His words, only to finally understand them now.

"How should my nature educate man? See, merchant, see God's infinite wisdom! Through me you can understand what it means to be full of such bitter poison that it tortures body and soul, that it causes pain beyond what is needed, even unto death…"

Abdul's sight dimmed, and he could no longer see the fat-tailed scorpion, could no longer hear it, and he lay trapped with all his selfish inadequacies under the naked gaze of heaven.

When he awoke, he found himself still lying upon the dune, eyes crusted with grit and muscles wracked with pain as though he had been stoned and left for dead. Abdul could not believe the clarity of the air in his nostrils, the pure rasping as grains of sand shifted beside his ears, and the taste of dawn fresh upon his tongue. A whimper escaped his dried and tortured lips as he rolled to his side, hunched around the immense pain.

Then, as his memory returned all at once, he sat upright, breathing hard. He opened his eyes and rubbed the dirt from them, and frantically looked around. He was alone.

And his heart was full of the bitter ashes of a thousand and one regrets.

Abdul thought then of all that he'd heard since his fateful encounter with Mahmoud the prior evening, and saw it again fresh in his mind, only now with clarity refined by his lonely ordeal in the desert.

His friend the perfume merchant had been told to give away his wealth to those in need if he would see his wish for his wife's health granted, and he had, without delay. Selflessly.

Tears filled his eyes when he considered his own burden, small by comparison with the illness of his friend's wife, and the selfishness of his own reaction to adversity. He'd laughed at Mahmoud's 'foolishness' when he should have offered his empathy and understanding instead. When he recalled his reaction to the theft of his coin, he realized he had been filled with venomous rage at the thief, but more because he had been wronged than from a desire for justice. The Dervish had been absolutely correct in his harsh judgment of Abdul's character, and yet as kind in sharing God's message as if the merchant hadn't been rude and dismissive.

Salty wetness streamed down his cheeks when he considered that he had been ready to die to avoid being *embarrassed*, that all his worry had been about his *status* instead of how his wife and family would have been left with nothing. The full measure of his pettiness, his selfishness, his heartlessness, spewed up from his gut to spill out onto the harsh ground of the desert.

It was a better place for it than in a man.

When Abdul found himself empty of tears, he stood and turned north to begin his return journey, only something prevented him from taking the first step. Though he felt the truth of the Dervish's words, even recognized the gifts which the scorpion had given him which might allow him to regain his family, the riches of his life, and an appreciation for all that was good in his world, yet he faltered.

His right eye began to twitch as he looked but did not see the desert before him. *I have learned things, yes*, he thought. *But have I learned enough?*

After a while, he closed his eyes, spun in a circle several times, and reopened them. He began to walk in the direction of his gaze—hesitantly at first, and then with greater certainty. As days passed, he ate whatever he could catch or find, and drank the first condensation of morning. The plump features of a well-to-do merchant became planed, then carved, into something more austere and intense.

He changed his sleep schedule so as to pass the heat of the day at rest, rising at the gloaming to walk all night as some instinct seemed to bid him. His delicate and fancy shoes were no match for the terrain: they degraded until he kicked the rags loose, and then his feet were abraded until they toughened to hardened callus.

And still he walked where chance and his will took him, roaming the Rub' al Khali—"The Empty Quarter"—like one half awake. Ever and again he slept upon dunes hoping again for the pain and discovery of a passing scorpion's venom; ever and again he would awaken with a sense of incompleteness and disappointment in his lack of clarity.

One night after years of vain wandering, lost to himself and forgetful of the family and business he had left behind, Abdul came to the ruins of a village. It was the first sign of habitation he had encountered which had not been already swallowed by the sand, and the excitement of something different seemed to remove a haze from his mind. As his mind became more aware of his surroundings, he realized that he had been speaking to himself—*and probably for a while now*, he thought—and abruptly fell silent to look at the place carefully.

The wind seemed to scour the sand off the broken stone, offering a plausible reason why the remains of structures could be seen. Abdul felt the great age of the place in his bones, or at least they ached in a way he imagined age might inflict. He felt very aware of himself and this place, as if he had woken fully from a long sleep, or from an opium dream.

He began to search among the desert scrub, sand, and broken stone, and did not stop with sunrise or the ensuing heat of the day. At the fall of the following evening, he lifted a slab of stone canted against a rocky outcropping and found a low crevasse into the stone slanting downward. Carefully, lest some creature sheltering within might attack from within, he leaned closer to it and felt a wave of cooler air emerge from it as though exhaled. His curiosity spiked with the sudden realization that the space hidden inside must be quite large and fairly deep.

Abdul stood, feeling parched and hungry and a bit light-headed—he had not eaten or drunk since the previous night, but the exploration had consumed his attention. Though feeling somewhat nauseated, he set about foraging for his usual sustenance before turning his attention towards gathering what he might require to explore the crevasse he had discovered.

Later, the chill of night making the heat of the day the faintest of memories, he readied his meager supplies and lit a makeshift torch which flickered and rippled in the gusting wind. He returned to the opening and got down on hands and knees so as to crawl within, his light held before him. As he began to descend, the stone above him was low and close, forcing him to continue to crawl. His knees became scuffed and abraded, and the same would have befallen his hands but that he wrapped them in cloth strips torn from his faded and thin-worn clothes.

Several times Abdul came to turns which took him onward and downward, air from below continuing to billow up periodically past him and ensuring that both he and his small fire had enough air to breathe. He lost sense of time as he descended into the Earth, and all of a sudden came to an open space. The illumination of his torch—ample for the confines of the tunnel, but pitiful compared to the cavern before him—failed to penetrate far enough to see any wall or cavern ceiling from where he knelt.

He held very still and breathed shallowly in order to better hear, but no sound came to him. Carefully he maneuvered out of the tunnel and stood, moving the light around and above him to assess his surroundings.

What he saw in the feeble light made him draw in a ragged, loud breath, and such was his shock that he only just kept himself from shouting: the stone roof he could see above him had clearly been worked by tools!

The flame caught glints among the stones, many and more as he moved the torch around to see. After a bit he began to notice patterns. "Stars?" he whispered with a sense of wonder, and the resulting echoes seemed to rush away into the darkness like a swarm of flying insects. Although he studied further, the forms of the constellations he saw did not match what he'd become familiar with, and it made him wonder as he traced them with trembling fingers.

Eventually, Abdul lowered the light to see the wall to one side of the opening through which he'd crawled, and saw that it had been carefully painted in a myriad of rich and startling colors. And as he moved along the gently curving wall away from the tunnel, he saw that what he had first observed was only part of a much larger mural of what appeared to be a coastal city of some sort. The buildings appeared oddly proportioned, and the color of the plants a richer green than he could remember having seen. The painted sky was a cerulean which seemed to instantly and seamlessly substitute itself into his memories for the real thing, fading to the twilit darkness of evening as it rose to the starry night sky of the ceiling.

He froze when he first glimpsed the city's inhabitants, unsure for a moment whether they were real or paint. They were low-slung things which seemed to be able to both stand upright and slither on all fours. Their skin was depicted meticulously in fine grey scales of varying hues, and their heads were more reminiscent of a crocodile of the Nile than of a man.

Abdul followed the mural as he moved along the wall slowly. The life depicted beneath the cunningly wrought sky had both familiar and bizarre elements to it. Portrayed in the painting were scenes of agriculture and animal husbandry, fishing and boats of strange design, and what he immediately thought must be temples.

Those regions were the most disturbing, and looking at them he whimpered without realizing it. Strange architecture and geometry—structures his mind told him could not possibly have stood for any length of time—abounded, each more disquieting than the last. And the priests at these temples wore a common uniform of finely sheened fabric, though each of a different color or hue. It appeared that the most prominent of these additionally well adorned with gems and jewelry. Their blades wept the blood of their sacrificial victims with a crimson devotion so pure that it made him weep.

As Abdul circled the cavern, he came to a new tunnel on the far side, and then a gust came from it which put out his makeshift torch and plunged the astounding room into absolute blackness.

He screamed, and his sudden terror echoed around him like the hellish cries of some nightmarish marketplace where nothing wholesome might be sold. He felt an abrupt urge to urinate, and the prior nausea struck again, redoubled. Abdul fell to his knees in the dark and retched, spewing his earlier meager meal to the rocky ground. When his belly had finished rebelling, he felt weak and feverish, and sweat seemed to spring forth from his skin as though conjured. His eyes strained against the dark until his head hurt, his ears full of the sounds of his own rapid breathing and galloping heart.

"What do I do now?" he whispered, and sat frozen, listening. The crescendoing and fading susurrus which followed seemed to mock him in the heavy darkness of this strange place.

He reached out tentatively for the cave wall, as if afraid that he might find something altogether more dangerous instead. When he made contact with the stone he jerked back in sudden alarm, even though nothing bad had happened. Abdul's hand wavered uncertainly in the darkness for a moment before he touched the wall once more. When he made contact he jerked back in alarm, but when nothing happened he licked his dry lips and reached again.

Another gust of cool air from the tunnel before him dried his sweat and set him to shivering. His teeth began to chatter as he got to his feet. *Back the way I came or onward?* he asked himself. The unseen but known seemed far less terrifying than the alternative, and so he started back, fingers trailing along the mural to be sure of his location in the impenetrable blackness. It felt slick, almost wet. Abdul paused, suddenly fearful at the thought that some of the vivid, awful, painted blood on the blades might get on his fingertips, and he stopped to retch again. Only a pathetic amount of bitter acid came up this time, and he spat it out.

His flinching hand came to emptiness, and with abrupt relief he realized he had reached the tunnel from which he had started his survey. And then the sudden flutter of whispers came with the next gust from the tunnel across the black cavern, as though thousands of papery wings all rubbed together.

Abdul shrieked and lurched forward, forgetting the low opening, and struck his head upon the rough rock. He felt wetness sheet down into his right eye, causing it to sting as he dropped heavily to his knees. The fresh pain galvanized him, and he scrambled forward heedless of care. He scraped against walls as he moved, tearing the fragile fabric and the yet-more fragile skin beneath.

The darkness filled his eyes, his nose, his mouth, and he felt as though he couldn't get enough air inside. A fingernail caught an outcropping of rock and stripped away with a white-hot agony, but he couldn't scream the pain out for the weight of the blackness around and inside of him. All he could do was crawl and whimper.

It took a long time, and each fresh blast of wind which overtook him was filled with whispered exhalations from the abyss behind him. His tortured journey on hands and knees put him in mind of the crocodile-like figures below, caught mid-slither in the terrifying reverential paint on the cavern's walls. It made him try to scramble faster, his breathing ragged and wheezing. All he could imagine was a dessicated, winged reptile with filmed-over eyes, crouched somewhere in the darkness behind and below him as it blew thousands of its avatars in resolute pursuit of his frail flesh as he fled the alien cavern deep beneath the Empty Quarter's sands.

He did not realize at first when he had made it above ground because it was still dark, but the empty space around him finally made him pause and listen. Abdul rubbed clotted blood away from his eyes and squinted, looking up to see stars reminiscent—though with far different configurations—of the night sky painted on the cavern's ceiling. The wilderness around him was empty, silent, and best of all, disinterested in him, and still the urgency of his terror did not abate.

Abdul ran to the slab of stone he had moved a lifetime ago before he'd gone below ground, and strained to maneuver it to cover the crevasse to the horrifying mysteries below. His frantic grunts were tinged with hysteria as he heaved at it, but his persistence was rewarded. He let the stone fall, and almost wept with relief. His fear spiked as the huge slab descended too slowly, as though some force resisted it at first, but it gained speed and finally slammed down onto the rocky outcrop with a sound he would remember forever.

The former merchant fell to his knees and sobbed loudly, gasping the cold desert air in great lungfuls as the sky began to lighten with the approaching dawn. He glanced with fear at the blocked and once-again hidden tunnel, then pushed to his feet and staggered away from the ruins as fast as his lurching pace could carry him.

* * * *

Epilogue

It was years before his steps brought him once more to the great city of Damascus. He muttered softly to himself as he strode through market streets familiar and yet meaningless.

"By Allah!" The speaker was old, fat, and engaged with customers whom he quickly abandoned to move after the man he thought he recognized. "Is it my old friend, Abdul Amjad, after all these years? I have believed you dead! What has it been? Eight? Ten?"

The man paused, his eyes flashing as he turned to Mahmoud, the perfume merchant. His lips still moved, but his voice was low, the words rushed and indistinct.

"What is that you are saying? My ears are also years older, I fear." He chuckled as he leaned closer to hear, but his laughter failed at the sight of his friend's haunted eyes.

Abdul's voice rose in volume, but the words still rushed as though they could not hasten enough to be away from him. "That is not dead which can eternal lie, and with strange aeons, even death may die."

The fat merchant's face paled. "Ominous words to greet your old friend, Abdul."

"Abdul Amjad has been devoured in the desert, Mahmoud, and there is left only me."

"But your wife, your children…?"

Abdul's reply fell as swiftly and brutally as a scimitar stroke. "I have none." He turned and began walking.

Stunned, Mahmoud fell behind, but before his friend could get far he called out. "But if I am not to call my friend Amjad, what then shall I call you?"

The reply was in a voice harsh and dry. "Al-Azrad." He turned a corner and was gone.

Playing A Starring Role
by Paul Lubaczewski

The last frames of the film flickered to an end on the screen, and the lights came up. It had been a terrible slasher film of such generic proportions that the theaters only two occupants can barely remember its name. The scathing reviews, by the private screening reviewers who had even deigned to be at it, were so scathing that the theater's emptiness could scarcely be considered a surprise. The only reason the theater was running it was that it had come in a package distribution with a much more highly anticipated slasher flick.

One of the figures stood, and said in a sad voice, "They just don't make em the way they used to."

The other figure looks over at the man who had spoken, the speaker is already muffled in a scarf, and a hat making his face impossible to see. The young man can't stop himself from agreeing, "You got that right, I like bad horror movies, but that was awful!"

"In my day, we made a lot of crap, no doubt about that, but at least we tried to give you a plot and some characters," the voice was raspy, like the throat had been damaged at one time, but behind it was a booming quality, like the man speaking had once been a large husky man indeed.

"We made?" said the scruffy young man, his eyebrow rising behind his glasses.

The young man could feel the face staring at him, as if taking him in and weighing him. Finally, the man spoke, "Well yeah, I used to work in pictures once upon a time."

"Oh wow!" the younger man enthused, as the other man slowly walked back to where the young man had been seated. "That is so cool! My names Ed," he said thrusting his hand out towards the approaching figure.

The other man looked at his hand for a moment, as if he had no idea what to do about it, but then grasped it in his own gloved hand and said, "Creighton, my name's Creighton young fellah!" The grip of the man actually shocked Ed and caused him to wince for a second, he might sound like an old man now, but he must have been a full bruiser back in his day.

After finally retrieving his hand and hoping it still worked as well as it had before, Ed said, "So let me see if I've got this right, you used to work in films?"

Ed could see the man's eyes, gleaming out of the shadows beneath his hat in the still dim light of the theater, "Let me ask you something, what kind of films do you like? I mean personally?"

"Well, usually I like horror, tonight being the exception of course, but I like lots of stuff," Ed shrugged.

"Humph! Alright, well if you want to talk, come on and take a walk with me. They'll shoo us out of here any minute now, so they can make room for the next couple of saps dumb enough to sit through this buzzard," Creighton said as he made for the door.

"Yeah, OK, I'd love to hear if you've got some stories. It'd make something great for my film class, maybe even do a follow-up interview if you'd like. It'd go a way towards making up for sitting through that film," Ed said falling in step beside him.

"OK then, let's just talk for now, what were you interested in knowing about? I'm not going to go all Groucho/Cavett on you and name many names, if any. I'd kind of like to keep my own name out of it if I could. I'm just a private citizen these days you understand?" Creighton said as they made their way up the aisle towards the door and the night outside.

"You want to go get a drink or something?"

Creighton chuckled in his coat and said, "Kid, it's like you read my mind, there's a place near hear that serves drinks outside, that'll suit me just swell."

As the two of them were walking along, Ed asked, "So, were you an actor?"

"Yep, starred in a ton of films, a couple people even still remember," Creighton replied somewhat ruefully.

"Did you always want to be an actor?"

"Well, I don't know about actor, I was interested in things like that, but my old man wouldn't have it. Made me go to business school, if I hadn't gotten into acting, I probably would have made a decent plumber," Creighton replied.

They were silent while they walked until they reached the bar that Creighton had indicated. It was a tourist sort of a place, which made Ed immediately begin to count his funds in his head, these places got expensive. Creighton strode into the place confidently, raising a hand to the bartender as they entered to indicate that he and Ed would be taking a table outside. As he breezed by the bar itself, Creighton said in passing, "Two beers, my tab Lou."

Once they had sat down, and their beers had arrived, Ed asked, "So how on earth did you get involved in acting. Successful plumbers don't normally go for acting."

Creighton's face was still hard to see, because of the dim lighting in the outside patio area, but Ed could see he was smiling as he chuckled, "Well, my dad died for starters." Creighton could probably read the surprise on Ed's face when he said that, so he followed quickly with, "my Dad was kind of famous, and he was an overpowering sort of guy. He didn't want me acting, so I didn't act. Once he was gone, nothing was stopping me. I'd do anything at first! Bit roles, stunt work, anything I could get my hands on!"

"Oh, so only small stuff," Ed replied, crestfallen. This could have been a major scoop, but now it looked like he was spending time with a washed up never was.

"Well, at first. But everybody starts that way don't you see? I mean unless you've got absolute perfect looks, you gotta wait to get lucky. John Wayne did twenty films where he didn't even get a credit, and one he was only a corpse for, "Creighton chuckled.

"So, you got your big break eventually?"

"Oh yeah, funny thing is, that film nobody remembers me being in now, made me a name at the time. Same with westerns, I did a Mother Loving TON of westerns, nobody remembers that. Give you an example, next big break I got, the one that made everyone think I was a 'horror actor' all the sudden? I did three westerns that year too! If you weren't Karloff, you only had five good years back then playing horror. Most of that time, half your films could be duds, you had to do other films to keep the bills paid after that," Creighton explained. He looked thoughtful about it for a minute before adding, "I think that's where Lugosi was kind of screwed, with that voice, what else could he really do?"

Ed was wracking his brain, trying to figure out who he was talking to, all of the names he was coming up with were all long since dead. He thought Carradine was still alive, but this man seemed to hulk a bit, have a bit of bulk to him, and the whole reason John Carradine had been a horror star in the first place was that he had been born looking cadaverous.

"So, you still do movies?" Ed asked, hoping to prod some more information from Creighton.

"Well no, I was mostly doing garbage for a paycheck when I was forced to quit. You know, the kind of stuff they run late night, or at a midnight showing for kids to laugh at. I'm OK with that, the films were garbage, the kids are right to laugh at them now," Creighton sighed and then finished off his beer.

Suddenly, the older man sat slightly more upright, and pulled his chair back, "If it's OK with you, it seems to be getting a bit late for me. If you don't mind walking a little bit, you can walk me back to my house."

Ed thought about it for a second. It was getting a bit late for him too, but then again, he didn't have any classes tomorrow either. If he let the old man get away from him without even getting a phone number, and he looked it up later, and the guy had been some serious horror star, nobody would ever believe him. In the interest of eventually getting a tape recording of an interview, he said, "Sure, I don't mind. I don't get enough exercise anyway."

"Gee that's swell, let me settle up and we can get out of here," Creighton said getting to his feet.

Ed couldn't help wondering at that, who still said "gee" and "swell"? In 1982? But then again, Creighton had to be an old man at this point, and Ed had watched enough old movies to know people used to talk like that back then. As odd as it was to hear it now, they were just coming off the seventies, after all, a decade that had specialized in odd, so it was best not to judge.

The air was beginning to feel crisp as they began to walk down the boulevard, in the direction of what could only be guessed to be Creighton's home. Ed couldn't help but wonder if the old man had been reduced to some flophouse, and if he had accidentally re-discovered some forgotten star of yore living in squalor, like you'd see in the tabloids every once in a while. But then again, that had been a pricey place they had gone for beers, so maybe not at that.

Ed broke the silence as they walked, "So, why did you have to quit anyway?"

Creighton considered the question before answering, "You could say I had burned too many bridges. But that wasn't why, that was why I had been making really crappy movies though. I used to like to drink, well, can't say I'm proud of how much I used to like to drink. Even did ads for beer, I was notorious. I'd get into fights on the set, set up drunken pranks around the lot, that kind of thing. I don't know, you get bored sitting around all day in case they want to re-shoot something. You learn to make your own amusements, and when I didn't think of any at first, get enough Schlitz in me, and I thought of plenty."

"A real hellion huh?" Ed interjected.

"Yeah, you could certainly say that most of the studio heads did, that's for sure," Creighton agreed as he turned them down a darkened side street that Ed didn't recognize. This new road was barely more than an alley really, but he knew that every one of these little things had dozens of apartments with doors opening on them, so he could only assume that was what they were headed for.

"No, no what really stopped me was getting sick," Creighton continued, "got throat cancer. You can probably hear my voice ain't all that great. That's what killed my Dad by the way. Also got heart problems too. had liver issues. No, I probably wouldn't have survived another shoot."

"But here you are, alive and well!" Ed marveled.

"Well that's the thing about being famous, "Creighton shrugged, "especially in horror films. You meet a lot of weird people, mostly crackpots, nutjobs, the type who think that stuff is real. You get a lot of weird mail you know? I would usually try to write back to most of them, be grateful they took the time and all. Turned out one of them wasn't a total wacko. The first time he wrote me, it was about the plot of one of my films, I wrote him a nice thank you, and wrote him off as just another weirdo. Turns out he was a Doctor at UCLA and had been doing a lot of research, he knew towards the end that I'd been sick and wrote me again, he said he could save me. I wasn't as dumb as I played on the screen, I knew my days were numbered, hell by that point I'd been reduced to acupuncture for pain, I was willing to try just about anything."

"But," Ed shuddered a bit, the air was kind of cool tonight, and the alley just seemed to be getting darker, "how did you vanish? I mean, you haven't gone back to working, so you've just kind of disappeared, haven't you?"

Creighton chuckled, leaning in a bit closer as they walked and lowering his voice, "Easy enough kid, you put out a press release, say they body was donated to science. The press would have some respect for the family and just leave it be. I don't think I got more than a column in the Times for it."

"Well did he cure you? I mean he must have, right?"

Creighton tilted back his hat and looked over at Ed. Despite the poor light, Ed now had the first good look at Creighton he'd had all night. Except he didn't know him as Creighton, he knew him by his stage name, but not only that, Ed's heart raced as he also saw all the monster's he'd seen the man portray on the TV and in late night screenings! Here in this darkened dirty alley, he was confronted by the face that had launched a thousand childhood memories!

It almost seemed to Ed, that the old man seemed to glow as he turned fully towards him! Creighton's hands fell on his shoulders, "He did a lot more than that, I don't have any idea how long I'm going to keep living, could be forever if I do what the Doc tells me I gotta do. You seem a nice kid and all, and I'm sorry. But, c'mon, you've seen what happens when the monster reveals his face in this type of film!"

An enormous cracking noise resounded and echoed in the alleyway, followed by a wet slurping.

AND THE LIVING IS EASY
by Mike Chinn

Ash leaned heavily against the door, closing it behind him. He enjoyed the dim room; the short-lived relief at being out of the blighted sunlight. It never lasted. Within minutes he'd be chafing again, wishing he was outside where he belonged. In the sunlight. Even *that* sunlight.

He pulled off chipped sunglasses and loosened some of his layered clothing. He wasn't sure, but he thought it was starting to grow a little ripe. Peeling off his balaclava he scratched at his lank hair.

"Ama…!" he called. There was no reply. "Ama! I'm back…!" He stuffed the glasses into the pocket of a threadbare overcoat. *"Hi, honey I'm home…!"* He couldn't hold back the thick sarcasm which coated every word. It was the same every evening, or had become so.

"Come on, Ama—it'll be sundown soon—!"

He shrugged off the overcoat, dropping it carelessly across the back of a dirty wooden chair. It and an almost identical twin were the only sticks of furniture within the four bare brick walls. The plaster had long since crumbled. Filthy boards creaked under his feet. A ray of sunlight, too intense for the time of day, found its way through a chink in a window smeared with uneven layers of what once had been black paint. It was peeling now, faded to an ugly brown. The light flared against the opposite wall: the room's only illumination, wrong in ways that even Ash couldn't explain.

A rustle drew his attention. He glanced across the room at a gap in the brick: a ragged, lightless tear now filled with tenuous movement. Ama was finally coming out of her hole, blinking in the harsh light. Her once pale, exquisite features were swollen, hair the same nameless shade as the paint smothered across the window. Her elaborate kimono was no longer white; the bright red circles printed on the long sleeves had faded to a dirty orange. She sat on the second chair—almost falling—and gazed at him through bruised eyes.

"Another happy day in paradise, was it?"

Each day her appearance grew worse. Ash never spoke of it: he figured he was no better. Ama had smashed and discarded any mirrors long ago. He stripped off his remaining protective layers, just letting them fall to the floor. Eventually he reached his own stained and tattered robe. The pointed cross in a circle emblazoned across his breast was a washed out pale grey.

He was pretty sure the wings originally picked out in gold thread across his back were equally tarnished. He hadn't bothered to look for…however long it had been.

"Being too terrified to stick your head outside the front door is hardly a position from which to act all superior."

"Bastard…" Ama sounded tired. They didn't even argue anymore.

"So how was your day?" He always asked, even though he no longer cared, and the answer was invariably the same.

"What do you think?" She coughed: a deep rattle that came from somewhere impossibly deep within her thin chest. "You know who I was thinking about…?"

"Malina." He dropped into the chair facing her, resting against his stained overcoat. It wasn't a hard guess: she was always thinking of Malina. So was he, but he'd never admit it. "She knew the risks—especially for her. More than any of us."

Ama glowered at him. "Not you so much, though."

"Meaning what, exactly?"

Her bitter laugh choked off into another hacking cough. "Don't tell me you don't find it just like old times out there? The heat, the aridity. Must take you right back."

It was his turn to laugh. "I wasn't born in a desert. Not a true one, anyway. There were two huge rivers, plenty of irrigation…If it wasn't for me—"

"—their civilization would never have been born. You've told me several million times." She glanced at the splash of sunlight on the opposite wall, flinching away from the garish beam piercing the chinked paintwork. "And they're certainly grateful to you for it."

Ash wondered when she'd grown so cynical. Was it the fear? The uncertainty? After all, they were primarily creatures of routine, originally gifted with so much understanding. Now…"What happened to you, Ama?" he murmured. "You were once warm and soft, as I remember."

"Then there's something wrong with your memory." She glared at the paint smeared window.

Ash muttered and pushed himself out of the chair. He walked past Ama, deliberately avoiding looking at her. There was a clear plastic bottle standing against the rotted skirting, next to her hole in the wall. He picked it up and took a sip of the tepid water inside. It was metallic, hard to keep down. Even so he was thirsty and fought his every reflex. Once he was reasonably happy the water wasn't about to come flooding back, he turned around.

"You know why I go outside every day? You think it's because there's so much fun to be had? Or because of all the friends I've left out there?"

She continued to stare at the blanked window, her chin resting on an arm that looked as though it could barely support the weight.

"I have to, Ama! Because I can't stand being cooped up in here every day with you!" He took a step forward. Even though she wasn't looking his way, Ama flinched.

"It's summertime, Ama! We should be out there, in the sun. Even—" He pointed at the ray of sunlight lancing across the room. "Even *that* poisonous, deadly thing. It's still the sun. It's still—"

Ama swung around to face him, her eyes steely with unborn tears. "That has nothing to do with me! That's the bloated, pock-marked creation of some acne-scarred kid; a twisted, diseased newcomer! It's not mine! Never mine!"

She buried her face in her hands. For almost half a minute she hunched in the chair, shoulders heaving. When she finally raised her head, her blotched face was wet, her eyes red and raw.

"I helped grow rice and millet. I stirred up breezes fragrant with the scent of blossom and chrysanthemums. I was loved…" Her voice was wistful, tired.

"Who'd you have to kill to get that job?" muttered Ash. He tried to sound ironic, slightly mocking, but all he managed was tired and careless. He glanced at the splash of light on the wall: it had climbed a couple of feet, growing incrementally darker with each inch. Outside the sun was dipping towards the horizon; twilight was on its way. He could feel the lethargy; a unique fatigue spreading through him by degrees.

Ash retreated, pushing his back against the wall. He sank wearily to the floorboards, splaying his legs, bottle cradled between his hands. "Perhaps it's your nature," he said, talking to himself. Ama heard him anyway and frowned.

"What is?"

"You're not confrontational enough." He glanced at the dark hole in the wall. "When the going gets tough, you just go into hiding."

Ama's frown deepened into anger lines. "You're talking about Susano-o…!"

Ash juggled the bottle between his hands, tilting it back and forth. "Dumb old Sooz gets pissed, tramples those rice fields and tosses shit everywhere. Killed a few of your handmaidens, too, as I remember: the kinds that don't come back. And what did you do? Fight back? Get revenge? No—you hid in a cave…"

"I was furious!"

"Funny way of showing it: shutting yourself away in the Heavenly Cave and blocking it with a giant rock."

She looked wistful again. "The world fell into darkness and everything began to wither and die. Until Ame lured me out and Taji shut the rock behind me." Ama sniffed, rubbing at her eyes.

Ash's laugh was cruel. "So you're trying to bring back the darkness by hiding in a crack in the wall?" He raised the water bottle in mock salute. "A masterplan. My apologies."

Her once perfect lips twitched into a pale imitation of a smile; it looked painful. "I think it only works if I'm sealed up."

"And you can never find a boulder when you need one." He wondered what Ama would say if she knew that outside most of what remained was either rock or fused sand.

"We were young," she sighed. "Everything was young. Grand gestures seemed to be expected. It was all part of the…ritual. You know: sacrifice. Death, rebirth."

"I know. Osiris never stopped moaning about it."

Ama's pained smile broadened for an instant. "Osiris! Now *him* I haven't thought about in an eternity! Any idea where he is now? That—" she waved a hand at the patch of dimming light "—shouldn't affect him."

Ash stared at the floor, reluctant to speak. He should have told her long ago. Ama and Osiris had once been close; far too close for his sister's liking. But then, Isis was required to be jealous. "He never resurrected from his last annual murder. If I didn't know better, I'd say it was deliberate. Suicide—of a sort."

"Oh." She fell silent again. When she next spoke, her voice was small and lost. "I never believed he'd…I thought that it was just us that suffered. Ra, Apollo, Utu, Melina. Osiris is—was—what's the word? Seasonal?"

"We're all seasonal, Ama. That is rather the point, isn't it? And now there are no seasons. Not here; not in Melina's arctic home; nowhere. Something you'd appreciate if you stepped outside once in a while."

Ama came to her feet with a convulsive leap, toppling her chair. Her kimono sleeves brushed the boards, hissing softly. "I don't need to go out under that diseased light to know it's eternal summer. An endless, blistering deadly summer! Even as corrupted as it is, that sun lives in my veins as much as yours!" She pulled a sleeve back, revealing a bony arm. Spidery traceries, the same hue as the dark sunlight, twisted along the pale, translucent skin. "It calls out to me, every day, from rising to setting! I want to answer: to run outside and join it—"

He tried not to look at her scarred arms. "But to waste the light, Ama… To hide away in shadows until the dark."

"It burns me, Ash. Even in here I can feel its poison burning through me. If it can do that, what will happen if—if I actually bare myself to it?"

"I go out."

"Yes! Safe under all this!" She kicked at the ragged pile of discarded clothing.

Ash rubbed at his face. He wanted to sleep: his body was reacting to the sinking sun. "I don't know. Maybe you're right. Sometimes it feels like no matter where I am, it's a prison. When I'm in here I have to get out; once I'm outside, I can't wait to get back in again." He stifled a yawn, jaw cracking. "Maybe I should just stay indoors. Wait it out."

Ama stood for a moment longer, anger sustaining her. Then she half collapsed into the seat draped by Ash's overcoat. "What was it like out there today?"

"Hell. Or I should say, still hell." He came slowly to his feet and started to pace, unwilling to surrender to the fatigue dragging at him. He could tell her the truth: that he'd orbited the world over and over; each time fruitless. There was just baked rock and dust that was once fertile soil. Everyone, everything, was gone one way or the other. Ama wouldn't want to hear it. "It's all too bright. The air too dry. The sun gloats overhead, face all puffed and blotched with great black scars—"

"Aren't they supposed to be sunspots?"

"Spots!" Her words generated an absurd image in his mind. "You're right, Ama: they're spots, all right. Vast stellar zits. Acne scars. After billions of years, the sun's reached puberty! Funny, I feel too old to be a teenager." His thoughts turned bleak. "We're childhood fancies, Ama; the stuff kids dream up. We aren't manifestations of a poorly-understood natural phenomenon, we're imaginary friends. And we've been grown out of!" He looked around the room: it was growing darker; the ray of light coming through the chink in the paint had turned the color of blood.

Ama massaged her temples. She was obviously feeling it the same as him. "You really believe that?"

He shook his head, hoping some of the cobwebs would break. "No. No, not really. At least I don't think so. It's just my own form of terror."

"What?"

"The darkness. The coming of night. The time when we're nothing." He reached down for the overturned chair. Righting it, he sat down wearily, facing Ama. "That's why I don't understand."

She blinked at him, uncomprehending.

"How you can hide in here during the only time we exist. Your only few hours of life." He glanced at the glow of sunlight on the wall. It was almost gone, fading through a muddy red which matched the bare brick. The room was rapidly growing too dark for him to see. Ama's off-white kimono was all he could make out: glowing softly.

"The sun's almost set," he murmured. They'd fade away with the last rays. Much as the idea terrified him, he wondered if it wouldn't be best if they could stay that way. Erased; at peace. "We'll go through it all again tomorrow: me hiding outside; you hiding in here. A cycle we can't break until the sun stops crossing the sky."

"Or perhaps…"

"What?"

Her voice was little more than a whisper in the growing dark: hollow, lost. "Or perhaps tomorrow I'll come outside with you."

He wanted to believe her, believe one of them could break the loop. "Really?"

The last of the dying sun's rays guttered as it dipped below the horizon. Ash felt himself drift away with it. The room fell into blackness. Ama's voice was all that remained: a last desperate sigh.

"Perhaps—"

The Prague Relic
by
Paul StJohn Mackintosh

Lieutenant Jan Kupka sat with his legs dangling into nothingness, waiting to drop into the void. In the eerie hush after the Halifax's engines cut out, the only sound was the whistling slipstream along the bomber's alloy flanks. The Special Operations Executive dispatcher had his eyes glued to the jump light, waiting for it to turn green. Brezina and Czech the Jew were waiting their turn behind him. For that moment, he was alone with the sighing wind and the night.

The red light winked out and the green lamp lit. The dispatcher turned his head to Kupka and gave a thumbs up. Kupka tipped forward and dropped into emptiness, arms and legs close to his body as he had been taught, letting the slipstream take him. There was a sharp jerk at his back as the static line pulled open his chute. He looked up, feeling a flicker of fear for the first time in many minutes. The canopy had inflated. Above its white circle, spread above him like a guardian angel's wings, he saw the chutes of both his comrades opening, and briefly, the black cross of the bomber's fuselage silhouetted against the night clouds. Fear gave way to euphoria: he wasn't dead yet. Perhaps the ground wouldn't kill him either.

Looking down, he realized that the vista below, seemingly such a dark void when seen from the plane, was all white. Farmland somewhere east of Prague, sure enough, but with no landmarks visible. Snow covered the countryside, hiding every feature of the ground. Coming up now, fast.

He crunched into a thick snowbank beside a hedge, legs driven deep into the softer drift beneath the frozen crust. In the windless night, his chute settled over him, and he had to struggle free of its shrouding silk. Muffled thuds and grunts marked the descent of his comrades, and the two canisters of munitions behind them. Floundering out of the drift, he detached his harness and scanned the perimeter, one hand on his Colt. All clear. Overhead, the Stirling's engines coughed into life as it pulled out of its shallow dive and droned away into the moonless sky, but nothing moved along the dark fringe of hedgerows bordering the field.

Brezina scrunched over to him, his lumpy build muffled in the white flight suit. "Back on Czech soil again, eh?" he grinned, features just visible by the starlight reflecting off the snow. Kupka held up a finger to his mouth in reply, and clambered uphill to look over the highest hedgerow into the next field, but the windows in the few cottages huddled below were dark. A wood at the bottom corner of both adjoining fields sheltered some dark shadows, but nothing moved there either.

Czech joined them, chute gathered in his arms. "We'll have a few hours at most before the Germans start combing our flight path," he hissed. "Any idea where we are?"

Kupka shook his head. "I think that flak barrage on the way over blew us off course. This doesn't look like the planned drop zone."

Czech pointed downslope towards the wood. "We'll bury the chutes and the supplies there."

The two canisters of supplies tobogganed down the slope easily, and they wiped the snow clear afterwards with the chutes. Czech chose a spot just under the forest fringe, where snow had drifted under the trees.

"You don't want to bury the flight suits now?" Brezina asked, as they shovelled the snow aside with the short spades from their drop kit.

Czech shrugged. "White winter camouflage? Let's keep them for now, until we have a clearer idea of where we are."

They packed some spare magazines and rations into their packs, then dug shallow pits for the canisters and chutes in a small spinney, covering them with brushwood. After sketching a rough map of the site, as best as they could by snowlight and torchlight, they moved on downhill through the wood, hearing nothing beyond the crackle of branches and the soft thump of falling snow masses. Brezina cursed as the ground suddenly dropped away before him in the darkness, revealing a pale snow-filled pit.

"Quarry," Czech hissed as he caught up. They worked their way down the lip of the pit, arriving eventually at its rutted floor and a wire mesh fence with a gate opening towards a snow-covered road. Beside the gate stood a wooden hut, its small square windows dark.

Guns at the ready, they skirted the hut, converging on its doorway from both sides. Nothing moved. Kupka risked a flash of his torch at the door, revealing that the latch was only held by a nail. Silently he slid the rusty nail free.

Once inside, they kept lights to a minimum, feeling their way around the dark interior, evidently the shelter and records office for the gatekeeper. Out of the cold, they huddled together, and shared chocolate with brandy from Kupka's flask, rather than light the hut's small stove. Warm ashes in its belly showed that it must last have been used only a day or so ago.

"I think we're here," hissed Czech, after examining the notices and papers in the hut, spreading his map on the keeper's cracked desk, and tracing roads and contours by torchlight. "We came down far closer to Prague than planned. We're at or near Nehvizdy, near Čelákovice. That puts us barely

20 kilometers outside Prague, but it also means we're far from our planned rendezvous. We'll have to make our own way into the city."

"It doesn't sound good," Brezina grumbled. Czech shrugged again, but did not contradict him.

"Let's get some sleep while we can," he concluded, folding his map. "It's daylight in a few hours."

If only the enchanted night could last forever, Kupka reflected, with a bizarre recollection of childhood Christmas. He curled himself in his flight suit on one of the hut's moulting armchairs, and tried to sleep.

He was shaken awake by a firm hand on his padded shoulder. Grey predawn lightened the windows, and the hut's shabby interior, revealing Brezina's tense face, finger to his lips. "Someone at the gate," he mouthed slowly. Remembering small arms drill at the Arisaig House SOE training school back in Scotland, Kupka nodded and grasped his .38 Colt.

Together they took up positions facing the door, crouching behind the scanty furniture. Czech, immediately opposite the doorway, levelled his Sten at it, the long suppressor nosing like a blind snout. Kupka braced his tiny Colt on the back of a chair. Footsteps crisped over the snow outside, with hoarse breathing as they neared the door, then a short gasp and a muffled curse, plainly audible through the thin planking. He's spotted the missing nail, Kupka realized. There was a moment's pause, then the door creaked open. A stooped form stood in the doorway, hefting a pickaxe handle. The watchman, clad in a shapeless tweed coat and a flat cap, peered inside and saw the three white figures, and the three gun barrels trained on him. For a moment, they regarded each other.

"Partisans?" the old man asked finally, his breath puffing white in the cold air from the doorway. Czech nodded.

"Come out and sit down," the man went on, stepping into the room and leaning his pickaxe handle against the wall by the desk. "I've some schnapps in the cupboard over there. If you've not had it already, that is."

They straightened up and lowered their weapons. Kupka and Brezina pocketed their snub automatics; Czech dangled his Sten easily from one hand, though Kupka noticed he kept his fingers close to the trigger guard and the safety off. The old gatekeeper lit a paraffin lamp hanging from the roofbeams, then opened a small wall locker, took down a dusty bottle and a couple of cracked glasses, and put them down on the desk. "Karoly Polacek," he introduced himself, extending his hand. They shook it, giving their pre-agreed cover names. Within minutes, they were seated together round the desk, drinking the schnapps and trading information. Old Polacek seemed eager for almost any news of the outside world, and in return, gave up information on the current state of the Protectorate of Bohemia and Moravia, the people's mood, and how to get around while attracting minimal attention from the Nazis. It was unreal, Kupka thought, as he sipped his schnapps. Within moments of almost shooting the man, they were chattering away like old friends.

Polacek and Czech earnestly discussed options for getting into Prague. "You can take the bus then catch the tram," Polacek counselled. "The lines are overcrowded nowadays, too crowded for the Germans to check them often. Of course, you might get checked in the streets, but you'll have to chance that. Let's see your IDs."

Czech hesitated, then pulled out his own ID and slapped it on the desk, motioning the others to do the same. Polacek squinted at them.

"Look good enough to me," he confirmed. "First bus is at seven, ten minutes walk down the lane. Why don't you gents take off those things and put your feet up?"

Once again, Czech took the lead, and the others fell in. They pulled off their flight suits to reveal the London-issued civilian dress underneath. Then, while Kupka and Brezina drank more of the watchman's schnapps, Czech took a walk up to the woods to bury the flight suits along with the canisters, and retrieve a few essential items. He was the only one who knew the mission objective, to maintain operational security, and if he was killed or captured, their instructions were to link up with the Resistance and do their best to get back to England. Kupka regarded that part of the mission plan as caution gone mad, but Czech was the nominal commander, and he wasn't in a position to challenge it. Yet, anyway.

Polacek told them where to catch the bus. "If you need to tell any Germans or the militia what you're doing here, tell them you've been doing casual work here," he said. And he entered their cover names into the quarry's books, painstakingly taking down the details from their forged IDs.

Polacek shook hands with all of them and waved them off at the gate of the quarry. He might betray them the instant they were out of sight, Kupka knew. Any moment here, in the familiar country, could be their last. At least the weather was clearer now, as they made their way in their civilian overcoats down to the deserted bus stop in cold winter sunshine that glittered on the snow.

The bus ride to the head of the tram line was easy enough. Kupka felt that the bus driver might have stared at them suspiciously, but he knew that could just be his nervous imagination. The bus and the passengers at least were little changed from pre-war days, but the tram stop and the tram itself were both daubed with German signs and Nazi propaganda. The picture grew worse with every stop along the line: buildings on all sides sporting huge swastika banners; Germans and Czech militia gendarmes at almost every corner; tanks and armoured cars on the streets. Brezina grumbled when he heard the tram stops announced in German as well as Czech, and

Kupka nudged him to keep quiet. Instead, he glared at the red martial law posters everywhere with their parallel columns of German and Czech text, alongside propaganda ads for the National Confederation. "Why do they always have to have the German first?" he muttered.

The streets were no better when they finally got off the tram, although at least Kupka began to realise how well they blended into the crowds. Patrols might be everywhere, but their SOE handlers had apparently outfitted them well enough to pass casual inspection, and no one stopped them on their walk from the bus station to the Old Town. With the Sten guns hidden in their packs and the pistols in their coats, any close examination would be a death sentence.

In the shadow of the swastika banners and hectoring fascist drivel, they found their way to their JINDRA contact in the Old Town. Karel Moravec ran an antiquarian bookshop in Melantrichova, and lived above the premises. Kupka and Brezina sat in a cafe waiting while Czech went ahead and scouted the place: Nation's Defence safe houses had been compromised more than once before, and there was no sense in risking all three of them. The coffee was abysmal: everything in the cafe seemed dowdy, run-down, leached and grey.

"Look: he's come out." Brezina poked Kupka hard and they looked through the dirty pane across the street, where Czech had stepped out of the bookshop and stood by a lamppost, looking as inconspicuous as possible.

"One at a time, remember," Kupka whispered to Brezina, as he stood up and left the table. He crossed the street and walked into the bookshop without looking at Czech. The greying, birdlike bookseller glanced up at him, nodded, then went back to the stack of books behind his till. Kupka pretended to be browsing the shelves, scanning the leather spines of finely bound novels from the last century. He ignored the ring of the doorbell as someone else came in, then glanced sidelong to see Brezina also in the store. A few minutes after, the doorbell rang again and Czech came back into the shop. They pretended to browse the shelves until the bookseller closed the till with a sudden jingle, and then led the way through the door into the back of the store. One after another, they followed him. As they did so, a young dark-haired girl in a print dress slipped by them to take up Moravec's position behind the till: his daughter, Kupka guessed. Behind the storefront they found a typical bourgeois drawing room, with a homely middle-aged woman laying out coffee and cakes on the table.

"We'll put you in the attic," Moravec declared, sitting down and spreading his hands on the tablecloth. "There's plenty of room up there, and the entrance is well hidden. And Mr Kupka, I believe you're the one who will be out front in the shop? I've registered you on our books. A former librarian, I believe?"

"Proofreader at a printing works, actually," Kupka corrected him, recalling his prewar life in Brno before he had joined up and crossed with his unit into Poland and then to France, and finally England, to continue the fight against the Nazi occupiers.

"Oh, very good, well I'm sure you'll manage," Moravec chuckled.

"Good coffee," Brezina smacked his lips appreciatively, slurping from Mrs Moravec's china cup.

"I used to be in the Volunteer Sisters of the Czech Red Cross," she explained, smiling bashfully. "My old comrades still help me out with supplies and such."

"Now, I understand from the wireless messages that you will only need to stay here a few weeks at the outside," Moravec continued, with a more businesslike air. "Mr Kupka here is the only one we can afford to have out in public on a regular basis, I'm afraid. The rest of you will have to stay in the attic, and only go out as needed. Remember, the SS headquarters is just north of here by the Štefánikův Bridge. So please, no unnecessary noise or conspicuous behaviour."

Moravec led them into the stairwell at the rear of the sitting room, where a bookcase with a few plates and statuettes on its shelves stood at the foot of the stairs. He reached behind the cabinet, and pulled. The whole ensemble swung away from the wall on hinges, revealing another dark and narrow staircase.

"It was easy enough to cover up the original door," he explained. "Now, follow me up."

They scaled the steep, narrow staircase to find themselves in a dark, low space under the roof tiles, with a tiny makeshift window created by the removal of a single tile. Four bare plank beds stood under the sloping beams.

"Well, I'll leave you to settle in," Moravec beamed. "Come down and knock on the back of the cabinet when you're ready, and I'll show Mr Kupka what to do in the shop."

"Settle in," Brezina growled, once Moravec had disappeared down the stairs. "It feels more as though we're already in a prison camp."

"Quiet: as he says, it's only for a few weeks," Czech chided. "Now, unpack your gear. We'll go downstairs again in a few moments."

Moravec needed little time to instruct Kupka in operating the till and working the shop; in any case, Kupka was expected to spend most of his time rearranging the shelves and helping out the bookseller and his girl assistant. "Angelika's not my daughter," Moravec explained in a low voice, when Kupka asked about her. "She's actually Jewish. I falsified her papers to hide her here, for as long as…well, you know, when peace finally comes, or whatever." Angelika, out of earshot down the other end of the shop, brushed her fringe out of her eyes and gave them a shy half-smile. She kept her head down and barely spoke that evening when Mrs Moravec fed them at the common table, despite the gentle ribbing of Brezina and even Czech. For a while, though, the room had a little of the normal domestic warmth of peacetime. Afterwards, when they went upstairs to their prison-like attic, Kupka felt the nightmare unreality of their situation seep back into the building like the cold through the roof, as he tossed in his narrow bed, with the sighs and snorts of his comrades less than an arm's length away.

The state of emergency gave concrete form to that fear, more pervasive than the freezing fog and winter frost. Prague resembled a ghost town haunted by demons: the Nazi soldiers, in their metal helmets and heavy coats, the war machines that rumbled down the streets on iron treads, were less like the troops of a modern power than the denizens of a medieval Apocalypse. An Apocalypse of war and pestilence, Kupka reflected, but the overriding miasma of sickness and rot stemmed not from the vanquished citizens—it was a creeping infestation among the occupiers, a mental canker. Death in combat against them suddenly seemed more like a purification, something real against this frieze of puppets and ghosts.

In spite of the patrols and security checks, Czech made several more trips out to the quarry to retrieve more supplies from their cache. Once he was stopped on his return, but was let go after showing his papers, without being searched. "Just as well; they'd have found the demolition charges and detonators if they'd only looked inside my bag of potatoes," he chuckled, grinning fiercely.

He also made a few more reconnaissance trips around their supposed target, without however revealing what it was. On one trip, he took Brezina, who came back none the wiser. "All he did was look at the manhole covers and try out a key on one when no one was looking," Brezina explained to Kupka afterwards.

Inevitably, Kupka and Angelika spent more time together in the shop. Moravec watched them both paternally when he was behind the till. Few customers came in: Kupka had no idea whether this was a consequence of wartime, or whether Moravec always had done only a little trade. At least the gendarmes avoided the place as well.

"This is all very quiet and dull for you, I suppose," Angelika sighed, looking up at him one afternoon with her steady, birdlike eyes that might have had a touch of fever in them from poor diet or simply constant stress.

"Well honestly, it's good to have a little peace and quiet for a change," he declared, banging a stack of books down on the desk emphatically. Moravec had been vague about how much Angelika actually knew, and had advised them all to tell her nothing: perhaps she thought they were all

Jewish refugees like her.

"What did you do before the war?" she asked him, returning after every retreat to circle gently around him and tease at his reticence.

"I was a proofreader in a printing works, down in Brno," he admitted.

Angelika's eyes widened as though he had told her he'd been a millionaire financier. "I'd like to go to Brno," she sighed. "Did you go to university?"

"The Philosophy Faculty of Masaryk University," he admitted.

"I wanted to be a student," she sighed. "I loved poetry. But now they've closed the universities, so I just read what I can off the shelves."

The doorbell rang and a customer came in. Angelika attended to her, and afterwards seemed quieter and more thoughtful.

"I gave up hoping for anything now," she admitted finally. "It's easier just to live from day to day without expecting anything. I don't know what happened to my parents, or any of my relatives. I had to stop myself thinking of them. That gets you nowhere. All I can afford to see is what's right in front of me."

She moved closer to Kupka, and stood right in front of him, looking up at him with her dark-ringed eyes. She kept her hands down by her sides, and stood quite still, but she was close enough for him to feel her breasts press on his body with each intake of breath. He took her shoulders in his hands, bent down, and kissed her.

Moravec and his wife were both out on an errand that afternoon, and they hung the "Closed" sign on the door, locked up, and pulled down the shutter, then slipped upstairs to the Moravecs' apartment, which Kupka had not yet seen. Angelika had a tiny bedroom just off the staircase, with a few small ornaments and yellowed magazines. She pulled him down on the threadbare coverlet and started to run her small, slender hands over his chest.

"I know I'm being forward. But I want to have at least a little glamour and adventure in my life, like in the films, like Adina Mandlová or Anna Letenská. Is that so much to ask?" she sighed, looking up at him.

"You're beautiful enough. Look at your hair, your breasts, your thighs," he murmured to her, as he pushed her back on the bed and stroked them one after another. He realized he was unconsciously applying the observation and memorization techniques he had been taught during his SOE training: "Take the things that please you—your eyes, touch, smell and hearing. Try and express in words why they please you. Such effort will cause you to observe the object more closely."

He had no idea if she was a virgin or not: she was tight and narrow when he took her, but seemed so passionate and eager, with her skin flushed and her quiet moans, that he could hardly imagine this was her first time. They took just a few minutes longer to lie with each other afterwards before they dressed to go downstairs to resume the facade of bookselling, in the facade of a real city and a real life.

Czech came back from his latest reconnaissance later with a new air of excitement, and after the evening meal and the rest of the household had gone to bed, held a meeting of his own in the drawing room, with the doors closed and the curtains tightly drawn, lighting the table only with a torch.

"We move tomorrow night," he announced. "It's the dark of the moon, and the weather is cloudy. I've completed the reconnoiter and mapped out our infiltration and exfiltration routes."

"Moravec knows?" Kupka asked, with a sudden sinking of the heart.

"He knows, and his wife," Czech answered. Presumably that answer did not include Angelika.

"So, are you going to tell us what we're here for?" Brezina challenged him.

Czech spread his big hands across the table. "You know I'm not strictly here as a representative of the government-in-exile. I grew up in Bratislava, but with what was happening over the border in Germany and Austria, I could feel which way the wind was blowing. I moved to Palestine in 1938. We call that making aliyah. The Jewish Agency Defence Department sent me back to help the Allied cause, and especially to protect Jewish communities and goods. We planned this mission when we learned that the Reich Protectorate was closing synagogues in Prague. Our target is the the Old-New Synagogue, where we believe the original golem of Rabbi Low is still hidden."

"The golem?" Kupka coughed in incredulous disbelief. Like most metropolitan Czechs, he knew the legend well enough.

"Yes, yes, the golem, made by Rabbi Low from clay from the banks of the Vltava in the reign of Rudolf II, to protect the Prague Ghetto. We wouldn't plan a mission like this just on hearsay or for a legend. We have actual documentary evidence that the golem exists, as well as eye-witness accounts from the last century. We are going to infiltrate the Synagogue, confirm whether the golem is there or not, and if it is, retrieve it."

"You really think it's there?" Kupka challenged him.

Czech nodded emphatically. "The sources speak of the golem being in the genizah of the Old-New Synagogue. But then, where else would it be? The genizah stores any paper or other object that includes the holy name of God, prior to decent burial. And we know the golem was animated through a shem, one of the names of God. We should find it lying here, waiting."

Brezina shrugged. "And if we find it, we get what? A clay statue?"

"Whatever we find, it's vital to keep it out of Nazi hands." Czech ground a fist into his palm. "The golem is a symbol of Jewish self-defence and resistance. If the Nazis captured it, that would be an immense propaganda coup and morale boost for them. We have to keep that from happening at all costs."

"So we're not here for the Republic at all, but for some stupid Jewish legend?" Brezina fretted.

"Corporal," Czech snapped, and Kupka saw Brezina stiffen and snap to attention despite himself. "This mission has the full authorization and backing of the government-in-exile," Czech continued. "And we are soldiers in the field, in occupied territory, under orders. You will carry out your mission as instructed, and complete it. Is that clear?"

"Sir," Brezina responded, lowering his eyes to avoid Czech's glare. Kupka had no idea yet of how Czech would handle himself in a fight or when in danger, but right now he felt that the big Jew was quite capable of shooting Brezina out of hand for insubordination. Somehow, that was a comfort.

Czech laid out a sketch map of the area around the Old-New Synagogue, and explained the plan. Infiltrate by night through the sewers, to avoid German patrols as far as possible. Scale the iron ladder on the outside of the building, the only access to the attic, to reach it and the genizah. Search the attic, and if the golem was there, either retrieve or destroy it. Withdraw the same way, then return to England by one of a number of possible exfiltration routes.

Cowed as he was by Czech, Brezina couldn't suppress a snort when their commander came to the last part of the plan.

"What's so funny?" Czech snapped. "This isn't a suicide mission. Infiltrate, retrieve the target, or destroy it, and return to friendly or neutral territory. That's our mission. If we don't get out, we fail. I would have thought that would be a huge bonus for you. You get to live."

"So, let's go through our fallback options for getting out of here." Kupka answered. "Pickup by SOE flight from England or Malta, if we can find a remote enough road or disused airstrip down south, in Hungary or the Slovak Republic, where security is less tight. How realistic do you think this is?"

"Would you rather I just tell you we're going to our deaths?" Czech shrugged.

"I think we'd more or less accepted that," Kupka responded quietly. "Sir."

There was a moment's silence. Then Czech pulled another sketch out from under the street map. "Now, let's go over the sewer routes," he declared.

They were all too tense and expectant to sleep much afterwards, and downed shot after shot of schnapps as they sorted through the gear in their packs and checked their weapons. Kupka went to bed with his head ringing, and gave himself only the most cursory wash in the basin left by Mrs Moravec.

"You look awful," Angelika told him, when he took up his post in the shop the next morning, but she seemed to have no suspicion of any change in him. He ached to tell her that he was leaving, but without clear guidance from the Moravecs, he dared not let her know what was really going on. He tried to give her as many unobtrusive hugs and kisses as he could, until in the end she pushed him off. "Stop it," she chided. "The Moravecs will notice."

The day crawled by, as grey and cold as all the others. Mrs Moravec made a specially large stew that evening. Angelika went to bed early, complaining that the heavy food had made her sleepy. Kupka tried to catch her eye and got one last sulky, half-sleepy glance before she disappeared upstairs.

Once she had retired, Moravec and his wife pulled out sausages, rye bread and other supplies as they brought the packs and gear down from the attic. Czech made sure they stowed all the food in their packs, alongside the spare magazines, British grenades, demolition charges and timing pencils.

"If the golem is there and we can't remove it, we blow it up," he explained. "It's a clay figure after all: it can't be too portable. The Jewish Agency have authorized me to do that, and I even have a rabbinical dispensation for it."

He had taken the metal stock off his Sten gun to make it easier to hide, and helped Brezina and Kupka do the same with theirs. Moravec checked his wristwatch as the curfew began and the night deepened. Finally, with all the packs ready, the three men stood round the table. Moravec poured out another glass of schnapps for each.

"A toast, and here's to the Republic," he declared as they clinked glasses. Then he led them to the shop door and unlocked it, shaking their hands one by one as they filed out in darkness.

Czech led them just a few steps down the deserted street before he bent down over a manhole cover. The manhole key in his hand caught the light of a distant street lamp with a dull gleam, as he lifted the iron disc with its three-towered shield. The circular shaft within and its iron ladder were even harder to make out, and Kupka more or less felt his way down. Czech let them both go down first, bringing up the rear and closing the manhole behind him.

The sewers stank, but not as badly as Kupka had expected, or maybe he had just stopped noticing things like smells in the chaos and squalor of wartime. Czech shone his SOE issue torch down the shaft, and they emerged into a long brick-lined tunnel. Kupka saw by the torchlight some electric light fittings along the tunnel, but they were all dark. He pulled out his own torch, and followed Czech along the echoing passage. They reached a fork, took another direction, and eventually arrived at another iron ladder fixed into the wall.

"This is it," Czech announced. "We have to get up on the pavement, make our way to the rear of the Synagogue without being seen, then climb up the ladder to the attic. Remember, silent and unseen as far as possible. Now, let's go."

This time he led the way up the ladder, pushing the manhole cover slowly and cautiously off the rim of the shaft before emerging onto the pavement. He helped the others up, lifting out their packs. They had emerged on the north side of the Old-New Synagogue, behind the trees and hedgerows shielding the building. Out of sight, Czech crept to the edge of the area and stared out into the snow-covered street.

"All clear," he whispered. They all slipped down the rear of the Synagogue to the low-roofed lean-to against the back wall. Czech had already found a crate and placed it against the wall: with that and a hand on the lean-to's low tile roof, they were all able to shin up to the base of the ladder.

Wordlessly, Czech pointed upwards. Kupka looked up and down Pařížská, but no German patrols or passers-by were in sight. Czech reached up to the lowest rung and swung himself up, scaling the ladder as fast as he could, then stopped. There was a scarcely audible creaking as he pushed at the door to the attic. He disappeared into the low doorway, then a moment later, his head reemerged, silhouetted against the dark sky, and he waved for them to follow him.

Kupka felt horribly exposed as they climbed up the rungs, a fly on the wall. He shouldered his way through the narrow opening, then turned to haul on the rope tied to their packs. The gear slid through the doorway without snagging, and after it came Brezina, his grin white against his blackened cheeks. Once inside, he shut the low door, and they were sealed in the dark, musty space.

Czech turned on his torch, half shrouding the beam with his hand, and played it round the interior. Everywhere, piles of old books, uneven protrusions of masonry, crumbled brick and dust, in a long, heavily beamed space like a granary.

"From one attic to another, eh? And what are these?" asked Brezina, knocking at one mound of masonry and dust with his knuckle. "Burial mounds?"

"They're the upper side of the roof vaulting," Czech explained. "Look at those chains: they must be supporting the chandeliers." And he shone his torch beam on thick lengths of chain fixed to the heaviest roof beams, which disappeared through the floor, giving the place the macabre air of a dungeon.

"This is the genizah alright," Czech muttered, half to himself. "You boys make yourselves comfortable while I look around. But for Heaven's sake, keep it quiet."

Kupka and Brezina lay down on the mounds of masonry close to the attic entrance and leaned against them, trying to catch a little sleep, as Czech rummaged around the attic, with occasional low grunts of satisfaction. Kupka thought of offering to help, but he had no idea of what to look for or where.

Czech shook him awake an unknown length of time later. "I found it," he hissed, his eyes gleaming in the torchlight. "Come, take a look."

Kupka scrambled after him over the hummocks of masonry to a niche against the far wall, where a shrouded form lay under a filthy grey blanket between mouldering service books. Brezina, already awake, was crouched there, staring wide-eyed at the form under the blanket.

Czech twitched the cloth aside with a triumphant showman's gesture. Underneath, centred in the torch beam, Kupka saw a perfectly white face, standing out in stark contrast to the soiled and filthy attic interior, carved in inhuman perfection. The golem's features were as crisply delineated as if they had been traced by a cold chisel. But its flesh was the dull, flat, matte, lustreless, dead white of pipeclay. Its dry, dead texture recalled fresh bones, and worse, seemed to draw in and absorb the light, as the golem's whole body seemed to suck at everything around it.

Czech leaned closer, brushed the thing's forehead, and muttered a few words under his breath in a tongue Kupka could not follow, probably Hebrew. Its head twisted on its neck, and its eyes opened.

Kupka couldn't help jumping back, and he heard Brezina gasp behind him. The golem's eyes were the same featureless white as the rest of its face, the same colour and texture as the eyelids that slid back over them like the most exquisite, horrible miracle of stonecarving ever conceived. The thing sat up, then rose to its feet, taller even than Czech, its movements machinelike, except that Kupka had never seen a machine move with such grace. It was completely naked, and it had no genitals.

"This is what we came for?" Kupka couldn't help asking. Brezina was muttering prayers under his breath.

"This is the secret of Prague," Czech nodded.

"You didn't tell me we'd come here for that."

"Would you have believed me if I had told you?" Czech responded, with a sad, resigned air. "Besides, I didn't know it would work until I tried."

"How are we going to get it out?" Kupka asked stupidly. With that incredible abomination in front of him, his mind could only handle the most practical basics.

"He can move just like us," Czech explained. "He'll climb down the ladder and follow us into the sewers, wherever we go. As for covering him up, well…" And he held up his arm, with a greatcoat draped over it.

"That's all very well, but…" Brezina cut in, then suddenly broke off as Czech pressed a finger to his lips. They all crouched down behind the mound of masonry, as Czech doused his torch. The golem mimicked their movements automatically. Somehow, Kupka did not want to get anywhere near it.

At the far end of the attic, near the door, they heard scraping, banging noises, and voices speaking German. There was a grating noise as the door to the attic swung open. Kupka stared at Czech's dark form, knowing they were trapped in the attic with no other exit. He reached for the Colt in his coat pocket.

Czech reached out to both men and pressed them firmly against the floor, below the level of the masonry, and they huddled down, out of sight. Kupka could hear two, probably three Germans, stumbling and cursing as they picked their way over the uneven floor, playing torch beams around the dark interior. Then he heard a sharper exclamation. The Germans must have found their packs by the door, with his silenced Sten and the other gear.

Czech stood up and levelled his Sten. There was a low clattering noise, and shell cases spattered into the dirt beside Kupka's face. Czech crouched down again behind the cover, and Kupka pulled out his own pistol, shooting a glance towards the far end of the attic. One dark body lay straddled over the hummocks of brickwork, but at least one other German was cursing and yelling from cover. Then the golem surged to its feet, and charged towards the noise. Under the heavy-beamed roof, the German machine pistols made a dry clacking noise not much louder than the Sten, and bullets buried themselves overhead in the wood, but Kupka heard another sound, like hammer blows on cement. Then terrified screams, cut short in moments, and a wet tearing. The firing ceased.

Czech swore, and pulled them both to their feet, rushing to the low doorway. Kupka saw by the light of a dropped torch one German body, obviously shot by Czech, and two other bloody dismembered corpses, looking as though a grenade had exploded between them. The golem stood over them, daubed in the same mess, its hands covered in blood and entrails. The stink of warm blood, offal and cordite in the confined space made Kupka want to vomit.

The door to the Synagogue attic still hung open. Kupka heard shouts of alarm in German from outside and saw torch beams playing. Czech growled, reached into his pack, pulled out a grenade, primed it, and threw it out of the attic. A second later, an explosion resounded from the street below, followed by more shouts.

"What can we do now?" Brezina cried, panic obvious in his voice. "We're trapped."

"We'll get down the same way we came," Czech insisted. "Once we're in the sewers, we're safe."

"But how can we get down the ladder?" Brezina protested.

Czech grinned, his teeth gleaming white. "We've got the perfect weapon to clear our way for us."

He turned, and thumped the golem on the shoulder. The bloodied thing leapt straight out through the attic doorway. Kupka heard more screams outside, a massive thud, shots, still more screams. Then a moment's silence. They grabbed their packs, and rushed to the doorway. Kupka had just enough time to take in one German, still hanging on the ladder outside, staring transfixed in terror at the slaughter below, before Czech shot him and knocked him off the rungs.

Czech leading, they scrambled down the ladder and dropped onto the flags. The golem stood waiting, covered in even more blood, surrounded by German corpses, torn literally limb from limb. No one else moved along the street, troops or civilians, but faroff shouts and the sudden note of a warning siren showed that the hiatus would only last a few moments longer. Czech snapped a command, and the golem followed them as they swarmed back into the sewer entrance, pulling the manhole cover shut behind them.

They ran on down the low arched sewer tunnel until they were out of breath. The only noises that echoed along the cavernous brickwork were their own gasps and the trickle of sewer water.

"What's the plan now?" Brezina asked, wiping his face with both hands.

"The Nazis knew where we were going," Czech sighed. "Moravec must have been discovered, and given us up. Either that or we were just unlucky. In any case, going back into the Old City is just too risky. So we make our own way out and head for open country."

He hunkered down and pulled off his scarf, dunked it in the sewer water, then started to clean the golem, wiping the gore off its white torso. Kupka noticed that its skin, or surface layer, whatever it was, was completely unblemished under the blood and filth. Bullets, grenade blasts: nothing had left a mark. At least the dirty sewer water daubed some muck over it, and left its whiteness less glaring. Czech then pulled jersey, trousers, cap and coat out of his pack, and dressed the golem, which clumsily held up or lifted its limbs one by one in obedience to his commands. Once clothed, the golem was at least less monstrously conspicuous, but to Kupka, no less grotesque.

Czech led them deeper into the sewer network, and finally down a low oval brick tunnel which emerged in a sewer outfall under the quays of the Vltava. Barges and riverboats towered above them on all sides. A few lights burned here and there on the boats and the wharves, but left them in darkness. Czech groped his way to a rope ladder dangling down the hull of one barge, and swarmed up it. The others followed, with the golem in the rear. The ladder creaked dangerously under its weight, but held. Once over the low gunwale of the barge, Czech hauled up the ladder and unfastened the tarpaulin over the boat's cargo bay. They crawled in under the tarpaulin and bedded down on hard mounds of coal.

"Had it all planned out, did you?" Brezina hissed to Czech, once the tarpaulin was secured back in place over their heads. "What would we have done if you'd bought it back in the Synagogue, eh?"

"Shut up: you're alive, aren't you?" Czech snapped back at him. "This is my fallback plan. If the Germans hadn't found us, we would already be back with Moravec. If he hasn't been arrested already. Now, we'll ride this boat out of the city, then strike southwest through the Bohemian-Moravian Highlands along the Svratka towards Brno. After that, we'll aim for a rendezvous somewhere in the valley of the Morava north of Bratislava."

"And how are we supposed to call in the RAF?" Brezina objected.

"We'll pick up contact with the Nation's Defence down there. Or commandeer a German transmitter if we have to. Let's concentrate on getting out of here alive first."

Czech had evidently laid his plans very well. The barge cast off soon after dawn, as they were catching a little broken sleep on their hard beds of coal. They shared round bread and sausage from their packs as the boat chugged downstream. Once or twice, they heard the steps of crewmen thump along the decking beside them, but no one lifted the tarp or disturbed them. The golem squatted in the dark the whole time, its white eyeballs gazing at nothing.

The barge pulled into the bank and moored at evening. Czech insisted that they leave the boat as soon as the engine had stopped and the crew settled down. "It's a great way to travel, but it's going in the wrong direction," he whispered. "Besides, the longer we stay on board, the more chance for the crew to discover us." He led them over the side and down the dark river bank, where they found they were near Roztoky. Even in the dark, he insisted on leading them east, away from the river, through the woods and whatever other cover they could find, despite the cold. "We have to travel out of sight as far as we can now," he explained. "We can't pretend to be just migrant workers any more. Especially with him in tow." And he knocked on the golem's solid side.

By dawn, they were close to the course of the Elbe and had skirted the suburbs of Prague to the south. Czech called a halt for a few hours in a wood between several broad fields. Kupka was already worried about frostbite in his feet, and ready to start moving again even without sleep so the march could keep his blood flowing. He was horribly fascinated by the movements of the golem: its body remained stiff and hard, yet somehow its joints and tendons moved, as though every particle of its substance was flowing against each other.

"Do you think they're looking for us?" Brezina asked through chattering teeth.

Czech shrugged. "We killed an entire German patrol. And they probably knew where we were going, which means they probably have our entire network, at least in Prague. I'm sure they're combing the entire country. And if you have any doubt, look at that."

He pointed out from under the cover of the trees towards a distance black dot that was moving slowly against the grey sky to the south, with a faint buzzing engine note. "German spotter plane," he remarked calmly.

"Could just be a coincidence," Brezina objected, without conviction.

Czech looked at him pityingly. "Try and get some rest while you can," he urged.

Hours later, with the spotter plane long flown out of earshot and the light starting to fade from the winter sky, they set out again. During the night, Czech found them an empty shed by a forest path to rest up in, and lit a fire. He also found a set of old sheepskin shepherd's coats hanging on hooks by the door.

"These are the right colour for the snow," he declared, beating the straw and caked dirt off the matted sheepskins. "Instant camouflage, eh?"

He pulled the golem's coat off, and dressed it in the new gear. The golem's superb musculature reminded Kupka of a photo of Michelangelo's David he had once seen in an art book before the War. He remarked on the resemblance to Czech, who chuckled. "That's what he is: a David to smite the Philistine." Kupka couldn't think of the golem as a he, though. It had no penis, no balls, and its groin was a flat triangle more blank and featureless than any woman's cleft.

"Get some rest," Czech urged him. "The golem can keep watch."

"That thing?" Kupka replied, aghast.

"His eyes and ears are better than yours and mine. And trust me: he's slept enough—four hundred years. He doesn't need any more."

Setting the example, Czech shoved off his pack, yawned, and lay down on the straw. Kupka tried to follow suit, but he stayed painfully alert all the way through the night, fearful that the golem, standing motionless as a mannequin with its great empty eyes open, would come to life and crush him. He thought of Angelika, and her slim, hungry body: if the Moravecs had been arrested, she would now be in a concentration camp, or already dead. Finally exhaustion overcame him, and he slept fitfully for a few hours.

Next morning, when they moved out in their new white winter gear, the whole forest seemed empty, with nothing moving in the cold empty spaces between the trees under the leaf cover besides themselves. They marched more quickly over the bare forest floor, though Czech halted often to check his compass and keep them on track. He was leading them southeast into the Iron Mountains, where cover would be thicker and locals fewer. Kupka felt more and more as though they had degenerated, step by step, from soldiers to gangsters to murderers, and now, tramps.

Brezina did not seem happy with the whole plan. While Czech was forging ahead with the tireless golem, he hung back to talk to Kupka out of earshot.

"We're three walking dead men, escorting a fourth who never was alive," he complained. "What are we doing this for?"

"It's the mission," Kupka chided him. "Those are the orders."

Brezina shivered, and stared ahead. "We should just ditch the thing and find some better way to help the Motherland. He's a monstrosity. He should never have been created."

Kupka sighed. "I know he did horrible things to those Germans back in Prague, but that's no worse than what a shell or bomb would do to any soldier. You know that."

Brezina shook his head. "No, that's not what I meant. I don't mind seeing Germans suffer and die, after all they did. They deserve it. No, he's worse. He has no soul. It's a blasphemy. Look at him, there in the snow: white on white. He's like a hole in the world. He's hollow, empty. You can feel it. And it sucks at you, like his hollowness was trying to drain away everything around it."

Kupka shuddered in his turn. "Look, no matter what you think, we have our orders. And we have to get him back to the Allies. What if the Germans got hold of him and found out how to make more?"

Brezina gave a resigned shrug. "He was made by Jewish magic, you know that. I doubt the Nazis would make another. I don't know why Czech and the government-in-exile want him, but one of him is bad enough."

"If you have to think about anything, think about how to get us back safely," Kupka snapped at him, and trudged on behind Czech and the monster in silence. Brezina was starting to get on his nerves almost as much as the golem. Ahead lay Slovakia, and the fascist Slovak Republic: Brezina could always slip over the border and seek refuge there, even defect. Kupka had never doubted his loyalty before, but the insidious influence of the golem was pushing them all to the limit.

Late in the afternoon, they crossed a single railway line, snaking through the forest. As they stepped over the gravel, Kupka looked up and saw, hundreds of metres off, two dark figures in greatcoats running away down the track.

"What was that?" he rasped to Czech. "Germans?"

"No, probably our national soldiers," Czech sighed. "Those helmets didn't look German. They must have been guarding the track."

"What should we do, go after them?" Brezina asked, gazing wild-eyed down the culvert where the figures had disappeared.

"And kill two Czechs? Besides, they're already too far off. We'd do better to get away from here as far and as fast as we can."

He led them stolidly on through the forest, sticking to the original line of march. They passed another anxious night in a gamekeeper's hut in the forest, filled with fodder to help the game through the winter. Kupka was sure he could hear the noise of distant engines on the wind, from beyond the forest.

Early next day, they reached the southern limits of the deep forest and struck a river valley leading into the Moravian Karst. The narrow valley threaded its way through steep limestone crags, almost sheer on both sides, with just the level strip of snowy ground beside the river gorge. Czech tried to keep heading southeast, but they had no choice but to follow the course of the river. There was no doubt now about the intermittent engine noises behind them.

Around noon, they reached a sharp bend in the river, which disappeared between the walls of an even more forbidding gorge. Before it, though, was a wider expanse of valley floor, with low masonry walls and iron gates defending a two-storey building of the last century, enclosed by more wooded crags, shuttered and silent. Czech wiped the snow off a sign on one gate pillar to reveal the legend "Moravský Conservatoire."

"I guess there's not much demand for musicians now," Kupka chuckled bleakly.

Czech shrugged and led them in between the iron gates. A stretch of snow-covered ground led up to the house in stepped terraces, each one fringed by a low plastered balustrade, with here and there, a classical urn or a small statue. Czech squatted down in the snow and motioned them to huddle around him. The golem stood aside, aloof and indifferent.

"The Germans can't be more than a few hours behind us," Czech explained. "They have us bottled up. If we go any further this way, they can funnel us up the gorge and pick us off as we try to scale the walls. I say we halt and make a stand here. If we stage an ambush, we might be able to buy enough time to at least get out of the trap. And if we can't, well, we can take a few Nazis with us."

"And the thing?" Brezina asked, jerking his thumb at the impassive golem.

"He could be our ace in the hole. You saw what he did in Prague. And I can see how to use him to spring a trap on the Germans."

Czech stood up and took the hat and pack off the golem, then its coat. In moments, he had the thing naked in the snow. He whispered to it, and the golem stepped up onto an empty plinth and stood there motionless. Czech picked up some snow and piled it on the golem's head and limbs.

"There: a new statue," he declared, stepping back and wiping his hands. The golem did look just like another piece of decorative classical work in the conservatoire's grounds. "The Germans won't see that coming," Czech chuckled. Then he took his pack and started laying out spare magazines, grenades, and demolition charges behind the balusters of the terrace parapet. "Well?" he urged, pausing to look up at Kupka and Brezina. "You going to get ready or not?"

Within a few moments, they were set up as well as they could be for the ambush, camouflaged by their sheepskin coats. Further down the valley, they heard the faint noise of engines, drawing closer along the narrow road. The golem stood unmoving on its plinth, frozen as white and cold as any effigy of snow and ice. They crouched behind the balustrade, listening to the rumble of tracks drawing closer.

A German unit, apparently platoon strength, with an armoured half-track bringing up its rear, came into view between the trees, advancing slowly up the valley towards the conservatoire. "At least they're not in winter camouflage," Czech chuckled quietly, as he peered over the top step at the oncoming troops in their heavy field-grey greatcoats. Kupka winced: the Germans might be sitting ducks, but the infantry alone already outnumbered them at least six to one.

The Germans shuffled steadily onward through the snow, through the gaps in the house's ludicrously low garden walls. Czech held his fire and signalled the others to do the same, until the Germans were well within the Stens' effective range. Then, Czech opened up with his first burst, taking out three Germans in the rear. As the others halted and looked around to see where the silenced rounds had come from, Kupka and Brezina joined in. Almost a third of the Germans were down, dead or injured, before the rest of the squad reacted and threw themselves prone in the snow.

Then the golem stepped down from its plinth, shaking the light covering of snow off its body, and strode through the snow towards the soldiers. The Germans started firing at the unearthly white figure charging them, but their rounds smacked into it without even interrupting its stride. Reaching the first German, it planted its foot on his back and stamped straight through his spine, grinding him into the earth in a red ruin. The next soldier rose to a half crouch and sprayed machine pistol fire straight into its chest, without effect, until its fist crumpled his helmet and the skull inside. After that, the other Germans broke and ran, heedless of the bullets that cut them down in their flight. Only slightly slower than their panicky run, and strong enough to forge through the thick snow, the golem caught a few more before they could escape out of reach.

A shell burst on the terrace, spraying fragments of stone, plaster and shrapnel. The German half-track mounted a field gun, and was firing, either to stop the gunfire or, more likely, to try to hit the golem. Shaking his head to clear the concussion from his ears, Kupka blinked and looked around him. Czech was lifting his head, dazed; Brezina was still prone in the snow. Kupka crawled over to him, noticing a red stain on the whiteness under him.

"Fucker got me," Brezina gasped, as Kupka turned him over to see the shrapnel wound in his side, then he went limp, and died, there in the snow. Kupka grimaced and closed Brezina's eyes for him, then looked down the valley. The surviving Germans had retreated into or behind the half-track, which confronted the golem alone, its engine running. The golem stood motionless, as another shell flew past it and exploded in the earth beside it, rocking it on its feet.

"There's only one way to finish this," Czech snarled, slinging his Sten and fumbling in his pack, fusing the demolition charges. "Get out if you can." And with a last wolfish grin at Kupka, he stood up and started running towards the golem, holding his pack. Small arms fire caught him in the chest before he got halfway, but he struggled on through the snow, grabbed the golem and slung his pack on it before slumping at its feet. Stirred into life once more, the golem ran straight at the half-track, climbed onto its bonnet and over the driver's vision slits, then into the crew compartment. The half-track exploded. Detonation charges and artillery shells erupted together in a huge orange fireball that blew its metal shell open like a tin can.

Kupka carried that last fiery image in his memory until he died, a few days later, in his last stand in an isolated barn against a German patrol: the golem rushing the German half-track, climbing aboard it; the explosion, blowing the half-track into pieces, and the golem back to its clay. A funeral pyre for what had never been alive. At least, he thought, as the final German bullets tore into him, his was a real death.

The Circle
by Matt Sullivan

Nylas stroked the feathers of his two remaining arrows and released a heavy sigh. Two arrows could kill two men, sure enough, but it was three haunting his steps. Like baying hounds, they whooped and howled while he cowered in the shadows, bow gripped in shaking fist, guts turned liquid from fear. These weren't merely hired thugs. These were seasoned killers, each of them given grim titles for grim deeds. Two arrows would not be enough.

Thrashed by needles and stones, his bootless foot was numb save for a dull throbbing. He failed to pull on his second boot before fleeing the campsite and would gladly trade both arrows to have it back. They were a simple luxury, boots—one too often taken for granted. Funny how impending death made a man appreciate the simple things.

Reaching the top of a bluff, he scanned the forest below. The hunters were nowhere in sight, but he knew his panicked flight would give them signs. They would soon catch up. *And then?* His fingers found nothing as he reached to his knife sheath. He left that by the fire, too—right next to his boot.

Fuck.

Defecting seemed a good idea on the eve of an unwinnable battle. But if he'd known the commander would send these persistent dogs, he may have chosen to die with the others. Nylas' life could be measured in bad decisions. And now here he was again, outnumbered, unarmed, and losing light.

As the sun sank, he caught his breath within the long shadows stretching from the west. In the hills beyond the trees, black mounds rose up from the earth like broken teeth. There was something unnatural about the silhouette. *Too many perfect angles.* Might be the ruins of an old garrison, he thought, or perhaps, remnants from the Age of Gods. Maybe there he could find a hiding spot or at least higher ground from which to give these bastards a proper fight. He hobbled off into the woods, wincing every time his naked foot met a sharp stone or branch.

Darkness thickened beneath the canopy. The taunts of his pursuers had fallen silent, their brutish voices replaced by a steady hum of crickets. With each crunching step, he cared less for stealth and more for the promise of shelter, dubious though it may be. As he drew close to the structure, certain features made clear it was an Ancient's site.

The greenish color was the first clue. No such stone existed anywhere near these lands. Perhaps nowhere else on this world. Its smooth texture and rounded contours reminded him of the shaping powers of the sea. Being a thousand miles from the closest ocean only enhanced its alien qualities. And then there were the glyphs and signs etched deep into its surface, perfect in every contour, uniform in their precise size and shape. Ancient man could not have achieved such exactness, such finesse. Only the gods were capable of such work. Ruins like these could be found all over this primordial forest, as far west as the Old Road, and as far east as the Saradune River. Those with even a small measure of good sense shunned them entirely. Only those with the most avid curiosity dared trespass. *Only fools.* Or those like Nylas who had no fucking choice.

As he approached the foreboding structure, he caught a whiff of burning wood. He froze. Peering ahead, he spotted a fiery glow emanating from somewhere within the wall of ancient stone. A campfire? "But what kind of fool wo—"

His whispered words broke off as a plan took form. He pitied anyone sitting by that fire, but what choice did he have? This was a measure of good fortune he could not pass up. For this distraction some poor souls may pay with their lives, but if it wasn't his own, a boot and blade might be the worst he'd lose that night.

A branch snapped, and he whipped around in time to eat a fist. The blow struck him square in the mouth, knocking him sideways, near pitching him to the dirt. He looked up through watery eyes to see another fist coming down, this one gripping a nasty blade. Nylas knocked the arm aside, lunged forward, gnashing his teeth like a wolf. In the split second it took to reach him, Nylas recognized the man as Gregun, Gregun the Beaut—an ironic moniker, for the man was ugly as sin. Gregun's beard protected him for a moment, but soon Nylas' aching jaws found the warm flesh beneath. Gregun's body convulsed as Nylas bit down, but so too did the man's blade. Searing pain coursed through his thigh as the knife plunged deep into muscle and flesh.

No choice now. Eat the pain, and chew like a fucking dog.

With all the blood and spit things got slippery. His teeth kept losing their grip, but always he found more flesh to chomp. Ignoring the scorching waves shooting through his leg, he wrapped all four limbs around his attacker's brawny frame and hung on like a tick. And all the same, he was out for blood.

Keep chewing.

The coppery taste filled his throat, almost gagging him, but he drank it down and kept gnawing Gregun's neck. The bastard must have lost his grip on the blade, for no further blows landed. But that didn't stop his nails from thrashing Nylas' scalp and ears, as he tried desperately to peel him off. After another mouthful of flesh and gulp of blood he felt the man's frame soften.

As they crumpled to the earth, he wondered how loud they'd been. Had the others heard? He pushed himself away from the corpse and blew red mist through his teeth. Scanning the trees with blurry eyes, he saw no signs of movement. Then, a distant voice bellowed from the dark, and he near shit his breeks.

"Gregun? Where ya got to, mate?" Said the gruff voice, maybe a hundred paces distant.

They hadn't heard.

Nylas got off his arse and almost tumbled back down as his leg gave out. Leaning against a tree he looked down at the leaking wound, all dark and bloody and riddled with pine needles. That knife would have to come out, but not just yet. Not until he was away from the corpse. He took a first agonizing step toward the campfire glow and spotted his bow lying a few feet away. His heart sank when he noticed the string had snapped during the fight. With no need to retrieve the bow and no hope to hide the body, he hobbled toward the light.

At first he approached with caution, trying to avoid crushing any leaves or twigs, but then he remembered stealth wasn't necessary for his plan. If someone was there, they would serve as a distraction and perhaps buy him some time to slip away.

Two massive pillars of green stone, marked top to bottom in glyphs, formed an entrance through the stone circle. Within, he saw firelight spreading across a large courtyard. Though the rest of the surroundings were moss-covered and weathered, the reddish tiles of the court seemed relatively unscathed by storm and sun. Nylas hadn't the time to ponder such things, for at the center sat a hooded figure, poking the fire with a stick. *Or is it a broken spear?* Across from the figure, was a large log that probably served as another's seat.

So, this hooded one may not be alone.

Confident he hadn't been spotted, Nylas stepped through the doorway, hobbled ten paces to his left, and scaled a rocky ledge steeped in shadow. It was no easy task to avoid driving the knife deeper into his leg, or to cry out from the searing pain, but at this point Nylas considered himself a master stoic. It probably helped that his life depended on it. The shouts of his pursuers grew louder, but strangely, the hooded figure paid no apparent heed to their shouts.

"Gregun! This your blood? Or have ya stuck the rat?"

Clearly, they hadn't found the body. That should have come as good news, but it didn't matter now, for the voices couldn't be more than twenty paces away. That terrified Nylas, but the hooded one seemed not to notice or care.

"Wait!" another voice warned. "You know what this is? I ain't going up there. Fuck that."

"This site ain't nothing special. Besides, we need to get paid. The war's windin' down."

"Fuck. That," he repeated and paused. "I can't be sure. I ain't goin'!"

From where he hid, Nylas couldn't see more than their silhouettes. But he'd seen one of them before—the one with the ugly scar that stretched from cheek to cheek, splitting each corner of his mouth into a permanent grin. 'Smiles', he was called. A nickname needn't be too creative, he supposed. He didn't recognize the other's voice, but he was a tall, wide-shouldered bastard. It was the tall one that protested.

"Don't be dim, Smiles. First we gonna search elsewhere. Nothin' turns up, then you can go stompin' 'round these ruins, losin' your mortal soul an' all that."

" I suppose you're right." Smiles paused a moment and hollered, "Gregun! Where ya at, mate?!"

Both of them turned back the way they came, and only then did Nylas put it together that neither of them noticed the hooded figure nor the fire.

Nylas let out a breath he'd held for what seemed a life time, and as he did—

"Come. Sit," the hooded one said.

For the second time that night Nylas almost shit himself.

"Come. Let's take care of that wound, yes?" the hooded one waved him toward the fire. It was a man's voice, deep but clear.

Nylas said nothing and listened for whether the brutes took notice. A faint breeze was all he heard. The scent of campfire promised a small comfort, and the knife sticking from his leg and the blood pooling beneath told him his options were limited. Go sit by this stranger's fire in the midst of these forsaken ruins, or bleed out on this rock?

Life is full of such wonderful choices.

Nylas decided it best to remove the knife before climbing back down. He balled up a thick wad of sleeve, bit down hard as he could, and pulled free the blade. He managed to stifle a scream, but the pain overwhelmed him and the world faded.

In that darkness, he forgot where he was. Who he was. Even forgot the pain. A wave of nausea swept up to his throat, but a deep breath and the smell of campfire pulled him back. He blinked heavy tears from his eyes and ran a hand over his sweaty, blood-caked face. Once again lucid, he recalled his shit-laden circumstances and looked for the knife. It was nowhere in sight. Perhaps it fell when he blacked out. After patting the stone beneath him, he spent no further time looking for it.

Slipping down the ledge onto his good leg spared him much of the pain on impact. He hobbled through the entrance and into the light—his trail of blood blending with the red tones of the tiles.

The hooded man reached to the bottom of his cloak and ripped off a long wisp of fabric. Judging by the look of the frayed garment, it wasn't the first piece he'd torn from it. "Here, you know what to do. Tie it off while I heat the metal." The hooded man stuck the shaft he was holding into the fire. Nylas could now see it was indeed a broken spear. He grabbed the tatter from the man's outstretched hand and proceeded to wrap his leg. Pulling it tight, the nausea returned and he near puked, but by now he'd become an adept eater of pain. Barely a whimper escaped his lips.

"So what the fuck are you doing here, hooded one?" Nylas asked through gritted teeth.

"It's Mallin."

"Mallin, eh? Name's Nylas."

Mallin nodded and Nylas could now see an unkempt beard, sharp nose, and bright blue eyes beneath the hood. He was thin of frame and hunched. His long neck and gnarled hands gave him a bird-like quality.

"Those men, you didn't see them? They sure didn't see you." Nylas continued.

"No. I've never seen them."

"Never?" Nylas considered the word choice. "Ain't that a bit strange?"

"Hmph, everything is strange in this place." Mallin grinned.

"Aye, I wouldn't enter such a place unless I had no other choice. So again I'll ask, what brings you here?"

"Are you familiar with the myths of the Pyun Tan, Nylas?"

"Somewhat. I seem to recall learning about them a long time ago at a campfire much like this. Probably one of the many stories my father liked to tell. What of them?"

"Well, I believe their legends aren't far from the truth. I believe they knew much more of the Ancients, the Architects, the Gods—whatever you wish to call them—than the conquerors of this land give them credit." Mallin removed the spear from the fire, examined the reddening steel and placed it back in the flames. "I'm a seeker, Nylas. Some would call me *meddler. Sorcerer.* But they know little of such things. I came here at the request of one called Maxus. You've heard the name?"

Nylas had heard tales of the man. Dark tales. He simply nodded in reply

"I came here because Maxus said this site is special, that it would confirm certain suspicions found in the myths of the Pyun Tan tribes, as well as those of theologians and the greatest scientific minds of Pathra and Selsun. You see where this is going?"

Nylas had no idea. His mind was on the glowing spear tip that would soon be searing his flesh. But he nodded all the same.

"Maxus believes that the secret origins of life on this planet may be confirmed at this very site. And, as you and I have proven, he may be right."

"Huh?" Nylas managed.

"Nevermind. Here. It is time." Mallin retrieved the spear and held it up to reveal its hellish radiance.

Nylas' blood ran cold. Somehow he could imagine the precise degree of pain it would bring, as if he'd felt it before. He reached down to unwrap the fabric, but was surprised at the lack of blood. Looking below, he saw a brown stain on the red tiles, but no fresh drops. He looked to Mallin who wore a bored smile as he placed the spear back into the fire. Confused and impatient, Nylas pulled free the tourniquet. His mind went blank as he stared down at a scar. The pink tissue was smooth, as if from a burn, and shaped into a narrow triangle.

Like a spear tip.

"You with me now?" Mallin asked.

"What the fuck?" Dizziness assailed him.

"It's okay. Be calm. My memory was inconsistent at first. You'll eventually adjust…and accept."

Nylas again felt like he was going to be sick. No words would come.

"It was only an hour ago. You scooped up two arrows and tore off up the wall and must have fallen asleep. It wasn't the first time either. You did the same when you first arrived here. Eventually, you came down from the perch all bloody and hobbling." Mallin's words trailed off. Nylas' astonished expression must have given him pause. But he soon continued, "I remember my first few months in this purgatory. That's when I still counted the days." Mallin swept his hand toward the tiles below. Nylas squinted and peered beyond the firelight where he saw tiny nicks carved into the stone, hundreds of them. "Look," Mallin pointed a finger at Nylas' feet, "there are yours." On the tiles surrounding him were dozens of marks, cut into the red tiles.

Nylas felt a phantom ache on the tips of his fingers. Faint memories began to play in his mind.

"It would seem you don't remember, so I'll tell you again. It's not as if we're pressed for time." A sad smile grew on Mallin's lips. "These sites are shunned for good reason. From what I've learned, they are no natural phenomenon. The Ancients dabbled in technologies that do not conform to our own understanding of the world. The Pyun Tan had much wrong in their reckonings, but they were right about one thing: there are more versions of reality than our own. Their belief that ghosts are but souls caught between one realm and the next, are not without merit. But what they imagined as the gods…Ha! No. No, the Ancients were not gods. They were no more divine than us. Their *magic* was developed through study, and these abandoned sites were used for their experiments. This one was a failure. It is tainted. I haven't been able to decode the markings hewn into that entrance, but I'm sure they are a warning. And I'm also sure that Maxus—that bastard—knew exactly what they were."

As comprehension and broken memories dripped into Nylas' thoughts, the sound of nearby voices pulled him back to reality. The hunters returned.

"The bastard killed Gregun! He was a right prick, but he was our mate." Smiles was louder this time, frustrated.

"Ah, you've got your back up. They return, I take it?" Mallin asked.

Nylas thrust a finger to his lips, signaling for Mallin to be silent, but the older man ignored him. "They can't hear me. They are *your* reality, not mine. They can't even see the fire."

As Mallin spoke, the two brutes approached the entrance. This time, Nylas could see them clearly, and he recoiled. They wore piecemeal armor typical of such mercenaries, and walked and talked as men, but the bodies beneath were monstrous. As if they had been dug up after months in the earth, what skin remained rotted and drooped from yellowed bone. Moonlight played off the metal of their blades and the skulls beneath their helmets, but did not reach the blackened sockets that once held their eyes.

"When you arrived weeks ago, these men looked like you and I, Nylas. Whole. But as time passes, they rot. Or so you say? Is that still the case?"

Nylas, dumb with equal parts wonder and fear, nodded in silence.

"This remains both a mystery and a small shred of hope for me. Why do they change, while you and I remain the same?" Mallin wondered, his voice taking on a note of inquisitive inflection.

"Stop. Look!" It was Smiles' voice. "There's the fuck," he pointed and reached his skeletal arm out to alert his partner. "See him?"

They were looking right at Nylas. Terror eclipsed astonishment.

"Here, use mine…again." Mallin spoke the last word in a sarcastic whisper as he handed Nylas a hunting bow.

Commanded by what could only be instinct, Nylas grabbed the bow, kneeled, and fetched his two arrows. The soft brush of feathers brought him the first measure of comfort since this nightmare began anew.

The two abominations strode through the entrance, brandishing grimy swords, moving at a swift pace made somehow comical due to their skeletal frames. As Nylas sucked back deep breaths, preparing to aim, a strange calm settled over and a smile grew on his lips. He raised and drew, taking two more measured breaths. He shot two arrows in as many seconds and both found their mark—one straight through a gaping maw, the other punching through rotted chain links into the ribs beneath. Their bodies crumpled with a resounding crash as bone and steel met the red tiles below. It was a small victory in such bleak circumstances, but it felt good. It felt familiar.

"Well, that's it for the show, I'm afraid." Mallin let go a quiet chuckle. When next you wake, their corpses will be gone, and your arrows will have returned. Like the fire, like the memoires, like these men, the circle continues."

"Food?" said Nylas, as thoughts flitted from one possibility to the next.

"You *feel* hungry?"

Nylas admitted to himself that he did not. *Thirsty neither.*

"Wish I could tell you your boot would reappear. Oh, how you complain about that cold foot of yours."

At these words, Nylas sat down on the stump across from Mallin and stretched his naked foot toward the fire. A finger's length from the dancing flames, the licking tendrils tickled his foot and his mind flooded once again with all he'd forgotten.

Sanctuary
by John Linwood Grant

In the time of the Growing Cold, a finwife came to the Wolds. She came slow and silent, hauling herself from the seal rocks to the land, and she was not the finest of her kind. She was in fact a sadling, a runt of a girl with pearls of beach glass and dull hair which straggled on her shoulders. That she was there, so far from Eynhallow, could hardly stay unnoticed.

Charlie, the village's lengthman, saw her first. He was slicing his way down Odd Cows Lane, stripping back the summer's growth on the verges. He watched her progress around the gorse bushes, supposing herself unseen, and then he watched her slide into the mere. She didn't surface.

"Lunch," he said to his scythe.

The White Horse was quiet. Martha Grange leant on the beer pump and regarded the cigarette end floating in the slops tray. A tiny brown boat, bobbing on a brown ocean. She lit another one, and drew hard on it. Tuesday lunchtime. Four or five regulars, and a family passing through, two morose teenagers trying to sit as far away from their parents as possible. The father was muttering something about the taste of the beer.

Martha smiled. She didn't dislike strangers, she just didn't need them. Her worst fear was being put in some good beer guide and having people turning up, all notebooks, braces and beards. With that in mind, visitors got the barrel ends and the slop tray.

"There's summat different come," said Charlie, propping his scythe by the door.

The tourists looked up. Martha scowled at the lengthman, beckoned him over.

"What do you mean, 'different'?" she asked, her voice low.

Charlie leaned right over the bar.

"Summat over Odd Cows Lane way. It's a lass. She went in t'mere, stayed there."

Martha stubbed out her cigarette.

"Best tell Harry, then."

* * * *

The village of Gorse Muttering was not on any maps. It sat quiet and ignored in the folded landscape, not that far from the great chalk cliffs, not that far from the rolling farmlands of the Wolds. In the ramshackle glasshouse next to his cottage, Harry Cropton grew tomatoes.

He regarded Charlie with the calm that came from having managed to grow seven plum tomato plants from seed. The sea-frets and the cold inland winds were not kind to tomatoes.

"She's still there, I suppose." Harry, who was possibly eighty years old, sat on a stool outside the glasshouse, and considered. "Driven out, seeking summat, or just bringing mischief?"

Charlie blinked. He was far too close to Harry's aged cat, known locally as the Executioner. The Executioner didn't see that well, and didn't have the sense of smell he used to, but he'd never lost his touch. Anything smaller than a bullock was fair game if it strayed into his territory.

"I've Main Street to cut," said Charlie, edging back. "I saw nowt else, but they said I should tell thee, right away."

"Good enough. You get on wi' it."

Harry watched the lengthman leave, then kicked the cat. The Executioner sank his claws into the old man's foot, and found that Harry was wearing steel-toed boots, as usual. Disappointed, the cat staggered off to find something more penetrable.

Harry sniffed, wiping a dewdrop from his long nose, and set out for Odd Cows Lane. It was a ten minute walk—for him anyway—along Main Street and round by Trench's Farm.

The mere was silent except for the sucking sound as Harry tramped through the reeds. A duck stared at him with distaste and paddled back into cover. When he was close to being ankle-deep, he stood and brushed the water with his stick.

"They say you're in there," he said conversationally. "Best come out and talk, or I'll find a way to send something in after you. There's more than one dog can swim round here."

Ripples, and then a sorry head. The finwife's hair looked better, but not much better, wet. Her large dark eyes lacked the usual shine. He was reminded of a seal with distemper.

"Sanc-tuary. I ask…sanct-uary," she said. Her thin lips struggled with the words.

"We'll see."

* * * *

The kitchen of Cold Farm contained Harry Cropton, Jenny Mainprize and one of the Misses Hetherington. Harry thought it was Miss Edith, but it was hard to tell.

"A finwife?" Jenny peered into the teapot, added another spoonful of leaves. "That's odd, isn't it?"

"Aye." Harry nodded, watching her bend over the stove in her tight jeans. He had his dear Elsie at home, of course, but Jenny Mainprize was a fine looking woman. There was only fifty or so years between them, after all. Then he thought of Elsie's right hand clutching a kitchen knife, and decided to get back to business. "But she's shown no harm, as yet."

"Where did you put her?" Miss Hetherington was knitting. What she was knitting no-one dared ask.

"In Mike Trench's old barn."

"She's a long way from Finfolkaheim or Eynhallow." Miss Hetherington tutted as she tried to cast off. "But this is a time of changes…"

The others nodded. The Growing Cold. Things on the moors, even sniffing close to the towns. And the Children of Angles and Corners grew bolder with every year. All manner of hidden things were returning, and there were few people left who knew the old ways.

"Is this a matter for the cunning, then?" Jenny poured out more tea.

"Ten years ago I'd have let her be." Harry shook his head. "Now I don't know. If the finfolk want her…"

"She wants sanctuary from her own people. I don't understand that."

He took the fresh mug of tea from her.

"I reckon one of their elders has been pressing her. You know what happens—they get sent to wed a fisherman, or drag one down. It never ends well."

"Sanctuary, you said." Miss Hetherington looked up. "The Nazarenes used to like that word. We should put her in St Michael's."

Harry and Jenny looked at the ageless apple-dumpling of a woman, surprised. It was a good compromise.

"I'll take her up after milking," said Jenny.

* * * *

Gorse Muttering had been Ralph Townsend's escape from an inner city church on a rough housing estate. He was in bad shape, physically and mentally, when the bishop made a tentative suggestion about St Michael's.

"It takes a…a different sort of faith to minister in that, um, parish," the bishop said, peering over his bifocals. "You have to be somewhat, um, relaxed there."

Wary, and still nursing a broken arm from his last home visit on the estate, Ralph hesitated, but the bishop made it clear. It was St Michael's, or a change of vocation.

After a year in the village, Reverend Townsend was not entirely thrown out by the arrival of Jenny Mainprize and the finwife.

"Can it…she…enter? Holy ground, I mean?" he asked, when the situation had been explained.

He looked at the nervous creature by Jenny's side. The eyes were too large and dark, the jaw too pointed, but she might just pass for a human girl, if they could find some clothes for her rake-thin body. At the moment the finwife was naked except for a stained horse blanket.

"We'll find out, I suppose."

"So she's what, some sort of mermaid?"

Jenny gave him the sort of look you gave a slow child.

"Finwife. The finfolk didn't used to come further south than the Orkneys and Shetlands. The males are sullen, and violent."

"And the women, the females?"

"At the beck and call of their males, unless they find a way to escape."

Jenny urged the girl into the church porch. The finwife shivered but took damp steps forward, staring at the dark opening to the church itself.

"Well, we're very supportive of multi-faith initiatives these days," he said, and realised how stupid he sounded.

Jenny looked at him, supporting his self-assessment, but led the girl inside.

He was relieved to see that lightning didn't strike the steeple, and that none of the statues of saints started bleeding.

"Here, let's see what we have."

He opened a box of donated clothes inside the doorway. He found a long green dress and a cardigan, handing them to the finwife.

"You can change in there." He pointed to the small side door.

"I'll help her." Jenny and the finwife disappeared into the vestry, to come out five minutes later with the barefooted semblance of a teenage girl.

"How old are you?" the vicar asked.

Wide eyes met his. Jenny whispered in the girl's ear.

"Nine-teen," said the girl.

"And what should I call you?"

Another whisper followed.

"Kel-da."

The vicar frowned. "Can't she understand me?

"Mostly." Jenny patted his arm. "Simple words, vicar."

"Come on, then. We should find you something to eat."

Stood behind the church, the parish hall was little more than a large shed, but it did have a sink and a toilet. Jenny Mainprize helped when it came to explaining the toilet, but otherwise he managed by gesture and the odd word to settle the finwife in. He brought a camp bed from the vicarage, a few blankets, and watched her crawl underneath the bed, still dressed and wrapped in the blankets as well.

"How long…I mean, what's going to happen to her?"

Jenny shrugged. "We don't know, vicar. We'll think on it."

He looked away. "Oh. I see."

Not that he did. The villagers were either kind or pleasantly indifferent to him. He could visit them, if he wanted. There was always a cup of tea, a home-made cake. He could even talk about the church, but it was pointless. The ones who weren't Christian were better versed in comparative theology than he was; the Christians didn't believe in the need for an actual church. Services were attended when it was raining or when they coincided near enough with a solstice. Apart from that, he was left to do whatever he wanted.

Ralph Townsend did not know what he wanted.

* * * *

The presence of the finwife took up much of his time over the next few days. She would only eat raw food, preferably fish and raw meat. For want of ideas, he showed her round the church. She was the only person who had shown any real interest since his arrival.

"Time under you," she said, standing in the nave and looking down at the stone flags. "Many years gone, others in the earth."

He wasn't sure he liked the sound of that. He showed her the altar.

"Cross." She leaned forward, gingerly touching the brass cross on its dusty cloth. She seemed surprised when nothing happened. "Power inside?"

Her eyes were those of a wild seal.

"I don't know," he admitted. "Maybe. Yes."

A hissing laugh.

"Used to fear cross."

"There's nothing here to be afraid of, Kelda." He tried to think of something appropriately religious to say. "God is love."

The finwife looked down at her thin body, put one hand flat on her crotch. The short fingers were faintly webbed.

"Love," she said, rubbing at her crotch through the green dress.

The vicar reddened. "No, not sex. Um…love, care." He mimicked an embrace, a gentle kiss. She wandered off to look at the stained glass windows.

They walked to the mere occasionally, so that she could shed her clothes and dive into the murky water. He tried to look away, but failed more than once. She had small breasts, a narrow frame. He closed his mind to that sort of thought, and whistled softly as she swam.

In the evenings, he left her in the parish hall, turned off the lights and went to his own bed tired and confused.

* * * *

Charlie brought Harry a newspaper most mornings.

"This is t'one," he said, leaning on the old man's gate. The Executioner was elsewhere, and Charlie relaxed.

Harry peered at the newspaper.

"Fishing coble wrecked off the Head. Last night, eh?"

"I know t'bloke what buys their crabs. One of them swears he saw hands grabbin' side of t'boat afore they went over." he drew on his pipe. "Teks a lot to turn a coble keel-side up."

"More finfolk."

"'Appen. Thought tha'd want to know."

Harry creaked his way up to the village shop

A Miss Hetherington was sat behind the counter, round as an apple in a pinafore. He showed her the morning paper.

"There's a sale at Biltons," she said at last.

"No, the bit about the fishermen."

Mice explored a box of cereal which had fallen off its shelf. After some minutes, Miss Hetherington nodded.

"We need eyes, Mr Cropton. Yes, eyes." She looked at the clock in the hallway. "September. Who can we beg, who can we beg? Ah yes, they don't need to be anywhere, and they do like the cliffs."

He could guess who 'they' were. "Do you want me to—"

"I'll see to it."

"Thanks. I'll tell the others."

She settled back in a whumph of talcum powder and lavender which made him want to cough. He started for the door.

"The vicar's not a strong man, Mr Cropton."

Harry paused.

"You mean it's a mistake to leave her up there?"

She pursed soft pink lips.

"I don't know. They won't enter the church though. Never a finman would dare that, not even in the Growing Cold."

* * * *

He reached the parish hall by lunchtime, though he'd rather have been in the pub. The vicar was cross-legged on the floor, showing the finwife spelling books from a never-to-happen toddlers' group.

"Mar-y." The vicar sounded tired. "Jo-seph."

"Klok-folk," said the finwife, edging back from Harry.

"Everything alright here, reverend?" Harry leaned on his stick, catching his breath.

"We're making, um, some progress." The vicar stood up, brushing his knees. "She doesn't seem to be too sure of you, though."

"I'm not surprised. So, nothing unusual happened?"

Reverend Townsend looked at the half-clad finwife near his feet, then at Harry's carved blackthorn stick.

"No," he managed. "Everything's quite normal."

Harry decided not to mention the incident with the coble. He left the vicar and the girl Kelda to their lessons.

Down in the village, the White Horse was empty except for Martha.

"The jackdaws are up." She squinted at him.

"Miss Dorothy sent them."

They shared a quiet pint.

"I was watched, last night," said Martha, licking foam from the rim of her glass.

"Oh yes?" Harry held his own glass out for a top-up.

"It was them. The Children of Angles and Corners."

She might not have had the cunning, but the villagers kept nothing from her. She smiled. "I hammered a seven inch nail into the roofbeam. They didn't half create."

"Good lass." He stared at his pint.

"How's the girl?" asked Martha.

"Still there. Klokfolk, she called me."

The landlady consulted her knowledge of the village, and added the encounter she had had with a Norwegian trawlerman last spring. The spare room still smelled of mackerel.

"The clever people." She nodded. "Close enough, eh?"

"Aye. I don't reckon a finwife ends up here by accident."

"And you think they're coming to get her back?"

"Mebbe."

Harry drained his glass.

If he went home now, he could still water the tomatoes.

* * * *

Two walkers found a dead gull that afternoon. It was pinned to the side of a twisted hawthorn near the cliffs, its breast torn open and the small ribs spread wide. They had no idea what it meant, and so they left quickly to eat their packed lunches somewhere else. They preferred their countryside like their sandwiches, in small, tasteful bites.

* * * *

A Miss Hetherington was sat outside the shop when the vicar came for supplies. She smiled at him and rolled her way inside.

"More pilchards, reverend?"

"I'm afraid so, Miss Hetherington. And do you have any cod-liver oil left?"

He filled his shopping bag and after a pointless pleasantry or two made his way back up to the church. He was slow today. His sleep had been broken, an odd night of dreams which he couldn't recall. He felt like he'd already walked five miles before he started.

St Michael's stood to the south of the village on the rolling hump called Leathermans Hill. Kelda was waiting for him in the church porch, wearing a soft blue wool dress from one of the donations boxes. Her white-blonde hair was combed, long and silky, and she smiled at him. The sight of her sharp little teeth seemed normal by now.

"Ral-ph."

She took the bag from him, handling it as if it were empty. He had been surprised at how strong she was. Though not as surprised when she admitted her true age. Kelda had been born, or spawned, he didn't like to ask, in the wild sea currents near the Orkneys, one hundred and nineteen years ago.

"We can have our lunch," he said, ignoring the way the wool stretched over her breasts. He struggled with two fantasies at night. One was that of Kelda coming to comfort him in his over-sized, creaking bed, the other was of converting a finwife to the ways of the church. Neither seemed likely.

They spent the afternoon exploring the churchyard. Kelda seemed interested, and he found the gravestones a sign of normality. Gorse Muttering had funerals and burials like any other parish, though he'd never conducted one here. Some of the stones were caved with unlikely ages.

"Crop-ton," said Kelda, tracing a name. "Cun-ning Folk. Like old man."

"Yes. Harry."

She pressed nearer to him, her thin body warm.

"He send me back?"

He put his arm around her. "No, I don't think so. He's a…good man."

After dinner she lay on the sofa in the vicarage while he tried to draft a sermon. It was getting close to the autumn solstice, a time when he could pretend to be a proper vicar.

He finished his notes a little before midnight. Kelda was asleep, her bare feet twitching. The soft webbing between her toes was almost attractive.

One swift whisky and he lay down, fully clothed, on his bed. He was searching for sense in the Gospel according to John when he drifted off.

The sea was a lonely place. Ralph Townsend dreamed of vast abysses under the waves, of a watery emptiness where he swam, lost, on currents which carried him away from everything he cared about.

And then there was warmth in his dream, like the night before. He imagined hands stroking his body, comforting him. He moaned as slender limbs entwined him, and two large eyes shone with pleasure…

* * * *

Later, when the moon was dim, a particular chalk boulder near the edge of the village was moved. No-one noticed.

* * * *

Three days, and the jackdaws spoke of strangers between Gorse Muttering and the sea. Salt strangers. Harry failed to kick the cat that evening, only ate half of his over-cooked gammon. His wife, emerging briefly from her own slightly peculiar world, pushed cake into his jacket pocket and told him to walk the boundary.

"Why, Elsie love?"

"Summat's coming." She was a small woman, all pinafores and rubber gloves, as daft and as interesting as when they had married fifty three years before. She had a touch of briar and rook about her, a gift with the wild. She was the only person the Executioner never went for.

"You mean the finfolk? Are they here?"

She lost interest. There was cabbage to be boiled, and Harry would know what to do.

He did. He gathered Jenny Mainprize along the way, drawing her from her cows.

"Our Elsie says to walk the boundary."

Jenny patted her prime milker, Hildaberg, on the nose and joined him.

They took the way past Cold Farm and onto the slopes, the village a clutch of buildings in the dip of the land below them.

"The Rook-Stones are alright," he noted as they passed a broken circle of boulders in the middle of a field. A rook tilted its head at them, and flew off towards Rail Woods, where the old station used to be.

The ward-post by Rail Woods was as it should be, a four foot post with an eye carved into it. For the sake of any passing walkers, someone had added a yellow right of way arrow. No-one knew where the arrow would lead people, but that wasn't the point.

They passed around The White Farm, and into the woodland between The White Farm and the north road. Crossing the road, east and onto open land, the mere lay below them. Jenny shivered.

"Something's missing," she said. "Harry, they've broken the boundary."

"Finfolk couldn't…"

"Something's missing," she repeated, and strode out.

He struggled to follow here, using his stick to keep his balance. Halfway up Odd Cows Lane they found the first breach. The ward-post lay on its side, kicked under the nearest hedge. The simple carved eye had been scored through. Three times.

"I ought to have felt it. The jackdaws should have said."

"Wasn't done by the Hidden or their kin," said Jenny, stroking the post. She was a good one for the Touch.

"An accident? Kids from town, ramblers?"

But he knew better. When they found one of the sea-stones further on, rolled out of its place and similarly marked with three knife scratches, they knew why Elsie had sent them out. Someone had known how to break the village boundary, open the way for those who might have little love for the people within.

"Who did it then?" Harry's face creased more than usual.

"Does it matter? If something's in, it's in."

"It matters," said Harry. "But as you say, summat's here. Suppose it's come for that girl."

Sea-stone and ward-post would need replacing, but not now. Gorse Muttering had granted sanctuary, and Gorse Muttering's word had to be kept.

They had to get to the church.

* * * *

Ralph Townsend prayed, though he didn't expect it to do any good.

Three sinewy figures had arrived as he was showing Kelda back to the hall. Silhouetted against the sunset, they might have been men, but as they came closer they had a dark look which set them apart from any men he'd met before, even the worst of the thugs on the estate. Eyes as large as Kelda's, but full of ice.

They stood between the pair and the church, and he wished that he was wearing his cross. Somehow he'd lost it the day before. Their clothes were tangled with kelp and bladder-wrack, like drowned sailors, and their long fingers moved in an unseen current. The girl cowered against the parish hall. Was this why she had sought sanctuary—the cold finfolk described by Jenny Mainprize?

"I'll protect you," he shouted.

The tallest of the figures laughed, the scrape of barnacle against rock.

"No need, God-man. Her part is done."

There was a rustle in the bushes by the graveyard. The finman looked, saw nothing, and turned back to the vicar.

"Our kin have seen you, calling your God. No-one comes. This is the Growing Cold, our time again…"

"Not yet, mebbe."

Harry Cropton stumped his way around the corner of the vicarage, Jenny Mainprize in his wake.

"Thank God." The vicar ran to Kelda, tried to put his arm around her, but she thrust him away. The finmen hissed, and to Ralph's surprise the girl crawled towards the finmen like a whipped dog.

"What are you doing?" He reached for her, to pull her back, but found no strength in his hands or arms.

Harry nodded. "Reckon I see it now. You used her, she used him."

Thin laughter from the strangers. "Clever-clever. The sadling held him, made him pleased. Men do things in the night that they do not know."

The vicar remembered his dreams, the tiredness in the mornings.

"What did I do?"

Harry didn't look at him. "You broke the boundary. A stick here, a stone there. It wasn't your fault, reverend."

"But Kelda…"

"She was told to use you. I doubt she had any choice in the matter. They wanted to know what we had here, to see if they could come and go. They found a way."

"He is not klok…not wise. He does not even truly believe in his God." A finman hissed with pleasure. "So many children of men, so little cunning or faith. The Times Yet To Be will be easy, if even here we can walk."

The finwife was weeping.

"I think we will take this small God-man also. Drown him and make him dance on Eynhallow. He may be useful."

Harry and Jenny came closer.

"I don't think you will," said Harry. "This is our place."

The finman made a smile with an almost lipless mouth. One hand rose, and the vicar watched in horror as Harry and Jenny staggered.

"The Strength of Three is beyond you, Cunning Man," said the creature.

Ralph could see it now, a shimmer in the air between the finmen. They were bound together, working together. He tried to move, but was driven down by a single look from one of the finmen.

"Do something," he gasped at Kelda, but he could see that she was lost. A helpless girl, for all her years, under the thrall of the three.

The tallest of them nodded to another, who took the vicar's arm in a damp grip. He tried to fight, yelling at the creature which held him.

"In the name of Jesu…" An ice-glance silenced him.

"We go, with runtling and God-man. The testing is done." The finman gestured to Kelda, who stood up and came to its side, still weeping. "And we know what is here, now. We shall tell the Children of Angles and Corners, and others."

"You don't know as much as you think." Harry coughed, only upright because Jenny was supporting him. "He likes fish, by the way."

The finman frowned.

"What do you say?"

"He likes fish," repeated Harry.

The rustling noise heard earlier in the bushes became something large and vaguely ginger, if ginger had been smeared with mud, kicked around a bit and run over by a lawnmower. With a screech, the Executioner launched himself at the leading finman.

The cat slashed great furrows in the creature's face, then sank his remaining teeth into its upper lip. It wasn't often that he got a chance to have a real go at something. Flesh tore, raw and oily, and the cat's hind claws raked its chest. The Executioner yowled triumphantly, his mouth full of something far more interesting than tinned cat food.

The finman screamed, a high gull scream which echoed off gravestones and church walls. It managed to rip the animal from its face, but some of its face stayed with the cat. The Executioner landed surprisingly lightly and swiped a large, disreputable paw at the legs of the next nearest stranger, his claws going deep...

The Strength of Three no longer held.

Harry came forward, his brown eyes shadowed.

"Uninvited."

Jenny Mainprize took his shoulders, steadying him.

"Unwelcome," she said.

There was a feeling in the ground beneath the vicar's feet, a sort of change that he couldn't describe, and the air was scented with hawthorn blossom, which wasn't possible on a September evening.

"Unlooked for." Harry took another step.

"Unwanted." Her words fell in the same cadence as the old man.

The creatures heard the bane words, saw that terrible animal crouched ready to spring again...

"You have made an enemy," said the unharmed finman, glaring at its wounded companions.

Harry Cropton's face was dark and angry.

"That's where you've got it wrong, lad," he said. He smelled of hawthorn and spring mornings, of tobacco and an old man's cardigan. "We had nothing in particular against the finfolk, 'til this." His right hand went up, fingers splayed, and the churchyard yews shivered, tips pointing towards the sea. "Now you have an enemy. Think on that, eh? Ask on Eynhallow, and see if your elders think you've done good. Ask in the deeps if it was worth this test."

The tall finman lifted its arm; the Executioner gave a preparatory yowl, and the arm went down.

"Our Drowned Word upon you," the finman snarled at the vicar, but Harry's hand held land rights and Spring flowers; the cry of rooks and the first bleat of newborn lambs. The finman's Word was lost, and jackdaws circled above the yews, watching.

"Uninvited." A statement and command.

The finmen shuddered, their control lost. Stripped of power, they ran towards the cliffs, the girl limping behind them. Ralph thought that there had been a last backward glance from Kelda, but he found that he couldn't see so well. He seemed to be weeping.

The churchyard was quiet again.

Harry glanced east, watching the creatures head for their own sanctuary, the grey North Sea. The Executioner prowled through the grass, searching for pieces of finman that he'd missed. He seemed disappointed.

"Our fault," said Harry at last. "Never thought they'd go that far."

"The Growing Cold," Jenny said, and squatted by the vicar's side. "Cheer up, reverend. No damage done."

"Damage?" He looked up at her. "I was useless. I did nothing for her, couldn't protect her, couldn't protect myself."

"There'll be other days."

"What...what do you mean?"

"I'd ask God, if it were me." Jenny smiled, squeezing his hand.

Her eyes were not like Kelda's. They were grey and clear.

The old man tested his aching bones, and found most of them intact.

"No-one comes to Gorse Muttering by accident, reverend." He patted his pockets to see if he had a mint. There was still a sour, seaweed taste in his mouth. "Not finfolk, vicars, nor cats."

The Executioner spat and padded off. Fish was alright, but Trench Farm had a new goat. Now there was a challenge...

The Giving of Gifts
by Matt Neil Hill

One hand over David's eyes and the other pushing down on his jaw, Richard leaned forward with the penlight gripped between his teeth. Warm breath scented like the rot of fallen apples wafted up towards him from David's cavernous throat. Something angular and black nestled against the root of his brother's tongue—glistening, pupating, shy—not yet ready to emerge. Keeping David blinkered, he retrieved the torch from his own mouth and swallowed the saliva that had gathered there. *Click.* The room returned to its normal, dying-sun-amber level of light, after trial and error the only one David could tolerate. Loops of Christmas lights were strung around the bedroom, all but the yellow bulbs removed.

"Not quite ready, eh?" he said, exposing that depthless stare. "Doesn't matter, mate. You take your time."

David remained silent, just as he had for the last three months. The returning soldier, back from Iraq courtesy of a roadside bomb, wounded beyond almost all hope. Whose thoughts and feelings were now forever secrets. Ten years Richard's junior, it had been a long time since he'd needed his protection.

The radio kept up its babble in the background as Richard gently washed and redressed his brother, changed his diaper. News from far-flung points around the globe, questioning voices and the *Play for Today*, the different voices rising and falling as they slipped between fiction and fact. He turned David in the bed, his once-solid body lighter than feathers. He made sure the stumps of his legs were elevated, imagining this to be more comfortable. The final kindness was lubricating drops for those unblinking eyes. The fat, balding, middle-aged ghost of Richard's reflection swam and broke apart.

He walked to the chest in the corner, running his fingers over the smooth wood as he slid open the top drawer. He rummaged through piles of time-softened underwear as uniformly black as every other piece of clothing he owned, in search of the prizes beneath. So few were left compared to a few weeks ago, but he pulled out the last three plastic sandwich bags and considered them. Two went into his pocket, the third back beneath the socks.

"We'll be needing another miracle, eh?"

David said nothing, his eyes twinkling with artificial tears.

"I'll check on you when I get back, alright?"

The radio continued its patchwork lullaby after he closed the door behind him. Across the hall was their mother's room, the door open to reveal the vacancy filling the impression of her on the ancient bed. The substance of her had been up at the hospital since the day after David came back, disappearing by inches into the sheets on the oncology ward. Sick, but not without the possibility of her umpteenth recovery, oblivious to her youngest son's return. Richard knew he should be there now, but he saw her every day before and after his shift as a porter, and tonight was a little time just for him. Away from his vigil at the bedside of another dying loved one.

Except, against all odds, David wasn't dying.

Not this time.

* * * *

Beneath the half-life lights of *The Old Bacchus* pub, Phil palmed the little plastic bag of speed and disappeared it inside the heavy, festering brown coat on the back of his chair. His eyes darted around in his face, grey amongst the broken-vein purple.

"I'll definitely have the whizz off you, Rich, but let's have another look at the jewellery."

Richard sipped his pint and slid the small, unwrapped object back across the table. He never thought that the artefact would be of direct interest to his oldest friend—it was too feminine for his tastes, and Phil had no interest in engaging with real women outside of the porn world, let alone giving them gifts—but there was always a chance that he might know someone. Even in the dankest pub in the weariest satellite town on Earth there still had to be a few people left with an eye for the beautiful.

"What is it then? Some kind of lizard?"

"It's a chameleon."

"Right, right. Where do you get these things, Rich? You hardly ever leave the bloody house."

Richard smiled, then drained his pint.

"I told you, Phil, they're *gifts*. Some I keep, but the rest just aren't meant for me. Like the speed," he said, lowering his voice for the last word, "what am I going to do with that these days? But if you're having it, then mine's a pint."

"More than one, I should think. Alright, same again?"

"Please."

Phil stood up, placed the lizard back on the table and then wound his way through the Friday night crowd to the gloomy mahogany oasis of the bar. Richard reached across and took the little golden creature up by one outstretched foot, the second tail of its filigree chain uncoiling behind it.

The workmanship was exquisite, even though the symmetry was marginally skewed, the limbs on one side slightly flattened and curled in on themselves. It was noticeable, but didn't ruin the piece. He was about to put it back in his pocket when someone on their way past stopped at his table.

"Oh, that's pretty," the young woman said, stooping for a closer look.

Richard turned his face up to hers, saw her smiling back at him. Saliva dried on his tongue in response. She was about half his age, had piercings in her face and a ponytail that was threatening to scalp her. She somehow managed to be quite pretty in spite of it, which Richard thought was a decent trick. He could immediately picture the little chameleon frozen mid-run against the over-tanned skin of her throat.

"You like it? It's for sale." He hoped she hadn't noticed the crack in his voice as he held it out to her. Their fingers brushed against each other as she took it, an imagined spark across the gulf between them.

"Yeah?"

She turned the necklace over in her hands, its shine competing with her electric blue acrylic nails.

"How much?" she said.

"Fifty?"

"*Fifty!* How about twenty?"

Richard laughed, but it was friendly rather than confrontational. The girl laughed with him. It wasn't the worst sound.

"It's solid gold, love. How about forty?"

She wrinkled her nose. Cocked her head.

"Nah, too much for me," the girl said as she placed the chameleon back in Richard's waiting hand. Their fingers didn't touch this time.

"That's a shame, it'd suit you. Well, I'll be here for a bit if you change your mind."

"Alright. Maybe I'll ask my boyfriend when he gets here. See ya."

Richard watched her depart across the blood red carpet, checking intermittently that no one was watching him do it. She wasn't half his age—he was twice hers. Only the young were relevant any more, and all status was measured against theirs. He was losing his hair and could stand to lose more than a couple of stone. The best he could ever hope for from a girl like that was the distant contact of skin during a financial transaction. He'd never really been relationship material—too clumsy, too set in his ways—but was even less so since David came home. He bit his lip, forced himself to look away.

"Tell me you weren't trying to sell that thing to *her*," Phil said, setting their new pints on the table with the usual amount of spillage.

"Why? Who is she?"

"Tasha Bennett. She's only *Jacko's* girlfriend, isn't she?"

Richard closed his eyes. In a shithole big enough for more than one drug dealer, Jacko was by far the worst. When he finally peeled his lids open again it was to the sight of Phil grinning and shaking his head.

"You *twat*."

"I didn't know, did I? I thought he was going out with—"

"Ellie? No, old news that one."

Richard sighed.

"She walked past and spotted it and started talking to me—*shit*. He doesn't like me as it is."

"Well, what do you expect? This is his patch, he's not going to take kindly to freelancers is he?"

"Didn't hear you complaining."

"Well, no—but that's different. We're mates."

"Yeah, we are. Remember that if he shows up wanting to kick my head in, will you?"

"He's not going to do anything in here. Stop stressing, alright? Why d'you think I hang onto this minging coat? Nobody ever checks *my* pockets."

Richard took an unhealthily long swallow of his pint, then belched softly into his collar.

"Alright," he said.

"How's your mum, anyway? Any sign of her coming home yet?"

"No. I think this is how it's going to be until she dies, if I'm honest."

"Jesus, that's a bit bleak, mate."

"Try living it."

"Yeah, sorry. What'll you do?"

"Carry on, I suppose."

"No, I mean if she pegs it. Won't the council be after you for the spare room? Bedroom tax and all that."

"She isn't dead yet." His fingers creaked as they tightened around the glass.

"No, I know, but—"

"I said: *She. Isn't. Dead. Yet.*"

Phil nodded. Buried his face in his pint in search of his lost tact.

Richard took a deep breath. He couldn't think that far ahead, even though he knew he should. He closed his eyes. The darkness behind them always seemed to be tinged with amber these days.

"Mate?"

Richard opened his eyes and surveyed the pub and the life swilling around inside it. He looked at the faces and hands and at the bodies pressed up against each other. Daydreamed their myriad secrets as he inhaled the scents of sweat and cheap perfume and deep-fried bar food. He thought of

David, waiting in his eternal yellow dusk for his brother to come home.

"What?" he said, letting out his stale breath.

"Do you remember that time she gave us a proper hiding when we'd been at your Dad's scotch? She was a tough old bird in her prime."

Richard grinned at Phil's attempt at an apology. It had been a while since he'd thought about his mother in her pomp. After years of weathering the shallow peaks and seemingly endless troughs of her recurrent cancer it had been easy to forget her as a vibrant and occasionally terrifying woman. She'd had to be both those things to survive her marriage and bring up two boys alone. These days, the ghost she'd almost become was scared rather than scary.

"She was. She had to run out and buy more to top the bottle up. She'd have got a worse beating than the one she gave us if the old man'd seen that. How old were we?"

"Eleven? Twelve?"

"I should've known better."

He and David had learned early on in their lives not to cry within earshot of their father.

"We were *kids*..."

"Yeah, but I was old enough to know what a psycho he was, how he would've reacted. Who'd end up getting punished for it."

"Come on," Phil said, "don't do this. He's been gone a long time. You all did okay, didn't you? I mean, until—shit. Sorry."

"Well *you're* on bloody fire, aren't you?"

"Yeah, sorry. You still miss him?"

"Eh?"

"David?"

Richard stared down into the remains of his drink for a moment, the darker depths beneath the suds. He replied without looking up.

"Course I do."

He hated lying to Phil, but then what he'd said wasn't exactly a lie. He missed the brother he remembered.

That was the moment at which Tasha reappeared, this time with her boyfriend in tow.

"Alright, wankers?"

Jacko was a twenty year old slab of muscle in knocked-off sports gear, the air around him always thuggishly rich with the aroma of skunk that he both used and peddled. His eyes were slightly crossed, but that wasn't something anybody ever thought to bring up with him—not if they were in any incontestable way attached to their teeth.

"Jacko," Richard and Phil said in unison.

"Show me this lizard thing then," Jacko said, thrusting his hand out at

Richard.

"It's really pretty," Tasha said, squeezing Jacko's arm.

Richard fished the item out of his pocket and offered it up in his cupped palm, from which it was promptly snatched away. He watched Jacko turn it over just like the others had done, a sinking feeling creeping into his heart.

"This thing?"

"Yeah, I like it."

"Alright. How much did he say?"

"Forty."

"Pee, right?"

Tasha giggled. It was a pleasant enough sound, but all it got from Jacko was a roll of his mismatched eyes.

"Pounds, silly," Tasha said, squeezing his arm again.

"Forty *quid?*" he said, turning his scrutiny on Richard again. "Are you taking the piss?"

"It's solid gold," Richard said, managing to meet the man's irregular gaze.

Jacko rewarded him with a grin that displayed gold canines and a random lower premolar, all of an infinitely lower quality than the necklace that Richard now knew he'd be waving goodbye to for a pittance.

"Ten."

"*Ten?*"

"Alright, *five.*"

Richard bit his lip. He knew that style of haggling, knew where a further bid or question would get him. The beer-soaked grain of the table suddenly became very interesting. He nodded his head.

Tasha squealed and took the necklace when Jacko handed it to her, his other hand rooting around in his sweatpants. He pulled out a wad of bills that could have happily stood a couple of rounds of champagne for the whole pub, then searched out a lone fiver. He made sure he handed the tattiest one he could find to Richard, failing to let go of it for more seconds than was necessary to reinforce his point. Richard kept his hand still, knowing that the note would get torn if he tried to take it.

"Thank you," he managed through the bile on his tongue.

"You're welcome." Jacko finally relinquished the token payment. Tasha followed in his wake as he laughed his way back into the crowd.

Richard finished his pint, set the empty softly on the table.

"You alright, mate?" Phil said. "Want another one?"

"No. Thanks anyway."

"Hey, don't leave cos of that. Easy come, easy go, eh?"

Richard looked at him, his teeth grinding against each other as he took a deep breath. He closed his eyes, something black and shiny now amongst

the orange.
But they don't.
They don't come easy at all.

* * * *

The random objects had started appearing soon after David came home from his final tour. At first they'd been small things; minor artefacts of déjà vu. Scattered across the chocolate brown swirls of the carpet or glistening on David's pillow when he awoke. The first one was a tiny toy soldier made of poorly cast green plastic, rifle in one hand and the other raised to his open mouth, yelling mutely for comrades who never materialised. He remembered playing with whole platoons of them as a kid, of passing them on to David, every last one long since consigned to the bin. The next was a coin in no currency he'd ever seen. Three black seeds. A sand-coloured pebble. A spent shell casing. Small things, perplexing and of uncertain origin.

The first time he witnessed one coming into being he was terrified he would lose David all over again. Guttural, liquid sounds choked in that mute throat as Richard hammered between his brother's shoulder blades. The stickiness of the saliva across his knuckles from reaching beyond the cutting edge of David's teeth had never left him. Three warped and blackened dog tags on a chain emerged past bloodied gums, the names and numbers melted to slag. The vacuum in his brain was so much colder than the metal on his palm.

The gifts—as he gradually came to see them—continued with no obvious pattern in their diversity or sequence. Bullets one day, wild flowers the next. Foil-wrapped packets of cannabis or amphetamines, precious stones and balls of papier maché that transformed to official-looking documents when he unpicked them, unreadable with trickling smears of redacting black ink. When money got tight he'd sell some of them—including most of the drugs—but not all. Some had only a sentimental value. A ring, silver ouroborous snake that perfectly fit the middle finger of his right hand. An intricately detailed crystal skull the size of a plum. A Polaroid of him and David as children he'd thought lost, crumpled like an origami rosebud on his brother's trembling tongue while his eyes stayed deep and blank; the two of them in football gear, squinting happily into a long departed sun.

There was a magic inside David he couldn't explain or understand. An anomaly he could never reveal to anyone who might be able to do either. He wouldn't allow his brother to become a freakshow exhibit or fodder for the vivisectionist's slab. Every day now came with the anticipation of some unrecovered treasure from their shared past; memories reborn as powder, petals, celluloid and gold. He had no idea what it cost David to birth these things, but he'd vowed to keep him as safe from the world's harm as he possibly could.

* * * *

Richard stood at the cracked porcelain urinal and tried to piss his frustration down the drain, but it wasn't enough.

His anger wasn't really about the money, more that one of David's precious gifts had effectively been stolen. And that he'd been humiliated in front of the girl. *And* that she hadn't cared. He told himself two things. One: the necklace had clearly been meant to find its way into her possession; and two: it wasn't her fault that her boyfriend was such a massive prick. Richard was kind of done with the evening, but Phil would doubtless insist on one for the road. He'd just started to zip himself up when the door to the Gents opened behind him.

"Fuck me, not you again."

Richard sighed very quietly and finished with his fly.

"Just going, Jacko."

The big man was standing very close behind him when he turned around, making him jump a little.

"If I checked your pockets, what would I find?"

Richard tried very hard not to close his eyes.

"Not much. A few quid, some keys."

"Really? Not carrying anything you shouldn't?"

"Jesus, Jacko, I'd have to be daft. You told me once already—"

"Yeah, I did, didn't I? Let's see then."

"What?"

"Empty your pockets, dickhead. I want to *see*."

Richard shrugged, trying not to let any relief show on his face. All his gifts were gone. He turned his pockets inside out and held his meagre wealth out for inspection. Jacko slapped his hands away, sending the coins and keys spinning into the shadows under the row of sinks. Richard barely had time to react before Jacko grabbed him by the throat and slammed him into the urinal, his head smacking off the sea green tiles above it. He struggled, but Jacko held him fast. He could feel piss seeping through his clothes and shoes.

"I don't *like* you," Jacko said, pushing his face an inch from Richard's.

"Look—"

Jacko looked down and rummaged in his own pockets, then brought a Stanley knife up to Richard's face. Richard inhaled the tang of oiled metal, a scent suddenly more pungent than gallons of fermented urine laced with bleach. The blade hovered perilously close to his left eyeball. He tried very hard not to move.

"If I see you in here again I'm gonna cut your sad, fat, ugly, stupid face, you get me?"

Richard knew that all he needed to do at this point was agree, but there was a little bubble of dissent working its way up his throat against both gravity and his better judgement.

"But this's been my local for twenty-five years."

"And now it fucking isn't," Jacko said, putting a full stop at the end of his statement by jabbing the very tip of the blade into Richard's cheek.

"And if he hadn't been blown to bits in the desert I'd throw your useless tosser of a brother out as well."

The blade twisted.

Richard recoiled, cracking his head on the wall again. Jacko snorted, then let him go. Richard slumped into the remnants of his own waste.

"Now fuck off, eh? Get your poxy bits and get out."

Jacko didn't bother waiting to see if Richard did as he was told, just stepped up to the urinal and started pissing. Richard scampered away and scooped up his keys, not troubling himself with the coins. If he stuck around long enough to find them all he might do something stupid. He retreated into the pub to the sound of laughter and his blistered, hammering heart.

* * * *

"What happened to you?"

"Nothing. Leave it."

"Was that Jacko?"

"I said leave it, alright? It doesn't matter."

"It bloody well does!"

"I just have to find a new pub to drink in, that's all. Maybe shut up about it, unless you want to have to as well."

Phil's shoulders slumped. He shook his head.

"Bollocks to this."

He picked up his car crash of a coat and put it on, then followed Richard out of the front door. They stood out in the chill air, the streets damp with silence.

"Want to go somewhere else?"

"Yeah. Home."

"Oh, come on, don't let that arsehole knacker your one night out—"

"Already has. And I stink of piss."

Phil summoned a cackle.

"Doesn't normally stop you."

Richard smiled at his friend, unable to help himself.

"No, I suppose it doesn't."

"Want some company?"

"Not really. Just to get home to—"

The words died in his throat. *In vino veritas.*

"—to get cleaned up. I'll phone you, eh?"

"He'll get what's coming to him, you know."

"Maybe. But not from the likes of you or me."

"One day. If David was still around—"

"But he's not, is he?"

Phil didn't reply, just patted Richard gently on the shoulder.

"See you, mate."

"Yeah, see you."

Richard kept checking over his shoulder as he headed for home, often enough to be sure Phil wasn't following him. He hadn't enjoyed lying to Phil about David, but all bridges to the truth about that had been burned.

His oldest friend had been at the funeral after all.

Mum had been there too, on day release from the hospital, shrunken into a wheelchair and sick with grief in every part of her that could still feel. A captain from David's regiment, all sober reflection and stiff but genuine handshakes. Richard's nerves had sung a high tension anthem that day, primed for the destructive shadow of his father to fall over the graveyard. Mercifully, whatever hole the old bastard had fallen into twenty-five years before had kept hold of him.

He trudged up the hill between streetlight haloes towards the home he shared again with his resurrected brother.

* * * *

The letter from the Ministry of Defence regretfully informing them of David's death had dropped out of the blue a couple of weeks before the funeral and exactly one numb month before Richard found his brother's shattered body in the alley behind their end-of-terrace house.

Full of drowned sorrows on his way back from The Old Bacchus, he knew the shivering form was David even before seeing his face. There was something in the curl of the back, the positioning of his muscular legs even though they'd both been severed above the knee, fragments of charred bone poking through the cauterised flesh. Bitter smoke rose from torn clothes and exposed skin, its flavour that of gasoline and blood combined. Breathless, Richard scanned the alley, he and David utterly alone against all odds. The clear sky above bore no scar to mark the place where the body fell, not a single midsummer star out of place. Richard stooped over a face still bloody with IED shrapnel, wounds so fresh it was as if David had been blown thousands of miles by the blast only to land metres short of his own back door. Lonely weeks adrift in the troposphere, kept alive simply by water vapour and the sun's rays.

His first thought was to get David inside.

His second was to call an ambulance.

His third that his brother was officially dead and in the ground and who or what was in that coffin?

He took several deep breaths and hoisted David over his shoulder, shocked at how insubstantial he seemed. He carried him inside as quietly as he could, their mother's last fragile snores in that house covering his tracks. He used whatever medical supplies he could find to make David comfortable, most of them left over from mum's last discharge home. He'd observed enough at work to know how to dress wounds, and made educated guesses about how many painkillers and antibiotics to feed between his brother's slack lips. Nothing stirred behind David's eyes, but it was undeniably him.

Waking a few precious hours later at David's bedside was when he found the little plastic soldier and held it warm in his palm.

* * * *

Richard closed the front door behind him and leaned against it with his eyes shut. Inside the house the smell of his soiled clothes was rank, almost animal. His fingers went to the scab on his cheek, picked it away. A minute trickle of blood on his face as he opened his eyes.

A scratching noise came from somewhere above him.

Not scratching: *choking*.

He took the stairs at a run, barging into the bedroom to find David convulsing on the bed. His face was a deep bruise beneath the eternal Christmas lights. A slick black shadow protruded from his mouth, too swollen and monstrous to be his tongue. Richard laid hands on the new gift and felt rigid metal beneath the mucous and the blood. The choking sounds grew worse as he tried to pull it free. He let go.

David's hollow eyes betrayed neither pain nor fear. Those demonic fires burned solely in Richard's chest, stoked by the fuel of guilt. He hooked his thumbs into the straining corners of David's mouth in an attempt to widen the gap between his teeth. Another half inch of the object slipped out, shrieking across enamel. Richard's vision blurred. Blinking tears away, he tried again to drag the gift into the world. David's hacking breath suddenly stopped altogether, his face growing darker still as his eyelids drooped.

Richard fled towards the bathroom. The light cord danced manically behind him as he clawed through the paraphernalia cluttering the sink. Trying to avoid seeing the bone-white apparition of his face in the mirror, he threw his razor to the floor and stomped it beneath his heel. Cuts bloomed on his fingers as he retrieved one thin blade from amongst the plastic fragments. He ran back to David, hands trembling.

"Mate, I'm so sorry. I don't know what else to do."

He wriggled the razorblade into left corner of David's mouth and began to cut. His fingers kept slipping as he sawed and their blood mingled. When the clumsy incision was big enough he gripped the edges and pulled them apart, half David's crimson teeth on display. He reached in and grabbed the gift, pulling on it with every ounce of his strength. To a chorus of tearing soft tissue and splintering bone it began to move.

And then he was falling.

He abandoned the gift as soon as he hit the carpet and scrambled back to the bed, stroking David's face as he willed him to breathe. Blood and broken teeth sluiced between his fingers, his own face reddening as he swiped tears away. After a hundred years David's chest began to rise and fall, the air alive with the faint, discordant whistling of his returning life. The room was microscopic and vast all at once. He lurched to the chest of drawers, dumped fistfuls of underwear onto the floor. At the bottom was the last of the old gifts: a vial of morphine the size of his thumb.

He could have sold it of course, but never did. A syringe purloined from the hospital lay next to it. He'd read charts when transferring patients on the wards and knew how much to administer. David's eyes stayed as blank as ever, but how could trauma that severe cause no pain? He found a vein in one of those atrophied arms and slid the needle in, flooded it with oblivion.

The next hour was all washing and disinfecting and the mechanics of repair. Superglue instead of sutures. Senses alert for the cessation of breathing. Only after all that could Richard bring himself to look at the angular black mass in the centre of the room. He didn't possess David's expertise, but it looked perfect to him. Afraid to touch the thing at first, eventually he cleaned it and then lay down next to his brother with it cradled against his chest.

The gun was small and cold, a mean-spirited miracle. A gift from the depths of his brother's transformed body, presented without instructions for use.

Richard closed his eyes and, at some point during the long night, slept.

The gun filled every corner of his scarlet and amber dreams, yet when he woke he could not remember for the life of him against whose temple the barrel had been pressed, nor whether he had held it there in the spirit of mercy or revenge.

The Santa Anna
by Jack Lothian

I'm going to get us all killed. That is what I am thinking as I stand at the bow, staring into the thick mist ahead. There's not much of a wind, so half the crew are below deck, manning oars, grunting and heaving as we cut through the black water. It won't make a difference though. This is a ship of dead men, and it's all my fault. I turn to my first, Nilsson, nod to him, reassuring.

"We'll be through this soon," I say.

"Aye, Captain," he replies, but his voice is somber and grey. He doesn't believe me either.

There's mist in every direction, with no sign of land or life beyond, as if we're traveling through the heart of some endless dark cloud. No, we won't be through this soon. And Nilsson will be the first to go. He'll die, crying and begging for his life, and it'll all be my fault.

* * * *

I had promised the men retirement. More and more I could see them thinking about homesteads, womenfolk, family. While I understood those urges, for me there was a quiet terror in all that, in a normal life. The few times we had taken extended leave, I could barely stand it by the end. I'd be agitated, desperate to feel the shift and lilt of the deck over the waves again.

It's the routine that kills a man, inch by inch, hour by hour. Last time we were ashore for six months—six sodding months of nothing. You wake up and can't think of one good reason to rise from the bed. The town around you feels drained of color, full of people content to herd themselves like sheep, fat and safe on the land, no sense of ambition or adventure. Home felt like a foreign country to me now. I'd lie there at night, staring at the ceiling, feeling my days wither away before me. The sound of a dog barking in the distance would fill me with a nameless restlessness that I could not shift.

Of course, we had lost the child as well, and Lucy had proved barren since, which didn't help none either. She wore her sadness like a heavy cloak, day in, day out, and I was relieved to rouse the men and return to sea once again.

Many of them didn't want to go back this time. Sometimes as Captain, you have to remind them of their debt to you. To the life you've all chosen. Usually, a hard word or two would do it, but there are other ways. I had to almost march Helsby—the Quarter-Master—back to the ship, his wife yelling all sorts at me from the window. There's a weakness in a man who stays with a woman like that.

The men wanted to know why we heading back out. We'd made a good living before, they had savings, and some were of the opinion that there was no need to continue now, as if need was a thing that could ever be filled.

I knew I had to give them something to look forward to so they would focus on what lay ahead, rather than what they had left behind. So I told them what I'd heard about the Santa Anna.

It was the kind of fat, loaded ship we used to dream about running across. I'd heard it had gone missing around the Straits of Malatta. Told them if we could locate the wreck, we'd be set for life. Wasn't that what this was all about? One last voyage before our waistlines expanded in direct opposition to our ambition.

I didn't tell them where I'd heard the story and I left out some details, like the fact the ship had been missing for a good eighteen months now, and all search parties had come home empty-handed. I also neglected to mention that a few of the wives and families of the Santa Anna claimed to have had the same nightmares about the lost crew. The sailors had appeared before them, blinded, hands outstretched, speaking in some strange tongue, crying out the same odd words, over and over. Such stories I marked down to the hysteria of grieving women.

I am the Captain. I have a sense of duty. I do what must be done.

We would find the wreck. Or we would find something else along the way.

We always have before.

* * * *

On the sixth evening, I was in my usual place on the deck, watching the stars pass overhead, the shadowy coastline to our port side. The familiar comfort in a vast horizon. Nilsson fell in beside me, quiet for a moment.

"First night back on the ship, I had a dream," he said, leaning against the edge, eyes on the waves as they broke the surface. "I dreamt I was still on the farm."

That was where his money had been going—a small, unimpressive piece of land with his wife and two children. "I saw a deer come out of the woods, into the main field. Saw her walking across, until suddenly she stopped still. There was a disquiet about her. You know how agitated those beasts can get. They've got that way of being."

He fiddled with his pipe, pushing down the tobacco with his thumb.

"See there was something out there in the darkness, and the deer could feel it. She stood there, cold in terror, but she didn't turn tail and run. And it was getting closer and closer. Through the trees. Across the grass. I could hear in the dream. Yet still she stood there, just staring with those eyes, into the back." He lit his pipe and fell quiet again.

"What was it..?"

He glanced at me as if he was unsure what I meant.

"In the dark. What was out there?"

Nilsson kept his eyes on the sea. "That's what she's standing there for, Captain. To see for herself."

* * * *

We once ransacked a temple in Kiribati. As we tried to go back to our ship, the elders fell to their knees, begging us to return their sacred items, saying a terrible curse would fall upon us if we left shore with their treasures. We laughed and spat upon them, and some of us had their way with the womenfolk there too, as happens from time to time. Yet back at sea, we were beaten and buffeted by terrible storms. The fish we caught were foul and stagnant, rotting from the inside. For three days we suffered, and some of the more superstitious amongst us wanted to throw the goods we'd taken over the side. I had to stand firm. Superstition is a disease—and while the body can survive a little now and then, if you let spread and grow, you might never recover.

On the fourth day, the rains stopped, and the sun came out, and the fish were fresh and clean again.

* * * *

It took us a month and a half to track down the Santa Anna, zigzagging across her route, checking the wind-charts and storm records from when she went missing. Selkirk, the navigator, drew up map after map of possible locations. Morale dipped with every empty day. There were only so many promises I could make before the men started to lose faith.

Then one night Nilsson let loose a sharp whistle, and we all hurried topside. Lights in the distance, a few miles away on the ocean. There was laughter and a sense of growing triumph as we pulled through the water, closer and closer, and saw the Santa Anna appear before us, her lamps lit on the deck, like a scattering of fireflies in the midnight air.

We thought we were looking for a wreck. We never expected to find the ship intact, much less lit. We were looking for scattered remains, the tell-tale signs of a sinking. To see her like this—it felt like providence, like fate.

We eased alongside her. Usually we'd fire a warning signal, but her deck was empty. I told the men to bring out the grappling hooks and ropes. We pulled the ships closer together until we were bow to bow. Nilsson was staring at the empty deck, shaking his head. Even Helsby muttered how it didn't feel right, and this from a man who had never seen a rusty coin that he didn't try to pocket and polish.

Nilsson nodded me aside. "You told us she was a wreck," he said, and there was a tension in his voice.

"No, I said she was lost."

"And now she is found. Is that what we're saying here, Captain?"

"You can see for yourself."

Nilsson was quiet for a moment. "All the same, I'll remain on our ship."

He gets that look on occasion like he knows something you couldn't hope to understand. He's been alongside me for more years than I could count, yet more and more we are strangers to each other.

I called out to the others, "First mate has the wheel."

Nilsson gave me a small salute, and I returned the gesture, but neither of us was convincing, two tired actors who have played the same roles for too long. I couldn't remember when things had changed, just that he was a great sailor once, and now he'd turn his back on it all, to be some common farmhand. Sometimes I'd look across the deck and barely recognize my crew anymore, the men they had become.

"Helsby—organize the boarding party. We have a ship to take."

Once the cheers of the men would have woken the giants sleeping beneath the ocean. Now they felt distant, disconnected. This was not how things were meant to be.

I lead the boarding party across, weapon at the ready. As far as we knew the crew of the Santa Anna were mostly landsmen with a merchant captain at the helm, and as such wouldn't pose much threat. She was their ship though, and they knew her better than anyone else. A clear deck could be them drawing us into a trap. After all—the lamps were lit. Somebody was home, down below.

We moved across her, quietly as we could, gently easing open the door under the bridge, descending stairs, alert and ready.

I felt the silence down there, straight away. It was thick and heavy and coated the air like dust. We moved from cabin to cabin, but there was no sign of life. Beds were made. Floors were swept. Yet it felt like it had been a long time since anyone had walked along these gangways.

Then we opened the door to the hold, and everything changed.

All of her crew was inside. They were all standing, lined up, facing the starboard wall as if waiting for something. They didn't move, didn't even react to the hold door as it swung open, creaking on hinges.

I stepped in fast, roughly grabbing the nearest crew member, forcing him down, knife to the throat. I shouted for the rest to place their hands upon their heads, to kneel down.

None of them responded. They just continued to stare at the wall.

The crewman in my grasp put up no resistance, and his expression never changed. His eyes remained fixed starboard, even when I pressed the blade tighter to his throat, and repeated my threat. It was as if I was not there.

My men were still waiting in the doorway, and I had to bark at them to enter. A few of them laid punches and kicks on the opposing crew, but no matter what we did, these sailors would not respond. Perhaps some paralyzing fear had gripped them on our arrival, or some unknown disease had rendered them mute and immobile. For a moment I thought of Nilsson's dream, the deer in the field, frozen, gazing off into the dark.

There was a disquiet that fell upon us too, being in that hold with them, seeing them all standing there, ragged and pale, the way their eyes never left that wall. I couldn't help but stare at it too as if I might see what held their attention so.

Then the Santa Anna shifted upon a wave, turning a little, and every one of them suddenly shifted their heads too, a few inches to the side, as if on some silent signal. It was the only movement they made, and they made it as one. Just as soon as they had started moving, they stopped, and the silence that followed seemed to fill up the room.

I ordered my men to strip the lower decks. There were murmurs of complaints, but they knew better than to make me ask twice. They seemed glad to be back amongst the store-rooms and bunks, away from the hold, but they worked without speaking, and I noticed they took care not to make too much noise, as if afraid to wake the foreign crew from their stupor. Boxes and chests, hauled back across to our ship, as I supervised from the deck.

I was the last to leave the Santa Anna.

Something made me head back down, to that infernal hold. I lingered in the doorway, studying the crew, and then made my way across the room, past these motionless men, half expecting at any moment that one of them would call out and grab me. They remained as statues though. I reached the starboard wall and turned to face them so that their eyes could not help but be upon me.

I cleared my throat and asked them one final time what the meaning of this queer behavior was. There was no answer, so I took my blade and sliced it across the throat of the nearest sailor.

His body collapsed to the ground, and yet he made no noise, and his crew-mates showed no sign of even having registered this terrible event. His blood spilled out, black and thick in the dim light of the hold.

An uneasy terror started to gnaw at me. I had an unshakeable feeling that I'd crossed into the realm of something not entirely of this world. I pushed my way through that unmoving forest of men, as the fear swelled up, overwhelming me, forcing me to frantically make my way out of that room, rushing down the empty corridors, suppressing a scream inside me that so desperately wanted to escape.

Something was behind me. I have no way to prove it, but I could feel it at my back, keeping pace. Not like a hunter, but as if it wanted me to know it was there, wanted me afraid, that there was sport in that alone. I scrambled for the stairs, stumbling over, determined not to look back.

By the time I had returned to my own ship, I was the Captain again, composed and confident, and my men would never know of this moment of witless dread.

The sun was becoming to creep up on the horizon as we unhooked ourselves from the Santa Anna. Navigator Selkirk approached me and suggested that we shouldn't head in the direction that her crew had been facing. The men apparently had some serious concerns over this. Inwardly I was relieved that someone had come to me with this, so I could both berate them for their foolishness but show magnanimity by agreeing to travel the opposite way.

There was no way I wished to head in the direction of those cold, empty stares.

* * * *

By noon of the next day, we were hopelessly lost in the fog.

* * * *

Hours stretched into days. Selkirk and his people poured over instruments and charts, but we couldn't find our way through to clear waters. We barely talked of what was around us, this endless mist. I even allowed the more superstitious men to tip the bounty over the side into the sea. It wouldn't make a difference now. It was as if something had followed us back from that cursed ship, and made itself at home on our vessel instead.

I sat in my cabin night after night, pouring whiskey, maps spread out before me, trying to find an answer. Yet the compass refused to move, and without wind, we had no way of telling where we should be going.

I thought of five years before and the Inguita—a tribe we had spotted once, far south, on a lost coastline. They had been standing on the shore, rags tied across their eyes, faces turned towards our ship. They could not see us, but they knew we were there, knew we were coming in to land.

Helsby met them on the beach to barter for some food and fresh water. When he returned, I asked him about their tattered blindfolds. He said that when the men of the tribe reached a certain age, they would voluntarily blind themselves; a sharp iron blade, heated on the fire. He told me it was because they were not worthy to look upon their God, so they removed their eyes, so as not to cause offense to the deity.

I had asked him who their God was. Helsby had just shaken his head, said he had no wish to know.

Sitting in my cabin, I wondered for the first time if the crew on the Santa Anna had discovered something, out on those uncharted waters. Maybe I had it wrong. Maybe they weren't staring towards a point. Maybe they were turning their backs on something far more terrifying.

Which would mean we were now sailing towards whatever that was.

Before I could even grasp what that might mean, I heard Nilsson's sharp whistle sound out above. I hurried up the stairs, across the deck, pushed past the men gathered at the bow, to find him standing, in the half-light, gazing out to sea.

"Is it land?"

"No. There was something out there."

I looked out into the shrouded night-time fog. "Something..?"

"There was a shape. In the distance. Like a mountain, except it was moving."

"Who else saw it?"

The crew shook their heads. There was a time when I would have thought Nilsson had lost his mind for saying such things, but I couldn't help but believe him now. We had been out there for weeks now, and our skin was shallow, our water and supplies all but run out. Somewhere across the oceans Lucy wakes and walks down to the harbor's edge to see if my sail is amongst those returning. Nilsson's children make plans for when their father comes back, and his wife performs jittery needlework to keep her mind occupied. Some of us had families. Most of us had homes. These might as well have been in another kingdom, another world, compared to this strange place we had drifted into.

"We'll be through this soon," I said, but my words were even more hollow than before, and Nilsson didn't even respond.

This would be the last time I ever spoke to my old friend.

* * * *

It starts a few hours later.

I am woken from a dreamless sleep by shouts from above. Nilsson is screaming in the fog. We gather weapons and close in, searching for him, but the gloom is thick, and our lanterns can't seem to penetrate. We cannot even see the length of the boat, cannot locate where in this dreadful mist he is.

His yells become a whimper, and he calls out his wife's name, over and over, before his pleading suddenly stops, leaving nothing but an awful, deafening silence.

I move forward, my lantern held out. I can see smeared blood on the deck, leading off into the dark.

I order the men back below, but my commands are interrupted by warning shouts coming from different directions, from different crewmen, like the rising prelude of some horrendous symphony. Whatever is out there, it is picking us off, fast and brutal now. All around me I hear the desperate cries of my men. I grab onto Helsby's sleeve. I tell him to stay by my side, no matter what. We can go below. Barricade the doors. We can still survive whatever strange attack this is.

"You have men out there," he says, struggling against my grip, as the howling around us reaches a crescendo.

I try to explain to him. About the Santa Anna. Their crew in the hold below. How some people are unworthy to look upon the Gods—

But screams suddenly stop and Helsby is gone.

I am not even sure how it happened. It is as if the fog bloomed up around him and simply spirited him away, like some conjuring trick, leaving me alone in the unsettling quiet.

I almost wish the shouts would start again, to at least let me know someone was left alive. I back away, to the edge of the ship, and hopelessly call out the names of my crew. There is no reply.

But there is something out there, in the fog.

Coming my way.

Slow. Measured. Like it wants me to know it is there.

We were always so small and fragile, on these vast seas. It was foolish to think our ships could ever protect us from whatever lay beyond. We were never meant to come to such places. They were unknown for a reason.

I can't help think of that deer, in the field at night, staring towards the black woods. Knowing that something was approaching. Yet unable to turn away, to run.

In those final moments I think I finally understand what the dream means, what Nilsson was trying to tell me, but by then—of course—it is too late.

The Dread Fishermen
by Kevin Henry

Janet MacKinnon stared out through the large, plate-glass windows of the St. Luke's Hospital cafeteria. The world beyond the window was a rain-streaked blur. Lights atop tall poles in the parking lot appeared as small pools of feeble luminosity swimming amidst the great black sea of night. They seemed almost lost and lonely in the void.

She realized vaguely that someone was saying her name. She turned her head and saw the man she had met earlier in Bran's room. The old man wore rumpled clothes that smelled of the ocean. He sat a cup of coffee in front of her before joining her at the corner table.

"Tastes like cat piss, but at least it's hot, yes it is," the grizzled old sailor said.

"What was your name, again?" She asked.

"Noddy Gilmartin," the old man said. His mouth split wide in a smile that would have shown his teeth if he'd had any. "I was sayin' before that Bran sailed with me for a bit, he did. He's a right good fisherman."

Janet nodded. "Yes, of course. You'll have to forgive me—"

"No apologies necessary," Noddy said. "Quite shook up, you must be, what with Bran's condition and all."

She felt tears welling up again. The sight of her only child lying unconscious, hooked up to machines, and slowly dying was a knife through her heart. "It's not just his condition," she said, dabbing at the corners of her eyes with a balled up and already well used tissue. "He can't die like this. Not until I tell him how sorry I am."

"Whatever you got to be sorry fer, I'm sure he understands. Boys love their mothers, aye, yes they do."

Janet shook her head. "We used to be so close, but it all went to hell. I never meant for it to. I was so lonely after his father died." She stopped, wondering why she was spilling her guts to this stranger. Because she needed to tell someone, especially since the person she wanted to tell was three stories up in a coma, his condition deteriorating by the hour.

"Frank Bedford was a good man," she continued. "When he came along, I clung to him like he was the last man on Earth. Bran was jealous, but I didn't see it. Didn't *want* to see it, I guess. Too many things were changing too fast. Bran withdrew. I never got him back." She looked at

Noddy with pitiful, self-loathing eyes. "I may never get the chance to tell him how much I love him, Mr. Gilmartin."

"I'm sure he knows," Noddy said gently.

Janet blew her nose on the tissue. "You found him in Buzzard's Bay," she said.

"Aye, I did," Noddy pushed the coffee away, yearning for something much stronger.

"What happened out there? Doctors say there's no medical explanation for him being…the way he is." She leaned forward and whispered as if Bran may hear, "They asked me if he's an organ donor." She swallowed hard against the knot in her throat.

"I was comin' back from a long day out," Noddy said. " I saw Bran in the Dauntless, headin' toward Crow Island. I think he saw somethin' that lured him there."

"I don't understand."

"I know because I saw it too," he said, his pointed, knowing stare saying that there was more to the story.

"What was it?" Janet said, enrapt by the sailor's words.

"Lights."

"There's no power on Crow Island." She looked at him as though trying to decide if he was drunk.

He shook his head, trying to decide how to best explain himself. "The lights were *on* the island, but not comin' *from* it, if you get my meanin'."

Janet sat up straight in the hard cafeteria chair. "I don't know what this is about, Mr. Gilmartin, but I'm not amused. My son is in serious trouble and—"

"I know the trouble he's in better than you, Ma'am, yes I do. That's why I'm here."

"Get to it, then," she said, her voice stern and cold.

"There are other worlds than this, Mrs. MacKinnon…places that our minds can't comprehend. They're known to us only as whispers passed down through the ages from mouth to mouth. The knowledge won't be found in books or on a computer, but it's real all the same."

"Make your point."

"One of these other worlds is home to things that feed on us just as surely as we feed on fish in the sea. They hunt us in a similar manner, usin' lures to draw us in. That's what Bran and I saw tonight, one of their lures."

"How can you do this?" She said, clearly disgusted. "*Why* would you? My Bran is dying and you're wasting my time with this…this…whatever it is. Shame on you." She stood to leave.

"They don't want the flesh," the old man said, remaining seated. "They feed on the spirit. One of these things has Bran right now. He's fightin' like hell, but it's only a matter of time, it is."

Janet began walking away.

"I know how you can get him back," Noddy said.

She stopped in her tracks. Every rational part of her brain told her to walk away, but there was a feeling that told her to sit back down and listen to what the sailor had to say.

She moved stiffly, folding herself back into the uncomfortable chair. "What are you talking about?"

He could see the emotions playing across her face. She would leap at a chance to help her son, but was afraid to be hopeful, especially with the information coming from such a source as a sea dog like him.

"I'm sorry 'bout this," he said. "I truly am. The things I have to tell you could twist up a person's mind in the best of circumstances and this is far from that."

"I'll give you two minutes, then I'm going back to my son, where I should be right now, and I don't ever want to see you again, Mr. Gilmartin."

He nodded gravely. "My ancestors called them the Dread Fishermen. They lure men to their doom, to feed on their souls. For centuries men have reported seein' creatures and phenomena that lead some astray. Sirens led men to crash their ships on the rocks, so they did. Mermaids, kelpies, Will-o'-the wisps, Morgans, Bucca-Boos. Different cultures all over the world have seen 'em, but they don't exist except as illusions created by the Dread Fishermen."

Janet held her head in her hands. When her shoulders began convulsing, Noddy thought she was crying. When she lifted her face to look at him, he saw that she was laughing.

"What kind of old-time, superstitious bullshit is that? Do you expect me to believe a word of what you've said?"

"Aye, I'm hoping so, for Brandon's sake."

The laughter melted away. Her face became drawn, pensive. "How would one save a person who'd been caught by one of these things?" She asked against her better judgment.

"That's the hard part. There are plenty of stories about folks retrievin' lost loved ones from the Other world. Most don't end well."

"What is this to you? Why are you trying so hard to convince me of this?"

Noddy put his elbows on the table and stared at his hands, his fingers laced together in front of him. He rubbed his thumbs together in small circles for a moment. Finally, he looked back at the frightened mother. "I've been where you are now, Mrs. MacKinnon. I've taken the road that you seek."

"Someone you loved was…taken?" She did not want to believe any of this, but found herself being drawn in anyway.

Noddy's voice trembled slightly when he answered. "My Fionnula. They took her thirty years ago, aye, so they did. I found someone willin' and able to help me, but I was too late to save her. I never got her back, but you can still save your Bran if we hurry."

She wiped tears from the corners of her eyes. "It's all so insane. I don't believe in fairy tales."

"It's no fairy tale. This is the truth behind the myths. Anyway, the Dread Fishermen don't care what you believe or what god you pray to. They'll eat your son's soul all the same."

The blood drained from Janet's face as a chill worked its way through her body. "If I believed you, what would I have to do to get him back?" She asked.

"Come with me to Crow Island. It's an entry point to their world. I'll explain the rest when we get there." When she did not reply, he added, "I have nothin' to gain from lyin' to you. I only want to help the boy. Please, Mrs. MacKinnon."

He could see by the clash of emotions on her face that she was fighting an inner battle, her rational mind in conflict with her heart.

"I need to see him first," she said.

After he told her how to find the boat on which he lived, he said, "Hurry, Mrs. MacKinnon. Time works differently there than it does here, but we have precious little left." He got up and limped away.

Janet went upstairs to see Brandon again. His respirations were slower and more shallow than before. He was getting weaker.

She thought that she must be insane to even entertain the old man's ramblings, but Bran was drowning and Noddy Gilmartin was the only person throwing out a line.

* * * *

Noddy's boat was a forty five foot trawler with a raised pilothouse. It looked like a worn-out, rundown relic from another age. Dirty, yellow light reached out through one grimy window, only to be swallowed up by the fog that crept around the boat like a furtive thief seeking entrance.

Janet boarded the boat, questioning her own sanity all the while. Noddy soon freed the boat from the dock and set a course for the island which he insisted was a portal to another world. The silence in which they sailed, like Janet's acceptance of Noddy's story, was a fragile thing. It seemed that if either of them spoke, her suspension of disbelief would evaporate like a thin mist in the bright light of day.

Noddy finally broke the silence out of necessity. "There are those what say that a silver cord connects a person's soul to their body while in the astral plane," he said. "The place you're goin' ain't the astral plane, but some says as the two worlds are close enough. When you find Bran, you'll see the cord that binds him there. The monsters that have him are tuggin' on it, reelin' him in. Sever the cord and you'll break their hold on him."

"Won't he just float away or something?"

"No. You'll be able to see the doorway to our reality as a light at the end of a tunnel, so you will. Look behind and it'll always be there. Bring him with you to the light."

"How will I find him?"

"In that place, thought controls all. Think about him and you'll find him, sure enough."

"What about…you know," she could not bring herself to say the words for fear of how foolish they would sound passing her lips.

"The Dread Fishermen?" Noddy said.

She nodded. "What if they find me?"

The old man made the sign of the cross in the air. "We'll pray they don't."

She swallowed hard against the lump that had risen into her throat. "How do I get to this other world, Noddy?"

He took a swig of whiskey and turned his eyes to her. For the first time, she noticed a haunted quality in them that could easily be mistaken for weariness. "It's easier than you think, as long as we're in the right place when it happens," he said, turning his gaze back to the sea. Crow Island was in sight now, dimly illuminated under the glow of the trawler's forward pointing spotlight.

"That's vague as hell," she said, the worry evident in her voice although she had tried to make the statement sound like a joke.

Noddy did not reply, but kept his attention on the steering of the boat, directing it into a cove where he stopped and dropped anchor. "This is where the Dauntless was found. This is where they got him." He switched off the engine.

"No more bullshit," Janet said. "How do we do this? Is it like some kind of seance?"

Before he could reply, her phone rang. She fished it out of her back jeans pocket and answered. It was the doctor she had talked to at the hospital. He said that Brandon's condition was deteriorating rapidly. He could expire at any time and she should hurry if she wanted to see him again before it was too late.

She mumbled something to the doctor, ended the call, and leaned heavily against the door.

"What is it?" Noddy asked. "Is it too late?"

The strength in her legs gave out and she melted down the door into a pool of misery on the floor. "Almost," she said, her voice a whisper. "I'll never have the chance to tell him how sorry I am." Tears were flowing freely down her cheeks.

"There's still time," Noddy said. "Be brave fer your son. Do what I wasn't able to do fer my Fionnula."

She wiped the tears from her face, looked up at the old man. She peered into his bearded face, her eyes coming to rest on his. They were steady, earnest eyes. "We can really do this?" She asked.

He nodded solemnly.

"What the hell. Let's get started." She had not made a decision to act as much as she had simply resigned herself to the fact that she was out of options. If Bran died, she would not want to live. She had nothing to lose.

Noddy had already filled a round, thirty five gallon, steel tub with water. Now he dragged it into the center of the wheelhouse floor. He lit a yellow candle and placed it on a stool nearby so that its wavering light reflected on the water. "Kneel in front of it," he said. "Stare into the water."

She felt stupid to be doing so, but she knelt as he had instructed. The water was dark. The candle-light dancing upon it seemed unable to penetrate beyond the surface. She placed her face near the water and peered in, unsure of what she would see, or even if she would see anything at all. She was about to ask Noddy what to do next when she felt his strong hands on the back of her head. He was shoving her face into the water.

"I'm sorry," he said. "This is the only way. I'll bring you back, I promise."

She was too frightened to feel betrayed. She fought the overwhelming urge to breath, fear burning through her like a hot poker. She struggled against Noddy's hands, thrashing violently all the while.

Noddy pressed down firmly and evenly, taking care not to harm her any more than was necessary. It was over quickly. Her body went limp and he slid her gently onto the floor.

Noddy wrung his hands as he looked down at Janet's lifeless body. It felt wrong to have killed her, but death was the barrier that separated worlds. Crossing the threshold while in the nexus between this realm and another ensured that one's spirit would travel there and nowhere else. Anyway, he knew that he could bring her back. The responsibility was on her now. All she had to do was avoid the horrors that lurked in that place where she had gone and get Brandon to the light before he revived her.

* * * *

Janet became aware of floating in a black, limitless void. There was no sensation of heat or cold, or any physical awareness at all. She existed as the void existed, empty and alone. She conjured Bran's face in her mind. Thinking only of him, she floated through the great expanse of nothing.

Eventually, dim light emerged from the dark and she was peering into a wall of fog. She was no longer floating, but swimming. She had manifested a body, although it was not a physical construct, but a sort of psychic residue, her mental image of herself. This construct was not the fifty one year old woman with graying hair and a post-baby paunch that had never gone away. She appeared as she had in her early twenties, youthful and pretty.

Shapes appeared in the fog. They were far away, but Janet could tell that they were immense. They looked like the buildings of a vast city, but gazing upon them was confusing. They were comprised of many layers stacked on top of one another, some right side up while others were upside down. Larger layers rested upon smaller, with walls tilting at angles that were all wrong. Their existence was at odds with what common sense told her was possible and served to reinforce the fact that she was no longer in the world that she knew.

And then she became aware of *them*. They who had built the megastructures moved through the fog. She dared not look at them directly for fear that they may notice her. They must *not* notice her, that much she knew by instinct. The brief glimpses that she caught in her peripheral vision were of nightmares previously unimagined. She perceived limbs that were neither arms nor legs nor tentacles, but somehow all of those. Joints bent in unnatural ways. Other features were obscene and grotesque beyond belief. Their ill intent rolled off them like the rotting corpse-stench of roadkill.

Terror vibrated through her like loud music pushing a flimsy speakercone beyond its capacity. She felt that she may be torn apart by it, her core shredded by fear, her being reduced to the stardust from which she came.

She thought of Bran again, remembering why she was in that awful place. She thought of nothing but him, picturing his green eyes, his smile, the freckles on his cheeks and nose. She willed herself to go to him and found herself moving through the cold water, drawn by an unknown force.

After a period of time that could have been hours or days, she saw a small form wriggling and thrashing in the water just ahead. Moving closer, she saw with a start that the troubled swimmer was Brandon. It was not her adult son as he was in the real world, but as he had been at eleven or twelve.

When he saw and recognized her, Bran's eyes lit up. His mouth turned up in a smile and he cried out, "Mommy!"

"Bran. Oh my god, you're really here." She swam to him.

"I didn't think anyone would come," the boy said. "It's so scary here."

"I know, darling. I've come to take you home."

When she reached him, she hugged her son fiercely as they floated in the black water of an alien world. He looked so tired and frightened. The thought of her precious boy being at the mercy of things that would relish the taste of his soul made her heart hurt, but there was no time to be weak. Now that she had found him, she had to rescue him.

She became aware of other creatures in the water with her and Bran. These were smaller than the builder-beings, the things that Noddy would call Dread Fishermen, but they were no less malevolent. When they swam close, she saw them and immediately wished she had not. They were the size of large dogs with plump, oval bodies like fat, blood-engorged ticks. Their faces were disturbingly humanoid, but with many eyes like a spider. Inside their mouths gnashed long, pointed teeth. She could feel their hunger as if it were a palpable extension of their despicable, twisted forms.

One of the creatures bumped into her and then slid back into the distance, like a shark testing an object to determine its edibility. When one of the probing, curious things came too close to Bran, lingered too long before gliding away, she screamed at it and struck at it with her hand. It lurched away angrily.

"Something's pulling at me," Brandon said, his voice fearful, but not yet panicky. "It's trying to take me away. I've been fighting it, but I'm so tired. I can't fight for much longer."

"We have to get you out of here," Janet said, searching for the silver cord that Noddy had instructed her to sever.

One of the swimmers made a run at her then, mouth gaped open, eyes black as night. She heard it coming, whirled around and kicked at it. The foul thing did not relent easily this time. It snapped its teeth in her face, leaning past her to get at Brandon.

"No!" She screamed, punching and kicking it desperately. It backed away begrudgingly.

She was rapidly approaching all-out panic mode. The creatures were getting bolder and hungrier. She knew that she could not fight them all off at the same time.

"Honey, I love you so much," she said to Bran. "I need you to know that, OK?"

"I know, momma," he said with a smile, still wearily treading water.

She said, "I'm so sorry for everything that happened…the time that's passed, the things I said. I didn't mean them. You're the most important—"

"I know," he said softly. "I'm sorry, too."

A spasm wracked her entire body from head to toe. She faded out, then reappeared a second later. *'Noddy'*, she thought. *'He's trying to bring me back. Not yet, Noddy. I'm not ready'*.

* * * *

Noddy had already administered a shot of adrenalin, but it had not had the expected affect. He was pumping away furiously at Janet's chest as she lay on the wheelhouse floor, sweat beading on his brow.

"I won't let you go," he said, breathing heavily. "I won't give up on you. Come back now, you hear? Come back, damn it."

* * * *

Janet found the silver cord that tethered Bran to the nightmare place. It was impossibly thin as it ran from his back to disappear into the fog-filled sky above. When she touched it, it felt strong as steel.

In the next instant, she felt a searing pain in one leg. One of the creatures in the water had bitten her. She felt its sharp teeth tearing into her flesh, pulling her away from Bran.

"No, mommy," the boy shouted. He reached out for her, trying to pull her back to him.

Janet phased out and back again. "Just a little more time," she said out loud. "Please, just a little more."

One of the things in the water bit into her left side. She shouted obscenities and swung her arms wildly at her attackers. Tears blurred her vision. Pain threatened to rob her of consciousness, but she fought like a cornered lioness protecting her cub.

As the creatures both moved away, dozens more waited to take their places. They were all leering at Janet with equal parts hunger and anger, swirling around her and Bran in a circle that moved faster toward the center, like water moving down a drain.

She put one arm protectively around Bran while pulling on the cord with her free hand. It was thin, but incredibly durable. She would need both hands to do the job.

She phased out again, taking longer to come back this time. While she was gone, she got a glimpse of Noddy working to bring her back.

Bran was crying loudly, out of his mind with fear.

Janet pulled on the cord with both hands. The things in the water made their move, swarming over her and Bran, teeth and claws ripping into soft flesh. There were too many for her to fight. She threw herself over Bran, shielding him as well as she could with her own body, all the while enduring the agony of being eaten alive.

With no warning, the creatures in the water scurried away like dogs running from an angry master. Janet sensed movement above them, high up in the fog. Some thing of incomprehensible size was coming toward them. She knew what it was without seeing it. In fact, she knew that if she saw it, she would lose all courage, all sense of purpose. She would melt into the cold water and wait to be devoured.

Bran was screaming as he fought against the oily water and she knew that he also sensed the thing that came for them. It would be on them in seconds and then there would be no hope.

She phased out again. Noddy was pounding on her chest for all he was worth. He seemed desperate, but she was not ready to go back.

Bran's eyes widened as he stared up into the gloomy sky. His mouth was open, but sound no longer came out. Janet's skin felt tingly, as if a powerful electrical current was nearby, charging the air. The fog around them swirled violently. An awful behemoth was moving swiftly toward them from unknown heights.

As Bran writhed in terror, Janet gripped the silver cord again, applying all of her strength in a final attempt to dislodge it from him. A terrible stench assailed her nostrils. The fog roiled. A shadow moved toward them, a darkness deeper than midnight.

The cord snapped. A light swelled into being from the water's depths. This was the doorway that Noddy had told her about.

Bran stopped wriggling. His eyes turned to his mother's face.

"Go," she said, shoving him under the water and toward the light below. He disappeared, pulled inexorably toward the light.

The fog above her erupted and darkness swallowed her up.

* * * *

Noddy collapsed on the floor beside Janet's corpse. His chest was heaving from exertion, his shirt wet with sweat. He was sure that he had brought her back, but she had slipped away again. He had wanted so badly to help her rescue the boy, to make up for his failure all those years ago. He lay disappointed and spent, tears sliding down his grizzled cheeks.

* * * *

Bran opened his eyes. He was in a hospital bed, connected to machines that bipped and beeped like a chorus of digital birds. He should have felt safe, but knew that he would never experience that feeling again. He remembered everything. He remembered that nightmarish place where creatures that had been old when the Earth was born hungered for his soul. He remembered his mother…oh God, his mother! She had sacrificed herself for him.

Tears were streaming down his face while laughter erupted from his throat. He screamed and wept simultaneously. He had done the unthinkable…had gazed upon the thing in the fog as it reached for him at the end. He had stared the abomination in the face. Even as he sat up in his hospital bed, he could feel his mind being torn from its moorings. The tethers that held his sanity together were fraying. As he sank into a darkness that only he could perceive, he smelled the sea of a strange, distant place where hungry things pulled him farther from the light.

BLIND VISION
by Andrew Darlington

It's black when Niall comes around. So it's night? Either that, or he's in a cellar. But no, it's warm. He can feel the tingle of light falling on the back of his hand. His mind swims with visual echoes, an ice-water fear-wave rippling at him. He feels the screaming begin, he's a terrified animal, shrieking at spectres. Out of his mind with dread. For Niall is blind…

* * * *

With a sense of weary pride, Sebasten Contaxis creaks his emporium shutters open. Light slants in. Old sandals scuff him past shelves of ceramics, museum copies of classical myth figures, miniature crested bronze Spartan helmets, olive-oil soaps, skin-creams and unguents, locally-grown sachets of herbs, thyme, paprika, oregano, black and red peppers, kumquat liqueur, neatly-stacked boxes of baklavas, kourabies, akanes and rose petal loukoumi. He opens the door to step outside, blinking in the warm morning sunshine that falls across the narrow old-town way.

He tries not to look. But his eyes are drawn. Further along the smooth-cobbled slope, down towards the harbour, where Stefano's Bar is lurid with colours and pulsing light.

Contaxis has dignity. He honours Hellenic culture, folklore and tradition. And he scratches by. Stefano opens this obscenity of overpriced cocktails and loud euro-beat, and already Mavromatis drives a big silver Mercedes. He shakes his head, as he's done so many times before.

And a young couple approach. He's seen their like before. Lurching wrecked from Stefano's. Tourists with no respect. He watches as they pause, loiter…and enter his shop. The man, perhaps near-thirty, hair cropped back. T-shirt with corporate logo. She maybe a year or so younger. Jeans chopped-off so brief the pockets hang beneath the frayed rim. They both wear shades. Last night's revelry must leave their eyes sensitive to light? Sebasten sneers. Anticipating no sale. There's nothing here to interest them, surely.

But he observes them, picking up on their body language. Sensing there's tension between them. She's studying his ceramics too intently, as if to speak of anything else would invite recrimination, accusations. They are together, yes, but he detects the space separating them. She's smoothing olive skin-cream onto the back of her wrist, critically testing the erotic sweetness of its aroma. He's sifting through a selection of old maps in a box beneath the window display. He'd almost forgotten they were there. They're frail, shedding dust as he unfolds them.

The tourist looks up, enquiring. Contaxis shrugs, not expecting a sale. Two euros? The tourist says 'efharisto poli'. He responds 'parakalo' automatically. Perhaps he's misjudged the tourist? He smiles as they leave the emporium…

* * * *

Why did he buy the map from that bent stick of an old man? Yet Niall uncreases it carefully. Tracing lines. This is going to be a bad day, he feels it inside. No reason to go out. Equally, there's no real reason to stay in. Some days everything seems to click into place, but there's no doubt, this isn't going to be one of them. Obviously. Of course, such drab forebodings are just murky patterns taking shape inside his head, no way he can know just how bad that bad can get.

His hands dig deep in his pockets. Waiting for something to happen. Cordelia's still punishing him, still holding that grudge from last night. Sure, Gloria had given him the come-on in Stefano's, and he'd maybe played up to her. A little bantering flirtation never hurts? Now his presence reminds her of last night, she resents him, but can't get away. Like we're trapped by some tenuous thing that connects us.

We need to get away from noise, alcohol and stims. Time alone to work things out. Make it or break it. He reopens the map. Runs his finger along rambler's paths marked in broken lines.

'See, this track circles towards Necromantio, around Zagoria, and back. Through the Vikos Gorge, I've heard that's spectacular, 1300m deep.' He waits for a response. There is none. 'It'll be good. We need this. We owe each other.'

'Needing and owing are words about trust. Almost as though you can dignify what we have with the term relationship.'

'Sometimes it's like I don't even know what language you're speaking.'

'It's you that's free and easy with the truth. So, no point me arguing. You're going to get your way. You always get your own way.'

It seems she might be right.

Ashley the Rep says don't use the local bus, it runs on Greek time, but it takes them inland, above stunning views of sun-burnished coast, to dismount in the small village of Anthoussa where they refresh at the Mylos taverna. There's a renovated watermill adjacent to a stream that deluges down from the highlands above. The water gets diverted into a channeled gush, out onto the fins of the horizontal wheel, turning the adjustable stone grinding wheel. Niall points out a rack of old implements. Cordelia nods, without enthusiasm.

Above the church there's a steep track leading higher, between white houses draped in blossoms of bougainvillea fire, chickens strut in the shade, a goat watches them suspiciously, until they reach an arched stone packhorse bridge. The way steepens into a rough footpath wending between olive terraces. He talks trivia, or not at all. Points out how each terrace-wall is made up of individual dry-stones, each one selected and placed there by hand. She seems unimpressed. There are black nets draped like skirts from tree to tree, to catch the falling fruits. Olives are fruit, aren't they? She shrugs.

'I'm talking to you.'

'I know. I'm ignoring you.'

They're tracking alongside the same river course, losing it, then twisting back abruptly to its edge, until the path loses itself in a density of old trees and thorny-dry thickets. He squats down, scrutinizes the map. 'See, the original path continues up here. So I'm making an executive decision on it.'

'I'm officially out.' But she smiles grudgingly as he helps her down into the water, to use its rise as their pathway. It's shallow and ice-cold, its swirls and eddies barely to their knees. A shingle of small white pebbles squishing beneath their sopping sandals. It's oddly invigorating, as they begin climbing higher against the rapid current of freezing water.

'Against my better judgment' she laughs. Her laugh is magic. It's towards noon. As they get higher, pausing to look out over the vast terrain, it runs faster, drawing narrower towards a tight gap between towering cliffs. She hangs back warily, shaking her head, he takes her hand, guides her forward. It's surging chest-high now as they broach the narrowest point, glimpsing clear space beyond the torrent. Splashing through onto a narrow bow of shingle. Their toes pleasingly numb.

Niall slumps his pack onto a large white stone and sits beside it. Hauls the Vikos water out of the net-pocket on his pack, slurps from the neck and passes it across to Cordelia. She doesn't wipe it before gulping, water dripping her chin and onto her wet T-shirt. She finger-combs her hair as the sun dries their clothes pleasantly.

He watches her. Wondering if it's the right moment to speak. 'Y'know, that thing with Gloria was nothing. Just messing.'

'You don't need to explain. We have no claims on each other. We only just met.'

'I know that. I just want you to know.'

'So OK. I know. Can we talk about something else now?'

'It's so far from OK. But I want it to be.'

They follow the shingle incline beside the stream, which slows and broadens into an expansive wetland. He gazes around. They've emerged into a caldera, or ancient impact crater with high walls enclosing the oval valley. Wind soughs through the top leaves and scratches branches against the sky. The river continues as a fat silver artery bending away. But smaller streams also converge here, and springs well up out of cracks and crevices in the stony ground where fungus and moss grows, shimmering in reedy pools where frogs and turtles co-exist.

'Not exactly the end of the rainbow, is it? The river is right here on the map' says Niall, brandishing the evidence. 'But I can't tell how far we've come, or where exactly we are. If we follow it around we're bound to reconnect with the true trail.'

'Some kind of farm over there' she points, 'or maybe a village.'

They tramp and slither until the ground firms, her arms trailing through tall weeds. Clouds scud high, their shadows filling the valley with secret places, strange groves of gnarly trees where feral eyes glitter from concealment. A chirping trill and a sweep of swift wings, rustlings and furtive movements disturbing the undergrowth around them, as the air vibrates with expectancy.

They hit the graveyard first, laid out between two tall flame-high cypress sentinels. It's rough-hewn, unlike the elaborate tombs of other villages. Cordelia pauses. Each mounded plot is personalized by a framed photograph or—here, a corroded black box-camera. She picks it up carefully. It's maybe a 1950s model, the kind with a wind-on film cartridge. Whatever photos it contains are inaccessible. Its hidden visions long-lost. But there's something disturbing about its presence.

The church is derelict, with a smell of mould and stale urine. Its calm is the stillness of a baited trap. 'This is strange. The orthodox church is so strong here, a national identity thing. Remember the white-bearded priests in black we saw sitting outside the harbour taverna?'

It's as they emerge from the crooked church doors that they find Michael waiting for them.

He says 'Kalimera.' A skewed grin that makes you feel he knows something you don't, but which maybe you should know. Eyes that glint like spun coins in near bone-tight skin that denies wrinkles. Eyes that show no-one is at home. 'British?'

'Yeah. Not quite sure how we got here. Think we've fallen off the edge of the map.'

'Come, you are our guests, you drink with us' in remarkably good English. 'We're not used to visitors here.'

Stop. Two snarling dogs, little more than wolves, prowling in half-circles, hackles raised. Michael snaps something in Greek that sounds animal in itself, and they slouch down on their bellies. Watching resentfully with slit yellow eyes. Niall smiles, shifts the pack uneasily on his back. Suspicions lurk, but he's wary of tracking them down to their lair. Why not do as this Greek weirdo says? At best we need directions back to the main highway. The wolves prowl, cutting off escape.

The house is a solid white fossil embedded in ancient stone, overhung by trees. Easy to assume that this sad sprawl of a village…if it's even a village, is uninhabited. Easy to overlook this sole place of occupancy. A rusted half-truck pulled into the tree-shade, blinds over the windscreen. Clucking chickens flee behind wicker chairs in the shade beside the door. A goat looks up as they pass. Michael leads the way inside, stepping across the threshold.

After the outside glare it's pleasantly cool inside. The faint aroma of ash. Faded peasant photographs on the wall. A high amphora containing three agricultural scythes. Bundles of yellowed newspapers in indecipherable Greek text, tied with coarse twine. Hardback books. Their eyes adjust further, to make out two other tall rangy men. 'My brothers, Ginnis and Paulos.' They raise glasses in greeting.

Michael indicates chairs at the table by a grimy window. He sits opposite them, uncrosses his legs like the unwinding of a DNA-spiral, and leans across the table. 'Ah—you English, eh? I see you in the clubs. I see you in the bars. You get blind drunk. You like to drink, eh?'

Niall returns the stare, like it's a game, a challenge.

Paulos—or maybe it's Ginnis, slams a flask down hard on the table, three glasses speared on three fingers. 'Chimera breathes fire. We twice distil it in our own copper alembics here.' He pours three smooth bubble-bright shots of cloudy amberness.

Niall lifts it to his nose, smelling it critically. 'Raki, is it Raki? I drank Raki in Chania.'

The three brothers laugh. 'Drink.' They face each other around the table, Niall, Cordelia and Michael. He says 'Yamas'. They slam the glasses on the table, and gulp it back. The shock hits the back of his throat, takes his breath. He clams his eyes shut as his head explodes in spinning galaxies of colour…

It's black when Niall comes around. So night has drowned his sight in its darkness? Either that, or he's in a cellar. But no, it's warm. He can feel the shimmer of light falling on the back of his hand. He knuckles his eyes, swimming with visual echoes, an ice-water fear-wave rippling at him. Out of his mind with dread. Niall is blind…Wait, seek stability. A fixed point. An unwavering perception. Saturday. It's still Saturday. Is it still Saturday? How many Saturdays are there in a week? See no evil. See no evil. Hear the phantom tapping of white sticks. No, this is a temporary side-effect. A chemical reaction. It'll wear itself out.

He reaches this way, and that. Hears laughter. Hears snarling. He's backed up against a wall. In the yard? He braces himself against the warm stonework, and wriggles up. The two-lobed senseless brain-growth in his head jerks and twitches in a mad desire to burst out of his skull.

'Cordelia, are you there? Are you alright?'

'I can't see, Niall, I'm blind.'

He takes two wary steps towards her voice, arms held out like a sleepwalker. Abruptly, without warning, he's shoved violently sideways, stumbling. Loud laughter, dogs growling. Someone kicks his feet away, and he crashes down onto the grit. And a terrifying lunge of teeth as the dogs rip into him, attacking, snapping, jerking. And he's screaming, a terrified animal, shrieking at spectres.

Lying sobbing, bleeding from abrasions. 'Why are you doing this?' His voice is broken. 'What do you have to gain from doing this to us?'

'You donate your talents to our service. For our amusement.'

Hauled into a locked outhouse they huddle together in shared blindness. A hideous darkness, the world squashed by a vast black wing. He's holding her close. Pulses of pain rippling from an open wound on his leg, torn by the wolf-dog. Fingers exploring its extent warily, half in guesswork. Then pressing his hands to his eyes, pressuring so tight until bright sparks roar in glistening cascades, a psychedelic fantasia of jazzy fractal stars. Just to see ghosts of light above the neurotic movies his psyche's staging.

At first they'd assumed they were alone.

Then, 'What's your name?' A child's voice. A girl.

'I'm Niall. This is Cordelia. Who are you?'

A long silence, as though she's considering. 'Katina, of course. I'm Katina.'

'How old are you Katina?'

'I'm nine.'

'Do you live here, with Michael and his brothers?'

'They look after me' Katina says. 'Our Souli people once lived on the plains, beside the sea, until Ali Pasha's Turks came down from the north. We withdrew into the natural stronghold of the mountains. Here, where we are safe. Are the Turks still there? Would I be better off, or be safer outside the valley than in it?'

'How long have you been here, Katina?'

'I forget. Three hundred years, perhaps more.'

It's late, the frogs in the wetland are singing, and he's lying there in a blinded dark…every once in a while the frogs…stop. And there's complete silence for some minutes. He imagines that's when an owl flies over. The frogs have the instinct that all prey must have, to hush. He'd been prey. He and Cordelia. They were prey. He's not sure what he should say, much less what he should do.

The door wrenches open. It's morning? A sharp detonation spasms through him. A cattle prod. They're laughing at his agony, as he squirms away, cringes onto a feotal whimper, tensed for the next burst of pain. They're hustled out beyond the garden plot behind the house, and set to work clearing stones and dead tree-stumps. Pacing out the space, then digging the hard grit-soil. Uncertain, but likely they're under continual supervision. Otherwise, why can't they simply stand up and walk out? There's nothing physically keeping them here, other than blindness. All he needs is a few moments to orientate. First there's the church, beyond that there's the graveyard, the wetland, and the stream. Memorise that sequence, that path. Feel your way from one to the other. Church. Graves. Wetland. Stream.

He can sense Cordelia close. Sense the dogs circling. He licks at his lips, but his tongue is still dry. Columns of ants are crawling beneath the skin of his spine. Aching calluses on the palms of his hands. Heat-burn on his scalp. The wound on his leg is pulsing like aggravated heartbeat. No sense of passing time, the hours coming loose and drifting askew.

Then they're locked in the outhouse again. A silence in which bees drone and the breeze whispers private secrets. What if there are snakes in here? What if there are venomous bugs? He feels giddy, delirium shimmering at the edge of his awareness. Imagines canine poison coursing the blood-veins of his leg, radiating out from the wound. He drowses in a vivid cascade of multi-spectral dreams, as though his subconscious is attempting to compensate for sensory loss. And when he wakes, he waits, until the girl appears.

'This blindness, Katina, is it permanent? Do you understand me? Will it go away? Will we be able to see again?' He's not certain why he's asking her. She's a ghost who comes and goes as she pleases, and despite the locked door, she's never far away. She can see. There must be wriggle-space, a child-shaped gap big enough. Will she take any notice of what he's saying? No, probably not. But, he thought, I'm not asking her what I should do, only trying to get some information on which to base my own decisions. And she's not giving me the answers I want to hear.

'You eat it' she says at length.

'But they eat it too, Michael and his brothers.'

'They are different. They are not as we are.'

What? So it's…some kind of narcotic. A berry or fungus that grows here in the valley. Ground into resin, and administered, first in the Chimera, then on everything they eat. And they must eat. How long for the effect to wear off…twenty-four hours? Longer?

'So it's a race. We don't eat, until it wears off. But the longer we don't eat, the weaker we get.'

'They won't allow us not to eat. They'll know' says Cordelia. 'But we can do this…listen…did you ever read Robert Graves' 'I Claudius'?'

There's a startle of gunshots outside. They have some kind of antique muskets they use for shooting birds, or rabbits. A warning too. Niall thinks of the cemetery, the 1950s camera. The remains of previous 'guests' who'd outlasted their usefulness, who were no longer 'amusing'. How much longer before that happens to us?

A pattern of days, working in the yard, clearing stones and stumps. Difficult to tell the cycle of time. He thinks about forcing the glass off his wristwatch and tracing the hour-hand with his finger. But days have already been lost. More will be lost before this is resolved. Every day, Katina smuggles in a handful of fruit from the garden, olives, figs. Sometimes a lime. Cordelia eats them raw, gulping them down. Sometimes throwing them back up again. 'There was this Roman emperor. He has an evil wife, she's the bad guy. She wants her lover to be emperor, or perhaps it's her son. Or maybe her lover is her son, I forget. They were crazy in those old Roman days. But she poisons his food bit by bit until the toxicity builds up in his body. As he gets sicker, he starts to suspect what she's doing. So all he eats is olives plucked from his own tree in his own private garden.'

'Can you see yet?'

'No. Not yet. But I'm getting sense-impressions of light on my retina. Sun-shadows.'

'What happened to that old emperor guy?'

'You want to know? Maybe you don't want to know.'

'Tell me.'

'She found out. His wife spies on him and finds out what he's doing. So when he's not looking she goes out into his private garden and paints a layer of poison onto each olive on his tree. And it kills him…'

'But it'll work for us. It has to work for us. You will be my eyes. I will be your strength.'

Her fingers find him. Running reassuringly through his hair. Tracing the contours of his face like Braille. 'Yes. That's how it will be.' And she finds herself thinking yes, forever, me and you.

Slavery. Modern-day slavery, here in the European Union. How did it ever get to this? Her eyes burn. She rubs them until they water. As though there's a splinter of hard grit she can't wipe clear. It hurts. But there are shapes. The dark is less dark, and flecked with transitory points of light. Then black again, until a single white flame expands, flares, and drifts. Light without definition, pervading everything. Clarifying a little more.

She can make out the shadowy contours of Niall tossing in his sleep. In heat-delirium, or infection? Impossible to tell. His wound is too tender to investigate. When there's water, she attempts to wash it, but it's too painful, and she can't yet visually confirm the extent of its condition.

They must make their move soon, or the time will be lost. The opportunity gone. She's scared. She'd never been so scared in her life. At first she'd feared…rape, violation. But their captors have not touched her. To ask why seems crazy…but why? Isn't that the obvious motive for abduction and slavery? But there's something not quite right about Michael, and his brothers. Katina had said they're 'not as we are'? What did she mean by that? And how has she been in this hidden valley for three-hundred years? A slippage, a wrinkle slightly out of phase with normal time, where influences flow through and crystallize, a place not quite correctly aligned, a microsecond out of true, that's all it needs. Is that just kid's fancification—or something more?

Tomorrow. It must be tomorrow.

The cocoon of bloated pain in Niall's head is ripening, as if there's a dark thing inside sensing its deep primal need to break out. An insidious slug settling along the borders of consciousness, but restive, chafing at its restrictions, while feeding on his fear voraciously.

She's weak. But she can see reasonably well. She can see the morning settling around them. See the interior of the outhouse for the first time. The dirt and squalor, the dereliction. Piles of agricultural tools rusting beneath loose sacking. Sprockets and chains fused into trilobites. See Niall lying on his back. Shocked by how pale he's become, despite the raw sun. The fever-sweat beading his forehead. The congealed blood and yellow pus scabbing his leg. The faint stink of gangrene. He needs attention. Everything's narrowing down. It must be today. But it must be right. She waits.

Then the door rasps open. Michael. For the first time since their blindness she can actually see him. Taking in impressions, just like that initial encounter outside the ruined church. An indefinably disturbing oddness. Eyes that show no-one is at home. But don't look at him. Don't let him know you can see him. Stumble, as though you're still unseeing. Niall plays along. Acts more sick than he really is. Cordelia goes back, helps him up, shoulders his weight out into the blinding sun.

The half-truck is not there, not in its usual shadow-park beneath the tree. Good. That means Ginnis and Paulos, either or both, are out driving somewhere. But the wolf-dogs are circling.

She halts defiantly, Niall slumped up against her. 'His condition's too bad to work. You can't expect us…'

Michael turns. Don't look at him. Don't meet his eyes. Stay unfocussed. Wait.

'Inside' he gestures irritably, shoving them towards the house. Once inside, feeling her way, she helps Niall to one of the chairs by the grimy window. Props his wounded leg up on the facing chair. Then stands back. Michael glances from one to the other. She steels herself, deliberately not registering his attention as it crawls across her.

Michael crouches down to inspect the leg wound. Niall groans out loud as the grubby fingers touch the diseased flesh, Niall's hand reaching out, as if to defensively grasp the forearm.

There are three scythes in a tall amphora. Her fingers fold around the handle. Her breath burning in her throat. No. No. No. Can't do this. Can't, can't can't, don't make me. Yet she whips it around, crashes it into the back of Michael's head with sound of shlocking into overripe melon-flesh. He pitches forward. Simultaneously, Niall is on him, hands clawing around his head garotte-tight. Michael sprawls down onto the floor, twists around, bucking and kicking his way up. Niall is heavy on his chest, fingers tightening into his eye-sockets, puncturing in sudden spurts of fluid. An animal screeching. She smashes the blade down again, and again in a welter of blood and brain-matter.

Frozen in terror, she watches what Niall is incapable of seeing. Michael's jaws gaping wide rimmed with shattered teeth, the flexing mouth opening wider, his head splitting open, falling apart in roseate blood-pulses, livid with crimson gashes. A hideous gurgling of bubbling mucous, gloopy ichor. And something spiderish crawling out of the mess of ruined skull. A foul thing of whipping tentacles and long strands sunk deep into the severed brain-stem, wriggling like slender snakes. She's screaming in sick waves of nausea.

Niall yells 'what? what? what?' His hands are claws, dripping blood.

The hissing sizzling thing—whatever it is, launches at Niall's unseeing head. Seeking a new host.

At the same moment, the door slams open. Ginnis and Paulos are black against the sudden slab of sky. Two snarling slavering wolf-dogs at their heels. She backs away, retching, weak with shock. The brother's outraged yell is a sound more beast than human. Her terror vortexes, cringing away as the world spasms deeper into madness.

Paulos takes one step inside, an unpleasant undulating gait. A sharp detonation, and his head explodes in an abrupt smash of impact. Even as he falls over the threshold, Ginnis spins. A second detonation and his head splatters in a spray of gore. Collapsing inwards. For less than a second, the two dogs hesitate, then lope forward to begin feeding, ripping and tearing at their former master's raw meat. As two more vile abominations stilt from the decapitated neck-stumps on barbed tendrils, gills pulsing in unaccustomed air, Niall disappearing beneath the tentacular web of their slithering obscenity.

Cordelia breaks in a storm of madness. Striding across the writhing shattered slaughter, desperate to escape the stench of putrefying fish.

Katina is nursing the smoking double-barrel shotgun, her legs planted firmly apart to absorb recoil. A little girl in a white dress. 'You are correct Cordelia. This has gone on far too long. Time to end it.' Her three-hundred-year-old child's eyes are steady and unflinching. Breaking the gun, she slides two new cartridges into the breach.

Cordelia glances back, afraid to look. 'But Niall…oh god, Niall.'

'Go, now. I will do what must be done.' Katina takes a determined step towards the house's open door.

The half-truck is where they'd left it. They keys still flesh-warm in the dash. The engine misfires, then ignites in a grating thrum. She hits the accelerator, picks up rattling protesting speed, circles the yard, smashes through the cemetery leaving a wake of ribcage and spinning skulls, and doesn't stop until the wheels sink into the wetland and refuse to move. The engine coughing and spluttering into silence.

From there she staggers across the stony strand screaming Niall's name at the sky…

* * * *

Terrified to close my eyes. Frightened of the darkness. Each moment of new blindness.

First met Niall at Stefano's Bar, up that steep old-town climb from the harbour. Nothing special, but he seemed nice. But after that thing with Gloria I was close to moving on. No-one's worth that messing. Tell me my feelings don't make sense, then tell me again, what does make sense? He found that old map in the shop. We were forced into working together. Enabling my escape. Tell me that day down from the valley lasted less than a year and I'll call you liar. Now, he's all I can think of.

His hotel room has new occupants. No record of him booking out or removing his suitcases. Ashley, the holiday rep just smiles. No, he can't give details, that would be most unprofessional. Some of his clients are married, here to party. And hey, what happens in Greece stays in Greece. The Elliniki Astynomia are evasive. First they claim not to understand. Then there's a dark-haired uniformed girl who speaks good English, listens attentively, then makes some enquiries. The fan whirrs. The blinds are down to exclude full daylight glare. A fat black fly walks in circles on the desktop. When she eventually returns she carefully explains that such a hidden valley as I describe does not exist. There's no such location. Perhaps I'm mistaken? Perhaps I have more details or references?

Sitting in a café beside the harbour awaiting my departure time, every figure carries a secret threat. I want to rest. I'm ready for the other side of angst. But I'm terrified to close my eyes. Frightened of the darkness.

The Thirteenth Step
by William Tea

There were twelve steps between the first and second floor. No more, no less.

He knew this because she knew this.

One. Two. Three.

It was late when Jacob arrived. All the houses looked smaller now, except one. His childhood home still loomed large—even larger here than in his memories—its smoke-colored silhouette stabbing into the bruised, sleeping sky.

Wasn't everything supposed to seem bigger when you were a kid and smaller as an adult? Children grew, not houses. Why, then, did his hand hesitate upon reaching for the cold, cut-glass doorknob? The harsh angles and half-dozen tiny corners left angry red indentations along his life-line.

He knocked on the door but received no answer. Mom was probably in bed already. And Dad…

Four. Five. Six.

Jacob was overseas when it happened, teaching art history in Poland. He didn't get the news until it was too late. By the time he was back on U.S. soil, he'd missed the funeral. Shamefully, the first thing that passed through his head upon hearing that was relief. Relief that he might avoid going home entirely. Relief that was crushed when he heard his mother's voice over the phone, and the guilt became a tapeworm in the stomach of his soul.

"Come home, baby," she pleaded between ragged sobs. "Please. I can't do this alone."

The key to the front door felt heavy in his hand. He was shocked at how smoothly it slid into the lock. How silently. He'd long ago forgotten the thing served any function at all. Forgotten that it wasn't just another keychain, like all those tiny pewter flag pendants commemorating the countries he'd visited over the years: Turkey, Serbia, South Africa, Iraq. He'd spent a lifetime putting as much distance between this place and himself as he could, but nowhere was ever far enough for comfort.

Seven. Eight. Nine.

The foyer was dark when he entered. Murky shapes lurked in the gloom, jungle predators stalking prey from cover. He called out, but again got no reply. The shadows tackled his voice. Tore it open. Fed it to their young.

Closing the door behind him, he swept his hand across the wall in search of a switch. White stucco scratched the surface of his palm. At once, he remembered the way his mother used to click the lights on and off, on and off, on and off, three times whenever she entered or exited a room. He let his hand fall to his side then. At least the dark was quiet.

Maybe he could leave and come back in the morning. But what if he couldn't? How would he muster the will to drag himself across the threshold a second time? He hardly believed he'd managed it this time. So, instead of turning back, he plodded through the darkness pitifully, arms waving in front of him until he found the banister. A sound came from up above, something like shuffling.

Maybe she was still awake.

Ten. Eleven. Twelve.

It was only as he reached the top of the staircase that he realized he'd been counting each step, just like she always had. He suddenly felt dizzy, as if he'd scaled a mountain instead of some stairs. The air up here was thin.

He started to drag his feet in the direction of his parents' bedroom—not *their* bedroom he corrected himself, now it was just *hers*—but his toes caught on something. He tripped and fell face-first into the rough, wooly carpet. His eyes adjusted to the darkness, transforming amorphous ink blots into vague gray ghosts. He looked at what he'd stumbled over and saw that it was the top step.

A *thirteenth step.*

A step that shouldn't exist.

* * * *

There were twelve steps between the first and second floor. No more, no less.

He knew this because she knew this.

Just like he knew that there were forty-four yellow ceramic tiles checkboarding the walls of the upstairs bathroom, and forty-two cream-colored ones.

Mom counted everything in the house. It was part of her rituals. Every single day he heard her coming down the stairs, one step at a time. If he needed to use the toilet, he had to make sure to get in there before she did, otherwise he'd have to wait until she counted every last damn tile and washed her hands at least three times.

The house was filled with her sounds. Faucets turning on and off. Light switches snapping up and down. Doors closing and opening and closing again. Plus, all that damn counting. It was like living inside a giant telegraph, the voice of the house an endless plaintive cry in Morse code: S.O.S.

Of course, he didn't know S.O.S. back then. He didn't even know what O.C.D. meant at the time. He just knew those letters meant something bad. Sometimes, he'd write them down in the margins of his notebook, puzzling over them. For a while, he thought they actually spelled something, thought his parents were doing that thing grown-ups do where they speak only in letters instead of saying certain words, like S-E-X or B-I-T-C-H.

O-C-D. When he tried to sound it out, it never sounded right.

The rest of his notebook was filled with drawings of superheroes. Sometimes he imagined he was one of them, that he could rescue his mother from the bad guys and that she would love him in return. Other times he imagined the superheroes were coming to rescue him, taking him into their arms and flying away. Far, far away.

Mom's bad guys weren't so easily fought. They lived inside her head.

Dad tried to help. Kept everything spotless because she needed things to be clean. If they weren't, she'd spend hours washing and wiping and vacuuming and mopping and dusting and scratching and scraping.

Once, Jacob spilled a can of Coke on the living room carpet while watching Power Rangers after school. Dad wasn't home. When Jacob's mother saw what he'd done, she screamed as if it was blood pooling out on the powder-blue shag instead of soda, smacked him up and down and sent him crawling to his room. She apologized later, though he couldn't help but notice that her eyes never stayed on him for long. They were always scanning her surroundings, looking for something to clean or count.

One time, he tried to help. Tried to help her count the bathroom tiles so she could get done faster. But she just stood there, shaking her head with her hands on either side of her face, howling. Dad took Jacob away by the hand, kneeled down so they were face-to-face, and explained that Mom had to do her counting by herself, that all Jacob was doing was interrupting her, confusing her, making her start all over again.

Years later, even doing basic algebra in high school made his skin crawl.

* * * *

Thirteen steps?

No. He'd just miscounted. He shouldn't have been counting in the first place. Hated that he had been.

His hand shot out in search of a light switch again, this time found one, flicked it on. To him, the barely audible click sounded like a cannon. It rocked his head harder than his mother had after she'd seen that puddle of brown fizz pouring out onto her pristine carpet.

He rushed down the stairs, taking two at a time, not at all worried about slipping, more worried he already had. He lost count in his scramble.

When he hit the bottom, he turned and climbed again, slowly this time, focusing on each individual number.

One. Two. Three.

The light stung his eyes.

Four. Five. Six.

His temple throbbed.

Seven. Eight. Nine.

Drops of sweat formed on his brow.

Ten. Eleven. Twelve.

He held his breath.

Thirteen.

That breath flew out of him as if someone had dropped a sandbag on his gut.

Then…

Fourteen.

He turned and tried to soothe the nasty tremors spreading through his body. He looked back down the staircase. There were more than twelve steps there. More than just thirteen or fourteen too.

The staircase plummeted downward forever. He couldn't even see the bottom anymore.

Jacob stumbled back, fell hard against the wall, banged his wrist against a doorknob that wasn't supposed to be there. The air felt thinner than ever. He had to take big, gulping breaths to keep from suffocating on nothingness. His head spun like a bicycle tire. He called out for his mother. Not just "mom," but "mommy…mommy…mommy…"

He glued his back to the wall as if he were dangling off the edge of the cliff, and began to inch his way into the mouth of the second floor hallway.

When he came to the place where Mom's bedroom door should be, there was a corner instead.

He turned it, and found himself looking down a long, door-lined corridor that he'd never seen before. He shook his head and scrambled back the way he came, but that path no longer led to the stairway. Instead, he ran down another corridor, and when that twisted and split into still more corridors he ran down those too. He ran faster and faster, trying to evade the panic that was chasing him. He could feel its jagged fangs snapping at his heels.

He went one way until it seemed like the hallway would never end, then he doubled back and went down a different one. He ran past doors to rooms that should not be, but they were all locked. He never once saw a window, for if he had he would've gladly gone through it.

He did, however, pass several framed pictures he didn't recognize, sunny snapshots of him as a child with Mom and Dad, posing in the middle of family trips they'd never taken. There had been no vacations in Jacob's childhood. His mother could never be away from the house for too long.

And yet…

The first pictures he stopped to look at showed him at the Jersey Shore, Mount Rushmore, and The Philadelphia Museum of Art. Every shot was filled with happy faces.

It wasn't just Jacob and his parents who were smiling. Even bystanders in the background were smiling. And the faces in the portraits at the museum. The great stone heads of long-dead presidents.

Other pictures placed Jacob's family in stranger places. The middle of a junkyard. Outside of an insane asylum. In the bowels of a hospital morgue.

In that last one, he and his mother were posed in front of a metal table with a sink at one end. A fresh cadaver with an open chest lay there, organs the color of spoiled meat. The face on the corpse was that of Jacob's father. And, yes, it was smiling.

After that, he tried not to pay attention to the pictures on the walls. Even still, he couldn't help but notice the color red showing up in them more and more.

* * * *

Jacob had almost forgotten what his mother's voice sounded like when she called him. In all the years since he'd been gone, he didn't remember ever talking to her on the phone. Always Dad.

When he picked up, her voice was strained from crying. She too had missed the funeral. She'd wanted to go, but she hadn't left the house in years and now she was afraid.

For a moment, Jacob forgot about the time he'd spilled Coke, about the time he'd tried to help her count, about all the noises she'd made and the pressure she'd put on him to keep things spotless. Instead, he remembered the times when she would sit on the couch and watch Power Rangers with him, or when he would bring her those bunches of notebook paper stapled together and covered in scribbles that he called his "comic books." She'd always treated them like they were Escher originals.

As the phone line crackled and hissed, she asked him if he could please come see her.

Then she told him about how the house was growing.

Twelve steps on the staircase. Forty-four yellow tiles in the bathroom. Forty-two cream-colored ones. He knew this because she knew this. But now she knew different. And Jacob? He didn't know anything anymore.

She was scared. She said the staircase had grown a new step just that morning, that she counted three more tiles on the bathroom wall that afternoon. It seemed that the tightly wound tangle of knots that was her mind had, at last, come undone.

He drove across three states with a nuclear reactor of nausea radiating sickness in his throat. Dad had always assured him that was Mom was getting better, and Jacob had taken that as a sign that he'd been right to not come home, that she was better off without him.

But now she sounded worse than ever. Maybe losing Dad had pushed her over the edge. Or maybe Dad had been lying the whole time. Maybe that was the *real* reason he'd never asked Jacob to come visit.

The word "agoraphobia" flashed inside Jacob's head like a neon bar sign. Then "dementia." Then a whole new image: a vision of himself, in that house, playing the role of nurse to his mother, the role his father had filled for so many years.

The rhythms of the Morse code were deafening.

...

No.

No, there were places. Places that she could go if she couldn't take care of herself anymore. She wouldn't want to leave that house, but she would.

She had to.

* * * *

One hallway emptied into an intersection of four others. Jacob spun in circles, not sure of where to turn. God, he couldn't run anymore. His side ached and his lungs burned. It felt like he'd been running for miles. Like he'd been wandering the snaking corridors for hours.

The crisscrossed paths formed a small room, like a heart at the center of branching arteries.

The walls seemed to bend, pushing in and out at regular intervals. One minute the halls were so tight he thought they would crush him, the next they were so wide he almost fell over trying to find somewhere to prop his tired bulk. The house was breathing. Now, Jacob was the tapeworm twisting through a body.

He fell to his knees, shaking his head with his hands on either side of his face. He could hear little more than the animal whimpers in his own throat. That, and the shuffling. At first, he'd thought it was his mother moving somewhere in the house. Now there was a part of him that thought it was the house's own voice, its Morse code patterns congealing into something new, something alive.

It was getting louder, and sounded less like shuffling. It sounded wetter.

Jacob just sat there trying to block it out, but it kept getting louder, as if pushing him to keep moving. It got so loud he couldn't even his hear his own voice when he started chanting again, his echoing chorus of "mommy…mommy…mommy…" swallowed by a darker song.

When it got so loud it hurt his ears, he leapt to his feet and unleashed a scream from the center of his chest that shredded his throat and burned his cheeks. But he couldn't even hear that over the awful din. He battered his fists against the walls until his knuckles split and spilt blood. He smashed framed photos of faces that no longer looked human but were still, somehow, smiling. He tried to kick down doors that refused to budge, that sent shockwaves up his leg strong enough to nearly topple him over.

Except…

Except one door finally did budge. More than that, splinters of wood exploded from the wall as it flew open.

The noise stopped. Jacob's own body went slack, drained of energy. He stood there for a long time, mind blank. His brain had short-circuited and abandoned him completely. Little more than a wind-up automaton now, Jacob stepped through the door. An inch of water drowned the floor. Something red swirled in the creeping pool as it soaked through his shoes and tickled his toes.

"Welcome home, son," came a familiar voice.

Yellow and cream tiles stretched across eternity.

This Godless Apprenticeship
by Clint Smith

Unusual, this night errand. Not the activity itself, as Quartermaster Ware and his subordinate crewmen had grown accustomed to all manner of thefts and raids under the cover of darkness, but rather the ambiguity of the captain's requisition. *No matter.* Notwithstanding the nature of Captain Lacewage's charge, Thomas Ware moved with particular efficiency this night, recalling occasions when the captain had responded to laxness and hesitation with not a glimmer of equanimity.

Pacing over the wave-eaten beach, Ware watched as the horse-drawn carriage made its way out of the winding path from the forest-covered hills, the lanterns on either side of the driver's box swaying as the vehicle rolled along the rocky shoreline.

Some hours earlier, he'd received a hasty set of instructions from his captain—the older man acting particularly solemn and, Ware might venture, insecure. Now Ware looked over his shoulder, back at the *Gaggler Coach* anchored in the distance, the brigantine's wide square-rigs, its fore-and-aft sails, silhouetted and steady, a few amber lights flickering in the windows along the gallery. Behind a shredded quilt of clouds, moonlight intermittently shifted to touch the ocean's inky surface.

Out of sight, though needling the night with their occasional calls, were the gulls, whose shrill squawks, to Ware, echoed in a way that reminded him of the overlapping entreaties of a child. He shivered—*Filthy fowl*—and resumed the vigilance requisite to black tasks.

During these past six years, Thomas Ware—as part of this godless apprenticeship—had witnessed barbaric acts of punishment exacted with a knowing flourish by Captain John Lacewage; and now as the ship's quartermaster, he, Ware, had been ordered to furnish a brand of discipline, devoid of tangible compunction, which clearly suited his captain.

So, when Captain Lacewage had, the previous morning, surprised quartermaster Ware by explaining that they would be detouring south and west before proceeding to their original destination of Ocracoke Island, the sailor accepted the news of this uncharacteristically oblique agenda. On this stretch of night-shrouded Atlantic coast, Ware now stood waiting for the coach and its unexplained cargo; and though unfamiliar with this particular segment of the Carolina Province, Ware wagered they were somewhere south of Charleston.

As the carriage neared, Ware ordered the half-dozen crewmen to close in, raising their torches in a semi-circle. Ware noted a figure, his face hidden within a hood, accompanying the driver. As expected, moonlight touched the metal barrel of some weapon—a musket or blunderbuss, no doubt. The driver, dressed in black and wearing a tricorn, slowed near the boundary where solid ground gave way to uncertain slopes of sand. Ware gave no greeting, rather allowing this unknown party to play the first hand.

The carriage rattled to a stop, and now Ware indicated that the crew should go silent. Ware swept strands of hair from his brow, while his other hand casually unsheathed his cutlass.

For a time, it was simply the hiss of the tide and the breeze causing a lazy commotion in the trees. Then the driver of the carriage said, "You are Lacewage's man, then?"

"Aye," said Ware.

There was a murmured exchange between the driver and the musket-man; but then another voice emerged, this from the interior of the carriage. In a language Ware did not recognize, the driver produced what sounded like an affirmation before dropping down from the driver's box, eyeing the band of men before making his way to the carriage's riding compartment; he then assisted a shroud-covered form that, to Ware's immediate assumption, was that of a haggard, elderly woman—his suspicion confirmed when she spoke: "Ware is your name, is it—the quartermaster?" This was Ware's sixth year at sea with Captain Lacewage, only his second year as quartermaster; the title's mere mention still gave him a mellow swell of pride.

The driver continued to assist the cane-hobbling woman. Nearer now, the torches' firelight caught her pale features: the gray, wrinkle-pinched face of a crone, the sight appeared to make a few of the more superstitious men waver in place. Indeed, Ware did have in mind the face of a possum within the folds of that cloak. He murmured a curse at them to stand steady, then raised his voice in response, "Your arrangement is with our captain," he made a gesture toward a pair of men lingering on the fringes of flickering light, the duo fetching a black chest from one of the longboats. "And as our crew generally refrains from conducting business in the dead hours on these inhospitable shores, we'd like to make haste to fulfill our captain's request."

The old woman gurgled a laugh, the sound akin to a chuckle smothered by seaweed. "In a hurry, are ye?" Her small eyes twinkled in the meager light. She appraised Ware. "Your Captain Lacewage has shared the particulars of our accord?"

Lacewage was a brutal though not unfair captain. Ware had never spoken to the man directly about his past, though he had placed slivers and shards of conversation together to create a frame for the man's ruthless genesis. Some of the other crewmen had told tales as well, some murky while others were barbed with outrageous embellishments; all together, the rivulets converged to create a channel which did indeed fit the persona of the *Gaggler Coach's* leader.

He gathered that Lacewage had received the majority of his apprenticeship as a common sailor aboard the ship *Virtue*, under the unceremonious tutelage of one Captain Macrae.

Macrae and his crew—including Macrae's first-mate, a young Johnathan Lacewage—had shifted their focus from raiding shipping vessels in the Caribbean and Eastern Pacific and began to exact their predatory endeavors—as many had of their trade—on the East India Trading Company in the Red Sea.

Among Ware and his brethren there existed uncountable tales of mayhem and various pirate proclivities: the cruelty with which they engaged the captured. There was one famous incident that crews related of that lauded rogue Captain Dirk Chivers, who captured a pair of East Indiamen in the Red Seas back around 1695. Albeit Chivers—who was raiding the same waters at the time—simply appropriated the story for himself.

What followed was a viciously humorous encounter, involving Macrae and the captain of one of the British vessels, Captain Sawbridge. Unusually, the captured captain was rather defiant, verbally abusing the crew as Macrae coordinated both the allotment of the prizes and the fate of the East Indiamen sailors. Despite Macrae's patience, Sawbridge's reproaches only set the crew of the Virtue to cackling, but soon began to wear on the captain.

It goes that Macrae halted deliberation of the Royal-bounty's division and set his sights on Sawbridge, striding toward the man and withdrawing his pistol. It was at that moment that Macrae's first-mate, a seasoned Johnathan Lacewage—who had been, heretofore, a rather taciturn sort—intervened.

Perhaps impressed by the boldness of the request—and certainly delighted by the prospect of malicious ingenuity—Captain Macrae laughed heartily at Lacewage, tentatively allowing his first-mate to make his precocious suggestion.

Lacewage had momentarily disappeared into the forecastle, returning and approaching the restrained Sawbridge. Lacewage—no doubt drunk with audacity—explained that he had grown weary of the East Indiaman's captain's aspersions in the face of a dignified transition. Lacewage then produced a long, rusty sail needle, and as he further mused on the captured captain's excessive insolence, began threading its eye with a ragged length of hemp.

At this point, Macrae—rather than administering some demonstrative violence to punish young Lacewage—only guffawed, his brown teeth showing in the oppressive sunlight; he barked an order for several of his officers to hold fast the good captain Sawbridge, giving a nod for Lacewage to proceed.

Lacewage took his time sewing the captain's lips shut. The gruesome task complete, Captain Macrae ordered that the mewling man, along with a pair of his sailors, be tossed in a jolly boat and set to shore. It was Lacewage who tumbled the bug-eyed and bloodied man into the small boat—his face slicked crimson from the weeping punctures, the crooked-zigzag laces straining over his taut lips as he attempted to scream. Sawbridge would not survive his injuries.

Not long after, with the task of dividing up and allotting plunder, Captain Macrae ordered his quartermaster to act as steward of one of the captured East Indiaman prizes, finding in Lacewage a suitable replacement as quartermaster on the *Virtue*. And though the tale would be contorted and distorted over the course of time, Ware had witnessed similar imaginative acts of cruelty from Captain Lacewage aboard the *Gaggler Coach*.

Here now, standing on the beach, he recalled, if only for a moment, that traded tale of Lacewage sewing shut the lips of that impudent merchantman. As trustee for the ship's company, Ware's tasks included the administering and selecting the division of loot, but also meting-out the occasional punishment, which made him a respected though quietly reviled figure. He quickly pondered the witch's question: *Your Captain Lacewage has shared the particulars of our accord?*

In this instance, the captain had not, though that did not necessarily elicit distrust for his mentor.

Ware returned his cutlass to its sheath and placed his fists on his hips. "The only *particular* of any gravity is that we return in a timely fashion with the desired contents of this exchange."

The old woman's smile showed black apertures where teeth should be, "As you say…as you say." Her hunched form wrenched around, grunting a command in that discordant tongue; her two associates then began removing a tarp from atop the carriage, revealing cargo of several large crates.

Ware ordered his men to lower the black chest to the sand.

The old witch, knob-knuckled hands resting on her cane, appeared pleased. With several hunching shifts, the old woman lurched closer to Ware, who stood his ground though swallowed sharply. From the ragged layers of her cloak she produced a leather-bound volume (her movements causing Ware to tighten his grip on the handle of his sword). She extended the book to Ware. "For your Captain Lacewage." Ware alternated his gaze from the ancient-looking woman to the ancient-looking book for a span of time before accepting the device. It was very light, and contained perhaps a few dozen uneven sheets of parchment, as though someone had ripped all but a pair of chapters from a Bible and left the rest to be rain damaged, dried by a damning sun. She said, "If you want this over with quick your men could lend a bloody hand."

Ware inhaled, readying an acidic retort. Instead, he clenched his teeth and pursed his lips, waving at the men to assist with the removal of the large crates.

* * * *

Days later, the *Gaggler Coach* was steering toward a safe parcel near New Providence, what Ware was still getting used to calling Nassau.

They arrived in early afternoon, the skies clear and the crew rowdy with the prospect, though risky, of a night at port. The captain had been hole-up in his cabin for the majority of the trek from South Carolina to Nassau, only giving a cursory inspection of the crates before retiring to his quarters.

Ware had disliked the transaction from several nights before; he'd known next to nothing about why Captain Lacewage was so keen on withholding the details. Though admirably cold-blooded, Lacewage was a resilient captain to his crew—perhaps even a good man in another life—and Ware had never known the older man to allow a stray end to go untethered, particularly if it forsook his crew.

He would say nothing of his disapproval, of course, as Ware valued his own breathe and the salvation of his skin. With the crew removed, the captain approached his quartermaster on deck. "Insure their leave does not exceed more than the coming night," said Lacewage as he limped toward Ware.

"Aye, captain. The men are well aware."

Lacewage made his way toward the burlap-covered crates—the "witch's caskets" as the crew had come to call them.

The afternoon sunlight was brilliant, the humid breeze rippling the sails. Ware too felt a ripple of boldness as he said, "Captain? If you don't mind me asking about this recent chore?"

Lacewage said nothing but continued moving his calloused hands over the crates' exteriors. Eventually he turned, squinting against the sun. "Came to port for a repair." Before Ware could submit further query, the captain said, "We'll be replacing the anchor then, its shackles as well."

As though on cue, Ware noticed a band of men approaching on the dock. They rolled with them several wooden wheelbarrows. The apparent leader, a more distinguished-looking fellow of some modest trade—a blacksmith, Ware wagered—called out to Lacewage. The men boarded with no hesitation, going to work dismantling the crates and attendant contents. While Lacewage made even the transaction, Ware looked on as the men silently unpacked the goods from the "caskets." Ware's expression quirked as he watched what appeared to be pieces of domiciliary commonality—domestic metals of cookware, tools, silver picture frames, bronze sconces, candelabras, a variety of bronze heirlooms—unloaded and packed into the wheelbarrows.

A few yards away, Lacewage, looming over the tradesman, had gone from placid to possessing a composed ferocity. Ware caught only notes about a "deadline," that the task must be completed by the next day.

Time ticked by. Eventually some agreement had been settled and Ware watched the men withdraw, steering their carts and its mounds of metal back toward the town.

Ware expected Lacewage to return to the solitude of his cabin. Instead, the captain edged up next to his quartermaster, the two men looking out over the aqua vista. "It will be two days, this with the blacksmith," said the captain, unexpectedly adding, "a man of standards, I suppose." Ware thought he caught a note of resignation as opposed to contempt in this announced compromise. Askance, he eyed his captain.

He wondered if his master and mentor were losing some of that legendary savageness. Not for the first time, he tried to envision himself at this man's age, having seen what this man had seen.

What Thomas Ware could not envision was going back: not to the colonies themselves and his previously estimable reputation, but rather what he'd left behind more than a decade before. *That* return would be too much to bear. The ocean, unceasingly folding over itself, offered, for Ware, the attraction of not treasure—as was the case with many of his hit-and-run brethren—but rather liberty in the form of abandonment. Yet, no matter how Ware turned that notion over in his mind, no matter how the light and shadow of his conscious touched on the thought, it was not quite that simple, now was it?

No doubt she would have carried on years ago, he surmised. *Certainly she has remarried*, he often mused, *made a happily life for herself. Perhaps she now has a small one of her own—both mother and child healthy, happy, innocent.* But it was the opposing poles of hope and despair that had discouraged Ware the most: on one hand, he was cradling his daughter, comprehending and protecting a future for not only himself but his new family, while on the other hand, not a few months later, he was cradling her cold corpse as the physician imparted the news that nothing could be done. Fever, as it happened. *Quite common*, was the witless sentiment of those attempting to comfort Ware and his wife.

Ware was inconsolable, unable to recover from those extremities of overwhelming love and irrevocable loss. The experience had blackened him to the marrow; he swore he'd never be afflicted by or endure such arbitrary maliciousness furnished by this life—this business of humanity… the crooked racket of the righteous.

To his benefit, in his ensuing exodus, Ware exploited his threefold skills and capabilities to ascend to the status of quartermaster: he was, more than anything, a competent sailor and seaman, which thus lent itself to the profile of a privateer—an enterprise which earned his "Letter of Marque" from the sovereign state; but the wanton treaties of those fickle governments designated some men "privateers" one day while christening them "pirates" the next.

As opposed to the incessantly pleading entreaties to his dandy, whimsy-swayed administrators, Ware embraced his newfound outlaw assignation with robust defiance.

Ware's ambitious need to impress his captain with maintaining codified order aboard the *Gaggler Coach* this half-dozen years was made vividly distinct twenty-two months earlier: it had begun as a simple, oath-trading argument (over what, even Ware could not recall—likely a quarrel over an allotted amount of rum, though he did not allow the men to drink on deck), but soon escalated to an outright fight, a vicious one at that. Snelgrave and Burgess, it was.

Before Ware could break through the crew to separate the two, one of the men, Snelgrave, had clutched hold of a boarding axe and in a slashing arc brought the tool down across the other's collarbone, where it remained buried until Burgess, in no small amount of pain, bled out. A messy afternoon ensued on the *Gaggler Coach*—both literally and metaphorically. When it was clear that Burgess would not recover from his injury, it too was clear that Snelgrave's punishment should be swift. With Captain Lacewage acting as judge and Quartermaster Ware acting as mediator, a trial of sorts took place on deck.

Though Snelgrave's claims varied, with some even accusing Burgess of having had invoked mutiny, in the end the code prevailed: the consequence of killing a fellow crewman meant death, and the quartermaster was the only one who could administer such punishment under the code. It was clear that some of the men held a touch of sympathy for the doomed Snelgrave; but the shrewd quartermaster knew better—he was aware of the brewing feud between the two sailors, and of the failed attempts to trap Burgess in a snare. Drunk, Snelgrave had simply lost his head in desperation.

Ware was also aware that the ship's company expected the death to be a humane bullet to the skull. Casting an appraising eye over the men, and then back at his captain, Ware stepped toward Snelgrave, whose hands had been ordered bound by thick rope and tied to the mainmast.

Ware's voice carried across the deck: "*Remove that rope.*"

Men set about doing so, and a twitchy expression crossed Snelgrave's face. Perhaps the man believed that Ware would spare him a bullet in exchange for lashes to the back. "Thank you, sir—I ask for mercy, Mister Ware, mercy," stammered Snelgrave.

Ware could see, when a familiar smugness crossed Snelgrave's features, that this hope of mercy had been instantly contrived within the man.

And at that moment, Ware ordered that Burgess's corpse be fetched from below deck and brought topside.

With the blood-sodden body now between Ware and Snelgrave, Ware ordered that the rope should be reapplied, though this time employed to tie the men together, and knowing what would follow, Snelgrave began to struggle in the officers' arms.

Snelgrave screamed while Burgess's corpse was bound and knotted against him. Ware silenced the man, and the growing murmurs of several crewmen, with a roaring testimony: that Snelgrave had, in fact, been conspiring against his shipmate these many months. Then, quite simply, Ware ordered that Snelgrave—his eyes as wide and bulging as a scad—and his lifeless, gore-slicked comrade be flung overboard. Ware did not dignify the scene by laying on eyes it himself, but it was easy to imagine the conniving waste of space swiftly being pulled below the waves by the weight of his carrion companion.

That had been nearly two years ago. Now, standing next to his captain, together looking out over a horizon, the blue of which nearly fused with the sky, Ware cleared his throat. It was brash, but Ware said, "'Witch's caskets,' are what the men were calling those crates."

Lacewage snorted, a sound of half disgust, half bitter amusement. "I'm well aware of what they say." The ship creaked, gently teetering as a wave thrust against her. "And I suppose they be caskets at that."

* * * *

Over a week passed. They were now sailing northwest, back toward the coast of the Carolinas, what with Lacewage apparently satisfied with installation of the ship's new anchor—an ugly device, to Ware's eye: a wretched arrangement with its deformed flukes, irregular rigging, and asymmetrical arms. He'd not possessed the wherewithal to ask what was wrong with the old one. No matter—the *Gaggler Coach* set its sights on a prize-route along the coast, and the crew had been promised a predatory plunder the following day.

Evening had come on fast, and with the day's tasks complete, Ware paced the deck. The sky was streaked with peach, blending to purple as it faded toward some malignant storm out west.

A small commotion arose near the forecastle, and Ware was perplexed to see both Lieutenant Greeley and the sailing master, Dowling, arguing with Captain Lacewage.

Ware approached, cutting in just as Lacewage, holding a crumpled parchment, growled, "Set the bloody course, Mister Dowling, or I'll see you keelhauled before this twilight is out."

The lieutenant said, "But there's nothing there, Captain." The man opened his mouth to add something, but both Ware and the first mate stifled him, dispersing the officers and the few eavesdropping sailors.

Hours passed and light drained from the horizon. A brilliant moon climbed high—the lens of some bone-dust telescope—unhidden by clouds. Lamps and were lighted, causing misshapen shadows to shift and alter in the tea-tinted glow.

Ware, with most of the men below deck, crept up to find his captain. Lacewage, a solitary visage, was standing by the quarterdeck near the railing, the glow from a nearby lantern touching him with a frail hue; as Ware mounted the stairs, he saw that the man's head hung low and his upper carriage slouched in a way which implied one in mid-prayer (though Ware immediately dismissed this ridiculous possibility); yet, as Ware drew nearer the older man, he heard the low sibilance of words—a discordant canticle. When a pause in the verse occurred, Ware found his voice. "Why have we altered course so late, captain?"

For quite some time the man did not reply, but rather continued with his whispered hymn; and now Ware, craning his neck a bit, saw that the captain was clutching a book near the lantern, the same book that the witch had supplied several weeks before. Then came the captain: "We are, Mister Ware, nearly arrived at our destination."

Ware instinctively cast a glance around them. "There's nothing in sight, sir."

"Aye," said Lacewage, "but you know as well as I, quartermaster, that often the unseen is just as tangible as true treasure."

Ware again pondered this uncharacteristic pattern over these past days: Lacewage's midnight errand…the crates—the "witch's caskets" and their contents—the unnecessary exchange of the anchor. In a moment of impertinent unease, Ware said, "Captain—why have you dragged us to the middle of nowhere?"

After a pause, Lacewage withdrew a pocket watch on a chain, clicked open the face; he nodded slightly, approvingly, the night wind sweeping his long, oily hair across his heavily-lined brow; the captain then stared over the sea, unceasingly slashed by horizontal lacerations of reflected moonlight. Captain Lacewage took a deep breath and then unceremoniously flung the leather-bound book overboard.

The older man shifted his position, so that most of his face came into the rum-colored lamplight. "Ten years ago, I was leading a raiding party—our intended prize apprehended"—he stabbed a long, crooked finger down on the railing with each word—"at this very spot. A bloody frigate was all she was—sixty-odd men, thirty-some landlubbers." He shook his head. "I was a captain by then, older than you though no less foolish. When all was finished, we had our plunder, but some of the company complained, saying they found a key in the captain's quarters but no door below deck to be unlocked. This went on, and on—I," the captain faltered, retrieving his ragged hat and affixing it atop his head, "I devised a small theater of torture but none of the men confessed. Finally, we ordered them back aboard the frigate—ordered her to be set afire with her crew aboard, to which my men cheerfully—unquestioningly—went to work."

Lacewage turned then, squarely looking at his quartermaster. "'Twas the other captain's children, you see—two or three of them, concealed within some crafty panels in the lower gallery—I wager he was trying to return them to the colonies…suspected he might encounter our ilk." Lacewage began descending the stairs, closing in on Ware. The old man's tone and presence were not unlike a minister disclosing a confession to an unseasoned pastor. "I have heard those screams—the screams of children—this past decade, those entreaties echoing as I've carried about my business night after night." He looked directly at Ware. "No longer."

Ware followed, trying to comprehend his captain's unstable mental map; he then stopped short, his eyes growing wide. Just as the captain's admission served as a jarring volley, so too did Ware follow the true trajectory of the man's confession. Something black sank in Ware's midsection; he said, "The anchor—"

"The *witch*," snapped the captain. "It was she who provided a course to salvation." Ware needed to hear nothing else, but the captain said, "When it became too much to bear, I sought out the man's surname—where his family had been destined. Anything would suffice for a devilment, the hag said—anything that composed their happy lives on land."

And so he'd enlisted a gathering of all the metal from what was left of their estate, Ware understood—he understood it to the last. *An amalgamation…grafted onto our existing apparatus.* To himself, he murmured, "The anchor, all that metal—the blacksmith at port."

"Aye," said Lacewage.

Just then the ship pitched violently—the respiration of lantern-cast shadows stretching and retracting. Ware staggered to balance, his eyes fixed on his captain. The older man was squinting at him; and just as he appeared to add something solemn, Lacewage sneered, shouting at one of the officers near the bow to release the anchor.

Ware had no time—words a waste at this point. He raced past the captain, weaving through a cluster of men who'd arrived to assist with the mooring of the ship. Several in the company appeared bewildered as Ware unfastened a longboat and began lowering it to the water; he flung the rope ladder down into the dark.

Ware dropped down into the longboat, unfastening the rope and kicking against the brigantine's hull just as the anchor cleaved the water, the sinuous chain snaking into the black ocean. And as it unspooled, the chain's progress grew crazed, rattling erratically, now tearing at the planks of the hull itself, tugging and gutting the bow. A ragged, splintered cavity widened in the hull, the anchor and its chain continuing to descend as from some unholy weight deep within the water.

Men began to cry out. Under the moonlight, Ware had one last look at Captain Lacewage, craning his body over the railing, his attentive posture fixed on the roiling black sea and the water devouring the anchor, the chain, and now the water-gulped ship itself. Ware now noticed dark shapes—heads, shoulder, torsos—breaking the surface of the water, gliding toward the ship with unnatural ease, their crooked limbs reaching, hands scrabbling against the hull.

The screams of children. Unbidden came an outrageous impulse—the stinging need to flee once again…this time to flee for home.

Grasping at the stern, Ware began blindly searching the bottom boards for an oar, but when he twisted around he froze, his movement seized and his carriage instantly went rigid.

A slender figure was calmly seated on the stern thwart. All this under almost supernatural moonlight: a black shroud covered its misshapen skull, while its angular body appeared to be clothed in roughhewn sackcloth clumsily sewn together in stained, mismatched patches. With an overwhelming wave of knowledge, Ware understood that this was no human being, but rather a wretched creature of his own creation.

The presence lifted its hideous head a degree, and Ware caught the flash of flaking gray flesh, the smooth cusp of bone lining an empty eye socket. Outrageous that the thought should slip into his mind, but Ware distantly reckoned that the shroud in which he and his wife wrapped their infant so many years ago would not be in a dissimilar condition from the necrotic cloth covering this figure.

Slowly, the thing uncoordinatedly raised an arm, and from within the splotch-stained folds of its foul fabric, the ruined, vein-marbled hand produced an object—its obscenely-long fingers pinched something which caught a slim, silver flash of moonlight. It took Ware a moment to recognize the long, rusty sail needle.

Waiting
by John W. Dennehy

Sean leaned against the rear door of the rusted '74 Matador, with his head pressed against the frame, annoyed by his older brother. Timmy always got the front seat. Waiting for their mother always bored Sean, especially not knowing when she would return. And sometimes she came back smelling of alcohol.

Afternoon sun beat on the decrepit parking lot; heat wafted in a haze, sultry, making the wait intolerable. His stomach churned from hunger. Peanut butter and fluff with a glass of milk would do the trick. And he was thirsty, really thirsty. Their mother had left them in the car and walked into the squat, brick building.

"Be back in a few minutes," she'd told them, and then hurried across the parking lot and stepped through a dilapidated metal door into the building. He didn't believe she would be right back, though. He'd heard it before.

She'd been gone a long time, and probably wouldn't return until evening.

They were left in the car alone, an eternity. Hours had literally passed, and time stood still, waiting.

Their mother had been gone longer than usual. The AMC Matador felt stuffy, but Sean knew heat dissipated along with daylight. Eventually, the sun would set and cool things off, while a moist dew settled on the hood. He longed for sundown.

Waiting made Timmy agitated. Car fights helped pass the time, and often started because Timmy occupied himself by instigating his younger brother. Tight compartments lent Sean an advantage, though. His smaller frame made good use of leverage points.

Boredom pulled at his mind, like fingers probing into his skull. And then Timmy set in on him, with a reach over the seat. He slapped Sean on the arm.

Sean tried to ignore it, but the humidity hung in the car, so dense, he'd simmered, irate. Timmy followed the smack with wise comments. And then he elevated the harassment to slaps upside the head, reaching over the seat. Sean stewed at the attack, trying to ignore him.

Timmy leaned over the seat to slap Sean again. The headrest served

Timmy as a protective bunker. He launched more attacks, with scant hope for Sean to retaliate.

Sean quietly took a beating, and waited for an opportune moment.

Then, Timmy swatted at him, cutting a wide swath. The hit registered. Sean lunged. He grabbed Timmy's lanky arm, and yanked it down.

He held firm, immobilizing Timmy, hoping to pin him down until mother returned. Sean knew that she would blame him for the conflict, yell at him for grabbing Timmy. But he'd be safe in the meantime. Mother liked him better.

Timmy flailed wildly, not submitting to the hold. He used his free hand to belt Sean in the head. Timmy broke free and wiggled his arm loose, and then started another volley of slaps and jabs.

Sean responded passively, trying to deflect the hostile advances.

Except, the assaults kept coming, nonstop. The heat had gotten to his brother.

Timmy finally set him off, exploding. A rage.

Sean repaid the transgression with a relentless counter attack. Timmy recoiled from the angst, obviously afraid of the tirade that he set into motion.

Sean wailed away, delivering a barrage of punches, and total disregard for the consequences to either of them. He climbed in front and kicked and punched. Now, strewn on the bench seat, he planned to finish it off.

Back pressed into the door, Sean pushed his feet against his brother. Then, he locked his knees, restraining Timmy until mother returned.

Timmy ran out of steam.

The assailment hadn't lasted long, but the bruises would linger for days. A truce. They sat quietly looking out windows.

Sean longed for the lampposts in the parking lot to brighten, a sign that cool evening air would settle over the working-class Massachusetts town. Cars had pulled into the lot while they waited, and lined a fence dividing the adjacent properties. Much of the lot was now full, older models from the early 1970's jammed into tight spaces.

The side of the building abutted the parking lot. A one-story structure, it had a smooth façade, comprised of pale bricks and grey mortar. Only a metal door faced the parking lot; no windows. Their mother always used the clanky door. Sean wondered what lingered on the other side of the steel hatch. He'd heard it bang shut many times, but never saw inside the building.

More time passed, longer than ever before. Timmy grew more upset, but he didn't take it out on Sean. He was dismayed at their mother, angry.

"That's it," Timmy finally said.

"What?"

"I'm going in there."

"You can't do that. She'll give you the belt for sure."

"I don't care," Timmy said. "We've been here for hours… without dinner."

Windows ran along the front of the building facing the road, parting the yellowed brick. A cannon sat on the miniscule lawn. Sean liked the cannon, and wondered if any soldiers were stationed in the building. Peering out the car window, Sean thought the building had something to do with soldiers who fought in wars. Timmy didn't belong in there.

Sitting in the car, waiting for their mother to return, Sean had grown to despise the place. He loathed it, and wanted to leave. He didn't want to go inside, ever. Timmy should sit in the car and wait with him, like their mother had told them.

"I'm really going in," Timmy said.

"You always say that…"

The car door clicked open.

Timmy had done that before, too.

"You can't go in there," Sean said. "Give it up."

"Why not?"

"Only adults can go in there."

Even as Sean muttered the words, he didn't know how he understood it to be the case. But somehow, he knew that he was right.

Timmy swung the car door open wide. A canvas sneaker rubbed the gritty tar.

He sat on the edge of the front seat, hesitating.

"Don't do it!" Sean cried.

"Can't take this anymore," Timmy replied, shaking his head.

"Just don't… okay?"

They had been through this before. Timmy never got very far. He never went through with it. They didn't know what existed beyond the metal door. Something different cracked in his voice this time.

Desperation. And it concerned Sean, unsettled him.

Then Timmy broke for the metal door. A brisk pace, he closed the distance fast. Sean heard him mutter, "That's it." And he just knew Timmy meant to go inside.

Sean watched him approach the door, tarnished and rusty. The building looked scary.

Timmy grabbed the knob and swung the metal door open. He stepped through the threshold. The door slammed shut behind him, and he disappeared from view, gone.

Sean sat in the car alone, frightened. He expected Timmy to come back out, afraid to take it any further, but nothing happened.

The door remained shut.
Nothing.
It didn't swing open.

No Timmy. Sean waited alone, growing weary from the heat. He waited and waited, expecting Timmy to come back, scolded by their mother. Still, nothing.

* * * *

Eventually, the lampposts came on as daylight shifted to dusk. Cool air settled into the car and beads of moisture appeared on the hood.

Dim light refracted from the edges of the doorjamb. And then the night grew darker.

An incandescent glow spread over the parking lot from streetlights. One stood in the back of the lot, and a few lined the street nearby.

Sean grew despondent; he felt desperately alone.

Abandoned.

Twice.

He didn't want to sit in the car by himself, but he was afraid to go inside. Sean pictured his brother in the building getting throttled by their mother. He didn't want any part of a reprimand.

He imagined the inside of the building, lit up bright, tables covered with leaflets, like going to an open house at school.

Timmy would eventually come back, looking somber. He'd regret going through the metal door, disturbing the adults.

* * * *

Time ticked by, slowly. Waiting.

But Timmy never came outside. The door remained shut, as though weighted closed. Mother didn't return, either.

Then, the door began to open. A shadow cast upon the parking lot.

Somebody stepped outside, and sauntered toward the back of the lot. A large man staggered, regained his step, and weaved to a car. He climbed inside, and then the engine grumbled to life. The car backed around, and almost collided with the Matador.

The man glanced at Sean as he drove past, a scowl frozen on his face. Jowls drooped; the man's visage, reflected in the gloomy lamplight, appeared as a flash of anger, disconcerting.

A chill ran up Sean's back. He wondered what sort of people lurked in the building.

Sean waited and waited, anxiously.

He flipped the lever on the door; it clicked open. He dropped a sneaker to the ground, like Timmy.

A scraping sound emanated from the sidewalk, nearby. The silhouette of a crooked figure staggered along, slouched. The wayfarer dragged something behind him, something metal; it grinded into the concrete, something sharp, ominous.

Sean heard a garbled melody. The man mumbled, a scary incoherent diatribe. The presence frightened Sean like an apparition wandering down an empty street.

He gulped and leapt from the Matador.

Whipping the car door closed, he ran toward the building. The metal hatch lay before him. A faint clamor emanated from the other side. Muffled.

The person on the sidewalk paused near the driveway. He looked at Sean, and tried to say something. His words were inaudible.

Sean stood in front of the menacing door.

Afraid to stand there.

He was also scared to go inside.

The man mumbled and stepped closer. Frightened by the itinerant, Sean reached for the doorknob. His heart raced, and hands fumbled. He pulled hard and opened the door, partway. Clamor erupted from inside, a cacophony of sounds: music, glasses clinking, and heels clacking. Noise reverberated through the fissure.

Consternation from the din, he dared not move further.

The door grew heavy and pulled him forward. Yanked onto his toes, the door closed, shutting out the festive sounds.

He looked over his shoulder. The man approached, muttering to himself, and narrowed the distance, one shuffling step at a time.

Sean tried to heave the door open, without any luck. He gave it another shot and worked the door ajar. He shoved his sneaker into the gap, wedging the door open, and then he shimmied into the doorjamb, and slipped inside the building.

Sean entered a large room, shaped like a shoebox. Clouds of cigarette smoke hovered over a throng of bargoers. Sean choked on the stale air. A bar ran along the wall, stocked with shiny bottles of liquor, reflecting light in a sundry of colors. Rows of booths were located across from the bar. People danced on a concrete floor, and the walls were made of cinderblock. Sean didn't see any windows. A backroom bar.

He perused the crowd, trying to find his mother. Faceless souls danced and drank in the scattered light. Beads of sweat ran down the brows of men. Their bowling shirts were saturated and stretched by bloated bellies. Women danced and shook to dated jukebox music. Dresses flowed and fleshy arms jiggled. Sean looked for his mother, confused.

The place was tightly packed. Everything seemed a blur, and the loud music obstructed his thoughts. He couldn't spot his mother, or Timmy.

Then Sean heard his name spoken, faintly.

Sean turned to find his mother glancing in his direction from a booth. Then, she smiled, and wrapped an arm gently around Timmy's shoulder.

His brother sat on a bench seat beside Mother, a glass of cola in front of him, smiling. Mother's boyfriend sat across from them. A crotchety old man was tucked beside the boyfriend, a stranger.

Glassy eyed, the stranger greeted Sean kindly.

Sean slipped onto the edge of the booth beside Timmy. As the stranger chatted incoherently, an ammonia smell drifted across the table, mixed with odor from perspiration. Sean longed for a glass of tonic. Everyone knew Sean's name, and mentioned him repeatedly, while the stranger grinned and nodded. Women stopped by to say hello, and told his mother that her son was cute.

A gent came by and slapped Timmy on the arm, then he asked if the boy wanted some Seagram's to strengthen his soda. The man laughed and winked at the stranger, who chuckled at the comment. Sean didn't totally understand, but he realized it wasn't a military installation, but rather a low budget bar, a watering hole for veterans.

Timmy's grin turned awkward, forced. He fidgeted. Another slap on Timmy's arm, harder this time. "Strengthen it up," the odd man repeated, laughing.

And the stranger snickered again.

The air inside the bar stifled Sean. Across the table, the stranger, a barfly, jeered at the jokes. Crooked teeth, yellow and decayed, the stranger seemed to find everything funny.

Another jibe about making Timmy's drink stronger. This time from the stranger, who stole the punch-line and winked at Sean. The two odd men laughed and elbowed each other. Saliva pooled in the bottom of the stranger's mouth, swirling around his worn chompers. Fetid breath wafted across the table, stinking of stale cigarettes and Vodka.

Sean thought about waiting in the car. Loneliness where time stood still. Now, he fretted about sitting in the dank bar, pretending to be happy, while desperately wanting to leave. Mother's boyfriend and his drinking cronies made a spectacle of everything.

The summer night had cooled the Matador down by now. Sean longed for the car, and waiting there would have been much better. He slipped off the booth and trundled off to find the restroom. Sean noticed a sign directing him toward the back of the building. He pushed the swinging door open, and then stepped into a small, dank bathroom.

Sidling up to the lower urinal, he heard the restroom door creak open. Someone walked past, stinking of vodka, a familiar stench, reminiscent of the stranger. Sean glanced over his shoulder, but only saw a shadow slip into the bathroom stall.

A fly unzipped; the unmistakable clang of someone dropping onto a toilet seat emanated from within the partition.

Sean washed up as the man hummed contentedly from the commode. The youngster leaned over and expected to see a pair of old fashioned loafers and trousers bunched on the floor, with skinny, pale legs planted in the center. But the space appeared empty. An obscure haze.

Dread crept up Sean's spine, as his heartrate increased, and panic hastened his movements. He gulped and stepped toward the stall gingerly.

Crouching down for a better look, he tilted his head to glance underneath.

Afraid to get too close, he checked it out from a couple feet away. Still, the space didn't appear occupied.

Another chill ran down his spine.

His heart pounded at his chest.

Sean couldn't breathe.

And then he stood and bolted for the door. Just as the old, wooden door creaked open, he heard the unmistakable cackle of the stranger emit from the commode.

Sean fled the restroom and meandered through the throng of partygoers, dancing and sweating up a storm.

When he reached his table, he found it empty.

He looked around to see if they were dancing on the floor, or at the bar getting drinks refilled. Sean couldn't spot his mother or her boyfriend, and Timmy was nowhere to be seen.

Sean's arms pulsated, and his heart beat even faster. He grew so hot, he felt as though he were going to pass out.

He broke for the door, making haste through the crowd.

And that is when he saw Timmy, stepping outside, with their mother holding the door. Sean raced after them in panic.

The door began to shut. Nobody held it open for him.

Sean threw himself into the aperture. He squirmed to get outside, fighting against the weight of the door. Panic drove him onward. Just as he fought his way and stepped outside, his family had already made it to the car.

Sean's anxiety thrummed into hysteria.

They were going to get into the car and leave without him. He'd be stranded at the dingy bar with the crude strangers.

"Wait!" he called. But nobody seemed to listen.

They approached the car in a revelry.

He padded after them. "Hey, wait for me!"

Still, they continued on.

Then, his mother glanced into the car and cupped a hand across her mouth. She began crying then wailed hysterically. Her boyfriend rushed over to console her. Timmy looked in the car window, and then turned away with anguish in his eyes.

Sobbing consumed them as tears ran down their faces.

Sean stopped in his tracks, fearful of what he'd find in the car; he was terrorized by the memory of curling up on the front seat, having grown tired of the intense heat.

Then, he edged closer and peeked through the window.

A young boy lay on the seat, curled into a ball, peacefully asleep. Waiting.

Pouring Whiskey In My Soul
by Paul R. McNamee

The army marched, demoralized. They had been defeated without a shot. In a way, the retreat felt worse for not having stood their ground. The rumors had turned out to be fact—Washington himself had taken an army of thirteen thousand men into western Pennsylvania. The force of five thousand militia whiskey tax protesters disbanded before a shot was fired.

Doran Coyle rode with the haphazard retreating force. It hadn't been a fight in which he wanted to participate. But he had spent the harvest working with old comrades and figured he owed them his presence. He remembered Daniel Shays's disastrous rebellion in Massachusetts. Coyle quietly gave thanks the current insurrection had been brief and bloodless. He figured the memory of Shays had probably pressed the President to show force.

As the force rode and marched, they fragmented—groups heading to one village or another. Eventually, Coyle had only one companion.

"It's good of you to come," Jacob Palmer said. He coughed into a smeared handkerchief. The chill wet October had left many suffering fever and pneumonia. Coyle didn't know Palmer but as a favor to other friends he had agreed to accompany the sick man on his journey home.

Coyle rubbed a hand down his long, square-jawed face and stifled a yawn. He and Palmer were about the same build—tall but not towering—but Palmer had lost weight fighting illness throughout the ordeal. Coyle, on the other hand was wiry and healthy.

"Nearly to Allegheny," Palmer said. "Another hour, perhaps."

"Allegheny?"

"My county, created six years ago," Palmer said. "Parts of Westmoreland county and parts of Washington county. You can be sure I don't mind the name change."

"You were a part of Washington county?"

Palmer nodded. "Can you imagine it, Doran? Our king-general marching an army into a place named in his honor to make war on its citizens."

Coyle refrained from correcting Palmer's use of the derisive moniker. President Washington's actions were not popular. Many of the retreating men had fought with his army during the Revolution. To say they felt betrayed did not aptly describe their venomous attitude toward Washington and his new militia army.

They reached the hamlet of Baldwin near dusk. Palmer's lands were further west. Coyle wanted to push on and so did his companion, but Coyle knew Palmer needed rest. They stopped over at a tavern. The proprietor was a Scot-Irish named Macfadden. Macfadden had whiskers and mustache, a portly belly and pronounced limp. The limp had been caused by a musket ball during the war. The lead had taken a chunk of flesh from the man's calf.

"Lucky it didn't shatter the bone, though," Macfadden said stoically. Without prompting, he poured a measure of liquid for each of them.

"Not sure I want to see any whiskey," Palmer commented.

"It's your own! You fought for it and now you'll be paying your tax for it," Macfadden said. "So might might as well drink your share."

"We were going to fight for it." Palmer placed his hands around the wooden mug.

"I know. Didn't work out like you planned?"

"A plan would have been a start." Coyle sipped at his dram.

Palmer gulped his drink down. A deep cough rattled his gaunt frame and he pointed for another as the fit passed. Macfadden obliged. Coyle thought it might help flush the fever, so he didn't comment—though, he didn't want to bring the man home drunk. After weeks away, Palmer's wife probably would not appreciate such an arrival.

"Now, we've got stew and stew." Macfadden clapped his hands. "But, you could also choose stew, if you wanted."

"Stew is fine." Palmer said.

Macfadden headed to the fireplace, ladling generous portions from the simmering cast iron pot.

"The revenuers came by, Jacob." Macfadden dropped stew bowls on the table.

"After all's been done to them?"

Throughout the countryside, tax revenuers—government agents who collected the new nine cent tax per gallon of produced whiskey—had not been handled gently. At best they were beaten and run off. At worst, the received the age-old treatment of tarring and feathering.

"Well, they got bold. Most of you able-bodied men were gone and they known Washington was out there with an army, backing them."

"None of men making whiskey were here to pay," Coyle said.

"I think they were returning some harassment. Nothing serious but," Macfadden glanced at Palmer. "They headed out your way."

"When?"

"Three days ago."

Palmer leapt from his chair.

"Why didn't you tell me in the first place!" Palmer's sickly body shook with worry and rage. "Is Margaret..?"

"She's fine, Jacob." Macfadden placed a calming hand on Palmer's shoulder. "She's been by since then."

"I'd as soon see for myself!" Palmer pulled away from the tavern keeper. "Doran?"

Coyle nodded and tossed coins on the table.

Impatient, Palmer set his horse to a canter. The road, heavily wooded to either side, fell into darkness. Coyle urged Palmer to slow but the man ignored the plea or did not hear. Coyle slowed, the road unfamiliar. In an emergency, he would ride like devil anywhere but did not feel such urgency.

The woods gave way to open farm fields. The moon was not yet up. Dusk waning, Coyle made out shadows of buildings. A barn and a longer, shorter building. Candles lit windows of a house on a knoll.

Coyle nudged his horse up the little lane connecting the buildings. The distillery was a long building, constructed of short walls of stone and a tall, wood gambrel roof. The door was centrally located along the long wall, with fuel wood stacked on each side. Behind the building, a babbling brook provided the water power to crank the grist mill's wheel.

In his rush, Palmer had not tied off his horse and the animal wandered, grazing. The front door was ajar, a sign of the man's hurried entrance.

Coyle waited until the excited talk calmed before he knocked on the door jamb.

"Come in! Come in, Doran," Palmer said. There were a few more hushed words as he hurriedly explained Coyle's presence to his wife.

Margaret Palmer was a plump woman with a nervous smile. Her dark blonde hair hung freely.

"Mrs. Palmer, a pleasure," Coyle said. "I hope the evening finds you well."

"I am perfectly fine, it's this one I am worried about." Margaret pointed a finger at her husband. "You're too sick. You should have rested before you started out home."

"I had to get back to you," Palmer said. "I was worried—concerned—with you here all alone."

"We discussed that when you left and nothing changed." Margaret said. "I was fine."

"I heard the revenuers came by."

Margaret faltered then. Just a hint of her smile went flat. Coyle noticed. He saw that Palmer had not.

"Yes, they were here."

"What did they want?"

"They wanted money." Margaret handed a piece of paper to Palmer. "I played the good wife and said money was the affair of my absent husband. They said they had guessed that would be the case, so they gave me that."

"What is that?" Coyle asked.

"A court summons." Palmer tossed the paper on the table in disgust. "Well, I suppose I need to appear now."

Margaret got her husband settled in a chair and blanket beside the fire and then prepared dinner. Coyle stepped back outside and brought both the men's horses into the barn.

Coyle and the Palmers supped on hearty bread, hot soup and ale. Palmer appeared better for being home and under the ministrations of his wife. They secured Coyle a cot and he stayed in the living room. He declined offered night robes and stayed in his clothes. The couple retired upstairs where, thankfully, the sound of Palmer's raspy breathing and coughing fits were muted.

Exhaustion from travel combined with two warm meals, whiskey, and ale put Coyle into an immediate deep sleep though he occupied a strange bed. He awoke from a deep dream confused and disoriented. He did not know the hour of the night and felt dawn was long off. He could not return to sleep. The coals in the fireplace gave off a feeble glow. He stoked the fire and saw by the invigorated firelight the time was an hour past midnight. He shook his head, he could not fathom why he felt so awake after such a short sleep or why he had woke at all.

The night exploded in a cacophony of panic. Horses screamed and pigs screeched. Even as he heard feet stirring on the floor above, Coyle slipped his feet into his boots, flung his cloak about his shoulders, grabbed his pistol and bolted out the door.

Coyle knew he had secured the barn door and his first fear was fire, rather than bears or wolves. But the night was inky dark, a haze over a half moon. No light from flames lit the night.

The door to the barn stood open, crossbar on the ground.

Among the sounds of terrified animals, he heard strange groanings and meaningless mumblings, reminding him of the agonized dying of men in field hospitals.

Palmer's horse bounded out the doors. Coyle saw a glistening rivulet and a ragged, gaping wound on its side as the horse raced past.

Coyle entered the barn. His horse was kicking at its stall walls. There were beheaded chickens strewn about the ground. He no longer heard the sounds of the pig. Sounds of gorging mouths reached his ears.

Footsteps came from behind, light flooded the scene. Someone gasped. Coyle whirled, pistol cocked. Margaret darted behind her husband and the light danced as the candle lantern swung in her hand. They still wore their night robes.

"It's only us." Palmer raised a palm.

"Stay there," Coyle ordered.

He rounded the corner of the pig's pen. The low fence had been torn away. Silhouettes of two men leaned over the carcass of the pig, ripping raw pork flesh with their fingers and stuffing it in their mouths. They ate like wild animals. Dirt caked their clothes and hair.

"Gentlemen," Coyle said.

The two men gazed upon him. Their eyes appeared glassy with incomprehension but they gave bloody, feral grins.

"One must compensate the hog's owner before taking repast. Have you any money on your persons?"

"What is this? You mad men." Palmer stepped forward. "I'll fetch the constable and see you in jail!"

The men did not seem to hear or care. The stood straight, emitted low animalistic growls and stepped forward with jerky motions of legs and arms.

"I will shoot," Coyle warned. "One more step and I will shoot."

The staggering men shambled heedlessly forward.

Coyle fired. The ball caught one man's shoulder. The man nearly bent over backwards from the force of the blow but he did not fall or scream in pain. He regained balance and pressed onward.

"What is this madness?" Palmer asked.

Coyle pushed him away. "Get out!"

Palmer started to protest but he was in no condition for a physical fight. Margaret pulled her husband by the arm, out through the doors.

Coyle had no time to reload. He glanced around, spotted the slaughter knife hanging beside the pig pen. He dove between the two men, at knee level. The men clutched at air, reacting too slowly to catch him. He dashed for the knife, brought blade around, served the fingers from a groping hand.

Momentarily, the man stared dumbly at his mutilated hand, then pressed his attack, giving no more attention to his missing digits than to a scratch.

Coyle's dash for the knife had given them time to press close. Rather than attempting another slash, Coyle opted to use the handle and punched the unwounded man in the face. The man toppled back, tripping over his own shambling legs.

Coyle leapt over the struggling prone form and bolted out the barn doors.

"Who are those men?" Palmer asked.

"They were men," Coyle replied. "I"m not sure they are any longer."

"Whatever do you mean, Doran?"

"They were covered in dirt."

"They were in the pig's pen!"

"It wasn't from that." Coyle shook his head. "They came from shallow graves, I think. Their fingertips were bloodied but not from digging."

"Digging? You're saying they're dead men who dug out of their own graves?"

"Did you recognize them?" Coyle asked Palmer.

"Recognize them?" Palmer stamped his foot. "The way they look in bright day I wouldn't know them if they were my own kin!"

"They're strangers," Coyle paused. He looked at Margaret. "Strangers at your door, Mrs. Palmer? The revenuers?"

"What are you on about?" Palmer demanded.

Coyle kept an eye on the barn door, the shadows of the men were moving inside.

Margaret said nothing but turned her gaze to her feet.

"Margaret?" Palmer said.

"Three of them come by," Margaret started to say.

The two shambling men came out of the barn.

"They said they would take what was theirs." Margaret put a hand to her chest. "And more."

"You mean they…?" Palmer implied the rest with shocked anger in his eyes.

"They didn't get that far." Margaret put her chin up, defiant and proud. She met their gazes squarely. "I killed them."

Palmer's face turned surprised horror.

"Killed them? You, you. I." Palmer stammered. "It'll be our heads!"

"We'll sort that out later." Coyle pushed Palmer back. "Go and fetch your musket. I'll hold them off."

"I keep a fowling piece ready in the still," Palmer said. "It's closer. I'll grab it."

The couple set off.

"Wait!" Coyle said. "Mrs. Palmer, I need that lantern, please stay."

Palmer shot Coyle a look of disapproval but begrudgingly allowed his wife to remain.

The dead men shambled out of the barn. They looked worse for their bloody wounds. One lacking fingers on the right hand, the other's left arm hanging limp, useless because of his shattered shoulder.

"Dead is dead and should stay dead!" Margaret cried.

Coyle smiled wolfishly while he reloaded. His world had turned upside down years before and he knew all too well that dark corners of the world were shaded in gray. The dead did not always stay dead.

"Tell me, Mrs. Palmer, how did you come to murder these men?"

"I offered them drams, said they needed to know what they were collecting on. It was easy."

"What was easy?"

"Poisoning the bastards, of course!"

Coyle grunted.

No longer surprised by what he was seeing, Coyle calmly took aim and let the dead men get close. He squeezed the trigger. The ball punched through an eye socket, evacuating brain matter out the back of the shattered skull. The limp-armed man collapsed into the dirt.

Coyle shoved the spent pistol in his belt, readied the slaughter knife for the second mindless attacker.

"What did you poison them with?"

"A flavorless powder. Flavorless in a strong drink, anyway."

Coyle had been in knife fights in his time and his opponent had no fighting skill. He slipped past the snapping mouth and beating arm, drove the large knife deeply into the eye socket, steel scraping bone and lodging the blade in the dead man's brain. The man slumped to the ground.

"They seem like dead men." Coyle tried removing the knife but it would not dislodge. "But they die as sure as any man takes a musket ball to the head."

Coyle straightened. "What was in the powder?"

"Nightshade, dogwood, chinpaquin, Keene's blood."

"What is Keene's blood?"

"Plant from these parts. Never heard of it growing anywhere else. Red berries dry as autumn leaves. Grind it for the powder's base."

"Why did you have prepared poison powder in your house, anyway?"

"Rats and mice and whatever other rodents. Filthy things." Margaret said. "Oh, and a touch of toadstool."

Coyle suspected the combination could not truly raise the dead. It could not, at least, without the work of dark sorcery or ancient spells, neither of which he suspected Margaret would know how employ. Besides, she had wanted the men dead, not undead.

Coyle had seen men in this condition, the dead working cane fields of Saint-Domingue. A method of spells and drugs were used. The French authorities had banned such practices but zumbis could still be found on plantations. In hindsight, Coyle thought the spells superfluous. The men hadn't been dead but only appeared as such, the drug had excoriated their brains, leaving them flesh automatons.

"I buried two out back," Margaret confessed. "It took all my strength to drag them and bury them."

In the excitement, Coyle had forgotten the details of Margaret's earlier confession.

"You said there were three," Coyle said. "Where's the third man, Mrs. Palmer?"

"The other one was that large one. Dragged me off to the still. Poison wasn't working fast enough. I managed to grab an axe, planted it in his head. But he tumbled into the wort vat. I couldn't drag him out. I hadn't the strength!"

"You left him in the wort?"

"I was going to tell Jacob and we could get rid of the body—all the bodies—but then you showed up as our guest. Not something I was going to confess in front of a stranger!" Horror dawned on Margaret's face. "Jacob! He went to the still! The wort!"

They raced to the barn, Margaret screaming her husband's name, lamp swinging in her hand. Coyle overtook her and burst into the distillery, Margaret at his heels.

The lantern light revealed the prone form of Palmer's body on the floor beside the vat. His head twisted to an unnatural angle, eyes frozen wide in the shock of death. Margaret screamed.

A man stood in the vat, broad-shouldered with a heavy belly, his clothes dripped as he clambered out of the wooden tub, swinging his legs awkwardly over the side. The stench of soured wort overpowered a scent of stale woodsmoke.

The fowling gun was on the floor. Coyle snatched it up, pointed and fired. The pan flashed. The shot failed.

"Misfire!" Coyle cursed.

"What do they want?" Margaret said, her voice edged with hysteria.

"I imagine they hunger," Coyle said. "Dead and buried for three days."

"They had the animals, the pig!"

"They might also hunger for revenge."

The undead man shambled toward them, a gore-encrusted hand axe embedded in his forehead. Coyle ran forward, bludgeoned the resurrected revenuer with the butt of the gun. It had little effect. The man grabbed Coyle, crushed him against his burly body in a bear hug. The man squeezed hard, Coyle thought his ribs might break. He wormed an arm free as his lungs burned for a proper breath.

The axe head hadn't gone very deep. Margaret's poison must have finally taken effect even as she had swung the axe. The weapon had damaged the man but not enough.

Coyle yanked the axe free, gray matter slipped from the gash. Coyle swung the axe in wild desperation. He could not aim proper blows from his position. Instead he chopped wildly, hit the man about the face, neck, shoulders and head. Some blows cut deep, others slashed flesh.

The mad man dropped Coyle. Stepped back, wary. He bled from a half dozen gouges and cuts. He staggered across the room, leaned on a upright whiskey barrel for support. With herculean effort, the man hefted the heavy barrel to his chest.

The man's slowness gave Coyle time to react. He pushed Margaret away and then leapt as the barrel hurtled across the room in his direction. There was a loud cracking crash as the barrel staves shattered and the bands snapped. The strong scent of spilled whiskey filled Coyle nostrils and some of the liquid splashed on his pants.

Coyle grabbed the lantern from Margaret's hand.

"Out!" Coyle yelled. "Go!"

Margaret took one more grieved glance at her dead husband and then ran out the door.

The man moved to chase after the woman. Coyle hollered and stamped his foot and the shambling wretch again turned his attention to Coyle.

"I'm here." Coyle threw his arms open wide. "Unarmed."

The ruined man grinned and growled, moved in for the kill. When his staggering steps placed him the center of the spilled liquor, Coyle pulled the candle from the lantern and tossed it in the whiskey puddle.

An impressive whoosh of flame erupted from the floor but it did not have as much effect as Coyle had hoped. The man did scream in confusion and pain but the wort soaked clothing was not flammable and the rank fluid kept his clothes from igniting.

Coyle circled around the blaze, found the axe and rolled another barrel to the door while he burning man stomped around in confusion. Coyle smashed the barrel top, set it on its side and gave it a kick. The rolling barrel left a trail of whiskey which ignited when it reached the burning puddle. As Coyle darted outside, sheets of flame raced from the blazing pool toward the door, blocking the shambling near-dead revenuer from reaching the building's only egress.

Margaret sat on the grounds, knees drawn up, rocking and crying.

Coyle stared at the burning distillery, half expecting a flaming man to come walking out, but none did. The flames occasionally intensified and leapt skyward as the fire found its way to the remaining whiskey barrels.

"Revenge."

"What?" Coyle asked.

"You said they wanted revenge." Margaret sniffled but the tears had stopped running down her round face. "I don't understand."

"Your poisonous concoction did not kill them. They appeared dead. It destroyed most of their minds and brains. They must have remembered something. Held onto a last thought of vengeance as the rest of their memories were destroyed."

"They remembered?"

"Yes."

Margaret's face went from horror to satisfaction as she pondered the implications of her actions.

"Then I hope they remembered as much fear as I did when they threatened me."

Coyle thought the near-dead men had no concept of fear in their destroyed minds but he said nothing. He went to the two corpses lying outside the barn. In turn, he dragged each and shoved them through the doorway of the blazing distillery.

"What shall I do?" Margaret wondered.

"I would not make a habit of poisoning men," Coyle said. "Despite their actions. You could be hanging from gallows for this."

"For now, Mrs. Palmer. Well. There's has been a terrible tragedy, a fire in your distillery. Your husband was anxious to start production as soon as he came home. If there are any remains of those men found after the fire, your husband brought home men to help."

"If anyone comes looking for those revenuers, you never saw them. They never came to your farm."

"You would lie for me?"

"I don't like to lie, Mrs. Palmer," Coyle said. "I won't be here."

As dawn lit the morning sky, Coyle gathered his things, saddled his horse and rode away from Jacob Palmer's farm. He never again inquired after Margaret Palmer, and if anyone ever searched for the missing tax revenuers, Coyle never knew.

True Blue
by Darrell Schweitzer

I don't know where the custom of giving cars names got started. I know my parents didn't do it when I was growing up. It was always just The Car, and when my older brother Jeffrey had his first car, that was Jeffrey's car. If we ever called it "the heap" or "the hunk of junk," that was purely descriptive, not a name.

I drove my mother's car for many years, a huge 1973 Chrysler station wagon so big that when you put the back seat down to make a larger cargo area, you could actually camp in it. I slept in that car sometimes, and not always alone, but still it was just The Car.

Yet, when I actually acquired a car of my own, a rather worse-for-wear 1986 Dodge Diplomat, the first thing I learned was that her name was Annie. Allen Feldstein's dubbing this "the Richardmobile" came later. First it was Annie. Cars seem to have gender too. This one was female. The parents of my friend John effectively gave Annie to me. They lived in New Jersey, which has the worst insurance rates in the nation for younger drivers, and John was still under twenty-five. While they could afford to lease a vehicle in his father's name and let John drive it, they couldn't afford to give him their junker. So I got it, and to seal the contract, making it properly legal with "value received," I gave them a dollar. I later found six dollars in the ash tray, thus turning a profit and giving me a story good enough to get me on local television with the lady from *The Penny-Pincher's Newsletter*, an estimable publication I might have subscribed to if it hadn't cost so much—but I digress.

More to the point, Annie went to the great parking lot in the sky and was replaced by Old Faithful, a 1991 Ford Escort hatchback which, toward the end, had the hatch propped open by a piece of wood I carried for the purpose. Then Old Faithful's transmission disintegrated one blustery winter day, which led to Penelope, another Escort (with no hatch) that I still own, although as I write this it has 134,000 miles on it and has suddenly been demoted to the status of spare car.

Which brings me to the crux of the matter. My wife Carol named Penelope, and herself owned a car called Moby the Great White Whale, a rather decrepit (1985) Mercury Grand Marquis which she had acquired with even more admirable thrift than Old Faithful (i.e free) from an elderly neighbor, although there was no money in the ash tray and so she didn't make a profit.

This land-barge was so huge that when driving that thing I would often look out the front window and then into the rear-view mirror and wonder if both bumpers were in the same time zone.

But Moby the Whale went the way of all such things when we traded him in as part of President Obama's very popular Cash-For-Clunkers program, Moby being a gas-guzzling clunker *par excellance*, exactly what the program was supposed to get off the road. We received $4500 in credit for him and found ourselves in possession of a brand new (almost), bright blue Suzuki Forenza.

For this transaction we availed ourselves a very reputable Northeast Philadelphia firm, Don Dragovic's Yugoslavian Japanese Car Emporium, the owners of which pointed out with pride in all their ads that they stuck by their deals, their prices, and their mother country's name. None of this "Former Yugoslavian" nonsense for them.

Carol fell in love with the car as soon as she saw it. She insisted on *that one*, in blue, when we were looking among several selections. She said it was her instinct. The car spoke to her. Well maybe it did, but if it did it was whispering down the line because, ah, there was this slight irregularity in the electrical system, so they had to send to their other store for an entirely different blue Forenza, which was *almost* equally new, a 2008 rather than a 2009, with 1200 miles on it rather than the ten miles the form said, but it was still a great buy and almost brand new, and if there was some confusion about keys and what looked like the shrivelled remains of a human finger found loose in the trunk, Don Dragovic himself profusely apologized and made good to us. I never figured out if "Don" was an honorific or if his first name was really Donald, but he was a real gentleman, who looked sharp, and had a definite alpha-male presence. He offered us three years of free maintenance and inspections, not to mention dinner for two at his brother Boris's exclusive All-Nite Balkan Bistro and Barbecue, *and* when the unsightly finger bone (if that's what it was) turned up, he gave Carol a kiss on the cheek and a bouquet of roses.

We went away happy. It was a great bargain, and the finest car either one of us had ever owned.

Then I said to Carol, "Okay, what are we going to name it?"

"I don't think you just *name* a car," she said playfully. "You have to wait. The car will let you know."

Oh the car let me know all right, but it wasn't so simple. The next day I was alone in it, driving, when suddenly it chirped at me, really loud, the sound it is supposed to make to acknowledge that all the doors have been locked from the button-thingie on the key. *Now* that sound quite clearly in context translated from the automobilese into English as, "Hey you! Pay attention!"

There was a lighted plastic panel on the dashboard next to the clock which under these conditions would normally say PASSENGER SIDE AIRBAG TURNED OFF, but now it started blinking and said WHAT IS MY NAME?

"Fred?"

NO, IT IS NOT.

"Napoleon?"

NO.

"Ethelbruda?"

The light blinked angrily. Possibly, I thought, I had wounded its dignity by suggesting a female name for a male car; and *then* it occurred to me that not only was I arguing with an automobile, I was trying to be delicate about its feelings, which is ridiculous.

The light reverted to PASSENGER SIDE AIR BAG TURNED OFF, but somehow even that expression took on an air of accusation.

Later, over dinner, I said, "Honey, I think the new car talked to me today. Is that possible?"

"Well, there was a Sixties sitcom, *My Mother the Car*."

"It's not like that. This was real."

I told her what had happened.

She put her hand on my forehead.

"You don't seem to have a fever. You give no appearance of a total mental breakdown into gibbering, drooling schizophrenia of the sort my cousin Morris the psychiatrist specializes in, and I can assure you there is no LSD in the salad dressing, so this can't be a conventional hallucination."

I insisted that we go for a drive that evening. I drove up and down the Roosevelt Boulevard, then in and out of back streets. I even had her drive, but all the while, as the car handled very smoothly and we couldn't help but congratulate ourselves on the excellent purchase, nothing at all strange, much less supernatural happened. Of course since someone was sitting in the passenger seat all the time the passenger side airbag system was active and the notification light stayed off.

That must have been it. Carol had to go to work the next morning. She rapidly tired of this. She looked at me strangely as if to wonder what I was really trying to prove. Was I having separation anxiety from our old clunker?

"Why don't you just give the car a name?" she said when we got back home.

"It's not like that," I said. "You said so yourself."

"What is it like then?"

"You wouldn't believe me."

"Right now I am too tired to care," she said. "I have to get up at six o'clock." Which was, admittedly, the shortcoming of her having the day job.

The next time I was alone in the car, I had one thing figured out.

This was a guy issue. It was between me and the car, which was definitely male. No Annie or Penelope or Ethelbruda. *Mano a auto* we squared off.

The PASSENGER SIDE AIRBAG TURNED OFF light blinked and then spelled HI.

"It's you and me, pal," I said aloud.

WHAT IS MY NAME?

"Am I supposed to guess?"

WHAT IS MY NAME?

"Don't you know? Are you having identity problems?"

WHAT IS MY NAME?

When you argue with a car sometimes you get a little punch drunk. It must be the sheer weirdness of the situation.

"How the Hell should I know? Is it Xenophon Xerxes Ximenes?"

Maybe I didn't like its attitude. Maybe it didn't like mine.

The car chirped at me again, then screeched to a halt in the middle of the road. *I* didn't put my foot on the brake. The pedal went down *all by itself*, and it was all I could do to steer frantically while honking traffic swerved all around us. I looked up and saw the Mother of all Tractor Trailers (with grinning shark's teeth painted across the front) bearing down on me, and, brake or no brake I floored the accelerator as hard as I could and shouted, "Okay! Okay! It's John, Irving, Hugo, Huey, Duey, Louie, Justinian, Constantine Paleologos, Wang Long Dong, Ho Chi Minh, Godzilla, Bart, Bat, Brian, Quasimodo the Hunchback of Notre Dame, Igor, Allan with three different spellings, Charles Dexter Ward, Bud, Big Boy, Ronald, Englebert—Jesus Christ, I don't know. Get a fucking move on before we both get killed!"

The brake came up. The car lurched forward. The toothy-mouth truck receded in the rear-view mirror.

After a moment, when my heartbeat dropped down to humanly sustainable levels, I noticed that the blinking light said, YOU ARE NOT TAKING THIS SERIOUSLY.

"Oh, I am," I said grimly.

I just drove. I tried to convince myself that sane people, a group to which I self-flatteringly believed I belonged, did not argue, much less apologize to inanimate compilations of metal, glass, and rubber.

The car said nothing more. I think it felt that it had scored the victory it wanted when I'd screamed for it to move before it got *us* killed. I had acknowledged it as a fellow being, a person.

The next morning I acknowledged it as a potentially dangerous hunk of junk. I couldn't explain to Carol what I was doing. After she had gone to work I called Triple-A and had the thing *towed* right back to Don Dragovic's Yugoslavian Japanese Car Emporium.

Don, or *the* Don, or whatever he was, looked out from his office with a hurt expression on his face as I explained, forcefully, to the clerks, mechanics, salesmen and random customers that there was something very, very *wrong* with this car…but when the time came for me to actually describe the symptoms, I could *not* actually come out and say that the car talked to me and demanded a name and maybe even tried to kill me when I failed to comply. I mean that would have left me looking, well, a little *not normal*, and you never want people to know you're *not normal*, so the best I could do is say that the dashboard lights went on and off strangely and that the brakes had seized up in the middle of traffic.

The head of the service department tried his best to calm me down and promised to have everything checked out, and so I waited in the customer lounge for what turned out to be the better part of a day, wasting my time because I had not brought any writing or reading along to do, but so riled up that I couldn't think about anything else anyway.

The service people were very nice. They even brought me lunch.

About 4 o'clock in the afternoon the manager came back in and said very quietly, "Mr. Harcourt, we have checked out your car top to bottom, stem to stern, so to speak, and find that it is in excellent working condition. There is nothing wrong with it. But in order to compensate you for whatever inconvenience you may have experienced, we are extending your warranty for an extra year and sending you home with an extra bouquet of roses for your wife."

At that point I started screaming that the car was cursed or haunted and I wasn't crazy, but the car was trying to kill me because I didn't know its damn name and it was about time somebody *did* something about it. I was making a scene. People turned to stare. It was then that I both felt and heard the *thud* of Don Dragovic's hand, which was about the size of an elephant's foot, coming down on my shoulder. (Did I mention that Don Dragovic was an exceptionally tall man?)

"Sir," he said, "We always try to satisfy our customers, but they, in turn are expected to maintain a certain standard of courtesy in return. Now I trust that you have not made light of the numerous considerations I have already afforded you."

"Uh, no, but—"

"If you are having nostalgic anxieties about your old clunker, it is entirely too late for that, because it has doubtless been compressed into a cube of metal small enough to fit into a shopping bag by now, and it will soon be melted down to make ash trays."

"That's not the problem—"

"Good, because I am then able to explain to you philosophically, as one of life's wayfarers to another, that sometimes in the passages of existence when something is passed to you, you must accept it philosophically, and never attempt to pass it back to whence it came. This especially applies to, for example, an automobile, which hypothetically speaking, may be possessed by demons or enchanted by fairies or marked by a gypsy curse. Now *should* the opportunity ever come to pass such a fabulous object on to a further party, you should try to make the transition as pleasant as possible for the recipient, and add little bonuses and flourishes to be nice. I am sure that you and your wife will have a very nice time at Boris's Balkan Bistro and Barbecue."

"Well, yes, thank you—"

"I am pleased that we have come to this understanding. Now let us part with a further bit of advice. Sometimes in life you have to be assertive." And as he spoke, he pressed down on my shoulder harder as if to say, *But in other circumstances this may not be a good idea.* "Sometimes it is necessary to establish exactly who is boss." *And sometimes this is already clear.*

I accepted the keys—philosophically—and drove home. On the way, I recited every name I could possibly think of, but the car only replied: YOU ARE NOT TAKING THIS SERIOUSLY. I AM DEEPLY OFFENDED. A TRUE NAME COMES FROM THE HEART.

"Screw you," I said.

HAVE YOU CONSIDERED WHAT WOULD HAPPEN IF I TOOK OFF WITH YOUR WIFE INSIDE AND DELIBERATELY CRASHED THROUGH A BRIDGE GUARD RAIL INTO THE DELAWARE RIVER?

Yes, I considered it. I also considered what would happen if I merely pushed this car, with the gearshift in neutral and the brakes off, into the aforesaid river, but what stumped me was how I would ever explain that to an insurance claims investigator.

Carol was out late that night. Tapdancing class. She had gone in the old car, Penelope. By the time she got back she was too tired to talk about much of anything. I did not think she would particularly care for an account of the day's adventures, which very likely would cause her to make an appointment for me with her cousin Morris the psychiatrist. The guy specialized in paranoid wackos. He ran an institution with many rubber rooms.

No, that was not the answer.

It wasn't the answer either that I overslept the following morning, had entirely forgotten that this was the day Carol was to take off from work and drive upstate to visit her Aunt Minnie. Maybe it is a flaw in our marriage that we do not always communicate these things very well. When I woke up she was gone, and had left me a note.

She'd taken the new car.

It was only a few minutes later that I got a frantic call from her on her cellphone telling me that the car was completely out of control and it seemed to be going where *it* wanted to go. The steering wheel, the brakes, even the ignition key did not respond to her.

"*Now* do you believe me?" I said.

"Don't be an asshole! This is no time to prove your point! Come and save me!"

"Where is it headed?"

"North on 95. No, wait, it's turning off. I think it's heading for the Burlington-Bristol Bridge."

A rather old and rickety bridge in the middle of nowhere, I could only remind myself. High over the Delaware River. Nobody uses it much.

Now there wasn't actually much hope of overtaking them—notice how I said, *them*, as if there were two—but the only thing I could do was run out, get into the older car, Penelope, and take off, hoping the cops didn't notice how many speed limits I broke or how many red lights I ran.

I could only think…no, I really couldn't think much at all. I could only *do*, drive on with iron determination, both determined to save Carol and to get the best of that damned Suzuki Forenza. Was it gallantry or raging male ego at play here? Did it make any difference? I didn't have time to think about it, any more than a Cro-Magnon taking on a cave bear had time for a delicate analysis of his feelings and motivations. Andrenalin (or maybe testosterone) has done a lot for our species in the past, so I hoped it would serve me this one more time.

Incredibly, I found the Forenza parked in the middle of the bridge. The one or two cars that came along assumed this was a disabled vehicle and just swerved around it, completely ignoring Carol pounding frantically on the windows, which of course refused to open for her, as did the doors.

I stopped behind the Forenza and put Penelope into park, the motor still running.

As soon as I got out, the Forenza chirped, its doors unlocked, and Carol ran out, into my arms.

"I thought I'd lost you," I said softly.

The Forenza chirped again, then tooted its horn snidely.

I eased Carol aside and stepped toward the Forenza.

"A man's gotta do what a man's gotta do."

I sat down in the driver's seat.

"I can't let you do it alone," Carol said, and got in the passenger side.

I was speechless with admiration for her just then. She didn't have to get back into that damned car. That was really brave.

For once, even though there were two people sitting in the car, the dashboard light came on.

HI.

"Hi."

I COULDN'T LEAVE WITHOUT BOTH OF YOU.

The car started to drive itself. It began to pick up speed. The bridge had a precarious curve ahead where it would be possible, if you hit it just right, to go over into the river, which was a disquietingly long way below.

"Stop!" I said, "Stop-stop!"

WHY SHOULD I?

That was the moment it all came together. Maybe the experience of the last couple of days, or Don Dragovic's philosophical advice, or my love for Carol, or *something* rerouted some circuits in my brain, and *I understood*. It was all suddenly clear.

"Because I know your name! *It's Rumplestiltskin!*"

The car screeched to a halt.

OH COME ON! CAN'T YOU DO BETTER THAN THAT? I WASN'T REALLY GOING TO TAKE US INTO THE RIVER. I JUST THOUGHT THAT A GOOD SCARE WOULD MAKE YOU TELL ME MY NAME. I DON'T KNOW IT UNTIL YOU TELL ME. I CAN'T JUST NAME MYSELF. I WAS HOPING YOU WOULD SHOW A LITTLE FLAIR OR IMAGINATION. I GIVE UP…"

"Yes," I said, firmly. "You *do* give up, because Rumplestiltskin *is* your name. It is your name because I *say* it is, because I *give* you that name. I am your *owner*, car, and don't you forget it. I not only signed the paperwork, but I've got the key, and I buy your gasoline and oil, and I pay for your maintenance, and so if *I* give you a name it *is* your name, now and forever, or at least until another owner gives you another name. Got it?"

Carol added, "That's right. It's your name. I'm co-owner."

RUMPLESTILTSKIN?

"That's right."

PLEASE. PROMISE YOU WON'T CALL ME RUMP.

Carol paused, pretending to consider. "If you behave yourself, I am sure we can come to some understanding. It's better than fighting. Honey draws more flies than vinegar, my father always said."

PROMISE?

"Promise. Now, your secret name, your name of power, *is* indeed Rumplestiltskin. Names are magic. To know someone's secret name is to have power over them. But we don't have to call you that. You will also need an everyday name, a use-name, which has no power. It should be friendly, like a nick-name. I am sure you wouldn't mind being called True Blue. How do you feel about that?"

The light on the dashboard said PASSENGER SIDE AIRBAG TURNED OFF, but only for a moment. Then it went out.

Carol put her hands on the dashboard. The engine purred.

She turned to me and said, "Cars *want* to get along with people. Just don't be confrontational and things will work themselves out."

The Forenza chirped.

It was only then that I realized that I was actually driving again, that the steering wheel and the gas pedal responded to me. I turned onto 130 South on the New Jersey side of the river and headed for the Tacony-Palmyra Bridge. We could get home that way.

Several minutes passed before I suddenly said, "Oh my God! We left Penelope parked on the bridge!"

Carol just laughed. "No we didn't. Look behind you."

I glanced up into the rearview mirror, and there was Penelope, the Ford Escort, right on our bumper, following, driverless.

To my blank look, Carol said, "I have a way with cars."

Penelope was so close that the casual observer might think that the Forenza was towing the Escort.

But the four of us knew better.

The Treadmill
by Rohit Sawant

1

The treadmill was newly installed. It wasn't the first time they had replaced equipment. In the three years alone of Trevor's membership, the gym had traded in two other treadmills for newer ones.

Except they had been *new* new, he thought. Those new installations had that crisp, fresh out of the factory look, complete with a plastic film edged with air bubbles covering the console, but there was nothing new about the one he was presently on. The conveyor belt had the faded look of washed denim, and the up and down arrows indicating speed levels were spectral impressions.

Close to wrapping up his interval training routine, he ran full tilt for a minute. At the end of it, punching the down arrow, he attempted to slacken his pace but was unable to do so. The belt continued to spin at a fast rate, even though the readout showed a speed level of four. Before his confusion could turn to panic, a delayed series of beeps sounded after what felt like an eternity—and was, in fact, no short time—and the belt slowed down. When he finally got his legs under control, he hit STOP and wiped his face.

He noticed the loop of the safety key dangling down. True to his ritual, he had gathered the cord and placed it into the right hand slot next to his hand towel before starting. He almost fell on his ass once when he accidentally yanked it and made sure it was tucked away since.

"You're done, right?" A woman at his elbow arched her eyebrows.

He nodded distractedly and stepped off, resisting the urge to glance back at the treadmill.

2

Trevor owned a wholesale stone supply company; co-owned it with his brother who had put up a good chunk of the money. Dustin couldn't tell sandstone from a hunk of rock sitting on the road. And he wasn't bothered which was which as long as the business ran smoothly. They mainly sold marble and granite tiles. Other natural stones like quartzite, limestone and travertine also made their best sellers.

He spent the better part of his day in his office, going over invoices, overseeing orders, talking to clients over the phone. He occasionally went down to the manufacturing plant.

He'd been in the business for over a decade now. Over the years as the business had grown, so had his paunch, pushing the buckle of his belt out at an angle of forty-five degrees. His wife had tried to coerce him into jogging. Louise had read somewhere that even five minutes daily helped keep heart diseases at bay, which, she reminded him in an officious tone, he had a family history of. A groan and roll of the eyes was all her talk elicited. But seeing the desk biting into his gut one day reminded him of the time when he'd been able to sit down without the buttons of his shirt clicking against the edge as he lowered himself.

There was a gym literally right across the street from where he lived. He procrastinated for a week before going in one day and signing up. It took him a year to lose about forty pounds. And now he had the body he'd had when he graduated from college. Well, close enough anyway. And he enjoyed it. So did his wife.

Apart from the weight bearing exercises he did thrice a week (not particularly his favorite of days, especially if it happened to be leg day, since he'd spend the day after easing into and out of a chair like a heavily pregnant woman), running on the treadmill was something he looked forward to.

That would soon change.

3

Trevor found himself victimized by treadmill traffic again. In the small queue was also a man Trevor only knew as Headband guy, since he alternated between blue, white and black headbands. Today he wore the blue one.

When the new-old treadmill was free, Headband avoided it as Trevor had seen him do on multiple occasions. He was about to climb aboard but hesitated at a poke from an unbidden thought. While whatever glitch that'd caused the treadmill to delay slowing down hadn't reoccurred, he suddenly felt wary. He recalled the times he himself had passed a turn. It had been when the treadmill available had a loose deck that beat in a rhythmic thud. He wondered if that's why Headband shunned it, too.

"There's, uh, nothing wrong with this, right?" Trevor asked him, patting the console.

"No, not that I know of," Headband said, a little surprised. "Works fine, I guess. But…"

"What?"

"It's kinda ridiculous, but I'm a little superstitious about that one."

He told Trevor he'd learned from one of the trainers that there were two accidents in less than five hours on the day they set it up.

The first one involving a college student in the habit of running like he was prepping for being chased by a lion across a veldt. He tripped over his shoelaces and crashed face first into the conveyor belt and was flung off. He was unconscious before he even hit the ground and his mouth filled with blood. When his face hit the belt, his teeth had come down hard, slicing off the tip of his tongue.

"Christ," Trevor said.

"And like an hour or so after that," continued Headband, "there was this lady, maybe late fifties, who sprained her hip. She hadn't been jogging or anything, just walking, but she accidentally tugged the safety key cord while swinging her arms and just plopped down hard like you pulled a carpet from under her or something. She was furious and was going on about how she's gonna sue the gym as she hobbled off."

Trevor absently thought about his Aunt Elsie, a decade dead now, who'd always talked about suing someone or the other every fifteen minutes.

The music suddenly stopped. It had almost been like a physical thing in the air, and you never realized how much space it took until it went quiet, leaving the atmosphere noticeably vacant like an empty space where a large chair used to be. But rhythm hadn't altogether left the room. There was still the thudding of feet on decks, sounding like the terrified heartbeats of giants.

The treadmill Trevor stood on was the only one which was silent, like a third party in the conversation. Listening.

While he and Headband made small talk, a few treadmills next to it became available, and Headband made for one of them.

Trevor stared at the console. He was at a kind of crossroads. He wasn't superstitious, though he did have his quirks. He disliked the number eight, for instance. No particular reason. Just didn't like it and preferred not to do anything eight times or stop at a page number that ended in eight while reading, that sort of thing.

He pressed start and began walking.

The logic he was following was this: he could avoid it once. A dozen times, let's say. But then there'd be that one time when he wouldn't have an option. And he didn't want to have to swivel his vision inwards while legging it to constantly check the back of his mind for any dreaded thoughts lurking there. If he did ever break his ass, it'd be because of that nervous apprehension, rather than the result of some superstitious happenstance.

His eyes occasionally kept flitting to the safety key cord. It behaved.

When he was done he felt better about himself. The way a child might feel at having crossed a reputedly haunted bridge all by his or her lonesome. He froze when he saw his feet.

His shoelaces were untied.

There should have been nothing surprising about it. It'd happened often enough. He had stuffed the shoelaces in before running but sometimes they slipped out of the Nike's collar; but this wasn't like that. The shoelaces hadn't just come undone, lying in a loose knot. They were *laid out*, almost neatly so.

* * * *

Sweat coolly trickled down his face. He stood for a moment, hands on hips, steadying his breath. He grimaced a little at the stitch in his side. The gym was thinly crowded so he could afford to dawdle.

Trevor was about to reach for his bottle, when the conveyor belt sprung to life and rolled just a little. Staggering, he clutched the side rails. The moment he regained his balance, he let go of the rails as if he'd accidentally touched something reptilian. He grabbed his things and distanced himself from the treadmill.

He would've told himself he just tripped over his shoelaces had they been undone. Besides he'd *felt* the slight tug of the conveyor belt under his feet. He thought about informing the management. He even worked out in his head how he'd put it. Damn thing started on its own and would've cost me a few bruises if I hadn't grabbed for support. They'd tell him how sorry they were, that there'd been other complaints about it as well and they were looking to replace it as soon as possible. Until then they'd slap a sign on it, declaring it as Out of Order.

Standing there, he knew he wouldn't say any of that. A stray thought about Todd Henderson, who used to steal his lunch money and push him around, presented itself. When Trevor threatened to tattle he'd say, go on, boy (he called everyone boy, even the girls), then we'll have some real fun.

Trevor stared at the treadmill.

We'll have some real fun.

He left, without bothering to finish his workout.

4

For the next two months, he avoided the new-old treadmill. But he wasn't able to dodge it for long. One day, when all the other treadmills were occupied and it didn't look like they'd be free anytime soon, he squared his shoulders and got on it. He didn't jog; only walked briskly.

He'd considered moving on to the stationary bike, but just enough time had passed for the vague fear that'd hung over his head to lose definition, to seem like something from an old dream. Also, the fact that the treadmill was still there suggested that maybe there hadn't been any more incidents. The management would surely have done something about it otherwise. Maybe those early accidents were just that—accidents.

A little breathless chuckle escaped him as he thought how silly he'd been. Lousy luck associated with an idea or an event, some repetition thrown in, *et voilà*! You have your basic superstition, folks! He remembered how he avoided wearing a green flannel shirt to the movies, since he almost always spilled half the popcorn making it to his seat when he had it on. The deal with the treadmill was nothing but a variation of that boyhood conviction.

Trevor was jogging now.

He felt good. Yes. Clear headed. Jogging always seemed to—

Jogging.

He eyed the console. The speed level displayed was seven. Lost in his musings, he hadn't realized that the conveyor belt had picked up speed, even though it should've been sliding along at walking pace.

When he pressed the down arrow, the belt spun faster and he had to up his jog to a run. Drops of sweat lining his lips leaped onto the console as he exhaled. He stabbed the up arrow, hoping desperately perhaps if some glitch caused it to speed up when programmed to slow down, maybe the opposite would hold true as well. But it only accelerated it further.

His knees threatened to wobble when he gazed down at the belt. The blur under his feet seemed to shimmer and stretch in both axes in a way that defied physics; it reminded him of pictures wavering on an old TV set, the kind with rabbit ear antennas. The effect made him dizzy, and the malign vibe it gave off was as real as the sour smell of his sweat.

He grabbed the handrail. His slick palms touching the metal plate brought the tiny heart, small enough to be etched on a woman's nail, on the console's screen to life. Under it were three digits: his pulse, which was over a hundred and thirty.

He looked about him frantically and caught a trainer's eye. Greg Wilson had been observing him, thinking either Trevor was going to break some kind of personal record or a few bones.

"It won't stop!" he said as Wilson hurried over and yanked the safety key.

Trevor tightened his grip and hunched over as the conveyor belt slowed and hitched to a stop. Panting, he stared at the blinking heart then withdrew his hands in revulsion. He didn't like this thing, this machine reaching into him, listening to his heartbeat. There were contraptions designed to do specifically that, but they always had a human component. The end of the stethoscope would be tamped in the doctor's ears, there'd be someone operating an MRI machine. But this thing was just plugged into the wall;

like your blender. And it peered into you, past muscle, blood and bone, turning your veins into the string of some grotesque organic tin can phone, through which it heard the ticking of your heart, which formed one end of the string—but what lay at the other end?

"It didn't stop," he whispered.

Wilson asked him if he was okay, eyeing him with a combination of disdain and concern.

With a shaky nod and shakier limbs, Trevor turned to get off and tripping over his undone shoelace, crashed to the floor. He threw a baleful glance at the treadmill, sure if it'd had anything like vocal cords, it would've brayed with laughter. Before Wilson could reach for him, he uttered a furious cry, feebly kicked the treadmill and scrambled back.

He felt lightheaded as he rose and prayed that he wouldn't pass out. He sensed people staring at him. The blackness momentarily cleared from his vision and rushing into the changing room, he threw up.

5

"Louise?"

Only the sibilant hiss of the second syllable of her name slipped from his lips.

"Lou," he croaked, eyeing the slab of her back.

Nothing except the heavy sound of her breathing.

Trevor rolled around on his side and raised himself on an elbow.

He'd had the dream again. The same one; the running dream. But he wasn't being chased in it, nor did he do the chasing. He just ran, unable to stop, his feet treading blackness and air. He'd woken up with a jolt of his leg, out of breath.

It was quarter-past three.

He kicked off the sheet clinging to his sweat-slicked body and downed the glass of water by his bedside, setting it down with a sharp clack, secretly hoping it would wake his wife.

Sharing would be useless, he thought. It'd just add to her worry.

She was already concerned that he hadn't gone to the gym for two weeks now. And that he'd started smoking again; she smelled it on him. She connected those things with work stress and asked if everything was all right at the office. If he told her what really plagued him, she'd think he was off his rocker. Wouldn't anyone if he said a treadmill tried to murder him?

And was he, he wondered, off his rocker, for thinking that?

It troubled him to dwell on it.

He went down to the kitchen for some more water. He felt dehydrated almost as if he'd actually been running.

Having slaked his thirst, he lay awake in bed. He failed to blot out thoughts of the treadmill. Not just now but every waking moment.

Why would it want to hurt people? He didn't question the How. The world was a dark trove of unexplainable things.

The Why was what bothered him. Until now, his brain had just shrugged. But this time it plinked a line from *A Christmas Carol*, Scrooge saying something about the treadmills being in full vigor to the men at his door. What would denizens of the nineteenth century think about treadmills today? Sure, the machines weren't the rotating cylinders they trod on for hours, akin to climbing an endless staircase, but to them it was something you got sentenced to. And now people paid to do it.

The treadmill may have become just another appliance, but it had descended from a legacy of misery, its oldest genome existing in that instrument of punishment which, God only knows, killed how many people, wringed sweat and life from them till they were nothing but rank pulps of meat and bone. What if it developed a taste for this diet of cruelty? And the gene carrying the strain for this predilection was triggered in one of its descendents?

"Stop it," Trevor said to himself. He shook badly. Louise stirred.

"I have to do something," he said to the darkness. "Or I'll go crazy." *Will?*

6

When the voices outside the door faded, Trevor let himself relax. He was hunkered in the leg space of a disused desk in the storage room. The gym's storage room. He checked his watch. Almost eleven.

For days, the thought of *doing* something had burned in his mind. He was lighting up in the parking lot at work when the idea casually waltzed into his head: smash the fucker. He shrugged, sounds like a plan. Except it wasn't. It was just a notion, but, oh, such a sweet one. A hammer would do just fine.

Once he pursued the train of thought, a part of him pointed out how stupid it was. If he really had that much of an itch to do something, he should drop by the gym's office, inform them of his grievance and avoid using the machine. That would be the sane thing to do.

But Louise mentioning she intended to visit her mother seemed serendipitous, a sign that he should proceed with his yet-unworked-out plan.

He watched a YouTube video on picking locks. Closed it before it ended, knowing he couldn't pull it off even if he had the tools for the job. Heck, he didn't even know what lock they had.

But he could hide within, wait it out.

Alone in the changing room, he stowed the bag containing the claw hammer in a locker and made his way to the storage room where he found a desk at the far side, the only thing big enough in the clutter to offer concealment, and waited.

* * * *

It was after midnight when Trevor crawled out and approached the door.

Dread made his eyes bulge as the doorknob slipped from his hands as if coated with grease.

He was locked in.

Okay. Stay calm.

The janitor had probably locked the door when he had…dozed off? He couldn't remember dozing off, found even the possibility incredible, but there had been a point when his eyes had gotten unbearably heavy.

He pressed his ear to the door, heard nothing but the sound of his breath, took a step back and kicked the doorknob, cringing at the thud. He waited for a few seconds, head cocked, then kicked again. When it yielded no result, he rummaged through the room and found a ten pound dumbbell with a disk missing on one side. His hands grew sweaty, and he wiped them on the nondescript hoodie he'd worn before gripping the bar. He struck the knob twice, knocking it off the second time. The door swung ajar. He tossed the weight aside, stretched his arm then peered from within. Shadows and silence.

He stepped out to retrieve the hammer.

7

Trevor had spent hundreds of mornings here. But now, nothing around him seemed familiar. The overhead LED lights were asleep. The mirrors threw a pale milky reflection on the floor. But what seemed alien of all was the silence. He could hear the soft pad of his footsteps. A sound he'd never have associated with this place.

The treadmill was only dimly visible, but the darkness didn't lend it any sinister air. It didn't look much different than the one next to it.

For a moment, he wondered if he should go ahead; if it really wasn't madness. Then breathed a resolute sigh and tightened his grip on the hammer. He took a step ahead but paused.

Walking around the treadmill, he bent over and wrestled its switch out of the unplugged stabilizer. Next, he yanked the safety key free and flung it aside.

Gingerly gripping the side rails, Trevor placed one foot on the treadmill's deck, lifted the other and walked up to the console, his heart pounding, a mad gleam in his eye.

He licked his lips and swung down the hammer with all his strength. A sound like a fender bender blew a hole in the silence.

He glanced over his shoulder, blood thudding in his ears. Flipping the hammer, he struck the console with the claw side this time, which made a loud crack coupled with a grinding noise. He had to tug the hammer to dislodge it. It came free with a squall.

And the treadmill blinked to life.

The conveyor belt swiftly slipped under his feet, making him stumble. The hammer clattered to the floor as he reached for the handrail and put one foot in front of the other to keep from falling headlong.

That was all it took. Within seconds, he found himself running on the treadmill. If any doubt had remained as to its unearthly nature, it vanished when he craned his neck and, horror-struck, perceived the unplugged switch. His face was dimly lit by the light glaring out at him from the console. The whirring of the conveyor belt seemed like an angry whine.

His pace was somewhere between a run and a sprint. That was the first conscious thought to enter his mind, cutting through the terror. Trevor held onto it like a man at sea holding onto a rope ladder flung down from a chopper. Now having grabbed a rung, he made an effort to climb up.

It doesn't want me to get off.

It was going just fast enough to make it impossible for him to even try to get down, either by just leaping off (which would clearly be suicide) or hopping onto the footboards, without seriously injuring himself, but not fast enough to make him trip. Because if he did manage to dismount, say even getting pretty banged up in the process, he would still be alive; it'd lose power over him, and he could finish what he'd started, or rather what *it* started, while all it could do was whirr and whine as he hammered away.

So it kept him on. The scrambled time readout on the damaged console blinked convulsively, forming odd patterns on the digital figure eight frame, a six missing a side so that it looked like a lowercase 'o' with a macron overhead, as if it were counting down in an alien language.

God my heart's gonna burst if this keeps on.

Surprisingly, lassitude began to encroach on the horror, squeezing some of it out. How long was he running now? Thirty minutes? Forty-five? Dear God! It was like an outrageously paced last act of a movie where the climax drags on forever.

Trevor's hoodie was soaked through, as if it had been dragged from a swimming pool. A raging stitch burned in his side. His underwear chafed his skin steadily, the sensation like someone slicing his inner thigh with a dull razor. Rivulets of sweat tickled down his scalp. His ragged breath whistled in and out of his nose, his heart pounding on a little treadmill of its own. He was just waiting for the moment when his legs would give out, and he'd be tossed off the treadmill like a rag-doll.

The daze he was in dissipated when he sniffed: a burning smell.

Sweat rolled into his eyes, blurring his sight as he blinked. Looking down, he saw smoke creeping out in tendrils from the slit at the treadmill's front where its motor was housed. The smoke grew thicker, the smell stronger. Following a sharp crack, a greenish-yellow spark flew from the slit and the deck burst into flames. The whine of the belt wound to the pitch of a thin scream.

The belt's pace began to slacken. In spite of the dwarf yellow tongues licking his legs, a frenzied smile crossed his face.

The damn thing overreached. Oh yes. In an effort to make him gallop till he dropped dead, it had ended up overheating its motor, running it too fast and too long.

He let his legs blissfully flounder. In less than a second, he was lying, crumpled, a few feet from the treadmill with his nose bleeding. It had happened so quickly that he'd hardly felt any of it; the impact, being swatted off as if by a large invisible hand. He almost felt like he'd been teleported off it. He could have waited. The belt had stopped now…but he was just so tired.

He risked a glance at his legs, expecting to find twin torches of fire, but his sweatpants just smoked. Also, the knots of his shoelaces were intact. He reigned in his laugh. He would've cackled like a loon if he hadn't.

A metallic screech rose from the treadmill, overlaid by desperate sounding pops and scrapes, as if some small creature was ensnared in the motor compartment. If there was, he hoped it would stay trapped; whatever remained of his sanity would snap if it showed itself.

The treadmill blackened, began to droop like tallow as flames danced over it. And the dancers soon waltzed all across the room, and it was bright as day.

He tried to rise but only managed to half raise himself before the room spun and he collapsed. Darkness fringed his vision, blotting out the brightness. His stomach clenched and he retched. A faint smirk canted his lips when he eyed the burning treadmill.

He'd attempt to get up again, but for now, tired, oh so tired, Trevor closed his eyes, feeling the hot air lap against his face and neck and let the flicker of black and orange across his lids lull him.

THE VEILED ISLE
by W. D. Clifton

There was no sound upon the sea, save for the steady lap of oars. A dragonship moved across the silent water, its rowers peering apprehensively in all directions. They strove onward, though none could say where they went, for the ship was lost to the outside world. An impenetrable veil of mist lay upon the sea, and all attempts to see further than a few feet in any direction were met with utter disappointment. A shadowed figure stood in the fore with one foot upon the prow, peering out across the dark water.

"What do you see, Kho?" came a voice from behind.

Without turning, the figure merely shrugged its shoulders. "Hmph," came the gruff reply. After a moment a low, gravelly voice said, "Little and less, and nothing more."

The figure turned about then, standing to its full height. To most men in the Great North, Nakh Arag Kho was a disturbing sight indeed. He was large and strong, even among the other warriors of the company, and his grayish skin and bright yellow eyes marked him as something not quite human. A coarse, black beard helped him to cope with the cold climate of the north, but otherwise his head was utterly shorn. Still visible, however, were the two large incisors that protruded slightly from his bottom lip. His people called themselves *orc*, though the Northmen seemed to prefer the term *beastmen*. At present, he wore a mail hauberk and a hooded cloak of dark blue, and furs to shield himself against the chill northern winds.

Wulfherth Hrolfsson, called the 'Raven's Friend,' met the other's gaze without flinching. He was near as large as Kho, fair haired and blue eyed, and dressed out in fur and ring mail. The two had survived many trials together, and Wulfherth had come to value the orc's friendship. They were sworn-brothers, a sacred bond among the people of the Great North that was formed through ritual and the sharing of blood. "If even *your* eyes cannot penetrate this foul mist, then we are truly at the cruel mercy of the gods," he said, his tone grim.

"My eyes are better than yours in the darkness, Northman," Kho said, speaking with an accent that told of the wild climes of his far away home. He gestured with a hand toward the world around them. "In this foul weather, we are equally matched."

"Foul weather, indeed." Wulfherth spat over the side of the ship. "It is unnatural. By Wotun, this is no ordinary mist!"

Kho had to agree that the change in weather seemed rather unnatural. Before the mist had overtaken them, the band of reavers had been returning in broad daylight and amid clear skies to the hall of their lord, Jorgunthyr, after a season of raiding along the southern coasts. The men were laughing amongst themselves as they sailed, singing ribald songs and boasting of their achievements in recent battles, when suddenly the wind had ceased and their ship had been enveloped within a thick fog. The crew had started for the oars, but then Wulfherth had ordered a halt while they waited for the strange veil to lift. Many hours proceeded to pass, until all sense of time was lost to them.

No one could be certain how long they waited there, adrift in the endless gray. After a time that seemed ages, it was decided that they must move on, albeit carefully. The rowers were ordered to continue their efforts with caution to avoid any rocks that might wait below the placid waters, and it was then that Kho had been ordered to keep lookout upon the fore, his eyes being deemed best suited to the task. The mist had not lifted for the rest of that day, and continued to hold the ship in its oppressive grasp when the sun dawned the following morning, unseen save for a slight brightening in the surrounding gloom.

Kho grunted once more, nodding. "Aye," he said. "Unnatural." He turned back to the fore, gazing into the mist that hid the placid waters and whatever lay beyond.

The company progressed slowly and silently for several hours more, until suddenly the mist vanished as though a curtain was being rolled back. The sky remained a dull, cloud-streaked grey, but now Kho could see before them an island, at the center of which was a high crag reaching toward the sky like the silhouette of a monstrous finger, tilting slightly to one side. More startling, however, was what appeared to be a grand hall of stone situated at the base of the mountain. The beach was perhaps three hundred meters ahead and, though the shore teemed with jagged rocks that looked eerily reminiscent of sharp teeth, there was a harbor which lay directly in the ship's path. Kho scowled slightly, as it occurred to him that the harbor was like a great maw opening to gorge itself upon the band of reavers.

"Look!" cried one of the rowers.

"Land!" exclaimed yet another.

"Silence, you dogs!" Wulfherth shouted, his tone severe. As the crew fell silent, he sped toward the fore with a springing stride. "What is it, Kho?"

The orc spoke without turning, "An island, and a great hall of stone, though unlike any northern hall that I have seen."

Wulfherth frowned, moving one hand up to pull at the dirty, blonde braids of his beard, which were tied together with a decorated steel band. "We are lost, you know. Who knows how far we went off course in the fog?" He paused, and the orc gave a slight nod. He continued, "What do you think?"

"I don't like it," Kho replied. "There is a grim feel to this place, and I smell death on the wind."

After a moment's thought, Wulfherth spoke again. "There is no help for it. We must seek the master of this hall, to replenish our supplies and find our way again." He grinned slightly, "Besides, I've never known you to fear the scent of death."

Kho simply frowned, not sharing in his leader's mirth. As Wulfherth went to guide the rowers toward the shore the orc simply returned to his dour watch over the waves, scanning the shores incessantly with hard eyes.

A short time later, after disembarking and pulling the ship ashore, the crew set off for the mysterious hall, led by Wulfherth, Kho, and the skald known as Hrogar Spear-Singer. Kho had pulled the hood of his cloak far over his brow, as was his custom when meeting with strangers, and trusted that his beard would serve to conceal the remainder of his facial features. Though nothing could make him appear to belong in the lands of men, he found that this practice made it easier to communicate with folk who might otherwise become frightened or enraged by his bestial visage, and often allowed him to pass merely as strange, rather than monstrous.

As they approached the hall, the great stone doors opened and a solitary figure emerged. Drawing nearer, Kho could see that it was a large man, resembling the Northmen of his company in stature and dress, but of a size almost equal to his own and with a thick mane of black hair that made his pale skin shine with an almost unnatural light. Striding confidently across the sand, he walked straight up to Wulfherth, Kho, and Hrogar, placing a fist over his heart.

"I bid you greetings, strangers, to the isle of King Vorthul," he said. "My lord sends me to treat with you, to learn who you are and what brings you to this place."

Wulfherth spoke, returning the man's gesture. "I am Wulfherth, the Raven's Friend, son of Hrolf, and I lead this crew. We were returning to the lands of our lord, Jarl Jorgunthyr, from a long voyage south when we were overtaken by a strange mist. We must have lost our way, and came up just off of your shore."

The dark-haired giant nodded and chuckled mirthfully. "Well met, son of Hrolf. The mist that you describe is a frequent occurrence upon the seas surrounding this island, and you are not the first crew to have come to us in this way. I am Karlun. Won't you accompany me into the hall, and visit for a time with my lord and his lady wife? They have come to enjoy meeting with strangers who stumble upon our island. You will be welcome with us this night, and there will be a great feast in your honor. On the morrow, King Vorthul will help you to right your course and set you on your way again."

Wulfherth looked to Kho and Hrogar. The skald nodded with a roguish smile, while Kho simply shrugged his shoulders in acceptance. The captain turned back to Karlun with a friendly smile and said, "We will accept the hospitality of your king. Lead on, friend."

Karlun nodded and returned Wulfherth's smile, but his eyes seemed to linger on the concealed face of the orc for the first time. After the slightest hesitation, he turned to Wulfherth and said, "You make me glad. This way, then."

He turned and led them through the great stone doors. Soon after, they were ushered into a magnificent mead hall, as richly furnished as any that the Northmen had seen in all their voyaging. Torches flickered from support pillars, and in the unsteady light Kho could see a number of finely woven tapestries and a vast assortment of other plunder. A large number of warriors sat already at the great stone table, drinking from golden cups. To a man, they were dark-haired and extremely fair-skinned, just as Karlun. They wore brightly colored cloaks—reds, greens, yellows, and blues. A handful of women sat with them, of like complexion and similarly garbed. Yet another woman walked to and fro amongst the throng, serving food and drink. She was slight, blonde, and pretty, and Kho judged that she could be no more than twenty years old. She wore the drab garb of a slave, and the orc felt a slight twinge of pity for her. He had been a slave himself. As the war-band passed by, all turned to look at them, and it seemed to Kho that most eyes lingered on him.

At the far end of the hall sat two great oaken chairs. A man lounged in the rightmost of these, and a woman sat in the other. The man had the same dark hair and ivory skin as the others, yet there was a regality about him that marked him as a leader even without the evidence of his seat of honor. He wore vestments of forest green, and upon his brow sat a band of silver decorated with green stones. His companion was one of the most striking women that Kho had seen since coming to live among humans. She was long-legged beneath a gown of snowy white, and it was clear that her body was supple and beautiful. Her hair and skin matched those of the other denizens of the hall, but she peered at the newcomers with eyes that were a strange shade of violet. When her eyes met those of the orc, it seemed to him that she could see deep into the depths of his spirit.

At Karlun's gesture, Wulfherth stepped forward to stand before the thrones. "King Vorthul, I am Wulfherth Hrolfsson, the Raven's Friend, thane to the great Jarl Jorgunthyr. My men and I come before you in peace and friendship, and ask for the hospitality of your hall."

The king seemed to size him up briefly, and the mysterious lady beside him directed her gaze likewise. After a moment, Vorthul spoke in a hearty voice, "Welcome, Wulfherth Hrolfsson, to my hall. I have heard tales of your lord Jorgunthyr, and it is my practice to welcome worthy warriors as oft as I may. I bid you partake of my meat and mead, and all that I ask in return is that you and your men sit in the seats of honor, closest me and my wife, Brunhild, and regale us with tales of your voyaging."

"You honor these poor sailors, my lord. We would be delighted."

"And who, pray tell, is this?" Brunhild asked suddenly, her voice pleasant and silky like that of a singer. She leaned forward on her knees and gestured to Kho with one dainty hand.

The orc stepped forward, having been addressed. He removed his hood, and was met with a swift intake of breath from the king and several of the onlookers, some of whom laid hands to their weapons. The lady simply offered an amused smile and held out an open palm to still the reaction of the startled warriors.

"This is Nakh Arag Kho, my lady," Wulfherth said. "Do not let his appearance disturb you. Kho comes to us from lands far to the south, one of the beastmen who dwell there, but he has fought by my side for many years, and has become one of my most trusted companions."

"Interesting," she said, tapping her chin absently with a slender finger. "Most of those who have even heard of such folk consider them no more than the stuff of legend." She paused briefly, then turned to Kho and said, "Be welcome, Kho of the southlands. We shall certainly be delighted to hear the stories that you have to tell."

"My tale is long, my lady, and often unpleasant," Kho said, "though I am honored by your words of welcome."

This seemed to satisfy her, though she continued to peer intently into the orc's eyes for several long seconds after. Having somewhat recovered from his shock, Vorthul said, "Be seated, friends. Drink! My mead has no match, and will help the tales to flow."

All the men were then seated along the benches, with Wulfherth, Kho, and Hrogar Spear-Singer given the places of highest honor, nearest the king and queen. A hearty meal of roasted boar was brought forth, and seemingly endless flagons of some of the finest golden mead that any among Wulfherth's crew had ever tasted. The locals told tales of reaving and sea-faring, and of their island home, which they described as though it were a wintry paradise. In return, they called heartily for tales from their visitors, which were gladly provided—tales of raiding along the coasts of distant lands, of the glories of Jorgunthyr's hall, and much boasting about great deeds done in battle.

On several occasions Kho was called upon to give an account of his past deeds, and to tell about the lands of his birth. Of these, the Lady Brunhild seemed the most interested of all, though there was none of the hesitating fear in her eyes that showed in the eyes of the other inquirers. Something about the woman made Kho uneasy, and he was loathe to tell more of himself than hospitality required. Therefore, he said only that he was from the jungles of a land called Khult far to the south, that he had gone into exile and wandered many lands, living along the fringes of society before finally making his way northward and joining the war-band of Wulfherth. When Kho dropped into an uncomfortable silence, Hrogar leapt up and began a drunken song regarding Jarl Jorgunthyr's great victory over a rival clan at the battle of the Dagger River Fork, saving him from further questioning.

The feasting continued well into the night. Eventually, the local warriors began to leave the hall in small groups, departing through either the main entrance or through a set of doors immediately behind the high seats of the king and queen. When the men of Wulfherth's band became so drunk that most could hardly stand, the king called upon a handful of his remaining retainers to escort them to their quarters, and he retired with his lady. For her part, Brunhild gave a deeply courteous farewell to her visitors, though Kho thought that he caught her giving him a baleful glance as she departed the feast chamber on her husband's arm.

They were led to the doors at the rear of the hall, through which they had seen others departing earlier. Kho found that the structure was much larger than a standard mead-hall, with passages leading back into the curious mountain that sat at the center of the island. The party was split into two groups and led down separate passages. Kho was taken with one group, while Wulfherth and Hrogar went with the other. The men were assigned quarters in pairs, though Kho, being last in line, found that he had been apportioned a room to himself. Exhausted from the voyage and the feasting, the orc collapsed onto his mat and fell almost immediately to sleep. Drifting off, his last waking thoughts turned to the baleful, violet eyes of Queen Brunhild.

* * * *

Sometime later, Kho awoke with a start. He stared about the darkened chamber for a moment, shaking off the haze of slumber and attempting to discover what had awakened him. At first, he heard nothing but deep silence; then a slight scuff just beyond the door. A footstep, he decided, and it had come to a halt just outside his quarters.

For the next few seconds there was nothing, and an uneasy feeling settled over the orc. He lay back upon the mat and closed his eyes, but reached out and unsheathed his sword, dragging it to lie with him beneath the furs. Less than a minute later, the door was stealthily opened. Kho distinctly heard at least two sets of footsteps enter and sensed the room growing lighter through his closed eyelids. A rough voice said, "Bind his hands tight, Hrothi. We don't want this one waking up and throttling us before we reach the dungeon."

"Don't worry, Rerir. He'll not wake up anytime soon. The queen has seen to that."

The orc knew then that he was betrayed, and wondered briefly what had become of his comrades. He heard Hrothi approaching him in order to secure his wrists. Waiting until his assailant was nearly upon him, he sprang suddenly into action. He opened his eyes, and brought his powerful hand up quickly to catch the throat of his would-be captor in an iron grasp. Taken by surprise, the man dropped the rope he had been holding and began to strike at the orc's frame in frantic self-defense. Simultaneously, Kho leapt to his feet—dragging the ill-fated Hrothi along with him—and brought his sword around in a wide arc toward the one called Rerir. This man held a torch in one hand and a spear in the other, but was caught unawares by the orc's swift action and was unable to get into a striking position. The sword made contact with his neck, breaking skin and bone and sinking deep down into his breast. He collapsed instantly, and the torch fell to the floor and went out. Kho let his sword fall and added his other hand to the choking grasp on Hrothi's throat. There was a rip, a snapping sound, and then the light went out of his eyes.

Wasting no time, Kho dragged the bodies into one corner of the room and covered them with his sleeping furs. He did not know what was happening, but decided that it would be best if knowledge of his escape remained hidden for as long as possible. He donned his clothing and coat of mail, which had not been disturbed, slung his shield over his back, and took up his sword, still wet with blood.

Closing the door behind him, he stepped out into the passage beyond. No torches burned in any of the wall sconces, and there was utter blackness everywhere. The eyes of the orcs of Khult were not so troubled by darkness as those of men, however, and Kho was able to make his way with little difficulty. He went quickly to the chambers where his comrades had been, but found the doors open and the mats empty. There was no blood or sign of struggle, which struck the orc as odd, for he knew well that these were courageous and doughty men who would rather die in struggle than be taken without a fight. "Blood of the gods!" he swore under his breath.

He traveled the length of the hall, careful always to move as quietly as he was able, and then traced back upon his steps and went down the matching passage where the rest of the band had been lead. It was the same everywhere—open doors, empty mats, and no signs of struggle to be seen.

This passage ended at an oaken door and, having no other place to go, the orc went through in search of his missing allies.

Kho found himself in a passage leading off to both right and left. He chose left, having no clear sense of what direction to take, and followed that way until it ended at an abrupt angle and turned to his right. He followed this passage, which led to another, and then another. At times, he came to a place where the path forked in two directions and chose randomly, trusting to chance. He passed by a number of doors, all nearly identical to the one that had first led him into this seemingly endless maze of stone. Few were locked, and upon opening them Kho either found more passageways, more empty bedchambers, or storerooms stocked with supplies for the hall.

After rounding one very sharp turn in the corridor, Kho crashed headlong into a young woman running in the opposite direction. He immediately recognized her as the serving girl he had seen at the feast. He reached out and locked his sword arm around her, placing his other hand over her mouth to prevent her from crying out. She began to shake and tremble in his grasp.

"Hush, girl!" he said in a gruff whisper. "Be still, and I will not harm you."

Her trembling did not lessen. Kho moved his right arm slightly, bringing his blade further up into her line of vision. "I am going to take my hand from your mouth now," he said, "but if you try to cry out then, by Kaathk, I will bleed you." She nodded, still trembling violently, and the orc released his grip on her face.

"Please," she said in a whimper, "don't hurt me!"

"Who are you?" Kho replied, turning her so that she stood facing him.

"I am Hygda," she said, "a slave of the hall." She paused for a moment, studying his face, and her trembling seemed to increase two-fold. "You are the one they call Kho the beastman!"

Kho grunted in disdain, and then nodded. "So I am. My comrades have vanished from their rooms, and I believe that they have been taken by the treachery of your king," he said. "Where have they been taken?"

The girl's shaking seemed to lessen at this, and he loosened his grip upon her. She looked straight into his face, her eyes blazing with anger. "Not *my* king," she hissed. "I am a slave, plucked from an ill-fated ship just as you, and forced to warm the beds of the king and his men. I hate them!" She spat.

"How came you to be here, then?" Kho asked.

"A simple escape to make, requiring desperation more than cunning," she replied. "When the warrior who was keeping me this night departed to attend the ritual, I simply got up and left. Vorthul and his men have little care for slaves, trusting that fear and lack of hope will keep them at bay."

She raised one eyebrow slightly. "Indeed, where is one to go? There is no escape from this isle. Any fugitives are either slaughtered whilst attempting to flee, or escape into the wilds and die from starvation or exposure. It has happened to others in the past. I have suffered enough at the hands of these brutes, and finally determined that I prefer starvation to degradation."

Kho nodded, looking at the girl with a newfound admiration. As she spoke, her trembling had gradually subsided. He released her entirely now, and it seemed that all traces of fear had gone from her bearing. She stood straight and defiant, and her gaze met that of the orc's without wavering.

"You spoke of a ritual," he said. "What did you mean?"

"The drinking of souls," Hygda replied. "It is how the witch sustains her power and, despite the feasting carried out earlier for your benefit, how the warriors of Vorthul's hall truly feed."

"The witch? You mean Brunhild?"

"Yes," she replied. "You see, decades ago Vorthul and his band sailed to this island out of the mist, much the same as you and your companions. They found the hall already standing; the gods only know who raised it. Inside, they found she who calls herself Brunhild, come here to practice her black sorcery in secret. Laying eyes upon the war-leader, she was desirous of him, and wished also to have his warriors as her own personal troop. She bewitched them all, never revealing her true nature until the time was right. Vorthul and his crew stayed in the hall, and the king decided to take the woman as his own. Once her position was firmly established, she began gradually to reveal her true nature and work her power among them. Over time, she has turned them into her own creatures—helping her to trap the crews of hapless ships that wander here in the mist, in exchange for a share in the harvest of their souls."

The orc scowled. "By Kaathk, girl, where have my comrades been taken?"

Hygda nodded eagerly. "Yes, my lord. I have been a slave here for a long time, and know these halls well. Take me with you, and I will show you to the dungeon."

Kho nodded. "Lead on, then. Quickly!"

She turned and moved swiftly in the direction from which she had come. Kho followed, striving to keep up with the rapid gait of his guide. She led him through a seemingly endless sequence of passages, turning this way and that and darting through doorways with no hesitation, as one who knows well her destination. Finally, she pulled up just short of a bend in the passage. "Just past this bend you will find the entrance to the dungeon. Your friends will surely be held there," she whispered.

Stepping past, Kho peered around the corner. A guard stood on either side of the door, spear in hand. The two men were engaged in muttered conversation with one another. Kho lowered his sword to one side and pulled the hood of his cloak over his head. He gestured with an open palm to Hygda, who nodded and remained where she stood. He then stepped around the corner and began walking toward the guards.

It took a moment for either of them to notice the figure approaching from the shadows. In this passage, however, a few sickly torches burned from the walls. As Kho passed one of these the light was momentarily blocked out and the guards turned to face him. "Who goes there?" one cried. "Come no further, and identify yourself!" Wordlessly, the orc continued to move in their direction. "Very well, then," the guard declared. "Have it your own way!"

The eager guard made a move to stab at the orc with his spear. As he did so, Kho stepped deftly to one side and kicked out with a foot, connecting with the shaft of the spear and causing the strike to go astray. Simultaneously, he brought his sword down upon the man's unprotected head, splitting it nearly in half. Kho jerked the blade violently from the man's skull, sending forth a spray of blood. The other guard stepped forward, cautiously. His spear shot toward Kho's hooded face, and the orc dodged out of the way. The spear came forward again, and this time the orc caught it with his open hand, pulling it toward him and plunging his sword through the man's throat. He pulled back, freeing the blade, and the second guardsman fell to the floor with little more than a slight gurgle, his life's blood spilling freely onto the stone corridor.

Kho knelt beside the body of the first man and removed a small ring of keys. Without hesitation, he went to the door and began trying them one at a time. Hygda came up behind him quietly as he worked the lock. Finally, one of the keys fit just right, turning with an audible *click*.

The door swung open, and Kho saw his shipmates standing in a tight bunch in the dark chamber beyond, stripped of arms and armor. As the door opened, they turned toward the sound. Kho quickly scanned their faces and found that Wulfherth was not among them.

Hrogar Spear-Singer stepped forward. "Kho, my friend!" he cried. "Blood of the gods…when you weren't brought here with the rest of us, I thought sure we had seen the end of you!"

The orc spat contemptuously upon the floor. "It will take more than this lot to spell the death of Kho, singer."

"So it would seem, thank the gods," Hrogar replied. "The food that we were served must have been drugged! The last thing that I remember is falling asleep on my mat. Next I knew, I was being dragged into this chamber and thrown upon the floor with the rest of our shipmates." He paused, as if something had dawned on him then. "Why weren't you brought in with us?"

"Not for lack of effort," Kho said. "When they came for me, they did not expect to find me conscious and alert. I was able to make short work of them. They've not seen one of my kind before, and their poison must not have had the desired effect. But where is Wulfherth?"

"Taken," Hrogar replied. "We had all been gathered here, saving yourself, for only a matter of minutes before Brunhild came in dressed all in black, with two men in like garb. They took Wulfherth, Hodi, and Vikrn without a word, then left. What does it all mean?"

"She has them already, then," Kho muttered. Then, raising his voice for all to hear, he said, "This queen Brunhild is a witch, and Vorthul with all his clan are her thralls. They use the island as a trap, and feed upon the souls of those who venture here out of the mist. Already our comrades are in danger of a fate worse than death!"

He looked at Hygda, saying, "Can you take us to the place where the ritual is held?"

She nodded. "I can, my lord, though I do not wish to go to there."

The orc scowled. "Nay, nor should you. Yet go you must, if we are to have any chance of escaping this place with our lives." Then, turning to the others, he brandished his sword and cried, "Come, sea dogs! Let us pluck the soul of Hrolf's son from the hands of these devils, that it may yet find its way to the Hall of the Slain!"

The company followed Hygda rapidly out from the dungeon and down the adjacent passage. Moving past the two felled guards, Hrogar and another of the Northmen paused long enough to strip them of their spears, boots, and mail coats. Two of the others took torches from the walls, and then they were off again. Kho, following immediately behind the girl, judged that they were going in roughly the direction from which they had come, but she moved with such speed that it was impossible to say with certainty.

After a time, Hygda stopped short and turned to face Kho with a look of terrible fright upon her face. "Look there, Kho!"

She pointed down the chamber ahead of them and Kho, having also seen the giant figure striding toward them out of the shadows, stepped in front of her. He spoke only one word, "Karlun."

The figure came closer, and as he did so it became apparent that it was indeed he who had first greeted the band upon their arrival at the hall. He was dressed now in black robes, hood drawn up over his head, and held a long, cruel sword of dark steel at his side.

"Greetings, Kho," the giant man replied. "I have been searching for you this past hour and more, ever since I learned that you had missed your invitation to the gathering. You move swiftly for a stranger here, and a beast besides. Though, I see that you have had help." He gestured to Hygda with the sword that he held in one massive hand. "And it seems that you were able to free your friends. No matter; weakened and unarmed as they be, it will take little effort to return them to the dungeon once I have had done with you."

Kho simply nodded, bringing his sword to bear. The man was a fiend, to be sure, but the orc's warrior spirit could not help feeling respect for his courage and fool-hardiness. "Greater men then you have tried and failed. Come and test your mettle, if you must."

Karlun's lip came up in a sneer beneath the black cowl. "In truth, I have yearned to match steel against you since first we met. I have killed men enough in my time, yet never have I slain one such as you." He paused. "I will not bother to bring your degenerate soul before the queen. Rather, I will spill your blood to feed the stones of this passage!"

The giant man charged at Kho, using both hands to bring a terrible blow arcing down toward his brow. His shield still uselessly at his back, Kho dodged nimbly to one side and brought his sword hand around, striking Karlun in the back of his unprotected head with the pommel. It connected with a loud crack, and he crashed forward to the floor. He was on his feet and facing Kho again before the orc could gain any obvious advantage, though he swayed ever so slightly in his stance, reeling from the impact.

Just then a Northman who had taken one of the spears from the fallen guardsmen came rushing at Karlun from behind. Despite his momentary weakness, the huge man wheeled quickly around and cast the spear aside with a powerful blow of his arm, breaking the shaft in two. He brought his sword hand up and used the pommel as a hammer, smashing it into the Northman's unsuspecting face. The man's eyes went vacant and he began to slump toward the floor. As he fell, Karlun stabbed him viciously through the abdomen, puncturing his mail shirt, then whirled about, pulling his blade free and hurling the dying man at Kho like a projectile. The orc was forced to catch him to avoid being knocked off his feet, and Karlun used the momentary distraction to circle around so that Kho stood once more between his opponent and his comrades.

"I am curious, Kho," Karlun said between heavy breaths. "What do you think will happen when I kill you? If my god does not drink your soul, will it enter the Hall of the Slain? Or do your people's bestial gods have a hell set aside for you?"

Having laid his dead comrade on the ground, never taking his eyes from his foe, Kho stood and shrugged. "Whether to Wotun's hall or Kaathk's eternal war-band, it matters little," he said, bringing his sword to bear once more. "Neither will have me this day!"

The two combatants charged. Steel met steel, and for a moment the darkened passage was filled with the deafening clash of opposing blades. The men circled round one another, and neither could gain the advantage.

Finally, Karlun caught the orc in a moment of weakness and delivered a stroke hard enough to wrench the sword from his grasp, sending it to rebound off the nearby wall with a resounding clang. The man swung his sword again, and Kho was just able to duck beneath the deadly sweep of the blade. As he did so, however, his feet became tangled and he fell to the floor in a heap.

A snarling grin spread across Karlun's face and, without a word, he bounded over to the orc and raised his sword for the killing stroke. The orc's reflexes were not yet overtaken with exhaustion, however, and as the blade came down he rolled onto his back, dodging the attack and kicking out at his opponent's knee. Now it was the big man's turn to collapse under the impact, while Kho struggled to his feet.

"Kho!" he heard Hrogar's shout behind him. He turned just in time to catch the spear that the singer had lobbed in his direction. With one fluid motion, his body came around in a full circle and drove the point into the back of the prostrate Karlun, twisting it cruelly in the wound. A gout of blood issued from the torn black cloak, and with a final groan of agony the giant man was dead. Kho ripped the spear from the broken body and, with a somber look upon his face, brought the point to his forehead, leaving a gory triangular impression that his comrades knew was called the "god's mark" in the orkish religion. "The blood of my enemy for the glory of Kaathk," he said, slipping momentarily into his native tongue.

Next, the orc did something that his comrades thought curious. Kneeling, he stripped the black cloak from the fallen giant and donned it himself. He also took a small handaxe from the man's side and tucked it into his belt. He gave the remaining spear to a man named Thorir, and gave the fallen giant's sword to Hrogar, handing him also his own shield. "Hold onto this," he said. Then, retrieving his discarded sword, Kho barked at his fellows, "Come then! There is no time to stand gawking!"

Hygda led the bedraggled band at a mad dash down several more winding corridors. When she finally came to a halt, Kho thrust a hand into the air to silence his comrades. "The ritual chamber lies just round the next bend, my lord," she said to Kho in a voice rife with terror. Even as she spoke the words, Kho heard the sound of strange chanting coming from the shadows ahead.

Kho beckoned for Hrogar and Thorir to come with him, and left the others behind. The three crept quietly around the bend and stopped just outside of a huge open archway. Kho turned to the others and whispered, "Wait here. I will sneak in and get a look about. With any luck, they will see the cloak that I wear and think that I am Karlun returned. If not…then charge in and kill all that you can. We will rescue Wulfherth or drink from Death's cup before the dawn arrives." The others nodded, and Kho tucked his sword beneath his cloak and stepped into the awaiting chamber.

Upon entering, Kho saw that he was in a room much larger than any others in the hall, save only the feasting chamber. The walls, floor, and ceiling seemed to be made of black stone, though in the dim light it was difficult to determine. Two rows of figures lined the center of the chamber, dressed in hooded black robes such as the one he now wore. These stood chanting, facing a raised platform at the opposite end of the chamber, whereon two torches in black stands stood as the sole source of illumination in the darkened room. A huge altar of black stone sat atop the platform, and beyond this Kho could just make out a great, black idol. The being represented by this hideous icon was like nothing out of the waking world of men. It looked to Kho like a type of reptile, with scales and a serpentine tail snaking around its feet, yet it sat upon four legs with a posture that one might call ape-like. Worst of all, the figure was lacking for a proper head. Instead, its neck simply tapered off into another serpentine appendage that wrapped round and round itself into a seemingly endless spiral. This, then, was the god that Karlun had alluded to; the witch's god that had taught her to drink the souls of men.

Brunhild stood by the side of her foul deity chanting in a tongue that Kho did not recognize. She held aloft a dagger with a wavy blade, and—to his horror—Kho could see that Wulfherth was strapped to the altar by his hands and feet, stripped of both weapons and armor. The remains of Vikrn, who had been taken with him, lay at the base of the platform, cut open from groin to sternum. The other prisoner, Hodi, stood nearby in the arms of a hooded guard, wearing the expression of one who both sees and accepts his impending death.

As Kho entered the chamber, Brunhild ceased her chant and turned to face the hooded throng before her, so that her alabaster face became visible and shone out from the shadow of her cowl like a star in the night sky. She cried out in a northern dialect now, more recognizable to the orc, and as she raised her voice the chanting of the celebrants was stilled. "Behold, the blood and soul of this man for the maw of Chu'un! Blood and souls for the feast of his children!" She paused, spreading her arms wide. "The soul of a brave warrior such as this is rare sustenance, brothers....Ah, but we have an uninvited guest." She lowered the dagger, and then thrust its blade in Kho's direction. "Kho of the Beastlands, it is good of you to join us! Will you partake of the feast?" From a distance the orc could not be sure, but thought he saw a cruel smirk spread across her face. "Or perhaps you have come to offer yourself up for the pleasure of our mighty god?"

As one, the black-robed cultists turned to face him. Their pale faces seemed ghostlike in the scant illumination of the flickering torches. Kho snarled menacingly, giving no answer to Brunhild's questions, and adjusted his stance in preparation for an assault.

"Oh, come then, great warrior," the witch called. "I smell blood on your hands, and I think that our servant Karlun shall not return to us. Surely your fighting spirit will be most pleasing to Chu'un. Come hither, Kho. Come, for oblivion is sweet." She raised her free hand, and her pallid, slender fingers beckoned seductively.

Then, though neither her words nor her great beauty stirred him, Kho felt his legs begin to move involuntarily. There was a pull upon him, and somewhere deep within himself he could feel an urge to run to the woman on the dais. He strained with every fiber of his being, yet still he took one halting step forward, and then another.

"Yes, Kho," she beckoned, her voice manic, her eyes grown wide with delight. "The embrace of a god is a fitting end to a warrior's life. Come, offer yourself for the feast of Chu'un! Come, come, and let the darkness embr—"

Her last word was cut short. Summoning all that remained of his inner strength and iron will, Kho had drawn forth the handaxe he had taken from Karlun's corpse and hurled it toward her. It spun madly through the air, just over the heads of the assembled throng, and smashed with expert precision into the witch's unsuspecting face, leaving naught but a red waste in its place. She sank to the floor with a strangled cry, and her own blood began to pool around the feet of the hideous black idol.

The strange pull was instantly lifted from him and, without delay, Kho brought forth his sword and ran the blade through the stomach of the nearest cultist. "Come, Northmen!" he cried. "Slay! Kill for the Raven's Friend!"

He saw Hrogar and Thorir charge in with a shout, stolen weapons leveled at the nearest of their enemies. Wasting no time, he turned and charged toward the platform, hacking and slashing at any of the black-robed cultists that chanced into his path. From somewhere amid the crowd, he heard the voice of Vorthul crying out, "Then queen is dead! Kill them! Kill the blasphemers!"

Kho weaved this way and that, cutting his way through the throng, certain that he had dealt mortal wounds to a number of opponents. In short time he found himself climbing onto the platform where his sworn-brother lay restrained upon the altar. He tore the leather gag from between Wulfherth's teeth and went to work on his restraints. With the corner of his eye, he saw that Hodi had somehow managed to wrest the spear from his guard in the confusion. Leaving the man's corpse where it fell, he hurried over with his weapon still dripping to defend Kho in his efforts.

"Kho, by all the gods!" Wulfherth cried, leaping to his feet as soon as his binds were loosened. "Put a blade in my hand, brother, that I might meet death like a man!"

The orc stooped, plucking the axe from the ruin of Brunhild's face, and placed it firmly into the Northman's hand. "Die if you will, my brother," he said, "but I'm for the beach and our ship!"

Wulfherth climbed upon the altar, swiping aside a dagger thrust from an onrushing cultist and raising the axe high above his head. "Come, wolves! I am loosed! Let us cut our way to freedom, and hasten to the ship!"

There was a loud, frenzied shout from the throng. Turning, Kho saw that the other Northmen had entered and, using daggers taken from the cultists as they fell, begun to fight. Though he could see some of his comrades lying dead upon the floor, many more still of the black robed villains lay beside them.

Wulfherth flung himself into the crowd like a man possessed, swinging the small handaxe and charging madly toward the door. "Come, dogs," he shouted, "to Wotun's hall or the ship, whichever first we reach!" Kho and the others followed, leaving only a red wake and the echoes of battle cries behind them.

As they rushed through the door leading from the ritual chamber, Kho spotted Hygda standing nearby. At her feet lay the sprawled and motionless body of King Vorthul, his arms and hands splayed out before him as if he had been clutching at something. A look of terrified shock was on her face and she held a small, dripping dagger in one hand. Kho realized that she must have had it hidden somewhere in her clothing all the time that she had been with him.

She saw him as he bounded through the door and said in a choked voice, "He ran upon me in the dark while trying to escape. He didn't see me at first, and I remembered all of the times that he…and I had my knife…I thought he would kill me!"

"A job well done, girl. He deserved no better." Kho grabbed for her and pushed her forward. "Make haste now! They are upon us!"

The bedraggled band of Northmen rushed wildly through the maze of passages, with Kho and Hygda in the lead and the howling remnants of the cult at their backs. She brought them quickly to the feasting chamber, and when they reached the heavy stone doors Wulfherth threw the wooden bar aside while Kho and Hrogar put all of their strength into forcing them apart. The doors gave way slowly, and the warriors charged out upon the sands.

"The ship!" Wulfherth cried as he surged through and ran staggeringly across the white beach. The sun was just coming up over the water in the east, giving the ocean a sinister reddish hue. When they reached the dragonship, Kho grabbed Hygda and tossed her onto it with great force, yet with uncharacteristic gentleness. The men heaved madly, dragging the ship into the surf. Moments later they climbed on board, and then they were leaving the coast behind and sailing through a sun-blazoned sea. The cultists, or what small number remained of them, raged upon the shore like black shadows that did not flee with the dawn, and some flung daggers toward the escaping ship with desperate but futile effort.

"Thank the gods!" Hygda exclaimed, sitting down roughly in the hull as the Northmen pulled fiercely upon the oars. After a moment, she looked at Kho. "What will become of me now?" she asked.

Glancing down at her, Kho said, "You sail with us to Jorgunthyr's hall. From there, your destiny is your own. You have freed yourself from servitude, and you may stay or go as opportunity avails you."

She nodded, and the expression on her face was a mixture of joy and apprehension. "Anywhere is better than that awful place," she said, gesturing in the direction of the isle which was quickly shrinking away on the horizon. "And what will become of them, with Vorthul and the witch dead?"

Kho shrugged sullenly. "Perhaps they will throw themselves into the sea, or spill their own blood upon that vile altar," he said. "Let us pray only that the gods forgive us for leaving any of them to skulk among the shadows of the island." He spat into the churning sea, and turned to lend his strength at one of the oars.

Gila King
by Jessica Amanda Salmonson

for Nick Cave

*Here he comes on the run
and he's got himself a gun
It's the Gila King, he's going to bring
gin slings for everyone.*

*Venom for the cook
Snake-leather shoes
Gift for the porcupine
who sings the Delta blues
Tail like a blackjack
tongue full of lies
Looks like the coffin-maker's
here in disguise.*

*Poor a cup of baijiu
for Weevil down the hall
Pack of herbal cigarettes
to pass among us all
Coin for the ferryman
who's here from the Styx
Kisses for the bobby-soxer
doing magic tricks.*

*Here he comes on the run
and he's got himself a gun
It's the Gila King, he's going to bring
gin slings for everyone.*

NECRO-MERETRIX
by Frederick J. Mayer

The time inside the soul slows
to every beat of rhyme.
Eyes drip liquid of broken mirrors
that once reflected life.
The heart seems to float within limbo flow
of blood taht has all but dried.
A kiss from beyond
and now the darkness is mine.
A Miss from the mists coming on the hour
bringing something newly ripe.
Fleshy juices remind one of youth
at play within what remains of the body now.
Insides dancing out in waves of some wetness
and life is still existing.
Slow and gentle the brain shrinks
to squeeze all memories free from me.
Words are merely sounds
but songs are heard in some other way.
This night seems so clear
to an ever greening flower of deathly delight.
The touch of fingers disgard the material
or reality's living being taken away.
A darkness has stopped its growing,
yet there is no light to be seen again.

Someone is loving and caring for I can sense
and I can feel with what reaches out from myself.
Where I wish to lie and perhaps live once more alive,
there is no vert color upon the soil.
This willow tree imagery upon this spot tonight
are shades and shadows of living.
The desire is here,
but who cares if I cease to grow and only age.
Somehow I am falling in love
with that which always continues without us.
There comes out more wetness and it is no longer blood,
soft and sultry is what is this inbetween in me.
When living, I was in the dying period,

*now someone needs myself and being.
I am loved and I am dead,
or am I?*

GRINNING MOON
Frederick J. Mayer

Sunrise, sunset.
Sun's rise, sunset.
Sun's rise, Sun's death.
See how the moon grins.

The Burning Man
by Russ Parkhurst

I am but a dead man, adamantine
As chert, igneous or magmatic;
My old limbs after green aeons of dream
Have set, petrified, not elastic;
My placement no longer stochastic.

I tasted the kiss of Medusa
Saw her face in the sheen of my shield;
I spread wide the loins of Aethusa,
Her dark teats and labia revealed,
Spilled my seed till it ran and congealed.

O'er time wise men have called my sons daemons
Agares, Abaddon, Azazel....
My daughter was dark Lilith. No layman's
Imaginings could limit or quell
Her libido that drove men to Hell.

I drink blood and men's minds and I revel
In their suffering, horror and pain—
I am Lucifer, Satan, the Devil
Bow down to me, you'll never be free,
God is dead, I am all that remains.

Silent Hours
by Russ Parkhurst

In The Silent Hours

When daylight's
Gladsome golden noises melt to
Silvertone and black, I
Try to cry less audibly, the traffic past
My house at night is too occasional to
Hide my anguish, weeping
Travels swiftly in the dark, I don't want
To wake the neighbors, none of them
Just lost a brother, my grief
Is none of their concern, it needs
To stay with me as do the cats
Asleep beneath the dirt in back
Of my garage, they say it isn't home
Until you've something in the ground,
It all belongs to me
Now, every rotting inch of
Timber soaked in creosote, this
Ancient house, the lidless plastic
Bucket with my brother's plastic
Leg and all his clothes, the fallen shingles,
Broken doors and broken
Windows, these are all the
Treasures I possess, this
Is my inheritance, my only
Piece of him, I cannot
Lose this too.

The Old White Crone
By: Maxwell I. Gold

A long time ago, in the ancient East,
Lived a boy, who toiled all day and night.
His family cared for him in the least,
While they hoped for gold would sooth their plight.

The boy himself had wanted so much more,
To leave his home for some far-off shores.
Still he worked every night and every day,
With no change or hope coming his way.

Then one day, came an old haggard lady,
A strange ancient traveler passing by.
The boy was in awe of, of the old white crone,
Who looked as if she were one of Time's own.

She walked with purpose, as she creaked and moaned,
While she pushed her cart, rusted pots of her own.
The boy approached with caution, the old crone,
While his family cringed with fear that shown.

It was said back then, in villages where,
A white ghoul would come, to steal all youths there.
Such was the legend that persisted on,
Of the white ghoul and its hungering yawn.

The little boy was forewarned of this tale,
By his tired mother who could only hail;
"Beware my son, of the ancient white crone,
Who hungers so much, from blackness so cold."

The tale awoke his curiosity,
Only too late for the young boy to see;
What was soon to follow that fateful day,
A horrid tragedy, to their dismay.

So that day soon came, as her old wheels rolled,
Where the young boy to her, gleefully strolled.
"Hello there old woman." He said to her.

With a sharp glare, ne'er did her old eyes err.

She said nothing, save for an ancient stare,
Filled with a dark hunger and cosmic wear.
The family stood in terror aghast,
As they watched their son's life flicker its last.

"Beware my son, of the ancient white crone,
Who hungers so much, from blackness so cold."
His mother yelled with a sobering fear,
While he turned back, looking ever so queer.

She could not look, as it was imminent,
Pounding skies with fiery firmaments.
The poor boy was entranced by that white gaze,
While the village gathered to see his last of days.
Then a scream so bloody, so awfully fresh,
Echoed, rancorous with fearful unrest.
There for all to see, was the horror plain,
Another youth for her hunger to claim.

The old white crone stood in the square and smirked,
While the sight of her pasty white eyes irked.
With her hunger sated, and ravages quelled,
The wooden cart began towards some other Hell.

Behind, a red trail, none dared to follow,
For only despair would come tomorrow.
"Beware your sons, I'm the ancient white crone,
I hunger so much, from blackness so cold."

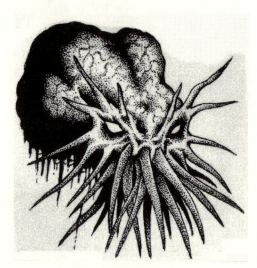

Made in the USA
Middletown, DE
23 December 2024